CRITICAL ACCLAIM FOR
THE THIRTEENTH HOUR

"Barbara Sofer has brought the Middle East to life in her moving and intelligent thriller. . . . Sofer's heroines are real people. . . . Her villain is as evil as they come, and the book has one of the best fight scenes ever." —Phillip Margolin

"Succeeds in conveying the psychological climate of a troubled land . . . timely and resonant." —*Publishers Weekly*

"A fast-paced thriller. . . . I was hooked. . . . Barbara Sofer writes with a great humanity and understanding of the complexity of the issues facing Israel." —*Woman's Day*

"Thought-provoking, intense, highly recommended." —*Booklist*

"SKILLFULLY MIXES THE PERSONAL AND THE POLITICAL . . . A MEMORABLE OUTING." —*Chicago Tribune*

"A HIGHLY INTELLIGENT THRILLER WRITTEN WITH REAL PANACHE AND A KEEN SENSE OF PLOT AND STORY. . . . SOFER HAS A REAL TALENT FOR BRINGING THE CONTEMPORARY HOLY LAND TO LIFE." —*Washington Post Book World*

THE THIRTEENTH HOUR

Barbara Sofer

A SIGNET BOOK

SIGNET
Published by the Penguin Group
Penguin Putnam Inc., 375 Hudson Street,
New York, New York 10014, U.S.A.
Penguin Books Ltd, 27 Wrights Lane,
London W8 5TZ, England
Penguin Books Australia Ltd, Ringwood,
Victoria, Australia
Penguin Books Canada Ltd, 10 Alcorn Avenue,
Toronto, Ontario, Canada M4V 3B2
Penguin Books (N.Z.) Ltd, 182–190 Wairau Road,
Auckland 10, New Zealand

Penguin Books Ltd, Registered Offices:
Harmondsworth, Middlesex, England

First published by Signet, an imprint of Dutton Signet,
a member of Penguin Putnam Inc. Previously published in a Dutton edition.

First Signet Printing, November, 1997
10   9   8   7   6   5   4   3   2   1

PUBLISHER'S NOTE
This is a work of fiction. Names, characters, places, and incidents either are the
product of the author's imagination or are used fictitiously, and any resemblance
to actual persons, living or dead, events, or locales is entirely coincidental.

BOOKS ARE AVAILABLE AT QUANTITY DISCOUNTS WHEN USED TO PROMOTE
PRODUCTS OR SERVICES. FOR INFORMATION PLEASE WRITE TO PREMIUM MAR-
KETING DIVISION, PENGUIN PUTNAM INC., 375 HUDSON STREET, NEW YORK, NEW
YORK 10014.

To my husband and children,
in love and gratitude.

ACKNOWLEDGMENTS

Many persons were very helpful to me in writing this novel. They offered everything from encouragement at critical phases to frank talk about explosives. I cannot thank them enough. My dear friend and mentor, Pamela Painter, taught me the difference between writing fact and fiction, and provided the nurturing encouragement for this book. Friends and fellow writers Sarah Wernick and Sasha Sadan were kind but meticulous critics. Rochelle Furstenberg and Rita Greenfield made valuable suggestions. My editor Michaela Hamilton's insightful, gentle, but firm guidance brought out the strengths of *The Thirteenth Hour*. Agents Deborah Harris, Beth Elon, and Jean Naggar believed in the novel from the moment they read the manuscript.

Biologist Shoshana Frankenberg at Hadassah Medical School, physicians Geoffrey Greenfield and Evonne Heitner, missile engineer Hillel Bar Lev, naturalist Ruthie Guthrie, chiropractor and martial arts master Rabbi Asher Leeder, Arabist Linda Israeli, Moslem *imam* Idries Abu Halid, sapper Chen Strasnov, my sister, psychoanalyst Charlotte Slopak, and my husband, scientist Gerald Schroeder, provided a wealth of specialized information for this book. The IDF spokesperson's office suggested military options. Thank you all.

Also, many thanks to my own self-defense teacher. Like Raphi's, his name is better suppressed.

Many incidents in this novel echo real events, but ultimately this is a work of fiction. Any resemblance to real personalities is coincidental.

1

Deborah Stern heard the first siren as she was getting into her car in the Hadassah Hospital parking lot.

Early that morning, her favorite work time, the Jerusalem air had been cool, and dew had covered the terraced hillsides. Now the noontime May sun was high overhead, making her drowsy. Hours of isolating and extracting nuclei from cells of infected rodents had produced only one test tube of a precious substance that might prevent the disfiguring and potentially fatal skin disease she was fighting. Her shoulders ached from so much bending over. Still ahead was the difficult phone call to her husband, from whom she had been separated for six months. She had to make it on his lunch break, before the children came home from school.

Her white Subaru station wagon had been standing in the sun all morning, and a blast of heat rose in her face as she opened the door. She spread a towel over the seat so the plastic upholstery wouldn't burn, then reached across to open the passenger-side window to let in air. Having the air-conditioning fixed was just one of many car repairs there was no time or money for. Would there ever be? she wondered.

That's when she heard the second siren. It was too close to the first.

By the time Deborah reached the lot exit, Yigor, the guard, was fastening an iron chain across it to keep the main road open for ambulances. He pressed together his thumb, forefinger, and middle finger and held them upward in a Middle Eastern gesture that meant she had to wait. God, he'd learned that gesture fast. Three months ago he had been designing ventilation systems as a mining engineer near Tashkent.

"How much longer?" she asked Yigor, leaning out the window. He just shrugged.

Sweat was already running into her eyes, and she lifted her arm to wipe it away with the shoulder of her short-sleeved blouse. Her back was wet.

A third siren blared and her heart beat in the hollow of her throat. In Jerusalem, three ambulances always meant a catastrophe. In the last two months a teenage girl and her father had been stabbed in the outdoor market. A bomb had gutted the city bus that passed her apartment, and a woman soldier had been abducted, driven to a garbage dump, and shot. Now the sounds of catastrophe were once again winding over Jerusalem's hills.

As Deborah watched, three orange and white ambulances sped out of the hospital lot. The sirens repeated a single sliding glissando wail, not like the two-toned sirens of Europe that brought back ugly memories to Holocaust survivors. Yigor lowered the metal chain and allowed traffic to pass. Driving fast, Deborah pulled out after the third ambulance, trying futilely to keep up with the ambulances as they disappeared around a bend of the road.

Hadassah Hospital, a building complex of pink stone mined from the nearby hills, dominated the southwestern edge of Jerusalem. In the forty years since it opened, neighborhoods had grown up along the old access road that linked the city's busiest hospital to the town like an umbilical cord, but the road had never been sufficiently widened to accommodate the increased traffic. It curved precipitously along a ledge carved out halfway up steep Judean hills, making it hazardous, particularly for ambulances.

Still another siren sounded suddenly and flashing lights filled her rearview mirror. The fourth ambulance was gaining on her, forcing her car against the jagged limestone wall blasted out of the hillside. The stone houses, vineyards, and churches of Ein Kerem, where Mary, pregnant with Jesus, was supposed to have visited, lay below. The ambulance raced by her, and once again Deborah was following behind.

Because Jerusalem was built on hills, a siren could be heard nearly all over the city, like the trumpets in the days of the two holy temples that had stood and were destroyed in this city. In the distance, other alarms were ringing.

This had to be bad. Very bad.

Deborah turned on the radio but only got a buzz. Damn. The antenna was broken off last week when she'd taken Ben to a basketball game.

Her fingers clenched and unclenched on the wheel as she drove the familiar road faster than she ever had before. Around another turn, the sirens seemed mysteriously louder again. As soon as she rounded the curve before the neighborhood called Kiryat Hayovel, the reason became clear.

On the road ahead, a pencil-slim policewoman blew a whistle and held up a white-gloved hand to slow traffic before a shady family park, home to a playground sculpture everyone in Jerusalem called "The Monster."

The Monster was a two-story play sculpture of white and black papier-mâché. Children climbed stairs up the back and slid down the monster's three red tongues. Children like Ben and Sarah. She caught her breath. But of course, they were still in school at this time. In the mornings, mothers with babies and elderly women sat there, not school-age children.

Screams and shouts were coming from somewhere in front of her. Lights from emergency vehicles flashed. Deborah crept forward a half dozen car lengths and then traffic stopped completely, trapping her into a front-row seat for the mesmerizing horror. Every ambulance and police van in the city seemed to be parked at odd angles along the right side of the road and on the sand of the park. Medics were lifting a stretcher from the spot where she often waited for Ben and Sarah to come down the slides. The medics' hands and the stretcher handles were slippery with blood. Other medics were hovering over another body on the sand. Behind them, more medical teams were working while policemen carrying submachine guns and walkie-talkies were pacing the perimeter of the park. More sirens wailed. A jeep full of helmeted border policemen pulled up from the other direction. A line of policemen in the khaki uniforms of the elite Yassam unit had formed a U-shaped barrier around the area where the medical teams were. Backs to the medics, they faced the frenzied crowd that shouted "Death to the Arabs!" "Who wants them here!" "Throw them out!" "Kill him who rises to strike you!" A middle-aged woman in the crowd dropped to her knees and clawed her face in frenzied streaks, a Sephardic gesture of mourning.

Deborah gagged as her car edged forward another length, bringing her even closer to the Monster.

This couldn't really be happening.

Now she could see a surgeon she recognized from the hospital leaning over a body. His sport shirt and pants grew red as he pressed hard on the patient's chest. He looked up, calling for assistance. All the medics were busy with other patients and no one seemed to hear him above the commotion. Maybe she could help him. Deborah was a biologist, not a doctor, but she'd taken the hospital's first-aid course and knew how to follow instructions.

She swerved to the side, parking behind a police van, and started to get out.

A traffic policeman with a mustache glanced at the Hadassah Hospital sticker on her windshield and leaned into her window, holding the door closed. "Nothing more to do, lady. Move on." His face was immobile. "Get back in line."

She started to argue, pointing at the surgeon, but he was already covering the body with a sheet. Before Deborah could pull out again, the crowd to her right tried to surge forward, and the Yassam policemen— at least twenty or thirty—linked arms and pressed them back. Deborah strained to see what was happening.

From behind the ambulances, two officers emerged,

pulling a stocky young Arab toward the van's open door. Each policeman held one of the Arab's arms. Two additional policemen walked backward in front to protect him from the crowd. Screams and curses rose in a chorus and the Yassam line strained to contain the men and women. A skinny young mother pressed a toddler to her breast and raised a bony fist in the air. A bald elderly man broke through the line and was grabbed on both shoulders by a policeman. The Arab kicked out at his captors, who arched their backs to step away from him. His eyes were bruised closed. When the policemen pulled him toward the van, he gave one more furious mad lunge and his knees hit the right fender of Deborah's car.

Suddenly, the Arab opened his eyes and looked up.

Deborah gasped. His eyes were black with loathing, narrowed to slits. She had never before seen such hatred. He sought her eyes and twisted his bloodied mouth, swinging his head back and forth like a caged bear. "You're next!" he shouted, then spat at her. Blood and mucus splattered on her windshield. Two more policemen rushed forward. One of them grabbed the Arab by the neck and pulled him down to the ground. After he was subdued, his hands cuffed behind, his legs shackled, five officers lifted him, shoved him into the van, and jumped in after him.

The door was slammed shut and the van pulled away.

The midday sun was drying the spittle on the windshield. Deborah gagged again, her body trembling with shock and rage. The policeman with the mustache slapped her hood. "I told you to get the hell out of here."

The gears scraped into second. Her knuckles were white against the sticky plastic of the steering wheel. A horn blared as she nearly sideswiped a car and for the next five minutes she struggled to focus on the road.

Finally, she reached her own neighborhood, Beit Hakerem, literally the "home of the vineyard," built in the 1920s as a garden suburb for those seeking peace and tranquillity. Even today, when the cottages had been replaced by apartment buildings, geraniums hung from nearly every balcony, and every walkway was lined with pansies, bay bushes, and roses.

A neighbor was emptying his garbage, tapping the upside-down pail against the canister rim. "Too many sirens. Did you see anything?" he asked Deborah. Unable to speak, she shook her head and searched for a paper, a leaf, a cloth, anything to clean her windshield. Amid the broken asphalt left over from the street remodeling was a torn cement bag. Leaning over the hood, she rubbed the dried spit until the last speck was gone.

The two flights of stairs to her apartment felt like six. Before the door swung closed she'd already flicked on the radio and rushed to the sink. Even the palmful of green dish-washing detergent didn't erase the dirty feeling from her hands. Water ran over her wrists and up her arms. The regular noontime radio program, *Mediterranean Mixed Grill,* was on. A Yemenite singer crooned a nostalgic ballad she usually liked. Now it seemed absurdly sentimental.

No emergency announcements yet.

She poured a glass of sour lemonade and paced back and forth, waiting for the 1:00 P.M. news to come on in English. Listening to the English broadcast was a habit, although after eight years in Israel her Hebrew was excellent.

On the refrigerator was a note marked "Urgent" from Inbal, the baby-sitter, who'd slept over the night before so she could get to work early. They were out of mayonnaise.

The radio beeped the hour. The announcer gave the time and his name in a strained voice. In Israel you could always tell if something horrendous had taken place by the time the announcer said the first few words. Deborah's glass banged on the granite countertop.

Four women were dead. One after another they had been stabbed by a Palestinian terrorist who'd shouted "Allah is great!" as he slashed into their hearts and lungs.

Deborah's wail chased away the pigeon feeding at her kitchen window box. Tears streaked her face, and she wiped them on a kitchen towel. She tried to breathe deeply to steady herself.

Israel was supposed to provide shelter for Jews. Were they any safer in their own land?

The attack had taken place fifteen minutes before her car had reached the park. What if she'd finished her lab work fifteen minutes earlier? Maybe she could have helped. But how? Run the Arab over with the old Subaru or race out to rescue the women? What a stupid idea. She would have been dead like the others.

Her eyes squeezed closed, and another scene formed behind the lids. Sarah and Ben were sliding down the Monster and the Arab who spat at her was aiming a butcher knife at their hearts. Could she have saved her children and run, or would she have stood there frozen and allowed him to kill them? Would she have taken her own children and left someone else's to face their doom? How could she protect anyone, particularly now that she was a woman alone?

She reached for the phone to call Joshua. He'd be back in the yeshiva study hall and would need to be paged. The problem about Ben's frequent school fights didn't seem pressing anymore. Now she was simply eager to hear her husband's voice.

In the early years of their marriage, before his accident, he would have left his law office to comfort her, to erase what she'd seen moments ago. She imagined him pressing her face into his strong neck, the smell of his lime aftershave, his half smile when he urged her to look at a problem in perspective. Today, instead of offering insight and sympathy, Joshua would be more likely to speculate about divine judgment. And he would never come home just to hold her.

She dialed three digits, then put down the receiver.

Ben's steps in the stairwell jarred her out of her despair. Yesterday a kindergarten classmate had knocked out his new front tooth in a playground fight. This morning a broken tooth had seemed like a tragedy. Now it was trivial. What mattered teeth, or even an arm or a leg? Survival was all that counted. Now she'd have to find the words to tell Ben about the terrorist attack.

Raba Alhassan, a petite Palestinian woman, carried her tea set to the shady patio of the white stucco house in Jericho. Her husband sat reading the *Jerusalem Post.* Around her, palm trees and orange blossoms dwarfed pink roses, hanging geraniums, petunias, and wandering jew. Her favorites were the long-stemmed bird-of-paradise plants. This is paradise, she thought, smiling at Ali as she placed the tray on a round rattan table covered with glass.

As was their custom on the days he was home at midday, Ali turned on the radio so they could hear the world news roundup on the BBC World Service. Four women stabbed to death in Jerusalem. The murderer was a nurse from Gaza who had a pass to enter Jerusalem because he'd accompanied a patient to a specialist at Hadassah Hospital. Raba's hand shook so much she nearly dropped the teapot.

Ibrahim, her brother, was a nurse.

"There are dozens of male nurses in Gaza," Ali said, putting aside the newspaper. He could always read her thoughts. He got up from the rattan rocking chair, went to Raba, and massaged her tense shoulders. "If you like, I'll call the hospital to make sure it isn't Ibrahim."

"Do you mind?" she asked, her voice unusually thin.

His smooth fingers caressed the line of her jaw. "Don't worry, sweetheart."

But his reassurance didn't banish the queasiness in her stomach. The patio no longer seemed cool. Raba felt sick. Nausea was expected in the early stages of pregnancy, but this was different—the gnawing stomachache of knowing something broken could never be fixed.

Could her younger brother have slaughtered four women? He'd once taken care of an injured bird, carefully mending its wing with homemade paste. After all

these years, he'd changed. The similarity between him
and their father had gone beyond their remarkable
physical resemblance. Now Ibrahim displayed a barely
leashed fury whenever she tried to talk to him. Like
their father, his fists came up more easily than words.

Out of habit, her fingers traced a childhood scar on
her ankle. When had they last seen Ibrahim? Exactly
three weeks ago at a cousin's wedding. They'd already
adjusted to Ibrahim's being cocky instead of grateful,
taking for granted the payments Ali had sent for nursing school and Ali's landing him the hospital job.
Other changes had followed. He'd started wearing traditional Arab dress and praying five times a day like
a member of a fundamentalist Moslem group. He'd
accused Raba of selling out to the authorities because
of her work at a government clinic for Palestinian
mothers and children, scorning her pride in using her
Western education for her own people. "What do you
know of our people?" he mocked her, one hand
pinching her shoulder. "You've been gone too long.
Half a year is not enough to learn the pain of our
people."

Maybe she had been away too long. So much had
changed. From the time she was nine until six months
ago on her twenty-seventh birthday, Raba had lived
in Detroit with her Aunt Fatima and Uncle Ziad. Her
mother's sister had rescued her from poverty and
abuse, selecting Raba from among her many nieces
and nephews in Gaza because she was the best reader
in the third grade. In the two decades they'd spent in
Detroit, Aunt Fatima and Uncle Ziad's business had
expanded from a grimy gas station to a string of modern self-service filling stations with twenty-four-hour
stores and coffee shops. Their own six children had
grown up and married. Raba's name had been short-
ened from Rabi'ah and she'd been sent to a private
Quaker school because that's where the mayor's daughter went.

Raba suspected that her shy uncle's involvement in
an Arab fraternal organization was undertaken for her

sake. The group's main activity was offering hospitality to visiting Arab students.

Ali, then a resident in cardiology, was among those Uncle Ziad invited for dinner. The colonial dining room table had been loaded with lamb and humus, eggplant dips and homemade pita. A taste of home, Aunt Fatima had said to Ali.

Raba was embarrassed by the obvious matchmaking, but she'd liked Ali because of his kind answers to Aunt Fatima's long string of questions about heart disease. On their first date they went to a Christmas party at the hospital. "An odd way for two Moslems to begin a friendship," he'd joked. Despite his years in British schools, Ali's spoken English was flawed with a heavy, almost comical Arabic accent. He was proud of Raba's perfect diction, her ease with American culture, and the doctoral degree she would soon earn in educational psychology. They talked about wanting to return to Palestine, but completing the residency would take another two years. Intimacy without marriage was unthinkable. Their Moslem wedding ceremony, with the mayor in attendance, had made the society page of the *Detroit Free Press*. Aunt Fatima gilt-framed the entire page of the newspaper.

When Ali's studies were completed, they returned to Israel. Palestine, they called it. Instead of the garbage-lined streets of her childhood, he brought her here to this garden smelling of orange blossoms.

Ali was still talking on the phone with his back toward the porch. Again and again, he patiently explained, "This is Dr. Ali Alhassan. My brother-in-law is a nurse at the hospital," before asking for Ibrahim's whereabouts. Without hearing the voices on the other end, she knew they were polite verging on obsequious because everyone at the hospital and in Jericho treated Ali with respect. His proud parents had prepared this beautiful villa for them in anticipation of their return. The elder Alhassans had been so afraid Ali would marry an American, they were more than willing to overlook Raba's inferior family background and had greeted her with warmth.

Ironically, her own brother had sneered at her connection with the Alhassans, whom he called "the old, rich ones." The aristocratic Arabs who lived in spacious villas would soon give way to the true believers, Ibrahim warned her.

Raba had been stirring sugar in the tea for too long and instinctively looked up to see if Ali had noticed. His broad back was rigid, fingers absently pulling the gray hair curling at his neck. What could be taking so long? Ali hung up the phone. He turned, avoiding her eyes. When he pulled his rocker close to her chair and reached for her hands, she knew what he would say. But she never heard it. The garden spun around her.

In the hall of the Economics Department of the Hebrew University, Raphi Lahav joined a group of his students huddled around a transistor radio to hear the one o'clock news in Hebrew. He'd been teaching when he'd heard the sirens, realizing immediately that something terrible had happened. When the announcer had finished spelling out the details of a terrorist attack, Raphi walked down the corridor to his office, locked the door, and slammed the marketing text on his desk, sending paper clips and highlighter pens scattering to the floor. Four women! Fucking bastards! This time they'd pay.

He dialed the six-digit Jerusalem number and then six more numbers to add the code. A female voice answered, "Tambour, Paint Shop." "Do you have any royal blue?" Raphi asked, his voice low. "Just a minute, I'll check," the voice replied.

In seconds, his commander in the General Security Service, also called both the Shin Bet and the Shabak, was on the line with details. The murderer, a nurse, had accompanied a patient to the oncology unit at Hadassah Hospital. The GSS figured he was a Moslem fundamentalist, probably from the Seventh Century, a terrorist ring they'd been unable to penetrate, hence the total surprise. More information would come in ten minutes.

"We're going ahead with civilian recruitment," said

the voice on the phone. "We've got to change tactics to penetrate the fundamentalist cells."

His office felt hot and stuffy. His fingers sweated on the receiver. "No."

"We've been through this before, Raphi."

"A three-two split isn't an agreement."

"It's four-one now. I just spoke to Gil."

A lie, Raphi thought. Someone, a student, was knocking at his door. His voice became even lower and more lethal. "It won't work. It's too dangerous."

"Cut the crap. You're going to need all your piss to follow this one up in Gaza. Try the small towns first. And set that plan in motion. Today."

Raphi dropped the receiver, flung open his door to sign a student's graduate application form, then locked it again. He took a minute to slow his breathing, then reluctantly dialed his cousin Rachel's number.

She answered on the first ring. The baby—Rachel's fourth—was probably sleeping. She'd heard the news. "Do you know how many times I've been to that park this year?" she asked, her voice shaking. "At least a dozen. What's happening, Raphi?"

Rachel knew, of course, that teaching economics was not Raphi's only job, but they never talked about the second life he'd maintained even before he officially entered the army at eighteen.

He told her what anyone who read newspapers knew, that the latest attacks were staged to derail the peace process, aware that "derail" was a euphemism. Blow up. Explode. Destroy. Those were more accurate words. With public opinion teetering between risking Israel's future on a peace plan or digging in for a long, ugly war with the Palestinians, each attack expanded like a mushroom cloud over the rare opportunity to make peace.

When he'd finished his analysis, Rachel asked, as he assumed she would, what could be done about it. He suggested she organize a self-defense class for women. Knowing it would look suspicious if the class were free, he offered to teach it for a moderate fee. Could she get a class together quickly? Her assurance

that she could get twenty, even a hundred names overnight made him feel hollow inside. Israelis used to
laugh off danger.

He forced a teasing tone. "Just make sure they're
all as beautiful as you." He hated lying to her about
the real reason for the class.

"Right, Cousin Romeo. Remember, I'm doing my
recruiting at the PTA, not stewardess school."

He'd told her he was dating a stewardess, but that,
too, was only partly true. Rachel suggested meeting
after dinner, but he insisted no one eat dinner before class.

"Just how physical do these classes get?"

"Physical. But no one will get hurt." *At least not
in class.*

"That's what you said when you took me inner-
tubing on the Jordan River."

"You loved it," Raphi said, realizing how long it
had been since he'd been on a vacation like that.

"Right. I loved the cast I wore, too. Hand-painted.
So long, macho man. The baby's waking up. I'll get
your group. Bye."

Raphi always felt better after talking to his cousin—
even on a hellish day like today. Why could he maintain
a loving friendship with her but not with the beautiful
women who walked in and out of his life?

He tried his commander again. The line was busy.

His car, a red Alfa Romeo, was parked in the underground parking lot. All of the Mount Scopus campus was built like a fortress. Like the older branch of
Hadassah Hospital, the university had been abandoned in the War of Independence. When the Jews
won it back in 1967, massive stone walls had gone up
around it so it could never again be taken. When he'd
gone to college in the United States, "education without walls" had been a buzzword, but in Israel, he
thought bitterly, we have to build campuses like military fortifications.

His eyes squinted against the brilliant sunshine as
his car pulled out. The Cebe sunglasses made of gold
titanium were in his glove compartment. His former

superiors in foreign intelligence, the Mossad, had fumed at the bill for them four years ago—200-dollar sunglasses when they were wearing plastic frames from the Carmel Market. Buying the sunglasses had been his petty revenge against his superiors for sending him alone against ridiculous odds to Boulogne because they had claimed a backup team "wasn't in the budget." How much was his fucking life worth in the damn budget, he wondered. He'd survived Boulogne despite eight broken ribs and the pulmonary emboli. The debonair French surgeon had warned him to protect his rib cage in the future.

There had been many close encounters since. His lungs and the glasses had somehow survived them all. Except for the ligaments of his left knee, which he'd stupidly torn getting out of a car at a friend's funeral, he felt fit as ever. God knows he worked hard enough at it.

Raphi cleaned the mirrored lenses on his sport shirt, annoyed that he couldn't call headquarters again. Anyone could listen in to a car phone.

The day was particularly hot and clear enough to see beyond the magnificent wilderness hills all the way to the Dead Sea to the southeast. Below, to the southwest, the Dome of the Rock reflected gold sunlight above the glazed blue ceramic tiles of the Temple Mount. The mournful call to prayer of the muezzin resounded on the hill. According to tradition, Abraham bound and nearly sacrificed his son, Isaac, there. But how many sons and daughters had been sacrificed since?

Two holy Jewish Temples had stood on that spot, the first completed 1500 years before Muhammad was born. Then the Moslems had built the Dome of the Rock shrine on the Jews' holiest site in the seventh century when Moslem Arab armies conquered Jerusalem. In 1967, when the Jews won the Six-Day War, Arabs had expected them to raze their mosques and build the Third Temple there, on the site of the previous two, but Moshe Dayan had handed the Temple Mount back to the Arabs, a magnanimous gesture of victory. Jews knew how to suffer, but they were inexperienced at winning. Giving away their holiest site had been a stupid mistake.

Now it looked as if they'd have to wait for the coming of the Messiah for the Third Temple and the resurrection of the dead. Among them would be many friends and colleagues who'd died in their country's defense, like Gil's older brother and Yusef Mana, Raphi's last partner, the best Druze undercover officer Raphi had ever worked with.

Raphi kneaded the bridge of his nose as he turned onto Highway One, the highway that erased the old seam between east and west Jerusalem, instead of his old favorite shortcut through Wadi Jose, a row of Arab car-repair shops where cars with Israeli plates were frequently stoned by teenage boys. He took out his frustration at the security establishment's latest foolish plan by blasting his horn at a black-hatted Hasid jaywalking across the road. The pale young man jumped back onto the sidewalk, his long curly sidelocks swinging in an arc below his black hat.

The way things were going, next they'd be recruiting Hasidim to run secret missions for them. This new "intelligence" scheme wasn't only idiotic, it was farfetched. A nonprofessional couldn't be trained quickly enough to handle a complicated mission. He'd argued for using one of their own women, slick, tough, and experienced. But the others had outvoted him. For reasons he wouldn't divulge, the prime minister himself had vetoed sending GSS operatives to Manger College in Bethlehem, where all intelligence reports were pointing the next attack would take place.

But having someone on the faculty, a nonprofessional who would report to them, wouldn't get them in the same kind of trouble, particularly if it prevented a terrorist attack. Although the GSS still had extraordinary, far-reaching powers, it was more vulnerable to criticism, both public and from within the government. Even if they did get a woman inside, no one could guarantee she'd bring back the right information. And who would be responsible if a *civilian* was killed working for the GSS?

Despite those questions, they'd decided that recruiting a nonprofessional was their only option. Of course, she had to have *some* basic training in case the going got rough. That would, of course, be Raphi's job. He was the martial arts guru. What would he teach Rachel and her friends? He drove with one hand and twisted his shoulders, throwing a few elbows. The women who'd studied martial arts alongside him wanted to be as tough as the men. They were lean and determined, not at all like Rachel's friends, whom he'd met at her kids' birthday parties, where they traded granola recipes and sweater patterns. Rachel had been serious in college, graduating with honors in archaeology, but she'd lost that exacting edge along with her figure.

Bulk, he reminded himself, would be an asset in close combat.

What if the class star turned out to be Rachel? Could he set up his own cousin to be a target for a maniacal group bent on the serial killing of women and children? No. He wouldn't let her go, no matter how much pressure his colleagues put on.

He leaned back in his leather bucket seat, caught in the traffic of the earlier catastrophe. Rachel wasn't the right type, anyway. Too softhearted and clumsy. Besides, there was something else. In addition to being strong, well coordinated, and well educated, the ideal candidate would also have to have a compelling patriotic reason for endangering herself for the country, say an older brother killed in the army, or a family with a strong military tradition. Then the GSS would have to find some excuse to get her on campus. The chance of finding the right woman, he realized with some relief, was minuscule.

He'd go through the motions of teaching the class. In the meantime, his personal search for the Seventh Century would go on. Two hours from now he'd be in Gaza.

*   *   *

Joshua Stern heard the sirens but forced his concentration back to the ancient text opened before him. An hour later, though, despite the prohibitions against listening to the radio for the religious, the news filtered in and was passed by word of mouth. A volcano felt ready to burst in his chest, but he capped it and said, "Blessed be the True Judge," the religiously correct response to death. He tugged at his beard in frustration, trying to decide what to do. His wife always drove past the Monster on her way to and from work. A sickening wave of fear lodged in his belly, but, he reminded himself, she never would have been at the park on a workday. Not Deborah. He still wanted to call her. It was 2:30, and she might be napping. Four would be a better time to phone. She usually went out with the children by five and they would eat a late dinner at seven.

In the large study hall, which smelled of old books and sweating men, Joshua picked up a tall book of Talmud: each page had a 1600-year-old text in the center and scholarly commentaries arranged around it. Today's section was about sacrifices in the Temple 2000 years ago. He thought of the four dead women. How many sacrifices did God require of them?

Joshua called on his iron discipline to get back to the material he needed to prepare for the rabbi's evening lesson. He spent from early morning until after midnight in the study hall, where students prayed and read passages out loud, making points with expressive forefingers. Some sat, but many, like Joshua, preferred to stand and rest their books on individual high wooden stands. The room was as large as a school gym, but spare except for the gilt rectangular ark against the wall, rescued in World War II from a synagogue in Italy. Inside were Torah Scrolls.

When he'd come here a year ago to try it out, he had suffered from the noise, from trying to think in a room with 200 men shouting out points of law. Subjects as esoteric as whether one could gather snow on the Sabbath were debated with seriousness. At first he wondered how the answers to the questions tormenting him could be found amid the web of fine points that obsessed his fellow students. Now he appreciated how the seemingly trivial points sharpened the mind to confront larger issues and that the constant study was in itself a way of serving God. The noise had the calming effect of background music, much like the Vivaldi concertos he listened to when he was at university. There he'd also studied law.

His study partner, Isaiah Teittler, walked toward him, sweat gathering on his forehead. He'd heard the news, too. "There's nothing we can do. Let's not compound the evil by wasting precious study time," Isaiah said, plunging into a precise reading of a text about the Temple grain offering.

What an odd couple they made, Joshua thought. Tall and broad-shouldered, he had maintained the build of an athlete despite his recent lack of exercise. Until three years ago he'd swum across the Sea of Galilee every spring in a national race, whereas he doubted if Isaiah could swim across a bathtub. Isaiah was at least fifty pounds overweight and short. His sole exercise was a nervous habit of picking up his skullcap and pressing it down again on his shining pate. At forty-five he was nearly bald, and the little hair circling his black skullcap was white. Joshua liked him immensely.

Isaiah read with enthusiasm, stopping where necessary to elucidate points, making the old text come alive.

Joshua listened, nodding his head. Then he read the Rashi commentary, a compendium of medieval insights in special script. In seconds they were lost in the sing-song dialectic. At 6:00 P.M., with an all-too-familiar sense of remorse, Joshua realized he'd forgotten to call Deborah.

Abed Shahada was just leaving Gaza when the one o'clock news came on his car radio in Arabic. Dressed in the summer suit of an Arab banker, he waited to go back through the Erez checkpoint. He pretended to look for something in his briefcase, so no one would see his face light up in joy. Ibrahim had done far better than he had anticipated.

The site on the road to Hadassah Hospital had been chosen to carry a message. In 1948, a caravan carrying seventy-eight Jewish doctors and nurses had been ambushed on its way to work. The Jews had abandoned the hospital on Mount Scopus. The current Hadassah Hospital had been built as a safer substitute. He bit back a smile. *Nothing is safe for you. We have beaten you before. We will beat you again. Jewish domination is at an end.*

Abed's Mitsubishi sedan was the third car in one of the long lines, and he pitied his fellow Palestinians who had to wait in the sun without air-conditioning. Every Arab in every line was carefully checked by Israeli soldiers. Both of the cars in front of him were Peugeot seven-seater station wagons carrying workers into Israel. The first bore a white Gaza license plate, the second, a blue plate like his own from the West Bank.

An officer was shouting commands to the soldiers at the checkpoint. The line would move more slowly now, since every person had to be checked before leaving the Gaza Strip. The General Security Service must have already discovered that Ibrahim was from Gaza and ordered more stringent checks of Palestinians entering Israel.

His papers, like his gray business suit and wing-tip shoes, were impeccable. At six feet, he was taller than most Arabs, and his trimmed beard and prominent Semitic nose made him look the exact image of the new Palestinian technocrats who advised sheiks about money. He lived in a village outside of Jerusalem and did indeed work in the investments department of the Palestine-Arab Saving and Loan Bank in Hebron, a job for which his Swedish degree in business administration suited him. But despite his projected self-confidence, Abed had been conditioned from childhood to feel nervous while being examined by Israeli soldiers. He was also uneasy because his plan to be safely out of Gaza before noon had gone awry. Bad luck. A routine patrol happened to pick on the house where he was counting his money, and he'd narrowly escaped arrest.

In the first Peugeot, one by one the men presented their identity cards for electric scanning. Abed rarely went into Gaza himself because the risks were so great. But his new, grandiose mission required money that was smuggled from Iran and Syria into the Strip.

He would continue attacking Jerusalem, showing how vulnerable the Israelis were in their own capital. And while he was hammering away, the real plan would take place in nearby Bethlehem. The little town of Bethlehem, a holy place for Christians, would gain them as much publicity. In contrast to Jerusalem, it had a sleepy local police force. Bethlehem had always been a low-profile military town because of the Christian minority that lived there. In the center of town and crucial to his scheme was a small college that the security forces had never closed, not even when all other West Bank colleges were shut down. The dean of Manger College was Christian and considered neutral in the Jewish-Moslem conflict. The student organization had already been infiltrated, but the faculty had proved impermeable.

To Abed's left, Israeli vehicles with their yellow license plates were passed through the crossing with the wave of a hand. Their line was much shorter than the Palestinians'. Nonetheless, one Israeli truck driver carrying crates of zucchini was trying to edge out another truck arriving with cement blocks.

Israelis despised waiting. They thought it was beneath them.

In contrast, Abed thought, waiting was a virtue inherited through an Arab's genes.

He had waited until the right link fell in place. To make his plan work, Abed needed one above-reproach faculty member on the inside. Someone he could control. He had heard that the dean was under pressure by American donors to increase the number of women on the faculty. Who would ever suspect a pregnant woman, particularly the wife of an aristocratic doctor?

Ibrahim was only a tool to bring Raba to them. Now they would go ahead at full speed. After Operation Manger, the so-called peace process wouldn't even be a footnote in the history books. The armed struggle to take Palestine would resume, more fiercely than ever. Islam would conquer not just Palestine but the world.

They would wait again. And they would win.

2

Deborah arrived early at the gym. She took a place in the front row and started stretching, flexing her arms over her head, bending back each leg at the knee so she could feel the pull in her thigh muscles. Moving felt good.

Deborah's hands gripped her waist, and she turned right and left. The elastic on the sweat pants hung loose. She'd lost her appetite since she and Joshua had separated. The blond ponytail flipped over her forehead as she curved forward, grasped an ankle, and held to the count of ten. Upside down, she smiled at Rachel, who'd come to stand near her. Rachel stuck out her ample chest and stretched her T-shirt by its hem to show off the neon MOMMY printed there. "I thought I'd remind Raphi whom he's teaching kung fu to."

Rachel hated exercise. The attacks must have shaken her deeply. When Deborah had first come to Israel, natives in sandals bragged about safe streets. Israelis now wore Nike Air sneakers, but no one felt safe anymore, Deborah realized, as the room filled up with rows of women.

Rachel copied Deborah's motions, breathing hard in the hot gym. "What are you, a jock or something?" Rachel asked.

Deborah slowed her toe touches so Rachel could keep up. Next to her Rubenesque friend, Deborah knew she looked boyish, a tight sports bra tethering her under a huge basketball shirt of Joshua's. It still carried his pleasing earthy scent. All his sport clothes had been left behind, even his running shorts and the beloved, scratched hiking boots he'd used whenever they'd scrambled up hillsides covered with prickly scrub. In the yeshiva, only black suits, white shirts, and black hats were worn. Even in a faded suit, Joshua looked so handsome that her throat constricted thinking of him.

The room suddenly fell silent. Deborah stopped doing toe touches and looked up as Raphi Lahav entered through a side door of the gym. No one had to announce him as the teacher. His footsteps were soundless, his erect posture broadcast authority. One of the women had whispered that Raphi worked for the GSS. Deborah remembered hearing something about that, one of those security secrets passed freely in conversation among Israelis but never revealed to anyone from outside the country. She'd assumed Raphi worked for the Mossad, Israel's secret service abroad, because Rachel's children often wanted to play "Cousin Raphi on a mission to France" with Ben and Sarah. A while back, hadn't Rachel mentioned something about Raphi being injured?

Deborah had last seen him at the *brit mila*, the circumcision ceremony, for eight-day-old David Getz, Rachel's son. Raphi had received one of the honors traditionally reserved for an elderly relative: holding the baby on his lap for the brief but delicate surgery. Rachel's husband, Dan, had wanted one of his uncles, but for once Rachel had held firm and insisted on Raphi as godfather. He'd worn an outrageous purple skullcap because Rachel had knitted it for him when they were teens. Tears had made his eyes bright while the religious surgeon was bending over the baby. Deborah remembered getting a lump in her throat because so few Israeli men, certainly not Joshua, would cry in public. Could today's teacher be the same man? Nothing but nothing looked endearing or domestic about him tonight in black T-shirt and black pants, which outlined a lean, muscular physique. His small eyes, brown bordering on black, displayed neither humor nor compassion, and his concise movements conveyed impatience, not a promising characteristic for a teacher.

"I'm glad to see some of you are already warming up," he said, nodding only to his cousin, irking Deborah. "But before we start in earnest, we have to talk."

The command in his voice was mitigated by his graceful motion, like a dancing master's, for them to sit on the floor. He remained standing and looked down at them. "The first rule in self-defense is to avoid conflict," Raphi said. "Always run away from a fight. Always. Someone calls you a dirty Jew, walk away. Someone gives you a lewd look, walk away. If I'm walking down the street with a woman and someone makes a pass at her, even puts his arm on her shoulder, I pull her away and we disappear. I don't react—and I have some experience in the martial arts. Wimps live a long life."

Give me a break, thought Deborah. The thought of him running away under any circumstances was as absurd as John Wayne collapsing at the sight of his first Indian. Is this all the course was about?

"Now you're all asking yourself why you have to come to a course to learn to run away," Raphi said with a smile. He paused again, looking at each of them in turn as if checking them for worthiness. "Many of you signed up for this course because of what happened at the Monster statue. Four women died. No more than one, maybe two would have died if they'd run."

Deborah's face burned with anger. What if you had to gather a kid from the sandbox and another from the swings, or your best friend was attacked?

Raphi went on. "In this course we learn survival, not heroism. So if you're disappointed, leave now. You aren't going to come out of this course Ms. Rambo, Jeanne d'Arc, or Jeanne Van Damme for that matter. Nor can I guarantee that you won't be paralyzed by fear and forget everything if you're attacked."

As he spoke, his eyes moved from one student to the next. Deborah's pulse accelerated with nervousness when they reached her. "In the final analysis, how you react is determined by, well, character." He paused after the last word, his lips pressing in a grim line.

"Nevertheless, those of us who are involved in martial arts do believe a certain approach can be learned, and that it might mean the difference between life and death. And, of course, training itself can transform character."

He walked around them. Grudgingly, Deborah admired his feline grace. "If you do have to fight, you fight to kill. There are no gray areas in martial arts. Pity the attacker and your family will be saying Kaddish by evening. Now, if you still want to take this course, let's get up and throw some elbows," Raphi said, again raking each student with those cold eyes.

"How do you like my cousin?" Rachel whispered.

"I'm reserving judgment," Deborah said, not wanting to hurt Rachel's feelings.

"No talking over there," Raphi said, his eyes on Deborah.

Drop dead, she thought, determined not to feel five years old no matter if he intentionally infantilized them.

She took her place in the front row. Raphi shifted his weight from leg to leg, pausing to massage his left knee. He lifted his right elbow high and patted it with his left hand. "Hands and arms are weak. Elbows are strong if you put your weight behind them. Just see what a little elbow tap feels like."

He walked down the rows and touched their foreheads with his forearm, an inch below the elbow. It hurt. Fuck off, Deborah thought, rubbing the spot. Why am I here anyway? The words that echoed in her nightmares since last week came back as an answer: "You're next!"

Drawing a deep breath, she swung her elbows as Raphi commanded. He talked about "harnessing power" as he stalked the rows, watching them, making corrections. "Aim higher," Raphi ordered when he stopped near Deborah. "You're shorter than most attackers and you have to target the face. Hitting a chest is a waste of energy. Smash an eye socket or break a nose."

You're not so tall yourself. He was about five ten,

at least two inches shorter and more leanly built than
Joshua, who had broad shoulders and a deep chest.
The whole class stopped to watch her throw her elbows under Raphi's gaze. Still dissatisfied, he changed
the angle of her arm with a grip that felt like a vise.
"Like that." Deborah let out her breath when he finally moved on to the next student. She rubbed her
hand over her upper arm muscle where she still felt
the bruising pressure of his fingers. Not one to be
bullied, she concentrated on getting it right, resolving
to practice at home in front of a mirror, the way she'd
taught herself to dance in high school.

When Raphi announced they should begin cool-
down exercises, Deborah glanced at her watch, puzzled. Two hours had flown by.

After class she felt wide awake. Sleep would evade
her for hours. She urged Rachel, her brown hair in
sweaty tangles, to come over for a quick cup of coffee,
but Rachel said Dan was bringing clients home. His
patent-law practice, like their family, was expanding
and Dan loved it, even if it meant eighteen-hour work-
days. Deborah handed Rachel her water canteen. "Do
you mind his obsession with work?"

"He's always there when I really need him," Rachel
said. Then she flushed. "Sorry, Deborah. Joshua loves
you. I know that one day he'll get over what happened
and come back."

Deborah squeezed Rachel's arm to show she hadn't
taken offense. "He'd better hurry," Deborah said with
exasperation. "I just might not be home."

Deborah knocked on her door before sliding the
key in the lock. The door was made of steel; the previous owners had bragged about it as an expensive feature when she and Joshua had bought the apartment.
She'd felt safe back then and they'd laughed at the so-
called extras, which also included revolting velveteen
wallpaper. Barefoot, in jeans, she and Joshua had
peeled the wallpaper, strip by strip, finally making love
on the floor, patches of wallpaper sticking to their
damp skin.

She was glad about the steel door now.

She knocked again and heard Inbal, the baby-sitter, turn off the TV. When Deborah was a teenaged baby-sitter in Connecticut, parents always startled her by opening the door without knocking. Joshua used to tease her ("Yes, you may enter your own house now, Mrs. Stern"), but after he'd turned extremely religious he'd learned of a Jewish law requiring that you knock at your own door, even if no one is home. "You see, you have an intuitive grasp of halakhah," he'd said, using with respect the word for the code that now bound his life. He yearned for her to be his companion on his spiritual odyssey. At first she'd welcomed anything that helped him combat the devils that had tormented him since the jeep he was driving hit a roadside charge and his best friend was killed. But then his personal journey took him spiraling far away from her. She ached to have him back, for the closeness they'd shared, and because having an intact family was important to her. Yet, unlike the biblical Ruth, she couldn't force herself to follow on pure faith. Guiltily, she felt more like Orpah, the other daughter-in-law, who went home and gave birth to Goliath.

Deborah locked the door, fixed herself an icy lemonade, and turned on the TV for the news. On the wall behind the couch was a family picture gallery. Soon after they'd met, Joshua took her to visit Christian Arab friends whose parlor was decorated with dozens of family pictures. She'd loved the idea and adopted it. In the center of mounted photographs was a wedding picture. How happy and confident the young, naive Deborah looked, staring adoringly at the tall, cocky sabra.

The news came on. Another Molotov cocktail had exploded on the road to Bethlehem. Two more Arab teenagers had been wounded in clashes with the army at the Dehaishe refugee camp. A predicted devaluation of the shekel would take place at midnight, shrinking her salary even further. Researchers' salaries were linked to a national wage scale and were modest in comparison to what private industry was paying.

The last item on the news was a renewed warning to the public for awareness due to terrorist attacks. Suspicious packages that might be bombs, particularly in buses and in school yards, needed to be reported immediately to the emergency police number, 1-0-0. It was written in black marker on the kitchen phone for the children.

She flicked off the TV and went to check them. Ben moved restlessly in his sleep, as if working through a nightmare. He still hadn't told her why he was fighting so much in school, making her worry that he was holding back some dark secret, like his father. Sarah was sunnier. She'd only inherited Joshua's dark curls. A single black strand had attached itself to her upper lip, and Deborah gently unstuck it.

In the moonlit room, the closet mirror caught her reflection. She looked a minute at the disheveled blonde, skinny and leggy, with vulnerable eyes who stood there. So different from the young woman in the photographs.

Her new martial arts master had warned them never to look vulnerable.

Silently, she threw an elbow at her own image.

After closing up the gym, Raphi caught the eleven o'clock news on his car radio, then tapped in Anat's number on the car phone. While the phone rang, he moved his shoulders in circles to get a kink out of his neck.

"Anat." He smiled into the receiver. "Are you alone? Want some company? In an hour. I'm going home to shower."

By the time he pulled into his driveway, he regretted calling her. Going to sleep in his own bed seemed a better option. He pressed a button in the driveway to turn on the light that led to his doorway. Like many lights in Israel, it shut off on a timer. He counted the seconds, and it shut off exactly at ten. There was one way, though, that his light switch was different from most others: if anyone had tampered with his door, it would switch off after five.

He paused at a potted lemon tree on the path that led from the driveway to his apartment on the ground floor, which was behind the main apartment building and had its own entrance. The sweet smell of his flourishing lemon tree pleased him. Lemons weren't supposed to do well in the cool Jerusalem climate, but his were thriving. He reached into the pot, checked the dampness of the soil, then pressed an additional button.

He pushed the door wide open. An old habit. His house was quiet and tidy, as it had been left. A light flashed from his answering machine showing he had two messages. A familiar voice. Gil. "The next fishing trip is on. Bring your line." Raphi scowled at the prospect of hunting terrorists. The late Chairman Mao had first called them fish. The second voice was his mother's from Zurich. His diplomat parents still did a lot of traveling even though his father had officially retired. Since the Israeli embassy had been bombed in London, he worried more than ever about them. He'd put in enough time working for the Mossad in Europe to realize how vulnerable diplomats were. His mother sounded cheerful, but then she always sounded as if she hadn't a problem in the world no matter how tough things got. Rachel was like her.

Tonight he'd been reassured that Rachel would never be chosen for the assignment. None of her friends seemed right, either. The only two who bore consideration from an athletic point of view were two heavyset women in the back row. He'd have to ask Rachel about them. The blond friend in the front row moved well, and the tautness of her arm muscles had been a surprise, but she was too skinny and high-strung. Also, Rachel had once told him Deborah Stern might be getting divorced. A single parent would never agree to a dangerous assignment.

Soaping his lean body, Raphi thought about Anat, whom he'd favored for the role. He'd been seeing her off and on, but not exclusively, for a year. She was much like him, all surface and calculation. The GSS had thought they were well paired and had used them on a mission as husband and wife. Going to bed hadn't been a requirement of the job, but their chemistry was right.

A half hour later, he parked in front of Anat's square apartment building, of the type built in the fifties when immigrants were coming so fast no one had time or money for imaginative architecture or the stone finish required on Jerusalem buildings. She lived on the fourth floor. There was no elevator, but Raphi would have taken the stairs even if there had been. Elevators were death traps.

"Just a minute," Anat shouted when he rang the bell. She smelled of duty-free Obsession and makeup. Tiny black lines of freshly applied mascara had smeared under her brown, almond-shaped eyes. A black tunic made it clear she was braless and just covered the crotch of red tights on long shapely legs.

"You walk like a cat—I couldn't hear you coming up the stairs," she said, kissing him lightly hello. "You'll have to show me how you do that sometime."

"What do you need it for? I thought you were getting out of the cat-and-mouse game."

"I have another three months working in airline security. Do you have nightmares?"

"I can't remember my dreams. My cousin Rachel, an amateur psychologist, says that's because they're too deeply repressed."

They drank beer and gossiped about colleagues—Gil's newest secretary conquest and the GSS commander's long-term mistress. Israel's security services had long ago lost the puritanical ethics for which they were known in the early years of the state. Raphi wanted to deepen their conversation, but as usual they couldn't get beyond the superficial—so they opted for the physical. He put his hand under her chin, softly caressing her skin. Her tongue ran over his teeth and greedy fingers impatiently loosened his belt, searching inside. "Ah," she said. "You never disappoint."

He insisted on locking the bedroom door, even though her flatmate, a genuine stewardess, was flying over Germany. Anat lifted the tunic over her head in one smooth movement, leaving her, in the red tights, like someone who had just stepped out of a hot bath. He unbuttoned his shirt, tossing it on a chair. Anat's long red nails ran over his chest and then lower down, her tongue playing in the corner of her mouth. She liked to push the fast-forward button, since neither of them had much patience for foreplay. Her preference was for bondage games, but Raphi rarely went along. Tonight she peeled off her tights as he pulled off his jeans. They were indeed well paired, he thought, sliding easily into her. He could feel her arch, and he held still so she could come before his own spasms began.

Raphi kissed her smudged mouth and rolled over, fighting the letdown he always felt after their sex.

As usual, Anat's breathing immediately evened. Like many who worked in airline security, she'd learned to fall asleep on command. He went to the kitchen. A roach scurried along the baseboard when the light went on. A former army chief of staff had once likened the Palestinians to roaches. Now he was a Knesset member and the head of a party opposed to the peace process that Raphi was dedicated to preserving.

His personal efforts, like most of the GSS's fight against the intifada, were not going well. Last week's venture into the Gaza Strip, like the previous ones, had yielded nothing of value. He'd been impersonating an Arab plumber with a gimp left leg because his own had been acting up. His fellow day laborers were so tired from the hard work, the long ride to Israeli cities, and the noise of their crowded homes that their vigilance was relaxed. Often they bragged about roles their brothers or cousins played in the anti-Israel resistance. This information was more accurate than the reams of copy that poured out of the GSS computer each day, collected from paid Palestinian informers. Israeli intelligence placed enormous weight on information gathering. An order of expensive beef to a refugee camp in Lebanon had once tipped them off to a high-level PLO meeting there, in time for navy commandos to attack. But the specific information

Raphi needed wasn't materializing. No one ever mentioned a group called the Seventh Century.

The GSS and Aman, army intelligence, had concluded that even though Ibrahim Masri had been sent by the Seventh Century to kill women at the Monster slide, he was a relatively recent and low-level recruit. Gil was patiently gathering material from him, but all of it was too low level to lead back to the organizer. The only effective way to stop a terrorist cell was to lop off the top, throwing it into chaos.

Raphi thought of an Arabic saying: *Iza ana amir, uinte amir, min yisuk alhamir.* If you're a prince and I'm a prince, who will lead the donkey? Ibrahim led the donkey. Raphi wanted the prince.

There had to be a clue or a leak somewhere.

Close to dawn, Raphi went back to bed and fell asleep for a few hours. Anat's wanting to make him breakfast the following morning should have pleased him, but it didn't. She chopped up tomatoes and cucumbers and heated frozen croissants to go with scrambled eggs. Somehow asking how he liked his eggs seemed more intimate than sex. But the morning sun streaming on her short hair and long neck enhanced her beauty as she moved gracefully in the tiny kitchen, and he felt the stirrings of arousal again. The clock told him there wasn't enough time.

"What are you doing on Saturday?" Anat asked, scraping the edges of the frying pan.

"Going fishing," he said.

"Wow, you're still doing that shit, even with autonomy coming? My sympathies. I tried it a couple of times when I was in the army—but nothing could make me do it again. I do a little play acting from time to time and a little eavesdropping, but for the most part it's passive observation." She stuck a fingernail into the smile line of his cheek. "Dangerous enough. Wasn't your last partner killed in Gaza?"

His face froze in anger at the casual mention of Yusef. Raphi had been unable to protect him. How could he protect an amateur, especially a woman?

*   *   *

The elderly obstetrician whom Ali had summoned to check Raba took her blood pressure, listened for the baby's heartbeat, and recommended bed rest. For a change, Raba accepted his diagnosis without arguing. She felt limp, and any excuse to avoid company was welcome. Nightmares spoiled her sleep, and guilt, lodged in her chest like cancer, plagued her when she was up. Would her brother have had a better life if she'd stayed in Gaza? Could she have helped him by visiting more often? Their visits had been brief and perfunctory.

Raba also felt deep shame over the scandal she had brought to Ali's aristocratic family. His parents were traveling abroad and she prayed they wouldn't read enough details in the *International Herald Tribune* to connect Ibrahim to her. But after a full day of weeping, Raba's mood began to improve slightly. Ali's Aunt Juni and Juni's married daughter presented her with a gift of hand-embroidered handkerchiefs. They seemed undisturbed by Ibrahim's crime, acting even more solicitous than usual about her health. Oddly, they even seemed more respectful. A maid had shyly presented her homemade citron jam, a sure remedy, she claimed, for troubled pregnancies. Blushing, she'd told Raba that *before* she'd been embarrassed to offer a folk remedy, but now, well, Raba was "more like us."

On the third day after the attack, Raba and Ali went to see her parents in the Gaza Strip. The poverty, filth, the smell of garbage always shocked her anew. How had she survived her first eight years here? There were no more children at home. Raba's oldest brother had been killed in a truck accident while she was in America. Two sisters, much older, were married and living in Khan Yunis, in the southern part of the Gaza Strip. They kept little contact with her parents. Her father, gray but still strong as a bull, gloated over Ibrahim's new status as a hero. "Boy was always a disappointment, but he finally did something right," her father said, his words slurred because of missing teeth. Her parents lived off UN relief funds. A mason, her father had rarely worked for more than two days running.

Raba tried to tune out her father's irritating talk, but she was ashamed in front of Ali. Aisha, her mother, looked helpless and old, even though she was only fifty-one. "Ibrahim, Ibrahim, what can we do for you?" she'd wept on Raba's shoulder. Later, when they were alone preparing the meal, Aisha's eyes were dry as she suggested Raba find Ibrahim a Jewish lawyer with a strong civil rights background. Raba was beginning to realize just how carefully her mother hid her quick intelligence from her father. Later, when they ate together, her mother was silent as she dished out the lamb stew prepared by Raba's cook in Jericho. They ate it with Aisha's homebaked pita, which still tasted better to Raba than any other bread in the world.

On the fifth day after the attack, Raba returned to work. She was the sole psychologist in a mother-child clinic for poor Arab families in east Jerusalem. The other employees called her Dr. Rab'iah, or *aldoctora.* Before Raba had started working there, mothers used to come only for their children's inoculations. She initiated developmental examinations, and personally saw parents of any children showing signs of a problem.

Images of her brother as a boy flooded her mind as she tested a three-year-old who didn't speak. The child's mother admitted taking him to a demonstration where he'd been exposed to tear gas. Raba guessed that shock was the root of his problem. There had been similar cases, and the staff knew Raba felt strongly that children should be protected from street violence. She believed mothers should keep them out of the line of fire—staying home themselves if necessary. Children would have time for politics when they grew up. The others found her cold and preachy. Ali had no idea just how foreign she felt among her own people. *Let me fit in here for Ali's sake,* she'd prayed.

The nurses and paraprofessional aides had always been respectful, courteous, but distant. Was she imagining new sympathetic smiles? A young woman who wore religious head covering drew her aside and begged her not to worry, that Allah would watch over her brother. Raba was surprised, and vaguely uncomfortable, as if the woman was suggesting she had complicity in Ibrahim's actions. At the same time, the warmth was pleasing.

She was delighted when nurses invited her to take tea with them instead of serving her with the single cup of fine china in her office. As she warmed to the subtle and overt changes in attitude toward her, she realized they were being kinder because of Ibrahim. Her shame over his actions was increasingly coupled by anxiety over his welfare. Raba wondered if Ibrahim was being beaten. She couldn't get her mind off the stories of Arabs tortured to death in Israeli prisons.

Then Najia, one of her older patients, a usually truculent mother of twelve children, had canceled an appointment because she was going to visit her oldest son in jail. Najia had mentioned the jail visit matter-of-factly, as an American mother might mention visitors' day at summer camp. To Raba's astonishment, three of Najia's twelve children were in prison. Najia wanted to know if Raba had visited Ibrahim in Jerusalem.

Somehow it had never occurred to her that she could visit a security prisoner. What was wrong with her? Despite all the propaganda, she knew Israel wasn't the Soviet Union. No one was shipped to the Gulag. Ibrahim was in jail in Jerusalem, all alone. The thought crossed her mind that she might be exposing herself to trouble, but she waved it away. After all, thanks to Aunt Fatima, Raba was an American citizen. Why hadn't Ali suggested it? He might object to her going. But a brother was a brother, murderer or not.

On Friday morning, his day off from the bank, Abed Shahada, leader of the Seventh Century, worked in his mother's grocery store. He waited until the other customers had left before addressing the veiled woman holding a baby. "So she was interested in visiting the jail?"

Najia nodded. She shopped daily at the grocery, and served as the contact between her large, nationalistic family and the Seventh Century. Abed thought of her as a perfect Palestinian woman of valor, quiet and steady, supportive of the two sons and one daughter who sat in Israeli jails. Another son, a mechanic, would carry out the next Jerusalem strike. Such families were the backbone of the intifada. Najia refused payment for the work she did for their cause. "God forbid that I should take money for holy work," she'd said. Abed was impressed, since she shopped on credit at his mother's store, and he knew her debt was large.

He counted out eggs, gently placing them inside a plastic egg carrier basket. Najia moved slowly, selecting tins of tomato puree and sesame paste from the crowded shelves. Abed's mother had expanded the store so that it carried school supplies and plastic hair barrettes, high-profit items his father had never thought of stocking. Above the store was a columbary, where pigeons roosted. His blind half sister Laila took care of them.

Abed's father, a heavy smoker, had died of lung cancer when Abed was five. Six months later, Abed's mother had surprised everyone by marrying his father's cousin, Burhan, seven years her junior and considered an unemployed gigolo by the villagers. Burhan had reformed after the wedding and had begun working long hours in the store. Even as a boy, Abed realized Burhan made his mother giggle in a way his father never had. His mother had four daughters with Burhan before having her tubes tied in a private clinic. Abed knew about this because he'd found the bill when he did the bookkeeping.

Burhan treated him with benign indifference, but Abed despised his stepfather. Despite his resentment, Abed outwardly accorded both his mother and her husband the respect Moslem children paid their parents. He worked in the store on his day off so they could go to the Dead Sea to ease his mother's rheumatism.

To his surprise, Abed doted on his half sisters, particularly the youngest, Laila, who'd been blinded by a rubber bullet in a riot.

Thinking about Laila's blindness used to make him feel helpless. Now it fueled his anger.

The store was an excellent place for making contacts. Most of the villagers bought on credit, paying when they could. His mother never commented, no matter how high the figures rose. "He who eats his fill while his neighbor goes without food is not a believer," she quoted the Koran. Nonetheless, debts were carefully listed in a hardcover ledger. Maybe he'd inherited his business acumen from her. Abed, too, loved to have people in his debt.

Najia heaved her purchases up on the short counter that held the scale and cash register. Abed rang up the bill. Then his long fingers reached into a square tin canister and came out with a *petit beurre.* Najia's baby grabbed it in his chubby fists, stuffing it so fast into his mouth that half fell to the floor.

Why, you're just like your older brothers, Abed thought.

Unlike their mother, Najia's sons' idealism did not preclude taking money from the cause. They'd grown up on salaries from the PLO youth groups, and then, when the Moslem organizations offered higher pay and more action, they'd become members of those. Five of her children were on his payroll.

The baby was chewing and looking toward Abed for another treat. Soon, Abed thought, there will be plenty of cookies and plenty of dinars.

3

A week had passed since her brother had massacred four women. It was time to face him.

Raba pulled together the gray cotton blazer to hide her pregnancy. She needed to be professional and to keep her feelings masked. Her best gold earrings were clipped on her ears, and a simple gold necklace was fastened around her neck. She buttoned two metallic buttons. Metal was a sign of authority. Power dressing, they'd called it in America.

Her adversaries would be wearing plenty of metal, too.

Looking professional should be a reflex by now, but it wasn't. For her mother, just feeding the children had been a daily challenge, and cleanliness was a low priority. In contrast, Aunt Fatima was obsessively clean and orderly. One of her first lessons to Raba had been the importance of looking right. Raba had her nails cut every Sunday night, and Uncle Ziad polished her shoes with a special cloth from the garage. As a result, her Quaker teachers often had used her as the model of what they expected from students. Despite such testimony, Raba had never banished the feeling that just below the surface, threatening to break through, was that girl from a Gaza Strip refugee camp with lice crawling up her braids.

Today her jet-black hair was stylishly cut so that it angled to a deep curve that fell in place below her cheekbones. Too bad she didn't feel as good as she looked.

Wassim, the Alhassan family driver, was waiting near the bright purple bougainvillea that bordered the driveway. Without her asking, the back door of the old but gleaming Mercedes was opened for her.

The moment the door closed behind her, Raba questioned the wisdom of her mission. Last night she'd argued passionately to Ali: "The police will question me anyway. Why shouldn't I initiate the contact, and show willingness to cooperate?" If handled correctly, her brother's actions might not jeopardize Ali's medical career. Ali had smiled at that. "Your brother's notoriety has lent your wimp husband new status among Palestinians," he said. "He's added prestige to the Alhassan family. Once wealth, intelligence, and a history stretching back to the conquering tribes was enough. In this new world jail terms, not graduate-school credits, count on a CV."

If convicted, Ibrahim would be transferred to a prison, probably the one south of Beersheba, Ali had found out. The death penalty had been applied only once in Israel: on Nazi mass murderer Adolph Eichmann. Did killing four women make her brother a mass murderer? Ali didn't think so.

Part of Raba had hoped Ali would convince her not to go. The thought of looking into her brother's eyes made her skin clammy. Nothing could justify what he'd done. Not to her. In Detroit, she'd refused to work with psychotic murderers during her psychology training, using her Quaker education as an excuse. In what her fellow psychologists, in their detached way, called her formative years, she'd known violence intimately. Nothing had been detached about the slaps, pinches, and pushes from her father's rough mason's hands. Once he'd broken a bone in her right hand just by squeezing.

Raba rested her head against the seat of the Mercedes, feeling threatened again by the violence of the past.

Wassim slowed and stopped. Raba opened her eyes and gasped at the sight of a teenage soldier with unsightly acne peering in her window, a submachine gun clenched in his hands. This was the roadblock north of Jerusalem where Arab cars were stopped for inspection. The soldier, judging her harmless, waved them on. Should she be pleased or insulted?

Jerusalem police headquarters, where Ibrahim would be detained until his trial, stood in the middle of town. Wassim let her off on Jaffa Road. Raba pulled down her skirt and straightened her shoulders. Two Arab women, their bosoms hanging low in embroidered black dresses, soiled white scarves over their heads, walked slowly toward the jail, on their way to visit relatives. Raba passed them, walking briskly out of nervousness. Her Italian heels clicked loudly on the sidewalk. She'd picked up Aunt Fatima's love of expensive shoes.

In Midwestern English she addressed the guard at the entrance to the Police Department. "I'm Dr. Raba Alhassan. I've come to see Ibrahim Masri, the security prisoner."

"Just a minute," said the policeman, looking her up and down. Don't react, she commanded herself.

The guard whispered something to a second policeman checking orange identity cards and pocketbooks. Raba handed him her American passport.

He told her to wait. Across from the guard station several dozen Arab women bided their time, their wide behinds hanging over the porch ledge, eating pumpkin seeds, breast-feeding babies while they took turns talking to their husbands and sons through the bars. Those were probably less serious offenders. The jails were crowded with Palestinians held without trial for twenty-one days. Men sat separately. She assumed they'd come for work permits or to visit relatives. The policeman motioned for her to follow him. She walked past the memorial shrine for dead police officers and into the main building. Inside was cool, in contrast to the heat of the day. The whiteness of the long halls came as a surprise, particularly the odd aesthetic concession of the delicate white wrought-iron staircase. The guard left her in a waiting area outside an office. The name on the door was in Hebrew so she couldn't read it. While waiting, she perused a trophy case where gold cups and photos of a police soccer team were displayed.

A tall police officer with the metal of rank on his shoulder opened the door to her. Red-eyed, his face unshaven, his mouth drawn down, he looked more like a prisoner than a jail keeper. But then, all jail keepers were imprisoned, too.

"I'm Inspector Gil. Can I help you?" the officer asked in British-accented English.

"I'm Dr. Alhassan. I've come to see Ibrahim Masri."

"What kind of doctor are you? The prisoner has already been examined by doctors. Are you from the Red Cross?"

"I'm a psychologist, not a physician. I'm not here to examine him. I've come to visit him. He's my brother."

The officer's brown eyes widened but he quickly recovered. "Ah, now I see the resemblance," he said, half smiling. "Come into my office. We need to fill out some papers."

Raba followed him down narrow halls to a small office. His desk was cleared, except for a shell ashtray and one rose in a glass vase. Pulling out a wooden chair, he waited for her to sit. "No one has come to visit him yet. We expected your parents."

"It's been a trauma for them. They're paralyzed from grief," Raba said, remembering to maintain eye contact.

"And you're not?"

"Each person grieves in his own way."

"Oh yes, you're a psychologist." Gil reached for an orange file. "We might as well get to it. I have to ask some questions."

Raba's fingers gripped her pocketbook. "I'd expect so."

He wanted to know when she'd last seen her brother and how Ibrahim had behaved. She admitted that Ibrahim had been agitated for the last five years, referring to the intifada. "Is anyone normal living under occupation?" she asked.

His jaw tightened, she saw with satisfaction. Israelis

were so predictable. Raba didn't care much about politics. It wouldn't do, however, to sound like a quisling. Raba groped for a handkerchief and pulled out a new embroidered one. She patted her forehead, clenching the handkerchief in her hand.

Gil leaned forward, tapping his pen on the desk. "We're not here to discuss politics. What do you mean by 'agitated'?"

"Short-tempered. Argumentative. Nervous. He avoided eye-contact, smoked jerkily, twitched his shoulders. Do you want a full diagnosis, Inspector? I have experience filling out forms."

"Did he try to recruit you?" he asked softly.

"My brother knows I am a feminist. We argued about it. Let's just say that there are conflicts between feminism and Islam that I had trouble resolving." Ibrahim, in fact, *had* tried to recruit her, accusing her of being a traitor, claiming that her years in America had compromised her, that she had a debt to pay, that if she believed women were equal she'd take risks, too.

Gil's eyes held hers for a long moment, then suddenly he stood. "You can go in now," he said. "But, I'm sorry—you'll have to be searched."

Her face turned hot. "Does your policy require humiliation?"

Gil didn't answer, just sighed wearily. He made a short phone call and a chubby, freckled policewoman he introduced as Yis'ka came in and led Raba to a dressing room. Raba froze as the policewoman, smelling of imitation Joy, lightly ran her hands over Raba's body, asked for her purse, examined it, then nodded an okay.

Raba's face burned in anger, and she felt another wave of exhaustion. She was too tired for what lay ahead. Facing Ibrahim would be a thousand times worse than a body search. She steadied herself and went with the policewoman, passing several guards as they left the main building and went into a cell area with a dimly lit corridor. No rats scurried in dark corners and there was no muffled weeping in the background. The halls were reasonably clean, smelling vaguely of pine disinfectant.

At the end of a hallway, closed off by cement blocks on all sides, two guards sat at a surveillance station. The one who actually was working the electronic board was missing fingers on both hands. Raba strained to see Ibrahim on the closed-system television, but the screens were turned away. The police-woman spoke to the guards. "Ze'ev will take you in now. Yoram will be watching, and I'll come back for you later," the policewoman said in English. "Good luck."

Yoram pressed a buzzer and Ze'ev, tall and broad as a fullback, pushed the heavy metal door open with his shoulder, waiting for Raba to walk through the narrow passage. She could smell the garlic on his breath as she squeezed by him.

Her heart pounding, Raba looked in the first tiny, narrow cell, but it was empty, as was the second. They walked to the third. Ibrahim! Despite all the prepara-tion, seeing him here came as a shock. She bit her fist to keep from crying out.

He paced back and forth in the small cell, as if unaware of them. At another electronic buzz, his cell door snapped open, and Ibrahim started as if a gun had been shot. "Raba!"

Tears were choked back in the first syllable of her name, and her throat filled. His large mahogany eyes were mirrors of her own. Even unshaven, he would have looked roguish and handsome if not for the lost, far-off expression in his eyes. Poor, poor Ibrahim. How could he have done it? Hadn't he sickened as life poured out of those women, he who trained to help the sick? Hadn't he cared that one woman was pregnant? She touched her own belly, and forced her-self to concentrate on his feelings. "How are you? Have they hurt you?"

"Zionist dogs. Allah will avenge me," he hollered at the two guards who stood silently outside the cell. "They beat me and electric shocked me. You must bring the International Red Cross."

He looked paler but fit, as if he'd gained weight. No signs of torture were apparent, but she had no reason not to believe him. Every Palestinian who was in Israeli jails came back with tales of being tied backward over chairs while being whipped, or horror stories of acid dripped into their wounds.

"Who can feel well?" he shouted. "I haven't eaten. They fry congealed blood and serve it with poisoned bread."

"Can I bring you anything?" she asked, worried that the walls would start spinning. She sat down awkwardly at the edge of a metal bed cemented to the floor. The guard moved closer.

"A knife to slice their Zionist throats," he shouted, clenching his fingers around an imaginary sword. Raba looked at the guard, who stood, eyes blank, his mouth twisted in a yawn.

"Let them hear it all. They won't be able to sleep at night, like me, waiting for the next torture."

Raba reached for his hand and finger by finger unclenched his fist, choking down revulsion as she imagined his fingers stained with women's blood. There were no scars or cigarette burns. In contrast to their father's hands, Ibrahim's were smooth like a woman's. She inched aside so he could sit next to her. "Can I bring you anything to eat. Maybe *za'atar*?" His favorite dish had always been dried hyssop in olive oil. Childlike delight brightened his eyes and he licked his lips.

Bending her head, Raba whispered that he could confide in her what was in his heart, that she would do anything she could for him, that all the resources of the Alhassan family would be used for his defense. When he wanted to know how their parents were taking his arrest, she told him about the visit, about their mother's good idea about the lawyer and how proud their father was. She asked about his being in solitary, and he said it was an advantage because he couldn't be raped. The drug addicts worried him most. Other prisoners had already offered him drugs. If he stayed much longer in jail, he was afraid they would get to him. You may be staying the rest of your life, she thought. Then they sat in silence, Raba holding his hand.

"I loved it," Ibrahim whispered to her, moving still closer. At her puzzled look, he continued, "The feeling of the knife cutting through the Zionist state. I could feel my own blood flowing through my veins, as if I was alive for the first time. I knew the spirit of Allah was in me."

Instinctively, she put her hand on her belly again, as if to protect her unborn child. Ibrahim's eyes followed the movement. "You must make your son a fighter for the cause. Make him tough. Islam is the greatest gift you can give him. Make him a soldier for Islam. If I die, name him for me. Don't let him grow into a weakling like your husband."

Recoiling at the insult to Ali, she stopped herself from answering back. Ibrahim's hatred of Israelis was only surpassed by his jealousy of aristocratic Arabs. His worst fear was that, when the revolution finally came, the same educated aristocrats would be back on top and he would have to serve them. He saw Islam as the equalizer that would make him achieve their status. "I'll come again, soon," she said. "And I'll tell Mother and Father that I've seen you."

She leaned forward and kissed his forehead.

He stared at her and began to declaim from the Koran in a loud voice: "Turn to Allah with genuine repentance in the hope your Lord will remove your evil deeds."

While the walls were still ringing with his voice, she heard him whisper, "Stay out of Jerusalem. We'll strike again very soon. Don't fear, my leader will contact you soon. You have an important role to play, dear sister. Only you will save me. Our family will be redeemed through you, praise Allah."

He threw himself at the bars and began to chant "*Idbah alyahud*," death to the Jews. The guard grabbed him roughly by the arms and pushed him back toward the bed.

"Leave him alone," Raba commanded. The policewoman had entered to guide her out. Ibrahim lay on his bed, weeping.

Raba wiped her lips, salty from the sweat on Ibrahim's forehead, with the handkerchief, but his image seemed to stay on the cloth, like Jesus' when Veronica wiped his face, on his way to the Cross.

Her wretchedness at seeing her brother as a murderer was overwhelming. What had pushed him over the edge? It was easy to blame his violence on the Israelis. But she knew better. Ibrahim's troubles, like her own, had started at home.

Maybe their father would have turned out differently if his parents hadn't forced him to marry his cousin when his older brother had refused. Abdullah, seventeen and madly in love with a village girl, had honored the family promise. He never let Aisha forget it. Raba's mother had fled his beatings once, but no one would take her in, not even her own parents. Her rebellion crushed, her dreams of becoming a schoolteacher gone forever, she had resigned herself to abuse as part of life's inevitable unfolding.

Lost in thought, Raba tripped and fell over an unshaven Arab wearing a dirty black-and-white keffiyah, sitting on the jail steps. The arm that caught her was so strong she assumed he was a construction worker, one of the thousands who wasted their lives building Israeli homes. He bent his face in embarrassment, and she thanked him in Arabic so he'd know she wasn't Israeli despite her stylish dress. He muttered an apology for getting in her way.

"Don't think of it," she said, no longer feeling aloof from the Arabs waiting at the jail portal. They'd been drawn together in a fraternity of agony, much like the unlikely friendships she'd observed among families of terminal patients in the Detroit hospital. She smiled at the man again, but he was looking into his lap, working mother-of-pearl *masbaha*—worry beads.

Outside, Raba gulped for air. Her anguish mixed with relief at getting beyond the barred walls. The perfect blue sky seemed inappropriate for such a glum day. She stood in the sun for a few minutes, warming up. Cars and buses crowded Jaffa Road, built on the ancient donkey path that led from the coast to Jerusalem, into the Old City. Wassim would be waiting around the corner, probably with a thermos of cold water.

Ibrahim's parting words rang in her ears. Who would contact her? And what would they demand of her when they did?

A few minutes later, the man Raba had tripped over was summoned by the name Abu Daud. Daud was Arabic for David. Abu meant "father of." Ever since Raphi had become David Getz's godfather at his circumcision ceremony, he'd been using this alias. He adjusted his keffiyah and, with his head down, followed a surly soldier down the hallway. He didn't like to be seen in his university attire at headquarters, and preferred to arrive wearing whatever identity he was currently using for his forays into Gaza. There was always the chance that someone would recognize the professor's face on a lame plumber. Safely inside Gil's office, Raphi pulled off the dirty keffiyah and tossed it on a chair.

Gil poured the coffee. It was, as always, strong and fragrant. How many cups had they drunk together?

Gil had surprised him by accepting a desk job. When he and Gil had first been young combatants, they'd ridiculed anyone not working undercover. But now Gil was working as a liaison between the Minorities Intelligence Department of the police and the GSS, as well as planning maneuvers for Raphi's unit, itself an anachronism. It was the last of the small teams reporting directly to the GSS commander. Today's General Security Services had been revamped. Most of the so-called combatants did little more than gather information from paid Palestinian informers. Like Raphi, they dressed up in Arab clothing to gather material on the ground, but many didn't even speak Arabic. Past thirty, Raphi and Gil were officially getting too old for fieldwork, but they had been so successful that intelligence had kept them on, leftovers

from an earlier era when individuality was prized over
high-tech solutions. Then Gil had changed sides of
the desk, too. Raphi couldn't blame him. Gil's only
brother's death on a mission in Lebanon had awakened in Gil a previously dormant instinct for self-pres-
ervation, something Raphi obviously lacked. You
know all the karate commands, but will your body still
take orders? Gil had asked him.

Raphi didn't know the answer. His left knee ached
from squatting. Gil's instinct had proved right about
one thing. Yusef, who had taken over for Gil, was
dead, while Gil was still alive.

Raphi took another sip of coffee. "Wonderful, as
always."

Gil nodded. "That woman was Raba, the psychologist sister. Our file says she has peace-loving tenden-
cies—went to a Quaker school, is working in an east
Jerusalem clinic for babies."

"She's expecting one herself."

Gil tilted his head in surprise. "How do you know
that?"

"She tripped over me. I got a close-up."

"Seeing her brother must have shaken her up. In
my office she was very composed. She spouted the
usual Palestinian line as if she were reciting a script.
Her clothes were calculated. Why wear a blazer, even
a cotton one, on a summer day? Yis'ka body-searched
her and classified her cosmetics as expensive, which,
according to her theory about women and makeup,
means she's not a social iconoclast. How did she get
a brother like him?"

"How the hell do I know? We're not exactly doing
Quaker work ourselves," Raphi said, sipping the black
coffee. "What would you be doing if you were born
on the other side, had been brought up in a hovel,
and had a violent parent to boot?"

"I wouldn't knife women."

"But you'd use them as decoys."

Gil rubbed a stiff neck. "Cut the shit, Raphi. You
know there's no choice. Every day more intelligence
accumulates that a major act of terrorism is going to

take place in Bethlehem. It's the eleventh hour, maybe the twelfth. So I changed my vote. Spare me the recriminations. How is the ladies' martial arts class working out?"

"About as well as your marriage worked out." Gil's impetuous marriage to a Turkish dancer had broken up almost immediately, but they still hadn't worked through the details of the divorce. The dancer turned out to be alcoholic, bisexual, and an excellent businesswoman, who wanted Gil's apartment and his balls "to decorate it," as Gil was fond of saying.

"You know what they say. Better to have loved and lost than never to have loved at all, Raphi boy." Unlike many of his colleagues, Raphi felt he could never get married while he was leading a secret life. All but a few were divorced, Raphi always pointed out when the subject came up, so what was the point?

Gil drank his coffee. "Not even one promising candidate? We only need one."

"There are two heavyset ones in the back of the room that look strong enough to defend themselves if the need arises, but they're probably troglodytes." He rubbed his eyes, as if to picture the class. "Maybe someone up front, actually the college type, but she's too skinny. We should go back to our original plan and dress up someone from the unit."

"Give it up, Lahav. You know it won't work. Not everyone has your talent for impersonation. Raphi, the Well of a Thousand Souls."

"You mean Raphi of No Soul, don't you? I hear dialect consultants are earning a lot of money in Hollywood these days. If I ever get out of here alive I'll head for California and the surf. In the meantime, we have a war on our hands and I'm teaching mommies to side kick."

Gil sighed dramatically, as if to say "poor Raphi," and brought out a blue file that included a shift in his identity. No more plumber. This time he'd pose as a job-hunting Palestinian student just back from studying veterinary science in Sweden. Included in the kit was a photograph of the Gaza refugee camp where he grew up. His house had been dynamited by sappers, making him a refugee with no place to go back to. Raphi admired the passport with its Swedish stamps, produced in a Tel Aviv workshop.

His goal didn't have to be spelled out in the package. He had to infiltrate the gang that had sent out Ibrahim Masri.

"Why Sweden?"

"Somebody in the identities department thought of it. Quite a few Arabs go there on scholarship. You know the language. They thought veterinary science was a creative touch. Unusual."

The ID department was always coming up with something new. Raphi could speak passable Swedish because his parents had worked in their embassy in Stockholm for two years. According to the dossier, he would offer his services for private lessons, a Gaza cottage industry, if you could call their ramshackle homes cottages. He studied the folder, already revolted by the thought of another weekend slapping flies in Gaza, hoping he wouldn't get his throat cut.

"After we break this group, I'm getting out," Raphi said, dropping the folder on the table.

Gil jerked his head up, looking startled. "Anything specific you don't like?"

"I don't like any of it, but you know that. Specific? I'm uncomfortable about the Swedish, but I suppose few Arabs who study there become masters of the tongue."

"Master of the tongue?" Gil made an obscene gesture. "Fuck off."

"So you'll start this weekend?"

"Sorry, I'm not available this weekend."

"Oh?" asked Gil, raising a sandy eyebrow. "Romantic engagement?"

"Believe it or not," Raphi said, "I'm baby-sitting."

Joshua phoned Deborah in the morning while she was making the kids' sandwiches. He started off friendlily enough, asking about her and the children. Then he'd presented an ultimatum. Either she tried his new world or he would file for divorce. He'd give her a month to decide.

She almost cut her finger slicing tomatoes. "I don't like deadlines," she said. Don't panic. Concentrate, she told herself.

"Divorce is decided in the rabbinical courts, as you know," Joshua said, his voice lawyer-like, informational. "Since I would guarantee Ben a strictly religious upbringing, the court would award him to me. They might be more flexible about Sarah."

The rabbinical courts weren't as biased against women as left-wing politicians said, but she did know one woman who'd lost her sons in a court battle. To be fair, how could the rabbis resist a plea from Joshua, who would impress them with his brilliance, woo them with his sincerity about religion, and touch their hearts with his love for his children. At best, she'd have an uphill battle. "Why don't we talk about it early next week?" she managed to get out, trying to keep her voice steady. He had the children from Friday to Saturday night, and she'd use the mental space to clarify her thoughts and legal position.

Deborah's hands were still shaking as she finished the sandwiches and sent the children off to school. She was running late. And then, as if the morning hadn't gotten off to a bad enough start, loud scraping sounds greeted her when she tried to back out of her parking space.

She got out to look. The tailpipe was hanging low, but there was no time to summon a repair service.

She squatted behind the car, trying to keep her clothes clean. The sidewalk was still littered from the road renovation. She looked around. Wires poked out of broken cinder blocks and asphalt chips. Hers had been a fix-it-yourself family. Her father had sold used auto parts, and her mother had applied her Holocaust survivor's resourcefulness in dealing with any household problem. Deborah found a heavy, mangled wire and straightened it, turning the end into a loop, and hooked it around the tailpipe, attaching the other end to the bumper.

The repair held as she drove. When the light turned red, she fixed her hair and lined her lips with a coral pencil. A tentative smile hurt her bruised mouth, still sore from yesterday's self-defense class, their fifth in a week. She'd managed to change hours with another teacher in the night school class she taught so she could attend them all.

The injury had been worth the retaliation she'd felt justified in taking. Deborah smiled as she thought of it.

Class had already started and she had to stand in the back.

"Try to locate the voice behind you," Raphi was saying, his military tone grating on her nerves. He was always mocking the class, picking on her in particular. Even Rachel had conceded that Raphi seemed to have it in for her.

"Make conversation. If you can, glance around. Guess which side the attack might come from." The point was to disarm the assailant, ridding him of a knife or gun so you had a chance of defending yourself. Raphi showed them how to turn swiftly to the right or the left to knock out a weapon. Surprise counted.

When they broke into practice twos, Rachel was up front, so Deborah had to find a new partner. Nurit, a heavyset woman with a mustache and one of the class stars, challenged her. In the first sparring Nurit kicked her in the shin and elbowed her mouth, even though they weren't supposed to hurt each other.

"Move farther apart," Raphi bellowed from across the room, glaring at her.

Go screw yourself, Deborah thought.

In the next encounter they were supposed to pretend an attacker was holding a gun to their backs. It was Deborah's turn to defend herself. She took her time, strolling the gym perimeter, listening to the heavy steps behind her, standing still as Nurit's fat finger poked her spine. According to Raphi's instructions, she was supposed to swivel, then hit Nurit's hand, as if knocking a gun away. Gently, of course.

Deborah stood motionless for a moment, listening

to Nurit's breathing and trying to imagine her opponent's position. Then in one fluid motion she spun around and hit hard, throwing her body weight, knocking Nurit on her ass.

"Bitch!" Nurit cursed from the gym floor.

Deborah smiled innocently and offered her a hand. Instantaneously Raphi was there, grabbing her elbow and scowling.

"Stop it. Someone's going to get hurt," he said so sharply his voice seemed to pin her in place. "I said to move apart."

"You also said to knock the gun out of our opponent's hand. Is it my fault she tripped? Make up your mind before you give us instructions." Deborah stood her ground and faced him.

His eyes turned gelid before an emotionless mask descended over his face. "Tap, don't massacre. I don't want any injuries in this course."

The final class was tonight. Raphi would test them. Deborah shuddered to think of the subtle way he'd get back at her.

The road to work turned past the Monster sculpture. Two women with baby carriages were sunning themselves in the park, which looked unchanged except for a circle of stones marking the massacre site. Why were stone circles, like fossilized wreaths, always the first memorials to victims of terrorism? Grimly she thought of a poem by local poet Yehuda Amichai:

> *Is there in this land a stone that was never thrown*
> *and never built and never overturned*
> *and never uncovered and never discovered*
> *and never screamed from a wall and never dis*
> *   carded by the builders*
> *and never closed on top of a grave and never lay*
> *   under lovers*
> *and never turned into a cornerstone?*

The country had too many damned stones, Deborah thought as she pulled into the parking lot. Yigor, the same Russian immigrant who'd been on duty the day of the terrorist attack, stepped out of his booth to wave her in. Deborah had talked with him in the cafeteria and knew he was taking a government retraining course, since there were no mines in Israel. Yigor's gold incisor caught the sunlight when he returned her smile. Behind her, a truck with a no parking sticker and Gaza Strip plates was stopped. It was checked for firearms and the passengers, an Arab couple and a blanket-wrapped baby, had to get out. The baby was crying and Deborah was about to see if she could facilitate their entrance—surely anyone with a baby couldn't be a terrorist—when Yigor waved them through. He must check hundreds of families a day, she realized. Nearly a third of all Palestinian children were afflicted by serious illnesses and more than half the children treated at Hadassah Hospital were Arabs. Since the massacre, pressure had mounted for guards to be more vigilant.

Deborah's research on a skin disease called leishmaniasis brought her into regular contact with Druze and Palestinian patients, with whom the disease was more common than Jews. At the least, leishmaniasis was disfiguring. The mild form left a round, ugly scar on anyone unfortunate enough to encounter a sand fly carrying it. Female sand flies, needing a blood meal, bit infected rats and passed on the blight to humans. If a "rose" formed near someone's eye, vision could be diminished. And if the sand flies fed off infected dogs instead of infected rats, they could pass along a potentially fatal form of the disease that penetrated the inner organs. In Sudan, an Arab country that might accept Israeli researchers if a peace accord was signed, hundreds of small children died of it.

In every Middle Eastern country leishmaniasis had a folk name. In Iraq, it was called "bud of Baghdad," in Israel "rose of Jericho" because the parasites that caused it lived in sand flies that in turn lived off rodents near the world's oldest city, Jericho. Rose of Jericho was really the name of a desert flower that could live for years without water, and then, with only a sprinkle of rain, fully blossom. Christians had made rose of Jericho a symbol of resurrection.

In Iraq, mothers exposed their babies' round bottoms so they'd get stung there first and develop an immunity, in order to lower chances of getting the ugly scar on the baby's face. Deborah was working on a more scientific means of immunization. The sooner she found the answer, the better. Last year she'd become close with Ichlas, a Druze woman whose only child had died of leishmaniasis. Pregnant again, Ichlas was desperate to vaccinate her new baby. In the last few months, there had been a breakthrough and the vaccine was almost ready. Deborah wished she could skip the staff meeting to work on it.

She was the last researcher in the staff room. Even so, they waited a half hour for the budget director, who was making a rare personal appearance. Without apologizing for wasting their time, he conveyed a stern warning that unless researchers brought in grants, work would be curtailed. When Deborah irreverently asked why, if times were so tough, they were spending millions on a new animal house, she got an impatient answer about donations being easier to raise for buildings than for research.

Lev, Deborah's immediate boss, slipped her a note. "This man controls your budget. Why antagonize him?"

Lev was right, of course. Her research could be eliminated. It affected third world children and not movie stars. The pencil in her hand snapped.

Her colleagues looked up, puzzled, and then gave her an understanding look that drove her mad. Ever since the rumor of her faltering marriage had circulated, coworkers had treated her with tolerance suitable for someone going through a breakdown. Was she? Her mind wandered and she quarreled easily. Would they fire her? When she and Joshua decided to have children, her modest research salary wasn't so important. He'd urged her to follow her heart into hospital research instead of taking a more lucrative job in industry. Now, instead of a successful lawyer's income, Joshua supplied a pittance for child support, living on money he'd inherited from his mother and a stipend from the yeshiva.

Maybe detaching herself emotionally from Joshua would be easier if she fell in love with someone else. But the irony was that she couldn't get involved with anyone if she decided, in the end, that she wanted Joshua back. According to the strict religious rules that Joshua lived by now, a separated man could not go back to his wife if she'd had a lover.

"Deborah." Lev was calling her name gently, repeating a question about animal requisitions. Miraculously, the correct answer floated into her mind.

Grateful that the meeting was over, Deborah looked at the clock and saw that it was nearly 3:00 P.M. The automobile garages would close soon because Palestinian mechanics left for their homes by four. Long lines of cars with blue license plates created daily traffic jams. She hurried out. She'd just make it if she was lucky.

4

Deborah's car mechanic had recommended a muffler specialist. "An old friend," Shmuelik had said. "He won't rip you off." Overcharging for car repairs seemed to be one area where otherwise nice persons of all races and nationalities shared a suspension of morality. "Use my name," Shmuelik insisted. Changing a muffler shouldn't be a big deal, she knew, from the hundreds of mufflers she'd peddled on vacations working for her dad. They'd sold used parts gleaned from Hartford Insurance Company write-offs. Her mother's lilacs and pansies flourished in their front yard, but the backyard of their rebuilt farmhouse was cluttered with wrecks waiting for dismantling. Weekend mechanics wandered through and picked out starter motors and taillights. Once a wrecked fire engine had joined the pile, and her friends had adopted it.

A metal sign advertised the muffler-repair shop in the middle of a narrow lane filled with garages. She had to laugh at the name of the garage: the X-Sauce Institute. Israel's garage owners had adapted a peculiar lexicon of mutated English automotive terms. Eliezer Ben Yehudah, the father of Hebrew's revival from an ancient to a modern language, would roll in his grave to see the biblical tongue so corrupted. One garage offered "overalls," which were total car checks, while another advertised bargain "fronends"—alignment of the front two wheels.

The narrow street resounded with the ring of hammer against metal and the buzzing of saws. Over the noise, radios blasted atonal Arabic music. Deborah maneuvered into the driveway of the repair shop, where a lone worker was on duty, his feet in shabby sneakers sticking out from beneath a car.

"Hello," she called, trying to be heard over the din, but not wanting to startle him. When he didn't answer, she shouted it. "Hello."

He slid out, sat up, and squinted up at her. She could tell he was Arab by the darkness of his skin and hair, plus some indefinable difference in his facial expression.

His narrow eyes sized her up. "What do you want?" His Hebrew was heavily accented with Arabic. She pointed to the tailpipe. "Is Jacob here? Shmuelik from Capital Repairs sent me."

The mechanic slid all the way out, stood up, and wiped his hands on blue overall legs. "He's clearing mufflers from customs in Ashdod and won't be back for an hour." He paused, looking at her. "I'll check the car. You can sit in the office." He nodded to a small room surrounded by glass partitions.

Deborah hesitated. Why did she feel so edgy?

Thick neck and back muscles bulged under the dark blue mechanic's suit, circles of sweat were marked under his arms. "What's your name?" Deborah asked, keeping her voice nonchalant. New England manners made her want to address people by their names. For some reason Deborah could not even guess, the question seemed to make him uneasy. He shifted his weight from one foot to the other. "Jamil," he finally blurted out.

"Well, Jamil," she smiled. "I'm Deborah. Call me when you decide what has to be done."

He smiled slightly and seemed to recover so completely, Deborah wondered if she'd imagined his earlier look. Her neck prickled. In class Raphi had talked about something he called "antennae of fear." "Pay attention to first impressions," he'd stressed. "If you feel threatened, leave." Easier said than done. What would she say? *By the way, Jamil, I think you might be a terrorist, no offense, so don't bother to fix the exhaust pipe.* She gave her head a shake. The damn tailpipe needed to be fixed. The mechanic hadn't said anything offensive. She worked with Palestinians at the hospital and never had a problem. Obviously, Jacob knew Jamil, and Shmuelik knew Jacob. The next garage was only fifty feet away.

There was, she concluded, absolutely no rational reason for her to be afraid.

So why did she feel so nervous?

Deborah turned on the light in the office. A certificate boasting that the garage had been chosen as an Outstanding Enterprise was pinned to the single plaster wall next to a girly calendar and a photo of three beautiful children at a birthday party. She took out a reprint on laser treatment for skin diseases, and sat in the single plastic swivel chair patched messily with masking tape. The desk was scarred with coffee-cup rings, and in the hot, airless room the overflowing ashtray stank. The old air conditioner chugged into action with a flip of a switch, adding to the cacophony of sounds on the street. Deborah felt sleepy. The mechanic was driving her car to the hydraulic lift. The car door slammed. *Gently* she thought, forcing herself to concentrate on lasers.

"*Giveret*," the mechanic called her, a few minutes later. Madam. "Come see what's wrong."

Reluctantly, she put down her papers and got up.

Jamil was standing under the car, pointing up at a twisted, rusty canister. "It's all rotted away. The whole muffler needs to be replaced."

She squinted at the muffler. "How could it have happened? There's no salt on the roads. It hasn't rained for two months."

"A stone," he shrugged.

Stones. Too many damn stones.

The cost made her groan. "Four hundred and fifty dollars for a muffler?"

"*Nerusta*," he said. The Hebrew for stainless steel. "Good for the life of the car. Guaranteed."

Was he mocking her? Jacob had probably said exactly those words so many times that Jamil had memorized the sales pitch. Car parts were imported and heavily taxed.

Sighing in resignation, she turned back to the window of the office where a decal advertised which credit cards they'd accept. Her own was on the list.

When Deborah looked back at Jamil, the cold, twisted expression that had taken hold of his face confused her. A wild glint in his eye made her heart lurch.

This can't be happening. A hot flash went through her body, with hysteria rising like steam.

"*Allah achbar,*" God is great, he shouted, raising one thick, grease-smeared fist above her head.

God. The word came to her mouth, too, but no sound came out. *He's going to kill me.*

Every instinct in her body said to crouch back from that powerful fist, but her brain told her to hold steady.

Raphi had ordered them over and over to take a strong stand at the beginning of any fight. *In your head, your opponent must already be dead.*

In a movement practiced a hundred times in class, she forced herself forward, crossing her wrists. The pocketbook she'd been holding slid to her elbow as she lunged toward his thick heavy fist until her hands struck it. "Help," she screamed, the pain running up her arm. Her wrists felt broken. The noise of the air conditioner, the radio, the hammering of metal from nearby garages drowned her voice.

The look of surprise on his face told her the move had been unexpected. *Men don't expect a woman to fight back. Use surprise to your advantage. Use everything.*

Her pocketbook had sharp corners. With her right hand she whacked it as hard as she could toward his face, but he grabbed the edge and tore it from her grip.

Her head was fuzzy. "Bastard!" she shouted in English, reverting to her native tongue. "Keep your fucking hands off me." *Run. Run. Run.* The word, drilled into them from the very first foolish-sounding lesson, buzzed in her head. *Run, run run.*

She turned to escape, but Jamil grabbed her wrist with what felt like handcuffs. A crazed light shone in his eyes. He's a madman, she thought in horror.

She tried to twist out of Jamil's hold, another technique they'd learned, but he was too strong. *If you can't break his grip, don't fight it. Try something else.* Raphi's voice guided her on.

Her arms went limp, and she turned slightly, lifted her leg, kicking hard just below his knee. Her aim was off, and she uselessly struck his calf.

He hissed at her through clenched teeth. The smell of oil and body odor filled her pounding head. The pain in her arms reverberated through her body. Then, as clearly as if a tape recorder were planted in her ear, there was Raphi's voice again, steady, quiet, urging her to act.

She spat at Jamil and twisted.

This time she broke free. Without losing a second, she tried to spin away, but her sandals slipped on the greasy floor. Again he bent her arm, and flung her back. She managed to regain her footing and break away from him by pulling her arm down and around as Raphi had bullied them to practice so many times.

Jamil looked at her with hate, gathering himself to spring.

Use surprise. Surprise, surprise. She kicked him with all her strength in the shin, scraping her foot down until she squashed his toes.

Jamil swore and pulled back, at the same time swinging out at her. She dodged and his blow fell wide, glancing her cheek bone. He swore at her in a familiar Arabic curse: your mother's cunt.

Deborah brought up her knee and kicked him in the groin.

He let out a strangled sound, cupping himself with one hand as he gave her a violent shove. She fell back against the wall, slamming her face. For a minute bright flashes of light filled her head. When her vision cleared, she realized her nose was bleeding. She wiped it on her arm.

I'm not dead yet. I'm getting out of here.

The door. Where's the fucking door?

Before she could turn and run, he lunged at her again.

The exit was too far. She'd never make it there.

She was going to have to fight to the death. Rage exploded inside her. *You're not going to kill me, asshole.* She wasn't sure if she said it out loud. Raphi's icy voice again. *Want to leave orphans? Don't wait. Kill him. It's you or him. Save your kindness for the elderly or you won't make it to old age.*

With every ounce of strength she twisted at the waist and elbowed Jamil in the nose, which instantly began bleeding like her own. Her arm swung backward again, this time into the eye socket. One-two, one-two. Cartilage squashed and blood oozed as her elbow hit, and her knees nearly collapsed with the sensation.

She took another breath. Her hands shaped into claws as she threw herself at him, her fingernails poking at his eyes, tearing strips of skin from his cheeks.

He fell to his knees. Tendons strained in his neck as he pulled himself up, panting.

The room was silent. Terror grasped her again. Her throat froze. Raphi had trained them to shout throughout a fight, to keep their adrenaline up and to make the enemy lose control. There was also the slim chance someone might hear her and help.

"You're crazy," she screamed at him in her broken Arabic.

He was distracted for a few seconds. Run. He was directly in line with the exit. She backed up to fool him.

"Cunt. Stinking cunt," he shouted, stumbling again, but rising. The eye she'd hit was closed.

His chest heaved, and he moved his head back and forth, just as the other terrorist had done when he'd cursed her. *You're next,* he'd vowed. No. He was wrong. She wouldn't die like those other women. No. He wasn't going to kill her.

Deborah tripped over a tire and saw his hands close on a car jack.

Then he was looming toward her. "All Jews are enemies. Allah is great. We will crush you."

She struggled to her feet, backing away from him again, looking around for a weapon but finding none. *Raphi,* she begged, *What should I do?*

The words echoed in her skull. Jamil was glaring at her from one eye like a Cyclops. "We will crush you. We will crush you."

His movements were slow and jerky as he lifted the car jack. She had the absurd image of a baseball player getting the feel of a bat.

They were now under the shadow of her car, still ludicrously poised for muffler repair.

Jamil stalked her, slicing the air with the heavy jack as if it had no weight.

And then she saw it, inches from her fingers. The red button for the car lift.

It hurt to make a fist, but she pounded again and again at the red button.

Jamil saw the Subaru descending and stumbled toward her, bent double at the waist to get away from the car. It was moving too slowly. He would get away.

Deborah braced her shoulders against the cement wall and summoned the last of her strength.

Her leg caught him on the neck. Then, as Raphi had taught, she struck him a second time in exactly the same vulnerable spot.

Caught off balance, he fell back beneath the descending track and the Subaru pinned him to the floor. His scream was muffled by the thud of the vehicle.

How long will he stay unconscious, she wondered.

For a long moment she leaned against the wall, staring as liquids pooled before her. Blood, she noted in a crazy observation, didn't mix with oil.

Five minutes later, when a whistling Jacob Turgeman strolled into the X-Sauce Institute, Deborah was bent over on her knees, heaving up her insides on a pile of shiny stainless steel exhaust pipes.

5

Raphi was sitting at his oak kitchen table, memorizing the alleys and hiding places of the Gaza Strip from a map, annoyed that another day was going by when he wouldn't work on his book about the potential for economic growth in the Middle East. He'd promised the department head it would be finished before a rival economist's book came out at Tel Aviv University, but he'd done little more than the outline. It would never get done if he didn't quit intelligence.

Not that ending an intelligence career was easy. Even if he begged out of fieldwork, there would be enormous pressure from inside the organization to continue in an administrative capacity, as Gil had. And there was his own addiction to action to cope with. What would get his adrenaline flowing after all these years of living dangerously?

His search for the Seventh Century continued to go poorly. Hard-to-penetrate Moslem fundamentalism had grown faster than anyone at the GSS had predicted. None of the foreign intelligence services with which they shared information had anything positive to offer, either. They, too, had underestimated the Moslems. The Americans were hopelessly baffled by the Moslem terrorism that had blown up buildings and airplanes in the United States. Christian fundamentalists were praying for the destruction of Islam as they had prayed for the fall of communism.

The phone rang, but he ignored it. His life depended on a mastery of the map. Keeping the streets straight was harder for him than it was a decade ago.

On the fourth ring the answering machine picked

up. "Raphi. This is Gil. I know you're there, schmuck. Answer the fucking phone. Better still, turn on the TV. Your favorite terrorist cell has already struck. But the victim outsmarted it. *She* is on the evening news. Call ASAP."

Raphi cursed and pressed the remote control. The TV announcer was speaking too loudly, crowing about how a Jerusalem woman had stopped a terrorist attack using self-defense techniques. The camera focused on a familiar face, now bruised and dirty, framed by honey-blond hair. Her white pants were stained with oil and blood, a navy-blue blouse torn at the neck. She stood crookedly as if her body ached.

Deborah Stern. One of his. He was flabbergasted.

The interviewer was begging her to tell what had happened an hour earlier at an automobile repair shop.

Her eyes were focused on the ground. She didn't answer right away. Then, in a shaky voice, as if overcoming revulsion, she gazed into the camera and summarized the attack, in excellent Hebrew with an American accent, using phrases like "use surprise," "strike back hard," and "hands can be fixed."

His words. Raphi couldn't repress a smile. His curriculum had worked. Even before the last of the lessons, Deborah had passed her solo flight. Still, he was surprised by her courage. In class, she'd looked pale, childlike, athletic but too skinny to be taken seriously. His memory shifted and he recalled her defying him by knocking down her sparring partner. It had seemed out of character at the time, but evidently there was more to her than he'd imagined.

The newscaster went on with questions about her job and personal life. He listened keenly, with growing annoyance.

Why was she baring herself to the cameras?

She answered, as if reading his mind: "I need to say that I couldn't have saved myself without the self-defense class. Women all over Israel should be taking this course."

God spare us from well-meaning amateurs. When

the interviewer asked the name of her teacher, Raphi
felt his breath stop. Here was someone who knew his
last name. In class he'd only called himself Raphi.
There were always rumors about him working for the
GSS. You couldn't help that in a small country. At the
university a lot of people had intelligence connections:
professors of linguistics, physics, chemistry, religion
who assisted espionage efforts. But being identified by
name on Israel TV, which was scrutinized by their
enemies, was different from having Israelis pass rumors about you. He cursed the newsman, who should
have known the censorship rules.

On the screen, Deborah hesitated, pressing her
hand to her forehead as if she were thinking hard.

"I'm really sorry. His name has skipped my mind.
This has been a tough day." Her eyes showed doubt
and her mouth pouted. The lie was given so charm-
ingly that the reporter apologized for tiring her out.
Raphi relaxed, and was impressed: Deborah could
think on her feet.

He dialed, and braced himself for Gil's baiting.

"So you were there all the time, dickhead."

"She's one of mine."

"I thought as much. Sounded like the sort of technique you would teach the ladies. Thoughtful of her,
too, not to mention your name. How do you explain
that? You must have done something right. Is she our
candidate for antiterrorist stardom?"

"She's the skinny one in the front row."

"Didn't look so skinny to me. Shapely, actually. Too
bad about the white pants. You could almost see a
breast through that torn blouse. I have it on tape if
you want to get a closer look."

"Drop dead. She'll need security, you know."

"Yes, we know, Raphi old boy. A blow to the pride
of a self-respecting terrorist organization to have a
member of their hit team defeated by a woman. The
hero died in the hospital ten minutes ago, being
prepped for surgery. Saved the government a hundred
thousand dollars in intensive care. What pretty revenge it would be to leave Ms. Stern gutted on the

steps to her apartment. She lives in Beit Hakerem, near your cousin, by the way. We have someone on her street already. I thought I might take the night shift myself and guard her from inside the apartment."

"She's too old for you." Rachel was thirty-two, so he assumed Deborah was around that age. Gil liked women twenty and below.

"Wrong again, Raphi boy. She's twenty-nine. Five years younger than you and me. Separated from her husband. Two kids. In addition to great boobs, she has copious gray cells—does biology research at Hadassah Hospital. Something with skin. You couldn't have invented anyone more appropriate for the plan. How do you do it? I bet she'll like me. I can be a British gentleman, you know."

"A veritable viscount. Maybe the earl of the Street of Prophets. Given your professed disdain for British colonialism, it's odd how you flaunt your blue blood."

"Women are fascinated by aristocrats."

"Stuff it. She's my student. I'll do night shift. After class. Just make sure the street is covered until I get there."

The instant the words were out of his mouth Raphi was surprised. What the hell did he care who guarded her? He'd promised Anat to go with her tonight to a friend's photography exhibit. Instead, he'd be guarding Deborah Stern and family. He remembered a little Stern girl playing jump rope with Rachel's daughter Talya. He wondered why Deborah had separated from her husband, unusual among Rachel's friends.

The students in the self-defense class were all talking about Deborah. Raphi put them through their final test. As he expected, that hefty woman named Nurit did well (how had Deborah knocked her down?) and Rachel did poorly. After wishing them never to need their new skills, Raphi waited for Rachel to leave and then drove to Deborah's house.

Damn Gil. He'd made doing his duty sound salacious.

Raphi walked soundlessly and knocked at the door. His hands ran over it. Metal. Good.

*   *   *

Dr. Raba Alhassan saw the interview with Deborah Stern replayed on TV. "Good for you, fighting back!" she said softly.

Then it struck her that Deborah Stern had taken a self-defense course because of the massacre at the Monster slide.

Ibrahim's massacre.

Ironically, her brother had fulfilled his childhood desire to have an impact on the world. Chills ran over her thinking of her half-mad brother in jail. When she'd come home yesterday, Ali held her tightly to stop her trembling. Sleep eluded her, a rare occurrence in her pregnancy. Ali urged her to take time off from work again. Instead, she'd decided to go to the weekly evening clinic where her patients' problems would eclipse her own.

Raba was pulling on support stockings sent from Detroit by Aunt Fatima when the maid came to her bedroom. "Excuse me, madam, but your husband's aunt Juni is here to see you."

Raba's face screwed up in puzzlement and annoyance. Why would Aunt Juni come now, especially without phoning? "Tell her I'll be right down. Serve tea and date cake."

She'd be late to work, but in Jericho, the need to get to work on time was not a good enough excuse to insult guests. Raba made an effort to hide her distress. Blush-on restored her color and cover-up erased the dark shadows under her eyes. She shrugged into the jacket of the maternity business suit also sent by her own aunt, thinking how different Fatima was from Juni, although they were about the same age. Ali's Aunt Juni had grown up among the aristocracy of Jericho, marrying a cousin, spending her time hosting other wealthy families. She had a reputation as a superb cook and had offered to teach Raba.

No one had eased the way for Aunt Fatima, a self-made woman who'd gone to night school, learned bookkeeping, and always worked alongside her husband. Aunt Fatima understood about working women. She would never make Raba late.

Aunt Juni was fanning herself in the garden, rocking in Ali's chair. Raba felt a twinge of irritation. Why should Juni's easy familiarity annoy her today, Raba wondered. Usually, Ali's relatives made her feel loved and secure.

"Little one, how well you look," Aunt Juni said, a broad smile revealing false teeth, well-crafted but with overly pink gums. "Your husband must be so proud of your beauty. How can it be true you are breeding? You do not look it."

"The monkey in his mother's eyes is a deer," Raba said, quoting an Arabic saying, which at once showed modesty and flattered Ali's aunt with the closeness she felt to the family. "So nice to see you, dear Auntie." Raba kissed the soft cheek. "If you had seen me doubled over this morning, you would be reassured that I am indeed with child."

"You are not well? Ali must give you something. But then he *has* given you something. You know what we say: the shoemaker is barefoot, the tailor is nude." Juni patted the seat of a chair near her. "Come sit with me. I understand you have visited your brother. I want to hear all about it."

Raba was jolted. How could Juni know? Ali's discussing the visit was unthinkable. Perhaps the servants had gossiped.

"You're surprised that I'm informed," Juni said, leaning back in the rocker. "Don't be. There are many things you don't yet know about the family. Your brother is a hero, my dear. We're proud of him. You were told to expect a message, I believe."

There was no way Raba could hide her shock. The smug satisfaction showed in Juni's smile as the heavy woman leaned slightly forward, her jowls rocking with the chair.

"Do you know where the livestock market is? Good. Be there tomorrow morning. Without Ali. Pretend you need a sheep for a family celebration. Someone will find you. Your brother must be freed quickly or something terrible will happen to him in jail. You must do this to help your brother."

Suhella was bringing a second pot of tea. Juni waved her back. "I know you have to get to the clinic. We are proud of your accomplishments, too, my dear. You will have a brilliant future with us. Now hurry along. I wouldn't think of making you late."

Aunt Juni lifted herself with surprising grace, smiling benevolently at Raba as if she'd just delivered a personal invitation to a prince's ball. How could Aunt Juni be involved in terrorist activities? The world had surely gone mad.

Raba had no idea what the animal market was like. The idea of shopping for live animals to slaughter frightened her. She neither wanted to buy a sacrificial lamb nor to become one.

The blood drained from Abed's face as he watched the evening news with his sisters. They were fascinated by Deborah Stern's ability to fight back and wondered if anyone could teach them to fight. He stifled a curse. The dead man hadn't been named on the news. He couldn't tell them it was Jamil. By tomorrow, the village would be in mourning, comforting Najia for the loss of her son. He would be eulogized as a hero, but the truth was that Jamil's failure had humiliated Islam, and was a setback for Abed's attempts to make the Seventh Century the working arm of Moslem terror in Israel.

Failure was never viewed generously by backers, who could cut off funds or have him killed. Deborah Stern had to pay.

On television, the newscaster bragged that she was a scientist at Hadassah Hospital and the mother of two children. Abed cringed at what donkeys that made his organization seem. Then it struck him that the Israelis' need to show off had been a stroke of luck. With so much information he could track her down easily. He'd regain his status as soon as he evened the score.

Later that evening, Fu'ad Zanoun, a Palestinian who cleaned Jerusalem streets, was fixing his son's tricycle. Abed came up behind him. Abed had been told that Fu'ad was on good terms with a lot of Israelis. Because Fu'ad was a married man with a family, even the frequent bans on Palestinians entering Jerusalem wouldn't apply to him. Fu'ad had too much at stake to become a terrorist, the Israelis reasoned. That also made him a perfect choice for Abed. Those who wouldn't cooperate with the Seventh Century paid with their lives. Their families would be impoverished and shamed.

"Good evening, Fu'ad," Abed said.

Fu'ad turned suddenly, fear in his eyes as he saw the masked man behind him. "Good evening."

"Allah is calling on you," Abed said. "You have been placed in an honored position to help your people."

Fu'ad stood silent like a fool. Inside the house, Abed heard a woman's voice rise over the crying of children. "You work on Herzl Boulevard." Finding Deborah Stern's whereabouts had been as simple as opening a phone book. "Do you know who Deborah Stern is, the woman who injured a Palestinian today?"

Fu'ad's eyes seemed uncertain how to answer. At last, he nodded.

"She gives me lemonade in the summer."

The answer surprised and infuriated Abed. His hands grabbed Fu'ad's collar. Fu'ad was a strong man, but no match for him. Abed could feel him shaking under his grasp. "Did she also spread her Zionist cunt for you? Have you collaborated with the enemy? For your own sake, and for the safety of your wife and children, you will submit to the will of God and serve your people."

Inside her apartment, Deborah toweled her wet hair and put the kettle on to boil. The bath was soothing. Her face, legs, ribs, and head ached. After heaping praise on her, Joshua's father, Dr. Stern, had examined her and told her to ice the sore parts. But hot water soothed her nerves best, and the lavender oil was reputed to have healing properties. Her neighbor

Ramonde Tzabah checked on her a half dozen times, and Rachel had come over to comfort her, insisting on making the kids' supper so Deborah could rest. The only one who hadn't called was Joshua. That hurt.

She knew there was no television in the yeshiva, but it was unlikely that he hadn't heard what happened. News always passed fast in Israel. Deborah had taken extra time putting Ben and Sarah to bed, assuring them she was safe, waiting for them to fall asleep as she swayed in the rocker Joshua had bought her for nursing.

It was so hard to take in. A few hours ago a man had tried to kill her and she'd fought back. She was still alive.

Deborah went back to the bathroom, trying to get the knots out of her hair. The face in the mirror was pale and bruised. She'd been on national TV looking a wreck. "Always look your best. You never know who will see you," her mother had lectured her, particularly when she was a teenager and wanted to wear nothing but jeans and her father's flannel shirts. Her thoughts lingered on her mother. Even the Holocaust hadn't crushed her mother's vivid European elegance, which had been wasted in their New England village, where she'd never made any real friends. Deborah had been embarrassed about her mother's solitariness. As an adult, she understood that a woman who had survived Auschwitz would have little in common with her Yankee neighbors. How many times had Deborah found her mother drinking coffee in the middle of the night to avoid bad dreams? Tears welled in Deborah's eyes for her dead mother, her dead father, her failing marriage, her struggle with Jamil, and the pain in her arm.

Suddenly Deborah heard what sounded like tapping on her front door. Her heart started pounding so hard it hurt.

There hadn't been any footsteps on the stairs.

It was probably just Ramonde, checking on her again, bringing mint tea and cookies.

But that wasn't Ramonde's knock.

Deborah pulled her cotton robe around her and padded to the door in slippers. An iron trivet stood on the hall table. Her fingers ran over it, judging its value as a weapon.

The hall was so quiet she wondered if she had really heard anyone outside. "Hello?" she asked tentatively, her hands shaking as she pushed the button that would light up the hall. Before her eye could get to the peephole she heard a voice.

"Hello, Deborah. It's Raphi."

Raphi! Waves of relief and anger coursed through her. Why the hell had he scared her? He could have called. He would want a battle report, blow by sickening blow, and she was too tired to go over the story again. At the same time she felt profoundly grateful to him. "Oh, hello, Raphi. Nice of you to come." She forced herself to sound calm. "I'm okay, really. I'm just terribly tired. Maybe another day would be better. Why don't you call tomorrow?"

"I need to see you, Deborah," he said in a voice that left no room for questions. "I have to talk to you."

He'd probably reprimand her for the wrong elbow technique, but she was too weary to argue. Again, there was absolute silence from the hall, not even a breath. "Oh, okay, then. Just a minute." She pulled the robe tie tighter and unlocked the door.

He waited for her to step aside before he entered. He was wearing his workout clothes. He must have come from class, but he looked as if he hadn't deigned to sweat. His movements were, as always, efficient and economical when he surveyed the living room, his hard eyes taking in everything, pausing at the trivet in her hand. She felt foolish.

"Deborah, you have to ask for more identification before you let someone in," he said.

She shook the trivet at him. "Goddamn you! Are you here to give me the lesson I missed? Don't bother. I've had a private tutor." Her free hand reached for the door handle to dismiss him.

He took the trivet from her hand and held the door

closed. "I'm sorry," he said. "You're one hundred percent correct. I'm out of line."

For a few seconds he actually looked unsure of himself. She relented. "It's okay. I was just making tea. Let's sit in the kitchen." She turned and he followed her. She pulled out an armful of herbal tea boxes from her cabinet and carried them to the table. They smelled of apple and forest berries. Raphi slid into the bench against the wall and Deborah pulled up a pine chair.

The phone ringing jarred her. Her hello sounded high-pitched.

"Hello, Deborah."

Joshua! She was flustered and embarrassed. Joshua had warned her about seeing men while they were still married. Raphi made an obvious pretense of reading the labels on the tea boxes to give her time for her conversation. Embarrassed, she caught his eye and put her finger to her lips for him to be silent. He nodded.

"Deborah?" Joshua asked again. "Are you all right? You might have been killed." The reprimand made her feelings shift from guilt to anger. You bastard, she wanted to shout. Don't you have a drop of sympathy anymore? But she wouldn't quarrel in front of Raphi. "I'm bruised but basically okay, according to your dad." *Your father was here when you weren't.*

"I'm relieved. I was worried about you."

She softened, smiled into the receiver, wished he'd get off the damn phone and come hold her in his arms to make her less afraid. The line grew silent except for the sound of distant electronic beeps.

"How are the kids? Is there anything I can do?"

"They're both asleep. The situation is under control." The words sounded hollow in her own ears.

"You realize, of course, that I've been telling you for some time that life is much safer within the community where I live. No terrorists or murderers. Everyone looks out for each other. If there's anything I've learned here, it's that nothing in this world happens by chance. What happened to you today could well be a sign that God is trying to get your attention."

"Well, God certainly succeeded," she spat back. The God she believed in didn't tap you on the shoulder with a tire iron to gain believers. At her change in tone, Raphi looked up and raised his eyebrows in question. She shook her head while Joshua mustered articulate arguments for her joining him at the yeshiva, even that night. When he took a breath, she cut him off.

"I have to go now."

He sounded suspicious. "Is someone there?"

"Of course not," she said, hoping he wouldn't hear the lie in her voice. "But today wore me out. I've never been so weary. I just made myself some tea and want to get to bed."

Joshua paused before he spoke. "Of course you're tired. I'm sorry. We can talk about this again tomorrow when I pick up the kids. Just remember, you'll have to make up your mind by the end of the month."

Her hand shook as she poured the water over the tea bags. Raphi wiped the wet saucers, both hers and his, with a napkin. She thanked him, feeling so fatigued that lifting the cup was an effort. "You do know what happened?" Deborah asked.

He nodded.

"I should have left at the beginning. I could feel the threat in the air—just the way you said. But I needed to get the car fixed—there was no other time. Doesn't that sound stupid?"

He put down his cup. "No."

She poked the tea bag with her spoon to avoid looking at him. The hibiscus leaves escaped the paper and spread like a fortune-teller's. "I should thank you. I kept hearing that obnoxious teacher's voice you used to egg us on."

He smiled, but the smile didn't quite reach his eyes. "You did great."

Outrageously pleased by his praise, her eyes went back to the tea leaves. "He was so strong. I felt like a child flailing against an adult."

Raphi gave her his full attention, his fingers pressing the side of his head to help him concentrate. His eyes met hers, and he spoke as if to a colleague. "It's hard in a course like ours to give students a sense of how fierce the attacker will be. The average person might not even bother if he realized how bad the odds were."

"If you ever give the course again, maybe you should bring men to act as foils."

His smile was genuine this time. "I can think of one or two volunteers."

It struck her they were speaking English, not Hebrew as he had in class. "How come you speak such good English? You sound American."

"I'm a diplomatic brat. My father was in the foreign service and we moved around a lot. You learn to speak languages to understand the taunts of your classmates."

She tried to picture him as a picked-on kid but couldn't. All of a sudden she knew what she really wanted to ask him.

"Raphi . . . ," she started. She'd never called him by his first name before, and it sounded too intimate.

"Yes?" he said, studying her, his own face inscrutable.

"There's something I want to ask you. Something we didn't learn in the course."

His fox's eyes didn't leave her face.

The words stuck in her throat. "The sound . . ." She was surprised to hear her voice breaking. "The sound of . . . the bones . . ."

She couldn't get it out.

"Cracking, crunching, snapping," he filled in for her.

She nodded her head, tears welling in her eyes.

"What about it?" he prompted.

"The sound. The sound of the bones cracking under your elbow . . ."

She didn't even see him move, but suddenly he was holding her and she was weeping onto his chest and she didn't care that he was Raphi, almost a stranger.

"How do you forget . . . do you forget . . . the sound of the bones crunching?"

He smoothed her hair. "You try not to think of it, and it goes away by itself."

She knew he was lying, but she didn't care. She muffled her cries against him so Ben and Sarah wouldn't wake. He held her for a long time, the tears making salty tracks down her face, wetting his black shirt. It seemed incomprehensible that Raphi was providing her with this comfort, but she pushed away logic and let her senses take over. Being held felt wonderful.

Deborah reached into the robe pocket for a tissue, and blew her nose. His arms settled around her again. She told him every detail of the fight, how frightened she'd been, what worked and what hadn't, how the most terrifying experience of her life had seemed unreal, as if someone else was fighting and not her.

The story came out in spurts, but he didn't rush her. A few times in the telling she dozed off, and when she jerked awake again she didn't know if a second or an hour had gone by. He was still holding her.

Then she must have fallen into a deeper sleep, because she realized he was carrying her toward her bedroom, and a conditioned caution made her fully awake. He was looking down at her with protectiveness, not lust, and she let herself fall asleep again, too tired to protest.

Raphi checked the windows. Deborah's room would be hard to enter from the ground. There was no balcony below, so someone would have to scale three flights of rock facing.

Her bedroom surprised him. Unlike the rest of the apartment, furnished in practical, Scandinavian-style furniture, upholstered in browns and beiges to disguise kiddie fingerprints, the bedroom was dominated by a king-sized bed with a brass headboard. A dozen throw pillows in arabesque designs gave the bed a harem's look. A jungle of potted plants stood between the bed and windows that had been widened to let in sunlight.

Enlargements of scientific photographs were on the wall.

The bed had been turned down on one side only, as if Deborah still expected someone to fill the other. When had her husband moved out? Why? A historical novel set in China was propped on the nightstand. The phrase "attar of roses" came to mind as he pulled back the sheets. Her bedroom was incongruous with his early image of her, or the fighter she'd shown herself to be.

After he put her to bed, Raphi watched her breathing even out. He was surprised how aroused he'd felt. But then he'd never put a beautiful woman to bed without getting in himself. Beautiful. Strange that he'd been oblivious to her, and she'd been in the front row. Where had she hidden that glorious blond hair that smelled like lavender? The breasts that had pressed against him as he carried her had been full and firm under her robe. Gil had noticed them on TV, for God's sake. Had she bound them for class like the Chinese in her novel? She was the way he liked women, leggy and slim, even after two babies.

He'd meant to tell her why he'd really shown up at her door—she might be the object of a reprisal for humiliating the terrorist. He'd never gotten around to explaining that she needed his protection. Raphi checked the room where Deborah's children slept. It was divided by shelves of books and toys, and smelled of Playdough. The single window was secured by wrought-iron bars, the French kind that looped outward. No one could get in here without a supreme effort. The living room windows had wrought iron, too. He stretched out on the couch, wishing it were a foot longer.

Raphi closed his eyes, willing his usual light sleep to come. His last good night's sleep had been sixteen years ago, before he'd been inducted into the army. He wondered if he'd ever sleep deeply again before he was dead.

Early in the morning a dark-haired three-year-old girl in a fuzzy pink nightgown walked into the living room. He kept his eyes closed, but he could see below his long lashes. An old magician's trick.

He opened one eye and she giggled.

"Oh," she said. "You're Talya's uncle."

"Second cousin."

"What are you doing here?"

"I came to make sure your mommy's okay."

"Oh, that's right. Talya says you're a secret detective."

Raphi groaned. An old Israeli joke was that the enemy only had to infiltrate kindergartens to eke out the nation's secrets.

"He was Mom's self-defense teacher," sneered an older voice.

Raphi opened his eyes fully to see a scowling six-year-old.

"That doesn't give you any right to sleep here."

Shot down so early in the morning, Raphi thought.

"Your mom might need a little help today."

"We can help her ourselves," grunted Ben. "My dad won't like it that you're here."

"No. I suppose he won't. But he'll be glad your mom is safe."

Raphi followed them to the kitchen where they got themselves cereal. Ben wanted to know if he had brought a gun, and Sarah revealed, to her brother's annoyance, that they were spending Friday night and Saturday with their father. Raphi was sitting at the kitchen table with the children when Deborah, flushed from sleep and looking angry, walked into the kitchen.

"Why did you stay?" she snapped, a red stain stealing up her neck to her face. "This could be very unpleasant for me."

"You're right. I hadn't thought of that. I only considered the unpleasantness of the alternatives. You had so much on your mind it didn't seem fair to spell them out."

Deborah sulkily made sandwiches and braided Sarah's black hair. The son was blond like his mother. Joshua was probably dark. Over both Ben's and Deborah's protests, Raphi insisted on accompanying the children to school, which was at the end of the street.

Deborah blocked his exit. "You didn't tell me any of this."

"Sorry, I'd meant to. Unfortunately, there are other security details to discuss, too. Deborah, in the meantime, don't open the door to anyone and don't go anywhere."

He saw Sarah into the nursery school, and perched on a hill overlooking the school yard until Ben reached the safety of his school building.

Raphi jogged back to Deborah's house. He had to ring the bell and wait. *Damn it. I should have taken a key.* In the two minutes and twenty-three seconds it took her to get to the door, he had already looked at his watch four times, worried that someone had gotten in, considered calling for reinforcements.

"Where were you?" he snapped when she opened the door.

Outrage flared in her eyes. "Impatient, aren't we?"

She'd changed to jeans and a loose tank top. Despite makeup her face was bruised and swollen. In her hand was a kid's wet undershirt. The clothesline was on the back porch. The doorbell was probably hard to hear.

"You'll have to excuse me. I have clothes to hang," she said, turning to go back to the porch.

He followed her, sorry he'd let his impatience show. This wasn't the time to quarrel. He leaned against the door to the porch. When she stretched to pin up the undershirt, a slim waist was revealed between her jeans and T-shirt. *How pretty she is. How well she hides it.*

Suddenly Deborah swiveled toward him. "What right do you have to invade our privacy? Just because I confided in you yesterday doesn't mean you can take over my life."

"I wish I could say this was personal, Deborah. I'm not exactly a secret detective, as Sarah so nicely puts it, but unfortunately I am here on assignment."

She slapped a wet shirt on the balcony railing.

"You're not my teacher anymore. The course is over, Mr. Raphi Lahav—you see, I did know your name— and I'm not an idiot to fall for any trap that's set for me."

"You can't see the attack on you as an isolated incident."

"Do you want to tell me that the mechanic knew I'd be coming in? I know, this was planned for months. Someone smashed my tail pipe in advance. Then he checked every day to know exactly when the muffler would corrode and arranged to have Jacob Turgeman out of the shop. If our enemies were that smart we wouldn't stand a chance. Isn't it just a little more likely that Jamil was one of those fundamentalists we keep reading about who dreamed he had to take on a holy mission, and who happened to find me vulnerable? So tell me, why do I have to be paranoid?"

She reached into the machine, keeping her eyes on him.

"I'll be succinct. First there's Jamil."

"How is he doing?"

"He died last night."

She dropped the clothing, and her hand jerked to her mouth.

"Jamil has eleven brothers and sisters. Several are too young to be a threat, but three are already serving prison terms. We're watching the oldest six. The baby seems fairly safe. Your being on television yesterday was a mistake. Someone should have warned you against it."

Deborah stared at him, her lips parted as if she wanted to say something but couldn't think what. He kept on.

"In addition to Jamil's immediate family, there are hundreds of cousins. Like most Arabs, Jamil's family is protective and clannish.

"To make matters worse, we suspect Jamil belonged to the most deadly terrorist cell of all, one with branches in Gaza and the West Bank, a group that's sought revenge before." His voice got softer. "One of my partners underestimated them."

"What happened to him?"

"We're not sure if they took his testicles off before or after his throat was slit."

They were both silent.

Her voice was wobbly. "But how would they find me?"

He shook his head at the foolishness of the question. "You're in the phone book. I checked. Also the Hadassah Hospital faculty directory."

"Shit." Her hands moved nervously through her hair. Her mouth tightened. "What now?"

"They'll realize soon enough that you're being guarded and won't make a move. For the near future we'll have a patrol outside your house. You'll be followed. I'll give you a few emergency phone numbers. I assume you pick up the kids from school? The guard will follow at a discreet distance."

Her eyes narrowed in thought. "I still can't believe all of this is happening."

"You're going to have to trust me on this. It pays to be cautious. The children told me they are spending the weekend with your husband. He'll be briefed about security. I don't know anything about him, but I assume he's a reasonable person who will be concerned about his kids' safety and yours."

"Yes. They'll be safe." Her voice was bitter.

"I apologize again for any inconvenience I have caused you. I thought having someone you knew— even slightly—would be better than having a stranger guard your home. Headquarters insisted someone sleep here the first night. If I'd thought it out better, I would have sent a woman."

He pictured Anat in his role and rejected it.

"By mere coincidence, I will be doing a few hours of baby-sitting for my cousin's children this weekend. That puts me nearby if you need anything."

"How very reassuring."

Bowing in the Oriental gesture of courtesy they'd used in class, he let himself out.

Deborah exhaled, relieved to be alone to think. Raphi had to be exaggerating. But maybe he wasn't. Someone might try to kill her, he'd said.

Deborah double locked her steel door.

The image of Jamil under the car came back to her. Dead! No specific sympathy came rushing to the surface, just the guilty disbelief that she'd killed a human being.

Deborah returned to the laundry with its smell of bleach. The next garment to hang was her pair of white pants. A night of soaking had done little to remove the gray grease smears. Her fingers ran over the irregular outline ridges of blood. Nothing would ever get them out. Somehow she found that terrifying.

6

On Friday morning, Raba's driver, Wassim, reluctantly, silently drove her toward the animal market. Wassim had complained that Ali was too liberal, permitting his wife to do whatever she wanted. Even though their decision to follow up Aunt Juni's bewildering summons was a joint one, Ali had looked worried as he kissed her good-bye. They had to pursue every lead toward helping Ibrahim. Ali had already contacted a Jerusalem civil rights lawyer to prepare a plea of insanity for Ibrahim, and on an upcoming trip to Egypt he would consult a cousin who had excellent PLO connections.

The public animal market was located in a field north of Jerusalem. For most of the year a desert wind toasted these hills. Any uncultivated land turned into a yellow brier patch, and one field had been converted into a livestock market where Arabs sold goats, sheep, donkeys, and mules. There were no stalls, just animals hobbled and tied to stakes in the ground, or penned in the back of pickup trucks. Since the animals had eaten the brush, even in the heat, piss and manure had turned the ground to mud. Sheep and goats bleated. Merchants hawked sheep in loud voices. Dozens of men milled around the livestock, but only one Bedouin with a green tattoo on her forehead represented womankind.

Except for Raba.

Raba ran her tongue over her dry lips. She had on a cotton blouse, jeans skirt, and leather loafers, which she already regretted wearing. Mud, straw, and droppings stuck to them. Had she grown up in Gaza, she would have been better prepared for this market. To an American, this felt like landing on Mars, except that she spoke Martian. The odor of sheep-dip made her reel. She bolstered herself with her mantra of "Raba you can do this" and walked forward.

A filthy man puffing on a home-rolled cigarette that smelled like hashish sat on a straw stool with his arms around a sheep. His fingers were yellow with nicotine and God knows what else.

"Lady, do you want a sheep?" he called, reaching for her. She stepped back. Could this be her contact?

"I need a sheep for a family celebration." Her voice surprised her. She was shouting.

Both Arabs and Sephardic Jews slaughtered whole sheep for private thanksgiving festivals. All the customers today appeared to be Arabs—the Jews probably bought their sheep elsewhere.

Sellers shouted, "Lady, a sheep," "Here's a beauty," "Mine's a fat one." The dirty merchant grasped a metal bar with a hook at the end and reeled in an animal. Clumps of mud hung from its brown wool. He smiled up at her with a toothless mouth and swore this was a healthy one. The radio had mentioned an epidemic of pox affecting sheep. Raba shuddered.

She wandered farther, trying to sidestep the worst puddles, and wondered how one selected a sheep. Several of the customers, tidily dressed men, were seriously examining animals. At one stall, an overweight man rubbed his hand back and forth over the back of a sheep that looked cleaner and fatter than the one she'd been offered. She watched fascinated as he looked the sheep over, measuring with his hands and eyes. He bargained with the owner, admitting this was a nice looking animal, but insisting it had passed its prime and would soon be old and tough. The owner and the buyer were debating just how fat the sheep was—fat appeared to be prized by both. When the buyer stood up and she saw his face, he looked vaguely familiar. Perhaps an old friend of Ali's? The contact person?

"I need to buy a sheep for a celebration," Raba

said, struggling to sound matter-of-fact. "You seem to understand these things. Perhaps you can advise me."

"With pleasure." The man nodded. "How large an animal do you need?"

"For a small party. Maybe ten. It's a family event." He nodded again and signaled with his hand for her to follow him.

Raba concentrated on keeping up with him through the busy field. Ahead, a large group surrounded what looked like particularly good sheep. This man was taking her too seriously. Maybe he wasn't her contact—maybe he was just trying to be nice. What if he negotiated for her and she wound up buying a sheep? How much would one cost, and did she have enough cash with her if this game went too far? What would Wassim say when she showed up at the shining Mercedes with a sheep? He would maintain his inscrutable expression as if she had handed him a dress box from an import shop.

In the tumult, a hoarse voice whispered her name. "Raba."

She turned, her heart already pounding.

A young redheaded man with a prominent facial scar was beckoning to her. He tilted his head in a gesture that showed in which direction she should follow him. She broke through the crowd and caught up to the heavy man, tapped him on the shoulder.

"Oh, thank you anyway. I've changed my mind. I have to go." She blushed with humiliation over the stupid excuse.

He scowled at her, but there was no use complicating the lie. She turned and hurried in the direction of the young man who stood on the side watching her, his middle finger up his nose. Again, he indicated with his head which way to go.

Her face felt flushed as she picked her way across the field where a line of battered trucks and wagons were parked. He hoisted himself into the back of an open truck and reached for her.

She couldn't force herself to take his hand, just

shook her head no, hoping he wouldn't feel her revulsion.

He sat down, swinging his legs over the side, facing her.

She recognized him then. Something in the gesture. And then there was his unusual coloring: freckled, redheaded Arabs weren't that common. He'd been in Ibrahim's class, which would make him around twenty-two. A long facial scar was an injury from a homemade bomb, she recalled. To her surprise, she remembered his name. "Sami Hamadi," she whispered.

He smiled. "I'm flattered that you remember me. Thank you for coming. Would you like a drink?" He nodded to a bottle of orange soda. Middle Eastern hospitality again. The rims of his drinking glasses looked fuzzy with dirt. Her horror must have shown, because he poured only for himself.

"Dearest Raba, our sister, we are so honored to have you back with us. You have been away from your homeland too long. What a shock it must have been to return and have your dear brother arrested by the Israeli swine."

Raba admitted it had been traumatic and replied to his polite questions about the health of her parents and finally her husband, whom he called "Dr. Ali Alhassan" with a sneer. Her fingers traced aimlessly over the edge of her leather pocketbook. Where was this conversation headed?

"Could we get to the point, please, Sami? Why did you want to see me?"

He wiped his mouth on a dirty sleeve, bristling, his manners fleeing. She had a tendency to control the pace of conversations, and rushing him had been an error.

His voice sounded like a parody of a marine sergeant's. "Here is your first instruction. You'll be taking a new job—teaching psychology at Manger College in Bethlehem."

Raba was silent, unnerved by the sudden change of tone. "Thank you, but I already have a job," she said softly.

"Yes, the clinic. We know. You can keep it. This won't take up much of your time. No more than six hours of teaching a week."

"If I wanted to teach, I would have looked for a job at the Hebrew University," she said.

From his acid glare, she knew the barb had hit its mark. The Hebrew University had more status than any of the Arab colleges. The smartest Palestinians studied there.

"You'll teach, damn you!" he shouted. "We have decided it."

She pulled back, wishing she'd learned self-defense like that woman in Jerusalem. Her feet were sticking to the mud, which oozed up around her stockings. An old oath sworn to herself propelled her forward: no man would threaten her like her father. "I make my own career choices." Her chin lifted.

He held a blackened fingernail under it, hurting her. "We need you inside the college." Then his tone changed again and he was more conciliatory. "Why resist the grace of Allah which comes to save you? Grasp the rope that Allah holds out to you. Affirm your faith. Dare not reject it. Turn to us, Raba."

The phraseology was from the Koran. How absurd to imply that she was a sinner and he a holy messenger.

"You will get more details soon," said Sami.

Her stomach curdled at the smugness of his smile.

What kind of infantile games were they playing? Then she remembered that her sophomoric brother had knifed four women. Her voice was steady and quiet. "So that's the way it is. Am I to know whom you are representing? I'm supposed to have myself tied up and trussed like one of these sheep for a secret meeting? I've never volunteered for the cause. I'm not my brother. I don't admire what he did. Leave me out of it."

Something moved behind him, startling Raba. A tiny goat pulled itself up from the straw inside the truck and shook itself off like a dog. Sami smiled and reached for the animal, stroking it sensually along its long neck. "Ibrahim belongs to an elite group. The best. You'll have to trust us. We wouldn't have called you if we didn't need you. Only you can help him. Think of it as a matter of family honor."

Family honor. The term rankled. Fathers and brothers used family honor as an excuse to murder daughters and sisters they considered wayward. They never had regrets, but told the police they were doing what any proud Arab would do to protect his family's good name. Her own father might have resorted to this primitive vengeance had she been in his clutches and dared to defy him. Again, she praised God for letting her grow up protected by her aunt and uncle's love, and now Ali's.

Sami poured more orange soda and drank it like a shot of whiskey. This time he didn't bother to wipe his chin. His right eye twitched. "Either you cooperate or we will kill your husband. Collaborators die a painful death. No one dares to attend their funerals. You know what we say: 'If I have ten bullets, one is for my enemy and nine are for collaborators.' "

Hundreds of Palestinians had been executed for collaborating, tortured by masked teenage boys. Their families feared reprisals and weren't allowed to mourn for them. The top leadership of the intifada admitted nonchalantly that there had been "mistakes" among the killings, but still they went on. The crazy thought of going to Inspector Gil crossed her mind. Sami looked at her like a wolf cornering a chicken. He seemed ready to spring, his eye twitching again as he tried in vain to recover his former poise. "We know this is new for you. You've been away so long. But everyone's involved. And you are such a treasure for us." His smile twisted as his eyes undressed her. "Had Ibrahim told us you had grown into such a magnificent woman, we might have called you back sooner to serve the cause."

Sheep and goats screamed as owners dragged them off. She realized now why they had summoned her here to deliver the message when they could easily have relayed it through Aunt Juni. They wanted to see her mired in manure before they enticed her into their den. She glared at him. "You underestimate me."

Sami let out a mocking laugh and leaned back in the straw, scratching his groin. The baby goat shied backward.

Her face burned with anger and humiliation. For all her brave words, she was terrified. There was something too knowing about Sami's jeer. Around her the sheep and goats bleated. Raba scraped the bottom of her shoe on a stone, realizing that cleaning them was hopeless. Then she turned her back on his coarse laughter and walked away.

Wassim opened her door, the lines relaxed on his face. Raba sat down sideways on the seat. Before pulling in her feet, she slipped off her shoes, leaving them by the side of the road. She watched them growing smaller as Wassim drove away, with the knowledge she'd lost this skirmish. Abandoned shoes were the symbol of defeat of Arab armies. Even when she could no longer see the shoes, the stink of dung clung to her all the way home.

Raphi walked fast, impatient to take off the "fat suit" at a safe house in Jerusalem's Old City. Every agent who wore this disguise drenched it in sweat, and despite dry cleaning, the smell never came out. He'd added his share: he hadn't expected Raba to approach him, making him so conspicuous. He'd damned near bought her a sheep. At least she hadn't recognized him as the man with the worry beads at the police station.

There were dozens of safe houses, places where Arab collaborators and costumed combatants could hide, relax, and change identities. The GSS used regular apartments in residential areas where students would pretend to live, taking in the mail, playing music, frying potatoes so the odor would send the subliminal message that someone was living there. Recently, a twenty-six-year-old GSS officer had been stabbed and hammered to death in an apartment in

Rehavia, one of the nicest Jewish neighborhoods. This safe house in the renovated Jewish Quarter, inside the gates of the Old City, was Raphi's favorite because it fitted organically into a part of the city where even normal people seemed to be wearing costumes—everything from Arab *dishdashas,* long flowing dresses, to Hasidic *streimels,* big fur hats. Likewise, if he ran into a colleague or student at the Hebrew University while wearing street clothes, no one would think twice about it since there were magnificent homes of lawyers, doctors, and professors who enjoyed the rich character of the area.

Raphi walked through Jaffa Gate, a two-lane-wide break in the stone walls. A jeep of Israeli border patrol soldiers was parked at the gate. They were as dark-skinned as the dozen Palestinian men lingering around the entrance. One kiosk was selling freshly squeezed juice. Christian tourists with a map were asking directions for the road to the Via Dolorosa from an Arab boy who was offering to take them for a fee. "Five deutschmarks," said the tiny businessman.

Straight ahead was the Arab market, a tapestry of spices, fabrics, blue necklaces against the evil eye, and T-shirts boasting I GOT STONED ON THE WEST BANK. Until the intifada, it had been a bright feature of Jerusalem. Now the doors locked at midday and tourists feared terrorist knives in their backs.

Raphi turned right, whistling, and took a shortcut through St. James Street to the Jewish Quarter. He couldn't wait to take a shower and put on jeans and a Hard Rock Café T-shirt, clothes a tourist in the Old City would wear. He opened a door.

A young woman with a submachine gun pointed at him was standing on the other side.

He scowled. "How many times have I told you not to point that in my face?" he said.

"Orders are orders," she said, smiling with bright orange lipstick.

"Any for me?"

She handed him a long white envelope.

"Should I swallow it?"

"Some swallow and some don't," she said.

"And what kind are you?"

"You'll just have to find out for yourself."

Sexual banter was part of the hello-how-are-you of the military. Raphi thought of it as just another dialect. Two messages were in the envelope. One was from Gil to call immediately. The other was a printout of Raba's school record. She'd earned good grades in everything but gym. Delicate, tiny, pretty, and smart. He wondered what role she was playing.

Raphi phoned his answering machine. There was only one message, but an annoying one. His cousin Rachel was going out of town for the weekend with her husband, and Raphi had promised to spend Saturday morning with the kids. Now the baby-sitter had come down with the flu. Could Raphi spend the night?

Perhaps he could make this dovetail. The unit commander wanted more information about Deborah. Raphi laughed so heartily the soldier at the door looked his way. Ever since seeing Deborah on TV, Gil had been obsessed with her. He'd probably requisitioned her kindergarten finger paintings and had them analyzed by a psychologist by now. Wait till I tell Gil I'll be sleeping around the corner from Deborah, Raphi thought. Gil might unretire from fieldwork.

Joshua Stern took a deep breath before he knocked on the metal door. A wonderful smell of curry told him Deborah was making their favorite chicken recipe. Hunger and nostalgia mixed in his gut. The rattle of pans reassured him. A jackass GSS operative named Gil had visited him in the yeshiva, suggesting that Deborah and the kids were in danger.

Not that Joshua was indifferent to what had happened to Deborah. He'd felt, in order, fury, helplessness, and guilt when his father told him about the attack. Had he been living with her, he would have taken care of the car repair. He blamed himself for being unable either to protect her or to convince her to seek a safe haven in religion, as he had. But he blamed her for insisting on being out there, exposed and vulnerable while he was offering a secure, constructive world.

Joshua knew he should have gone to comfort her, but how could he be a hypocrite and express sympathy for her plight when he thought she was unreasonable for not joining him?

They still had such strong feelings for each other. They'd built a life together and had children. He was in love with her. Perhaps if he shared his most private torments with her she would understand him better and trust him again. But he couldn't chance telling her what had really happened in the accident. She might despise him and he'd lose whatever affection remained. Who could love a man who had essentially murdered his best friend?

The door opened and Deborah smiled hello. Seeing her, as always, exhilarated him. "Great smell. The kids won't get curry from me."

"I'm indulging myself this weekend. They hate Indian food."

I don't, Joshua thought. He should be here eating with her. Making love afterward or during. "How are you feeling?"

"Sore. Do you like my shiner?"

"Impressive." He almost lifted his hand to touch her cheek, but held himself back. His new codes didn't actually forbid their touching, but he felt uncomfortable treating her as his wife when they weren't living together. He ached to put his hands inside her cobbler's apron as he used to, but he bit back desire.

Her voice was soft. "Your dad came to examine me again today. He says I'll be fine."

Deborah's ability to maintain such a close relationship with his father had always surprised him. Dr. Stern was polite but cold to most people outside of his immediate family. Deborah had broken through his Germanic barriers, and the awkwardness that paralyzed Joshua's own communication with his father since their separation only seemed to drive his wife and father closer.

He and Deborah lapsed into a familiar, wretched

silence. He looked at his watch. "I'd better get going. The buses stop running in an hour." After a long pause, he forced out the words. "Deborah. You can come, too."

Pain crossed her face and tore at his heart. "You know I can't. It wouldn't work. We've been through this so many times before."

His children appeared carrying new, brightly colored tote bags. He could imagine Deborah taking them to the store to pick out new cases, as if visiting their father was an adventure to plan for instead of the bitter fruits of a separation. She could turn anything into an adventure.

"Daddy," Sarah shouted, and ran to him. He swept her up in his arms and flipped her upside down before lowering her to the floor again. His heart was doing somersaults, too. Two weeks had gone by since he'd seen her, and she looked bigger. Ben, too, seemed amazingly to have grown. Deborah bent to each of the children, talking quietly, pressing bags of cookies into their hands, hugging them, telling them not to give Daddy any trouble.

What trouble could children cause? Joshua's throat thickened.

Ben shook his head when his father offered to carry his bag for him. Sarah handed up her own bag with a warning that it was "terribly heavy" because she'd brought all her Barbie dolls. His insides wrenched as he walked away with the two children, leaving Deborah behind. The reckless thought came to him of falling on his knees, burying his head in her apron, and begging her to come with them. But when he looked up, Deborah was chopping onions, two hands on the blade, her head bent to avoid his gaze, pretending the tears were her eyes watering, looking alone and vulnerable.

He followed the kids down the stairs. Outside, the Arab street cleaner was gathering leaves and popsicle wrappers into a metal dustpan. Idly, Joshua wondered why he was working on Friday afternoon when civil servants got off early. But then Sarah and Ben began telling him stories at the same time. About school. About Mommy's fight. Sarah was saying something about a secret detective who'd slept on the couch, and Joshua was so intent on listening that he didn't think of the street cleaner again.

Deborah fought the engulfing sadness as she closed the door. No, she wasn't going to mope. This was going to be a recuperative weekend. No speculation about how her marriage could be saved or how terrorists could be thwarted. Let Joshua take care of the former and Raphi the latter.

Curative solitude was what the doctor had ordered.

A long, hot shower helped. She twisted her hair, still wet, up above her head. It would come out full of banana curls the next day, but who cared, since she wasn't going out. Peach-scented lotion soaked into her arms and legs. Purple bruises marked her thighs and midriff. They hurt if she touched them.

Every day is a celebration of survival, her mother would say, and *she'd* survived Hitler.

A shocking pink sundress usually made her feel cheerful. Like all her clothes, it was too big now, exposing more cleavage than Joshua would approve of these days. The image of her wearing a pink dress in the somber Hasidic world made her smile.

Simple brass candlesticks held the Sabbath candles. They'd belonged to her father's mother, but her own mother had used them. Her maternal grandmother had glorious silver candlesticks, according to her mother's stories of their wealthy Warsaw home. All the silver had been confiscated with the other household treasures early in the war. Deborah's father had volunteered to have a replica made by a silversmith in Meriden, Connecticut, but her mother had always refused, saying she'd come to grips with the loss. Nonetheless, those silver candlesticks had loomed large in Deborah's childhood imagination. Often, she tried to picture them as she lit her own candles, saying the prayer the way her mother did with her hands pressed to her eyes.

Although her parents weren't Orthodox, Deborah's childhood home had been more traditional than Joshua's, where religion was eschewed as superstition. The Sterns had left Germany in 1932 to settle in Palestine, and had fit in easily among the European intellectuals in Jerusalem. She'd never met his mother, who'd died at fifty. His father had been shocked but typically tolerant when his only child had turned religious. In the beginning, Deborah had been happy with the change, agreeing to use a timer to turn off the lights on the Sabbath and to immerse herself at the ritual bath once a month. She believed in God and preferred a traditional home. But then he'd wanted them to enter the insular, Hasidic world where the secular was denigrated and she rebelled.

Deborah ate her dinner alone, grateful for the quiet. Afterward, she retired to her bedroom where all her simple comforts were ready: pillows puffed, books stacked, a brown bag of pumpkin seeds on the side table.

The knocking startled her five minutes after getting into bed. "I don't believe it," she muttered. But there it was again. She cursed all the way to the door. Whoever was out there heard her coming and cleared his throat.

"Hello, Deborah. It's Raphi. Raphael."

Raphael. The name of the "healing angel." Some healer. What was he doing here again?

She leaned one shoulder against the wall. "I'm sorry. I need more identification than that."

"I'm carrying Leah Getz, who has a birthmark on her left thigh. She's just fallen asleep after an hour of screaming. Her mother's middle name is Faigel, but if you ever use it she'll stop talking to you."

Deborah's laughter betrayed her and she opened the door. "We have to stop meeting like this."

"You're right," he said softly, looking down at the sleeping child, her face smeared with tears. He began a long tale about how he'd gotten roped into babysitting. Deborah's name had been the first on the emergency list.

Deborah sighed. "There's light in the bedroom." She cleared the books and her reading pillows, smoothing down the bedspread. Raphi bent to lay Leah down.

"Her ear," said Deborah, pressing her lips to Leah's forehead. "See how red it is. I have some kids' pain-killer. There's not much to do until a doctor decides if it's infected."

Leah whimpered. Her breathing was ragged from crying.

Deborah sat on the bed, leaning back on the head-board.

"What's so funny?" Raphi asked.

"Look at you."

The front of his shirt was splattered with ketchup. Leah's wet drooling had turned the shoulder of his natty white sport shirt brown. His hair was tousled and dirty. He laughed, too, surprising her with the richness of the sound, his usual arrogance banished into boyishness. The fine lines around his eyes crinkled, and cynicism was turned on himself. "Rachel predicted it. Her troops vanquished me in short order." Raphi sat at the foot of the bed, Leah between them.

Deborah picked up the brown paper bag and leaned toward him. "Have some seeds."

He turned his palm up and she poured in a handful. His even white teeth broke the seeds in two, thumb and index finger extracting the shells. Despite years of practice, Deborah couldn't do it perfectly.

"Do you have a newspaper?" Raphi asked. "I'd better check to see which hospital is on emergency duty tonight."

"You don't have to. My father-in-law is a physician. I'm sure he'll see her in the morning if I walk over with you."

"I don't want to take your time."

"For you I probably wouldn't do it, but Rachel's my best friend. Besides, I never mind visiting my father-in-law."

"Thank you." Raphi got up to examine the giant framed photographs on the wall.

"Leaves?"

"Sand fly wings. Don't you like them?"

"Interesting. Maybe they're an acquired taste," he grinned.

Leah stirred in her sleep. Deborah put a finger to her lips to caution him not to speak.

Raphi lifted the sleeping toddler and followed Deborah to the front door. The Sabbath candles had burned down, casting the living room in shadows. Deborah held up her fingers and mouthed the words "ten o'clock." He nodded. His lips formed "thank you" and "good night."

This time when the door shut, she didn't feel quite so alone.

Raphi was waiting outside the Getzes' building with his four charges when Deborah arrived. Fancy pilot sunglasses hid his eyes. Today's white shirt was French cut, and tight jeans outlined his muscular legs. No signs of spilled cereal or, if her guess was right, that he'd slept very little. David rode easily in a backpack that looked as jaunty on Raphi as a Danish schoolbag. How fast he adapts to different roles, Deborah thought.

"I like your curly hair," he said.

They walked toward the Valley of the Cross. There was no breeze and the leaves were immobile on olive trees posturing like aged ballet dancers on a green hillside dominated by a Crusader monastery. As they climbed up the hill, Asher begged for a turn to push the stroller. He was doing fine until he lost his balance close to the top and the wheels began to slip.

"Raphi," Deborah began to call. Before the word was out, Raphi was there, the stroller recovered. She'd never seen anyone move that fast. Even when her heart slowed down, Deborah felt the aftershocks of her uneasiness. Normal human beings couldn't move like that. There was something hidden and forbidding about him.

Samuel Stern, a man of steady habits, was pruning roses in the garden where Deborah and Joshua had wed. He did it every Saturday morning, but the hands holding the shears were no longer steady. The charming youthfulness he'd maintained until she and Joshua had separated was gone, Deborah realized guiltily. She reached out to him for a warm kiss and hug, and saw Raphi watching her curiously.

"*Opa,* this is Rachel's cousin, Raphi Lahav. Raphi, meet the world's best father-in-law. You can call him Herr Professor Samuel Phineas Stern for short. Raphi's brought you a patient."

The men shook hands. Then Dr. Stern turned back to Deborah. "Let me take a look at you first." He held her away from him so he could look her over, and then lifted her sunglasses, before sighing and replacing them.

"Healing, I see. Sturdy stock. Must be a hearty Cossack on the family tree somewhere responsible for those green eyes." Dr. Stern turned his penetrating gaze on Raphi. "I thought I prescribed a quiet day. Which of Rachel's brood needs examining?" Raphi was holding Leah. "Just her," Raphi said.

Dr. Stern ordered his housekeeper to serve juice in the garden. He offered a box of imported chocolates to the children, who looked at Deborah for approval and then reached in.

Between listening to Leah's chest with a stethoscope and looking in her ear, Dr. Stern questioned Raphi about his background and university teaching. Deborah was surprised to learn that Raphi had studied undergraduate at Yale, not far from her Connecticut home, and that he'd played soccer and fenced. She couldn't picture this abrasive sabra amidst ivy-covered brick buildings with names like Timothy Dwight. But who could tell with an enigma like Raphael Lahav? Perhaps he belonged to a secret society like Skull and Bones, or maybe he was spying on them.

Dr. Stern confirmed Deborah's diagnosis of Leah and supplied a sample of the right antibiotic, saving a trip to the lone pharmacy open on the Sabbath. When the children complained about walking home, Raphi offered to race Asher and Talya up the hill—giving them a head start. He came behind them, scooped them up, and carried them to the top.

"Leave me all the hard work," Deborah shouted from below, pretending she was struggling with the stroller. Raphi left Asher and Talya at the summit, and with David still on his back, he ran down, picked up Deborah under one arm and pushed the stroller with the other.

"Put me down, show off," she yelled, laughing. But he wouldn't let go until they reached the top of the hill. Clowning, he pretended to stumble under her weight.

"Are children always this exhausting?" he asked, lying back in the grass.

Talya and Asher jumped on top of him.

"I've always had a soft spot for Gulliver," he said, flipping over and pinning his two giggling cousins beneath him. He got up, brushing grass off his jeans. His eyes met Deborah's.

"Think you can manage on your own for lunch?" she asked, as they reached the garden path to her apartment building door. To her amazement, he reached for her hand, bowed and kissed it, and thanked her for rescuing him. She removed her hand a little too quickly and hurried home.

Sometimes her stairs seemed like Mount Everest, but today she could take them two at a time. She realized she was still holding a bag of the kids' stuff that included Raphi's keys. Her feet swiveled in place and she tiptoed back down. Most people were sleeping or resting now—Saturday afternoon siesta. The streets were nearly empty. Raphi was thirty yards away, jogging down the road toward her. She waited for him by the garbage cans. He must have realized she had his keys and left the kids with a neighbor.

Deborah saw the glint of metal in the sunshine from behind the garbage cans just before Fu'ad leaped out.

He rose above her brandishing a kitchen carving knife. There was no time to think. All she could do was raise her arms, hands locked together, over her head and lean toward the knife. Her arms braced for the pain.

In the single long second before the blow would fall she realized it was Raphi's name, not God's, she was screaming.

The pain never came. Instead there was a snap, a horrid gurgling sound, and a thud.

When she could finally bring herself to look, Fu'ad lay on the street, his head twisted like a broken doll's. Raphi hovered over the body, massaging his right hand.

"Fu'ad," Deborah whispered, sound barely coming out of her hoarse throat. "I knew him. I even brought him lemonade." She was dazed. The whole thing had taken seconds. She was still clutching the plastic bag with the house keys. A man she'd always liked and trusted was dead. Pressure built in her chest.

Raphi flexed his fingers. "Poor fool. I don't think he even wanted to do it."

She tried not to look at the body, but her eyes kept wandering back to his face. Dead. The word echoed in her head. Raphi looked pale. He stopped massaging the wrist and shouted into his watch, "Where the hell are you? I have a dead body here and it could have been Deborah's!" A voice came out of his wrist. "We figured she was safe. She was with you, for God's sake. Saul went to piss."

Deborah lost her battle with nausea, and pitched herself on the grass to empty her stomach of Dr. Stern's imported chocolates. She was still gagging when a battered blue station wagon pulled up. Two men in black suits jumped out, just like the movies, and dumped the body in the trunk. One drove away and the other moved toward her apartment building.

"Are you okay?" Raphi asked quietly. He handed her a folded handkerchief, monogrammed RL.

She wiped her lips and forced herself to stand. "This is becoming a habit," she said. He put his left arm around her as if to say things would be all right. "Sorry, Deborah. We got sloppy."

He offered her the choice of coming back to Ra-

chel's with him or going home, with a couple of his
men guarding her doorstep. Something snapped. She
flung out wildly at him—lashing at his chest and arms
with savage movements. He reached for her hands and
held them against his chest.

"What's happening here?" she sobbed. "I didn't
want to get involved in your cops and robbers show!
Make it stop. Leave me out of it." She looked down
at her hands, shamed that they had struck him. "I'm
sorry," she said.

Her fury spent, she felt leaden. He held her elbow
and supported her to the door. After a nodded good-
bye, the metal door slammed behind her.

Sleep wouldn't come. Her mind was too troubled,
her heartbeat too fast, her palms and soles itched too
much. In the medicine closet was an out-of-date bottle
of tranquilizers, prescribed after Joshua's accident.

She thought of that day, too tired to keep the painful memories at bay. The phone was already ringing
when she'd banged Ben's stroller up the stone stairs,
trying to imagine who could be so persistent. "Deborah Stern?" asked a deep voice on the phone. Already
she knew it was trouble. Joshua had been on reserve
duty for a week. An officer from the infantry corps
introduced himself and said something about an accident, but her head was already pounding too hard for
her to take in details.

"Is he alive?" was all she could say. Her brain felt
frozen. "Is my husband alive?"

Pregnant women didn't normally take tranquilizers,
but the army psychiatrist left them on the counter before driving her all the way to the Haifa hospital
where Joshua had been flown. Joshua and another officer had been driving near the Lebanon border when
they'd run over a roadside charge. The other officer,
Oren Elitzur, was killed. Oren! Joshua's closest army
buddy!

She'd stood over Joshua in the intensive care unit,
trying to make sense of the machines, calling on all
her faith. His "signs" were strong despite the head
and chest wounds. After two hours of waiting, he re-

warded her by opening one of those magnificent blue eyes.

Haifa was two hours away, but she visited Joshua every other day, rejoicing that the wounds were healing. Stories about Ben made him smile, but his eyes remained sad. He kept asking about the Elitzurs, who lived right there in Haifa. Had Deborah spoken with Oren's wife since the funeral? She hadn't. Nina wasn't answering the phone yet.

The doctors assured Deborah that Joshua would be good as new. When he was well enough to leave the hospital the army sent him to a convalescent home near Jerusalem for two months. Deborah brought Ben twice a week. Joshua would be waiting for them, first in a wheelchair and then in a deck chair. He played with Ben on the grass until Deborah put Ben to sleep on a blanket and they made light talk like two old friends.

There was a strain in their conversations. Deborah brushed it off, attributed it to his injury, to their lack of intimacy, to her own exhaustion from the late pregnancy. Joshua surprised her one day asking for the Bible he'd gotten when first inducted into the army. Then a week later he asked for a prayer book.

Birth labor began one afternoon when Deborah was at home in Jerusalem. There was no slow buildup, as with Ben. She went outside to hail a cab and, when the bus came by, impulsively hopped on. The driver stopped the bus at the emergency room, while all the passengers were screaming out advice. Sarah was born five minutes later.

That, too, had been over so fast she could scarcely believe it. Alone for the birth. Alone now. She felt weighed down with sadness and stared at the bright capsules in her hand. Then she thought of her children and poured all but two pills back into the jar.

Her nightmares were full of Fu'ad. She was offering him her homemade lemonade and a package of old clothing for his children. But then his broom turned into the curved saber, the symbol of Islam. She tried to scream, but couldn't force a sound. At last she pro-

duced a hoarse shriek loud enough to wake herself
up. Once again, there was knocking at the door. The
voice sounded annoyed and angry. "Open up, Deborah. It's Joshua. We're back."

Joshua, Ben, and Sarah had eaten their Sabbath
lunch at the home of Yocheved and Isaiah Teittler in
Kiryat Sanz, a row of thickly populated apartment
houses near the yeshiva.

"You need to make a fuss about it," Isaiah said
after Sarah and Ben went off to play with the eight
Teittler children. Isaiah and Joshua drank tea, while
Isaiah's wife stacked dirty dishes in the kitchen sink.
She wouldn't wash them until the Sabbath ended an
hour after sundown Saturday night.

"A fuss about what?" He was used to Isaiah's jumping subjects and expecting him to know what he was
talking about.

"A man sleeping over. The rabbinical courts wouldn't
allow it. You could get the children to live with you."

Joshua felt his face freeze into what Deborah always
called his liquid-nitrogen expression. "Deborah and I
haven't decided to get a divorce. And if we do, I'm
sure it can be amicable, without wrangling over child
custody. I'm a lawyer, don't forget, and I saw too
many children injured by parents' selfishness. Besides,
Deborah is a good mother."

"There's no such thing as a friendly divorce,"
Isaiah said.

Yocheved came into the living room, untying her
apron bow. It was her signal to Isaiah to retire for
their Saturday afternoon nap together, Joshua guessed.
Isaiah's cheeks turned red. Joshua got up to go. He
envied their intimacy. Although he'd never seen them
touch, they shared small, electric glances that left him
no doubt about how their eight children had been con-
ceived. When he'd once asked Yocheved if having
such a large family bothered her, she'd answered with
a question. "Would you rather have one million or
eight million dollars? Aren't children more precious
than money? I studied social work in college. Why

shouldn't I prefer taking care of my own children than those of irresponsible strangers?"

He tried to think of Deborah with eight children. She could handle them, he was sure. The thought of conceiving them made him restless. He should never have agreed to the separation. He'd confront her about the detective when he brought the children back Saturday night. She'd have to listen to him.

When Abed learned that Fu'ad, like Jamil, had failed him, he felt so hopeless that he worried that the depression that had plagued him off and on since he was a teenager was returning. Abed was six years old when the Israelis marched triumphantly into his village. He remembered his mother and Burhan hoisting a white bed sheet at the window. He'd been frightened by the word "surrender" and he'd felt shame because the sheet was torn and stained. He'd been a timid, glum child, but the black periods started when he was fifteen and had grown so tall that soldiers began hauling him over, hands on the wall, for questioning. They provocatively pulled the orange identity card from his pants pocket, mocking him. Unlike friends who sneered at the soldiers, he'd become timid and obsequious, offering cigarettes and pitas from his mother's store. He got very thin and his mother had had to coax him to eat.

Ironically, he'd only burst out of his chrysalis and become a true revolutionary two years after high school, when his math scores won him a Swedish university scholarship provided by a human rights organization. In the freedom of Stockholm he'd turned politically and sexually active. Kerstin, a pink-cheeked Swedish woman with enormous breasts, had taught him to overcome his reticence. He thought back on her with a mixture of gratitude and guilt. Once he'd become a well-known Palestinian speaker a circle of political groupies were eager to sleep with him, frequently two at a time. He'd cheated on Kerstin so often she'd finally refused to see him. That's when depression came back, worse than ever. He'd lost nearly twenty pounds when, to his good fortune, the invitation for training in Libya had arrived.

In Libya, talents he didn't know he possessed were uncovered: his memory, skill with weapons, fierceness. Like a distant cousin, an illiterate shepherd from Hebron who, in 1948, kept one hundred Israelis pinned down in the St. Simon monastery in Jerusalem, Abed was a natural sharpshooter and fast with a knife. And for reasons he didn't understand, he could kill without a twinge as long as he was fighting for the glory of Islam.

The memories made him feel better. He got dressed. Abed drew a deep breath and steadied himself. He was picking up Raba. Setbacks were temporary. The conquest of Islam was unstoppable.

7

Raba peered out the window into the dark. It was 9:30, an hour later than the contact should have arrived. This is the Middle East, she reminded herself. People come late. In Detroit, she'd always thought Arab casualness about time made them pleasantly easygoing, but not anymore. She realized how much Western preoccupation with time she'd absorbed. At the clinic she found herself scolding mothers who arrived an hour late, with one squalling baby wrapped in a blanket, another clinging to their hips. The women looked at her without comprehension. None of them understood her pie charts on child development either. Her work was a flop. Maybe she was trying too hard. She could just stay home and be pregnant.

As if in response to her thoughts, a flutter stirred her abdomen. The first baby movements had come two nights ago, when Ali was eating a late supper in the kitchen and Raba was reading in bed. At first she thought her tummy was rumbling. Then, unmistakably, the feeling came again. She shrieked, and Ali ran up the stairs. He put his hands on her belly, and he blinked his eyes with emotion when the baby kicked. Later, she'd found olive oil prints of Ali's broad fingers on her cotton blouse. Usually so fastidious, he hadn't paused to wipe his hands, she realized, smiling. She should have worn that blouse tonight, stains and all, for good luck.

Ali was in Egypt. His was the central paper at the regional medical conference in Alexandria. She'd assured him that coping three nights without him would be no trouble. It was bad enough that he had to toler-

ate her family problems without them chipping away
at his career. "*Our* family problems," he'd gently corrected her. "If it had been my sibling, you'd have
given me your full support." Aunt Juni had brought
a message that someone would pick her up that evening, but warned her not to mention it on the phone.
Thus Ali didn't know she was going tonight.

Was that a car motor? Raba's pulse was loud in her
ears as she listened, peering down the long driveway.
The scent of roses from their bushes felt oppressive.
Her seersucker maternity suit stuck to her neck.

Suddenly, a noiseless presence was behind her and
a cool hand covered her mouth. A second hand
squeezed her waist. Her heart beat so hard she could
hardly breathe.

"Shh. Don't say anything," a soft voice commanded,
moving in closer behind her. She knew his scent: 4711,
a German aftershave she liked. Recognizing it somehow reduced the terror. She forced herself to relax
her shoulders as he slipped a blindfold over her eyes
and tied it tightly. He led her along the roadside,
squeezing her hand once as if in reassurance. His
touch made her recoil. A door opened. The voice was
soft, conciliatory, mesmeric, and unfamiliar. "You
need to get into a car now. It's high. A Fiat."

The driver's door opened, and she heard him slide
over the rough cloth, shifting with a floor stick, turning
on the engine. The upholstery beneath her thighs was
torn and the car reeked of smoke. He backed up,
turned, and drove away confidently. "I'm sorry about
the blindfold," he said, and his voice sounded sincere
to her psychologist's ears.

A caution light flashed. *Psychopaths usually sound
sincere.*

He kept talking. "We have so many security problems we need to be careful. It's in your best interest,
too. I'm sure you understand. We mean you no harm.
We appreciate your trust and share your devotion and
love for Ibrahim."

"We?" She swallowed, hoping her voice would

come out without squeaking. And when he didn't answer, "Where are we going?"

The warm breeze in her face brought in the scent of fertilized fields. From the grinding of the tires she knew they had moved off paved roads to dirt paths. Which direction? She had no idea. She hated the blindfold.

"How is your work at the clinic coming along?" His tone had changed to casual, as if they were two old friends catching up.

She was blindfolded, being driven to an unknown destination, and he wanted to chat about her work? *Think of anything. Say anything.* "It's going okay, for a beginning. I always wish I could do more, and there are patients I can't reach."

"We have our old ways which have served our people well. Perhaps you've forgotten in your life in decadent America. For decades Western companies promoted baby formula while our babies were suckling milk at their Moslem mothers' pure breasts."

Christ, A Moslem fanatic.

"You seem to forget I'm a Moslem, too. A Palestinian. A refugee." He was scratching something, maybe a beard.

He cursed as the car hit a rut. "Remember that you're an Arab who has been corrupted by Western myths of our people. Romantic, self-righteous, condescending myths created about our so-called mentality and behavior by their experts. It is a phase in our mental liberation, before we return to our true Moslem roots. Have you read T. E. Lawrence?"

"No. But I've seen the movie."

His laugh was pleasant and infectious, but his rapid mood changes worried her. "The true Lawrence maintained that Semites have no halftones in their register or vision. They exclude compromise and pursue the logic of their ideas to their absurd ends, without seeing incongruity. What is your analysis?"

"I'm a psychologist, so I see problems in terms of internal conflicts. To use psychological terms, we have a basic conflict between our fierce, warlike Bedouin heritage and our submissive, humble Islamic teachings. To compound our conflict, we Arabs believe that we and not the Jews are God's chosen people and look down on those around us, even though they often appear more successful."

Everything except the last sentence came from a seminar paper she'd written in a course on ethnicity. The paper had earned her an A, but its true worth would be tested now.

"Do you believe in instinct?" he asked.

"Yes. Modern theories suggest that instinct only means getting in touch with your unconscious. We perceive many things at the subconscious level, and later can call them up. What used to be called feminine intuition may be an ability by women to tune into their subconscious. If this is hormonal, genetic, or environmentally conditioned, we don't know yet. Why do you ask?" She let out her breath. The blindfold was cutting into her forehead. Without thinking, she tried to shift it.

"Leave it alone," he ordered, his voice rough. Then he softened. "Please. I know how it is annoying, but think of it as a parable. We hate the darkness, so we build a fire. But the flame dies, we are in greater darkness than before.

"Your husband, Dr. Ali Alhassan, is he enjoying his conference in Cairo?"

"Alexandria." If this was a test, it was infantile. "Yes, I believe he is."

The brakes squealed as the car came to a stop, and she had to repress a whimper of dread. Her door was opened, and the man's hand on her elbow was firm and strong. She stumbled against him. He seemed unusually tall for an Arab, but she was a petite woman and might misjudge. A door squeaked open and he helped her over a step. For a brief second Raba had the delusion that she was in her parents' home in a refugee camp near Gaza City. The room had they odor of perpetual dampness, kerosene, cooked rice and onions that had permeated the mud-baked shack of her childhood. They'd only driven ten minutes or so. There were refugee camps outside of Jericho. He told her to sit, and helped her onto a low, square straw stool, dragging a seat near her. She could feel his breath. She swatted mosquitoes that swarmed at her ankles. Her fingers stretched down to trace her scar.

"Raba. Our sister. We need your help. Your intelligence. Your training. You graduated magna cum laude."

Summa, she thought, but didn't say anything as he continued. "We want to save your brother and thousands of others who are decaying in Zionist jails. Only in unity can we find strength. When there is a storm, you can only cover your ears for so long before you hear the wind blowing."

Keep calm, she reminded herself. *Breathe deeply.* "I don't see how I can help."

Her anxiety rose another notch as Abed circled her wrist with strong, smooth fingers. He whispered, "The Israelis like to exchange prisoners: a thousand Arabs for one Jewish soldier. They believe they have come out ahead because in their hearts one Israeli is worth more than a thousand Arabs."

Her head pounded. "We must have someone to trade. Hasn't there been an Israeli pilot sitting in Lebanon for years?"

"Zionist lies. We have no one they care about. Hostages. We must take hostages."

"I can't be a party to violence." Even to her, it sounded flat and cliched.

His voice was gentle. "Raba, I swear no one will be hurt. Ibrahim will be freed. Your little brother will live like a hero in Tunisia. When we have our state he can return. Think of the alternatives. The Zionists will torture him. They have machines that will leave him half a man. He will prefer to die. We will regain his honor. You've been lucky, escaping the occupation in luxury in America. Can you deny your brother a chance?"

The mosquito bites were bleeding. She felt dizzy and grabbed the stool.

His voice dropped even lower but she heard the

threat in it. "Dear Raba, our goals are holy, our demands are simple, our penalties are great."

She inhaled. "I really can't take on another job. The clinic is counting on me, I'm still getting used to life here again, and my pregnancy makes me tired."

He stood suddenly. "So tired you would let your husband die?"

Raba instinctively pulled at the blindfold, but his hand caught hers. With the other he stroked her arm. She sat rigid, not showing how her flesh crawled nor giving him the satisfaction of a useless struggle.

"You will apply for a job at Manger College this week. The college is small but growing, with a dean so ambitious he'll hire you midyear. Once you're on the inside, you will get further instructions. In general, we'll need reports on faculty meetings and student activities. Much greater sacrifices have been asked of others. You must choose sides, Raba, and you will choose ours."

Going home, he laughed when she promised to answer soon.

"Why, my dearest Raba," he said, "I already have my answer."

He took his time removing her blindfold, fussing over a knot that had caught in her hair, "Don't turn around until you can't hear the car anymore. Otherwise, like Lot's wife in the Jewish Bible, you'll be turned to a pillar of salt."

Her eyes took a minute to focus. She was on the main street of Jericho, near a stand where tourists stopped to buy fresh orange juice. It was closed at this late hour. Across the street a boy was washing the entrance to Oasis, an outdoor grill. The air still smelled of roast lamb. Raba rubbed the back of her head, where her hair was pressed down and damp. She forced herself to take stock. His speech was educated and his hands were smooth. Maybe he was a teacher, a lawyer, or a bank clerk. Someone with a short fuse who was trying to overcome it. He'd probably come to religion late, like her brother Ibrahim. Gooseflesh rose on her skin despite the heat.

Since when did fundamentalists wear aftershave?

*   *   *

On Sunday morning, Deborah slept through her alarm, but the persistent ringing of the phone woke her. Joshua's ugly accusations had kept her up much of the night. His hurtful words were still repeating themselves in her head. She forced herself out of bed, remembering the special complication of the day: reaching two jobs without a car. The Subaru was still in the garage—Shmuelik and Jacob Turgeman, the muffler man, insisting on putting it in shape as a tribute to her bravery. Her arm paused above the phone. It might be Joshua. She debated not answering, then picked up the receiver.

Raphi. She let out her breath as he apologized for waking her and for nearly getting her killed yesterday. Could he make it up to her? Some of his friends were having a party tonight, and he insisted she come. If anyone deserved a night off, she did. He waved away all her objections, suggesting he'd pick her up after her night school class and they could go from there.

Parties bored her, but this was the perfect revenge. If Joshua was jealous, she'd give him something to be jealous about.

Deborah took the bus to the hospital, arriving late. She got to work immediately. Oddly, the results of one set of samples were confounded. She left a note for Lev asking him to put her samples through analysis at the central laboratory. At four, she took a taxi to her teaching job, quarreling with the driver, who wanted her to agree on a price without using the meter.

The students Deborah taught were Israelis who'd never finished the matriculation exams that would allow them to enter college. Consequently they spent thousands of shekels doing what they should have gotten free from the public system. Most of them worked all day and were too tired to concentrate on the fine points of high school biology. Deborah believed they'd been deprived by a system that didn't cater enough to differences. Her self-evolved teaching method was to reduce the material to core concepts and then dramatize it in a comical, exaggerated way so they couldn't possibly forget it.

Fueled by lingering anger over Joshua's behavior and nervousness over Raphi's imminent arrival, Deborah was outdoing even her own exaggerated style, rhapsodizing about genetics.

"Just think of the majesty of it," Deborah said, pausing as if she was considering it, "genes hiding away in the wings—one generation, sometimes many— like sitting on the bench for the whole season and then, in the final playoff, becoming the star forward on the Maccabi Tel Aviv team."

Raphi was leaning one hip against the doorway. How long had he been there? The clock said class had ended five minutes ago. "Oops. Time's up," she said. "Leave your homework on my desk."

"Sorry I ran over," Deborah told Raphi, slipping the papers into her briefcase.

He held the door for her. "Don't apologize. I enjoyed it. Do you always teach so flamboyantly?"

"Only when most of my students have been working two jobs and are so tired they deserve medals of valor just for staying awake. Exaggerating helps them remember."

He looked thoughtful as they walked to the car, a sporty Alfa Romeo that took her by surprise. It was shiny, red, and wildly expensive in Israel, where cars were heavily taxed. Something subtle would have seemed more in character with a spook. He stopped to open the passenger door before moving around to the other side. The bucket seats smelled like real leather as she slid in and buckled her seat belt. She tried to stay immune to the easy way he adjusted the mirror, leaning an arm insolently over the wheel and cocking his head to listen to the engine. His sandal-wood aftershave came her way. "Nice car," she said.

"I bought it in Italy and shipped it back," he said. "I've always had a weakness for sport cars."

"I'm relieved to hear you *have* a weakness."

The slow smile spread over his thin lips and showed off his even teeth. He drove to an old-fashioned apart-

ment building in the Kiryat Hayovel neighborhood.
She could hear the music as she climbed the four
flights of stairs with him. Raphi knocked, and a tall,
stunning brunette he introduced as Anat opened the
door and pecked him on the cheek. A half dozen couples were already dancing, but not close like lovers.
Raphi said the party had originally been planned in
honor of Anat's roommate's being promoted to head
of the El Al cabin crew, but when at the last moment
she'd been offered a free seat on the new service to
China, they decided to have the party anyway.

The music changed to something fast, and Raphi
walked right out to the dance floor, turning for her to
follow him. Deborah felt a moment of sharp embarrassment—something akin to the first time she got into
a bathing suit at the beginning of a season. She hadn't
done this for so long. She started slowly and conserva-
tively, and he matched his pace to hers. First her feet
moved, then she added shoulders, arms, hands, belly,
pelvis, and ass. He gave her a teasing look and she
turned her back and sent him one back over her shoulder. God, she felt good. She couldn't remember the
last time she'd done something for pure fun. Raphi
was a great dancer. Sometimes athletes weren't. Joshua
was a tireless hiker and great swimmer, but he never
looked relaxed on the dance floor.

Just thinking of her husband made her angry. His
voice from last night came back—a voice she used to
admire in the courtroom. She'd never believed he
could turn that tone against her, but he had. "No man
sleeps over at the apartment. I will meet you in court
the next morning."

"I'll do what I please," she'd shouted back.

"Not if you want my children!" he'd countered, hot
rage in his eyes. Ben and Sarah, who'd become used
to silence between their parents, had run to the
kitchen to hear what was happening. *Damn you.
Damn you, Joshua Stern.*

"Is anything wrong?" Raphi asked quietly.

His sensitivity to her mood triggered stupid tears.
"Yes. No. It's just been a bitch of a week, you might

say, and it's only Sunday." Deborah brushed the tears away with her fingers, as he held his arms out to her.

The over-sentimental slow song "Teen Angel" was playing on a compact disc. Deborah felt tired. It was a long day. She found herself dancing with her forehead within the damp curve of Raphi's neck. She closed her eyes, but her conscience nudged her. She leaned away. "Where did you learn to dance?"

"Another necessity of adapting to different cultures. Like learning the language and playing soccer. Ask any foreign service or military kid. The faster you prove you're a jock the sooner you are accepted. If you want to avoid taunting, then you have to dance and make the soccer team."

"Did you always?"

"Yeah." A grin stretched his thin lips.

Deborah went to the bathroom. When she came back Raphi was dancing close with the hostess. Annoyed with herself for minding so much, she went to the kitchen where drinks were on the table. She took a bitter lemon soda to match her mood. Raphi had introduced her to several of the men and women, young professionals or graduate students, but she couldn't find anything to talk about with them as they compared charter packages to Turkey.

When the dance was over Deborah asked Raphi to take her home. He drove in silence, as if sensing her need for space. Deborah spoke only when he passed her apartment building. "Where are you going?"

"A little surprise. Do you mind? Can your baby-sitter stay?"

The problem wasn't Inbal. Raphi was driving north into the religious neighborhoods in a conspicuous sport car. She'd be seen for sure, she thought in panic. What if she ran into Joshua, who could be walking along one of these streets? Her body slunk lower in the seat. "I really have to go home," she said.

"Twenty minutes, please. Your husband doesn't get out of night class until near midnight. You won't run into him, I promise."

She jerked up straight. "How do you know?"

His tone was matter-of-fact. "It's routine for us after an attack to have a target's immediate family watched."

The reminder that she was at risk jolted her. For the evening she'd forgotten it. Now as he circled through Meah Shearim, a Hasidic neighborhood of crowded buildings with rickety balconies and narrow streets, the men in black coats and the women in black scarves who were still pushing baby carriages along the narrow road despite the late hour, became objects of envy. Maybe Joshua's safe haven had something to offer after all.

Raphi turned right again, and the massive stone walls of the Old City rose up in turrets and arches before them, golden in the night. They were still breathtaking after eight years of living in this city. Raphi parked near the Dung Gate, seemingly unconcerned about leaving such a fancy car in an unprotected lot. As if he were reading her thoughts, a huge smile spread over Raphi's face, and he reached under the dashboard. "Almost forgot. My ignition gives off three thousand volts of surprise to anyone unwise enough to try to steal my car."

"What do you do, step it up from the coil?"

He studied her. "Yes. How do you know that?"

"My father sold car parts—in fact, he smuggled them into Israel in the War of Independence. I worked summers and vacations. Enough twelve-volt batteries passed through my hands to know you'd have to tap the output of the coil. Where does an intruder get the shock?"

"It gives a different meaning to 'buck-it' seats."

Deborah felt a laugh bubble inside her as she walked with Raphi to the wide plaza before the Western Wall, the last remnants of the Second Temple. A baker was selling doughnut-shaped rolls, smelling of fresh dough and sesame seeds. Even at this late hour, the plaza was crowded. A swearing-in ceremony of paratrooper cadets was just breaking up. Despite the day's heat, the air had turned cool Deborah shivered. Below, at the Wall, men and women on separate sides divided by a fence were limned by light in chiaroscuro relief. A box of scarves, used to cover heads and bare shoulders of women who came incorrectly dressed to the holy place, spilled over. Devout worshipers who came at night wore their own head covering. Above the prayers, a woman's weeping echoed against the stones. Deborah turned. "Raphi," she whispered, "what are we doing here?"

"I come here a lot at night. It helps me think." He was looking toward the Wall, his legs spread, his shoulders relaxed.

Of all she'd learned about Raphi, this admission sounded the most incongruous. Visiting the Wall was for the religious, sentimental, and emotional. Deborah had come here to pray for Joshua when he was injured. Raphi's expression was obscured by the shadows. Her gaze followed his. Three doves suddenly rose from the plants growing between the stones and circled in the moonlight. All evening she'd suspected a hidden agenda. She repeated her question. "Why are we here, Raphi?"

"Why did you move to Israel, Deborah?"

For another moment she watched the Wall, where more bearded men were gathering for night prayers. She was sick of games. Her voice came out hoarse. "For as long as I can remember, I've been obsessed with the Holocaust. At the dentist, I pretended I was in Mengele's chair, trying to be strong enough to endure the pain. I had to succeed on every school test because only the best and the fittest survived. Like my mother. She survived Auschwitz."

When he remained silent, she went on. "My father was my mother's second husband. She'd been married to her childhood sweetheart, the son of a raincoat manufacturer, and had a child named Deborah, shot dead by the Nazis. My mother had studied chemistry with medical students, and had successfully pretended to be a nurse in the death camp. Once she was caught by the Gestapo 'wasting' drugs reserved for the Nazis on Jewish children and was beaten to near death. She survived the war weighing eighty-five pounds and sick with typhus. I was named after my dead sister.

"I didn't know until I was sixteen and she thought telling me would bring us closer. You know how horrible teenagers are, I was in my rebellious stage, having been a model child up to then. I blamed her for my sister's death. I became more fiercely American, but at the same time I began focusing on Israel, believing that having a Jewish state was the only answer to the Holocaust."

The night breeze blew hair in her face and Deborah brushed it away with the back of her hand. "By the time I was mature enough to appreciate my mother's bravery, her love, her sophistication, she was sick with Alzheimer's. My father died of a heart attack the same year."

Deborah watched the shadows playing on the Wall. "I swore I'd become an Israeli and bring up my children where they'd feel safe and secure as Jews. And until recently I thought I'd succeeded."

The chanting of the mourner's prayer took on a quiet rhythm in the background. A night bird squawked. Raphi took her hand. "Recently?"

"Since the massacre at the Monster slide I've had Holocaust nightmares of Sarah and Ben being torn from my arms, calling out to me." She couldn't talk about Joshua's threat.

Raphi squeezed her hand. "I hear what you're saying. I'm named after my father's brother, who died in Bergen Belsen. He was an actor in the Yiddish theater, believe it or not."

Deborah returned the pressure in his hand. "At least you're doing something. I feel so helpless waiting for the next attack."

Something changed in his eyes and made her nervous. He spoke slowly. "But you can do something for your family and your country, Deborah," Raphi whispered, running his thumb over hers. "You can join us."

He said it once, but she heard the words "join us" over and over in her head. After that, the words were distanced, as if they came through a tunnel. The fun of the evening, the closeness, the tentative first steps

of romance were gone. He was saying something
about the GSS and Bethlehem, and how they needed
to get someone like her inside a college there. All she
had to do was teach a course . . . something like the
biology class she was teaching in night school . . .
except the pay would be better. She couldn't concentrate because she needed to reevaluate the whole evening, like a short story when you realized the hero
was really a villain or that movie where the voluptuous
woman was really a transvestite.

"We need you, Deborah. It's that simple." He tried
to squeeze her hand again, but she pulled away from
his touch, which now seemed cold and dirty. She ran
toward the taxi stand.

He ran after her, catching her in a second, holding
her arm tightly. Deborah's teeth gritted in fury as she
realized there was no escaping him. "Take me home,
you shit."

Joshua's study partner, Isaiah Teittler, had skipped
evening classes to accompany his wife to the Wall.
Sometimes Yocheved would take a bus there and
spend hours reading psalms and praying for sick
friends. Isaiah stood in awe of her spiritual side, unsul-
lied by croupy babies and mountains of foul socks.
Coming to the Wall recharged her spiritual battery,
she told him. Since the massacre he wouldn't let her
come by herself.

His own prayers were more perfunctory, so he finished them and waited for her in the plaza, passing
the time by reciting psalms. The rebbe who headed
the yeshiva had called him in recently to ask if he
was having spiritual problems. There had also been
complaints about his gossiping. He'd been matched up
to teach Joshua Stern the religious life so it might help
strengthen his own, the rebbe had said. Isaiah glanced
over at the women's area of the Wall and watched
Yocheved rocking back and forth gently, her eyes
closed in prayer, so like an angel.

Isaiah studied the crowd around him. A group of
French tourists was listening to a guide. An elderly

woman collected alms for the poor. Nearby, a fair-haired woman engaged in deep conversation looked familiar. But she didn't resemble anyone from inside his closed yeshiva world. He wondered if he'd met her at a doctor's office on a rare foray into secular Jerusalem. He wouldn't have recognized the woman if he hadn't heard the words: "We need you, Deborah." He was almost certain that woman was Joshua's wife, holding hands with a man.

The phone was ringing in Raphi's apartment when he got home. Gil. "Did she go for it?"

Raphi was angry at the question. "Hook, line, and sinker. Until I sprang the punch line and she nearly punched me."

"Anat says you looked companionable on the dance floor. You must have warmed her up for the sales pitch. I'm jealous."

Raphi flinched at his implication. "My approach was clumsy, and I felt like a pimp."

"Is she the right type . . . idealistic?"

"She wrote the book on idealism."

"Why do you sound so gloomy then?"

"I've been against this plan from the beginning."

"And you were outvoted. Peevishness doesn't become you, Raphi boy."

"She hasn't agreed. She was pissed. She wouldn't talk to me on the way home. I played on her conscience and decency. Finally, I said that since our unit was risking lives to protect her children, she could have the courtesy to hear out the plan. Then she'd be free to say no in person. The option of saying no in person to the famous Israeli secret service appealed to her."

Gil laughed. "Say no to us. That's a good one. About as likely as rain in June." Gil was still laughing as Raphi hung up on him.

8

The long-awaited dedication of Hadassah Hospital's new animal research center began on Monday. Deborah and fellow researchers had received stern memoranda to be present for the ceremony. There were a lot of speeches. Thanks were given to the principal donors, a middle-aged American couple. The story was told of how Hadassah's founder, Henrietta Szold, also an American, had visited Jerusalem in 1909 and had been so shocked by seeing patients examined by doctors seated on the backs of mules that she'd galvanized American women into an organization called Hadassah, the Hebrew name of the heroic biblical Queen Esther. Today's researchers were carrying on in her tradition of self-sacrifice, according to various speakers, all of whom predicted wonderful health changes in the region because of the ongoing peace negotiations. Deborah half listened, until she was jolted by hearing her own name mentioned by the hospital director. "The future will bring a cure for thousands of men, women, and especially children suffering from leishmaniasis, the so-called rose of Jericho," said the hospital director. "Scientist Deborah Stern, an American woman not unlike Ms. Szold, is near the completion of a vaccine."

The rare praise and recognition felt wonderful. In a reflex, she wanted to share it with Joshua, who had initially encouraged her career. She wondered how he'd feel now.

That afternoon, Deborah got her first chance in the new animal house. Despite her caustic remarks at the R and D meeting about the millions expended on buildings, she was excited by the new facilities and whispered silent thanks to the donors. Deborah chose a stylish olive-green lab coat from the new lab wear, slipped blue plastic shoe covers over her sneakers, and pulled on rubber gloves finger by finger. An important feature of the new animal house was its improved security system. Contagion was the fear of every animal researcher. The animal house at the prestigious Weizmann Institute in Rehovot had been closed down for two years. All the millions of dollars would be worth nothing if bacteria infected their work. A central computer recorded all comings and goings. Deborah punched in the codes she'd memorized to open the front door: a general code and her own researcher's identification number, 1620. No one but a New Englander like her would remember the year the Pilgrims had landed. The door clicked open, letting her into a central hall. A second digital pad was attached to the door of her private research room.

She stepped in and the door closed behind her, pushing hard to counter the positive airflow that kept everything but filtered air from entering. The room was only eight square meters but clean and efficient. Her mice cages had been stacked on her wire shelves. One cage was left uncovered as a monitor of airborne infections. A clipboard mounted near the door showed that an attendant had been inside that morning to report on the welfare of the mice and to deliver new ones Deborah had requisitioned. The attendant had her own code. Mice arrived twice a week from America and England, and were given ten days to recover from jet lag before she injected them with disease.

Deborah took down one cage at a time to count and examine the new mice: CBA, the gray ones, and C57 black, the shiny ones. These strains cured themselves when injected with leishmania. A second cage held BALB/c, white mice, which inevitably died of the disease. Someday, we won't need any of this, Deborah hoped. Yet her work was proof that animal experimentation was often necessary. She thought of Ich-las's baby.

If the current tests went okay—she still hadn't heard about her last batch—Deborah might have a trial vaccine within eighteen months. Teva, Israel's largest pharmaceutical company, would submit the vaccine for FDA testing in the United States. Deborah lifted a cage of white mice onto a sterile stainless steel flow hood, where air ruffled their fur, protecting them from airborne bacteria. She reached for a mouse, examined the fur near its tail, and found a lesion that confirmed that it was infected. Normally this mouse would now be doomed as the lesions spread internally. But before she'd injected it with leishmania B, a month ago, she'd administered four weekly injections of the vaccine.

Again, her fingers ran over the mouse. It was thinner than last week, but as it wriggled around the flow hood, it seemed healthy enough. The vaccine just might be working! She examined the mouse closely, wondering if her evaluation wasn't just wishful thinking. Impressions weren't good enough. The internal organs needed to be checked, she realized with regret.

Ether was the usual method for killing mice. Ether spared her the repulsion of touching the mouse, but the animals would writhe and suffer. Lev had recently shown her an alternative method: pulling the mouse's head sharply away from its body to quickly break its neck. She grasped the small white mouse in one gloved hand and held its neck with stainless steel tongs. She closed her eyes until she heard a tiny snap. The sound reminded her of Fu'ad's neck being broken. She gagged as she put the mouse in a bag.

It took time to shed the lab coat, gloves, and shoe covers and to go through the new checkout procedure. Finally, she carried the dead mouse through the long agar-smelling corridors to her lab. The door was open. That was odd, since her assistant was away.

Lev was inside, pacing back and forth, his brow wrinkled. He had a master key but he'd never used it before. "Deborah, I'm so glad you're here." He spread his arms as wide as if she'd returned from the space shuttle, and she hugged him. He smelled of body heat and pipe tobacco. Deborah laughed. "But, Lev, I work in this laboratory, not you."

He ran a hand through his thinning hair. His voice squeaked. "We have an answer to the problem in the lab analyses."

She put the mouse down on the dissecting board. Lev tended to overreact to problems.

"Is that the good news or the bad news?" Deborah asked, smiling. Cheering up Lev had become a habit over years of working together.

"The good news is that we have an answer. The bad news is that it's mycoplasma."

Deborah paused so long that Lev called her name to see if she was okay.

Mycoplasma was the plague of hospital laboratories because its presence in cultures distorted results. "Are you sure?" she asked. "It can't be. We're too careful."

"Lab monitors found the source this morning. Your incubators. Has anyone used them but you?"

She was about to answer no when she remembered that someone had asked to use their incubator just last week. A short, freckled woman working for Professor Schwartz in the neurology unit had begged to use it. Deborah had owed Schwartz a favor, so she agreed. Now she could kick herself.

"I know you're not going to like this, but the hospital has gotten very tough about contamination since the animal house was opened. You have a mandatory closedown of a month while a professional cleaning team comes in."

"A month! I can clean up in a day!" She crossed the room and grabbed a spray bottle of alcohol.

Lev shook his head. "I'm sorry, but no. You can catch up on writing, or take time off. Isn't there a conference coming up? Maybe we can scrounge up travel money." He patted her arm and left.

Deborah was stunned. Tears of frustration stung the back of her eyes. There would be a stop order on anything coming out of her lab. No one in the radioactive tracing department would accept material from her. The experiment with 200 mice would be useless. Her grant might be canceled because she'd produced no results for all her expenses. And, worst of all, how many babies would be doomed? Her eyes fell on the dead mouse wrapped in the plastic. It was all such a damn waste. She covered the tiny body and buried it in the container for contaminated waste. The stupor gradually transformed to anger. She spent the rest of the day furiously cleaning the lab, spraying counters, weights, microscopes, test tube racks, even file cabinets, with alcohol. Her head ached from the strong smell. Let the experts check her lab. They wouldn't find anything. It would be a cold day in hell before anyone ever used her equipment again.

She phoned the neurology unit and demanded to speak to Professor Schwartz. His secretary explained that he was out of the country on a six-month sabbatical. How could that be? He'd sent them a researcher just last week. The secretary asked if the assistant had given her name. The telephone slipped from Deborah's hand. When she picked it up, the line, like her mouse, was dead.

It was the hour before dawn. Abed woke to the sound of the village muezzin calling out the time for morning prayers. He was sweating and anxious. Flying always made him nervous. He comforted himself that if all went well, he'd be back by tomorrow evening, with Raba eating from his hand.

He washed his hands three times, then his mouth, nose, cheeks, forehead, forearms up to the elbow, head, ears, neck, and finally his feet. "I am prepared to pray," he announced, falling on his knees on the rug near his bed. His head lowered in the direction of Mecca, between the south and the east. In Mecca, the sun rose earlier and Moslems had prayed fifteen minutes ago. In Egypt, where he was flying to, they would begin in three minutes.

Abed rose from his mat. He thought about today's target, Dr. Ali Alhassan. Why had Raba married an older man, even an aristocratic doctor, when Detroit was full of young, rich Arab students? The old goat was proud that Raba was already carrying his brat— Abed knew that from the tapped phone tapes, and that Ali's voice was high and nasal, his Arabic aristocratic and annoying.

By rights, Abed shouldn't be carrying out this mission himself. According to the KGB espionage model, Abed was too high in the organization and the risk of getting caught was too great. But the KGB had tens of thousands of case officers and could afford to be doctrinal. Abed's assassins had failed him twice, and he couldn't risk another embarrassment. Besides, he was curious about this husband of Raba's.

The Air Sinai flight was filled with Arab businessmen. Jews preferred to fly El Al, which left on alternate days. The Palestinian woman behind the desk looked vaguely like a cousin his mother was pressuring him to marry. Abed asked for a seat in the back because it was the safest place on the plane.

The clerk pressed computer buttons and concentrated on the screen. "I'm sorry, they're all taken."

Abed worked his best smile. "Can't you rearrange something?"

Her color deepened and her fingers hit the keyboard again, making a mistake and correcting it. "I did find something."

"So kind of you."

"It's nothing."

He fidgeted in his seat before takeoff. The Bedouin in him felt better with his toes on the warm Palestinian soil. Out the window Jerusalem was fading below. In 638 Moslems had conquered Jerusalem. Then the Christian Crusaders had beaten them back. But in 1244 Moslem rule had returned. A tannery was built next to the Church of the Holy Sepulcher and a slaughterhouse next to the Ben Zakkai synagogue so that an evil smell would ever plague the infidels. Out of habit Abed touched his empty armpit. He hated traveling unarmed, but carrying a weapon on board was risky.

The plane dipped, and his hands gripped the attaché

case. Hands can be lethal, too, he thought, examining his trimmed nails. He'd strangled a man once, a fellow cadet, in a training exercise. The man's sphincter had released before death and his waste had splattered Abed's feet, but, despite his fastidiousness, Abed hadn't been offended. He'd felt free. Euphoric. If he could strangle a fellow cadet for his holy cause, he could do anything.

The Egyptian stewardess was passing out lemon-scented hand wipes. He pressed one to his face, feeling happy anticipation for the work ahead. In an hour he'd be in Egypt, a country he admired for its tradition of power. The pharaohs had been gods on earth with the Jews as their slaves. Soon the wheel of history would turn against the Jews again. It always did.

A mute teenager selling wooden camels at the airport led Abed to the car that would drive him immediately to Alexandria, 110 miles northwest of Cairo. Ali Alhassan had flown the second leg, but Abed hated small airplanes. His driver stopped before a villa in the most beautiful residential section of Alexandria, not far from the Cleopatra Beach. A tape recorder on the coffee table had been retrieved from the doctor's hotel room. Abed listened, disappointed. He'd hoped the phone tap in Egypt would reveal a mistress or boy lover, since the doctor had married late. But Alhassan appeared to be the model chaste husband. The only call not related to the medical conference was to a well-connected cousin who chaired the Pyramid Bank. He and Ali would meet at noon on Tuesday.

The meeting suited Abed's plans. His stated business in Egypt was to attract new investments for the Palestinians. A rumor was floating that Saudi businessmen wanted to open a new bank in Gaza and were looking for Egyptian partners as a cover. Using the false name on his passport, Abed made his own appointment at the bank for 1:00 P.M. There was nothing else to do tonight. Alexandria was more Mediterranean than Oriental, so he spent the evening in a nightclub, where the dancer stripped down to her panties and did a writhing dance on the floor. To his chagrin, he got hard right away. Islam's elevation of physical abstinence was difficult to keep. He'd been four months without a woman. Before that he'd carried on an affair with a widow. He couldn't get used to the bad taste of her breath, so different from Kerstin's sweetness. Social life was so restricted that some Palestinians visited whores in Jerusalem. Although Abed fantasized about having an Israeli woman go down on him, the risks were too great. He worried about disease and being watched. There were rumors of the GSS making films which were used later to blackmail Palestinians.

The villa was stocked with tins of pork and vodka, left over from Russian military advisers. Moslems weren't supposed to eat pork or consume alcohol, but when he couldn't sleep, Abed drank a glass of vodka, refilling the bottle with water. He dreamed of the afternoon Kerstin had discovered him in bed with her two friends. But in the mixed-up dream, he was in bed first with the belly dancer and then with Raba Alhassan.

He woke up feeling dirty and showered before prayer. He dressed in a business suit. His steel-toed shoes were highly polished. The traffic was thick, and Abed's driver blew his horn and shouted out the window. At the bank, a short man who looked like the photo of Ali Alhassan jogged up the stairs in the heat. He wasn't handsome, but he had protruding Arabic cheekbones and a high nose with a prominent ridge. At forty, Alhassan looked more like a soccer coach than a cardiologist.

Abed followed him. He looked forward to the cold shock of air-conditioning but the bank still used ceiling fans. In the reception area was a leather sofa and a grouping of low-backed chairs. The walls were covered with framed diplomas. Egyptians were obsessed with degrees.

Abed could see into the manager's office through a glass partition. While the secretary left to bring cold drinks, Abed adjusted the listening device he wore in his pocket like a penholder. Abed frowned as the wealthy cousins shook hands rather than embracing the way true Arabs did. They talked about PLO connections—they'd both been steady contributors—that might help Ibrahim Masri.

At exactly 12:45, a prearranged phone call came for Abed. "I'm so sorry," he said to the secretary. "Something urgent has come up. Please apologize to the manager for me."

Abed waited outside. Finally, at 1:10, Ali walked toward the market. He turned in an alley, then ducked into a sweets shop. Maybe the doctor wasn't so naive after all.

Abed waited in the appliance store across the street. On impulse, he bought a steam iron for his mother.

Across the narrow street, Ali emerged with an oversized box of All-Sorts licorice candy. The doctor was looking surreptitiously over his shoulder. He *was* definitely trying to lose his tail, walking faster now, scanning the street, probably for a taxi, jogging toward the open-air market and the illusive protection of having people around. Ali circled around the front of the souk, corridors of shanty stalls shaded by roofs of corrugated iron. He's a sitting duck now, Abed thought. He put down his briefcase, but held the steam iron in one hand.

Just then Ali, still walking fast, turned in his direction. Contrary to what most persons believed, it was easier to surprise a victim face to face than from behind. He pulled the keffiyah over his face, and walked toward Ali. At one foot away, he stepped in front of him. Abed's right hand sent a chop to the side of Ali's neck, but amazingly the doctor only stumbled. Abed brought the steam iron down on the side of Ali's head. Ali fell down. His eyes were closed tight in pain as Abed used the steel toe of his shoes to kick him repeatedly in the balls. Abed left him writhing. By the time a woman with a basket of sardines tripped on Dr. Ali Alhassan, Abed was watching the scene from the backseat of a taxi.

Because Dr. Alhassan was such a prestigious patient, the hospital director personally called Raba about her husband's injury. Thugs, the Egyptian police thought, had followed him from the bank to the market.

Raba insisted on speaking to Ali. When she got off the phone she shouted for Wassim to get the car.

As Wassim drove to the airport, Raba concentrated on what Ali had told her. His assailant was a tall, well-dressed man with a melanoma just below his beard. While he'd met with his cousin, Ali had noticed him sitting in the bank waiting room and wondered if he should warn a stranger about fatal skin cancer.

Raba had thought the man who contacted her was tall. But whether he was the assailant or not, she had no doubt the attack was related to the threat she'd received. She should have warned Ali, she thought guiltily.

Security was tight at Ben Gurion Airport. At the gate, Wassim had to show their papers and open the trunk. "Let's see your flight tickets," the border policeman ordered.

"I don't have them yet," Raba said.

"For which flight?"

She thought fast. "Air Sinai. To Egypt."

The soldier went back to make a call.

"There's no Air Sinai today. Just El Al."

Raba tugged her hair in exasperation. "El Al, then! What does it matter!"

He motioned for the car to pull over, asked for her passport again, and then made phone calls. At last, the car was motioned forward. Raba took her overnight bag and ran inside. Her eyes scanned the digital board. An El Al plane was taking off for Cairo in twenty minutes! She felt uneasy flying an Israeli airline, but what choice did she have? Then, to her frustration, as soon as she'd paid for her ticket an hour's delay was announced. The clerk only shrugged at her distress, and suggested she get the security-check over with in case there was another change.

An anorexic-looking man doing security checks closely examined her passport. "Why are you going to Egypt?"

What's it your business? "My husband was injured at a medical conference, and he needs me urgently."

He asked her three times if anyone had given her a package to carry on the plane.

"Why would I even consider taking such a risk?" she finally asked in exasperation.

"An Arab in London sent his pregnant ladybird on a flight with a suitcase full of plastic explosives, curled like little fetuses in the lining. Go over to the booth there and have yourself felt up."

Raba felt herself flush. "I'd like to see a supervisor, please." Surely this type of questioning couldn't be official policy.

A tall dark-haired woman in a blue-and-white El Al designer suit stepped forward. She seemed out of breath, as if she'd been hurrying. "What seems to be the problem here?"

"I'm being unnecessarily and rudely questioned. And I don't want to go through a body search. I've noticed that the Jewish women in line aren't being body searched or humiliated."

"Stop harassing her. Let her go through," the supervisor ordered. Amazingly in this male chauvinist culture, she outranked the security man.

It was time to board. The empty seat beside her was filled with the dark-haired supervisor.

Raba was surprised, but held out her hand. "I'm Raba Alhassan. Thank you for your help."

"Anat Ben-Dror. You looked a little pale back there. Is everything all right? Are you going to Egypt for business?"

"No," Raba said, feeling obliged to answer, since the supervisor was being so friendly. "My husband is there for a medical conference and he was in an accident."

Anat gasped. "Was he badly hurt? A traffic accident? The driving is terrible in Egypt."

Raba hesitated a minute and nodded. "According to the hospital he is doing well, but I had to see for myself. Thank you for your concern."

Anat had more questions, but Raba shut her eyes at the takeoff, making it clear she didn't want to talk.

She needed to think. The first time she'd flown in an airplane, she was eight. She'd worn her blue school dress and one leg was bandaged. On the day before she was to leave Gaza, her mother had surprised her by cooking sweets for her, a rare gesture of affection. The cooking was done on an open fire, and Raba had accidentally stepped in the pan, scalding her ankle and spilling the sweets. Her mother had put a homemade ointment on the burn. In America, the scar had become magical for her; touching it transported her to her home. At the same time, it always made her sad. When Aunt Fatima sent her to a psychologist because of her nightmares, the therapist had, through storytelling, helped her transform the scar into a mark of her strength, of love, a reminder that she had overcome the difficulties of her past. Looking back, Raba wondered if that's when she'd decided to become a psychologist when she grew up.

Her fingers traced the scar now, and reminded her that she was no longer helpless. She and Ali were a team. Ali had been attacked to frighten them. How surprised they would be to find out it had the opposite effect. Her experience with bullies taught her that if she and Ali gave in now, the evil forces would crush them like summer beetles. Together, she and Ali would face them down.

Raphi reviewed his notes. An alert gate guard had checked Raba's name in the computer. The plane was delayed until Anat could arrive. Raphi felt disgusted that no one in the GSS had even known Dr. Alhassan was in Egypt, let alone hospitalized.

They were making too many mistakes. Deborah had been left vulnerable at her doorstep. Killing Fu'ad had been an error, too. Even his commander, for whom death was a technical not a moral issue, had raised eyebrows at Raphi's savagery.

The Seventh Century was always one step ahead of them, playing the game like Israelis. Yusef, his dead partner, had always said that "You wanted to make Arabs into Jews. Now don't complain." Yusef had been Druze, the secretive Arab sect loyal to Israel. He'd been betrayed by a veteran Palestinian contact who had sold out for a higher price, or decided the Jews were no longer the winning side. The hardest day of Raphi's life had been visiting Yusef's mother in their village. Dressed in black, she sat staring over the vineyard, unwilling to believe her favorite son wouldn't be coming home.

Raphi would have liked to interrogate the turncoat collaborator, but his balls were packaged along with Yusef's.

The Palestinian opponents had become formidable, and as if the stakes weren't high enough, word had come from the prime minister himself for the GSS to be on high alert—public pressure was building against the peace accord, and the future of the Middle East could be gravely affected by a terrorist attack. They needed results fast. Raphi thought of an Arabic expression Yusef used: *Al a'jaleh min alshaytan.* To rush is the wish of the devil.

He shook his head. All his colleagues had to offer was a far-fetched plan that depended on recruiting Deborah Stern.

9

Deborah was glad Ben and Sarah were spending the
afternoon with their grandfather. She wanted to slam
doors, not make peanut butter-and-jelly sandwiches.
Tonight was the meeting with the GSS, so her angry
energy could be put to use. She drank two cups of
coffee and had no appetite for dinner. Good. Mean
and hungry was how to confront Raphi and his con-
federates. The GSS commander was never named, but
referred to mysteriously as "the head of the GSS."
What would he and the others look like? Her mental
picture was of paunchy European-born career spooks
with rheumy voices, in out-of-date suits, chess champi-
ons with Einstein's IQ and Don Corleone's morals.

Raphi had said *they* wanted to meet her because of
her command performance at the muffler shop. They
were probably confident of convincing her of anything
once she was within their power. Well, they were in
for a surprise. Suddenly, she was impatient to get it
over with, pushing the hangers from one side to the
next, wondering what to wear. A severe gray cotton
suit seemed right. Deborah had bought it for a regional disease-control conference. "Dress conserva-
tively. You'll be the only woman in a room of Moslem
men," the Foreign Ministry official had stressed. In
the end, one of the Jordanian scientists was a woman.
The official had mistaken the Arab name Hanan for
a man's. Hanan had worn a bright purple designer
dress, looking cheerful and confident.

Deborah pulled back her hair into an unflattering
bun, put rose lipstick on her too-wide mouth, and then
wiped it off with a tissue. Which shoes? Traces of the

sparkling toenail polish applied by Sarah shone on both pinkies. She laughed, spoiling her furious mood, leaning back on the bed, wriggling her toes in the sandals. Sparkling polish it would be.

Soon it was time to leave for the meeting. Deborah started the motor. Her station wagon had been returned with a ridiculous metallic trim glued along the chassis. The inside was now draped with zebra-stripe seat covers with the Playboy emblem. A green perfumed paper tree made the interior smell like a pine forest. She hadn't wanted to hurt the mechanics' feelings by criticizing their taste. She twisted to hook in her new, complicated seat belts when a tap at the window made her jump.

Raphi was leaning close, his face distorted by the tinted glass. "I came to pick you up."

It was painful to see him. Last night she'd opened herself to tender feelings toward him. She was angry at herself for the conceit of imagining he was really interested in her. Romantic stirrings had blinded her and left her wide open to his manipulation. She bolstered her determination to be clear-eyed tonight. When he reached for the door handle to open it, her hand came up to stop him. "I'll take my own car. I'm not staying long."

He paused a minute, then shrugged. "Okay. Follow me."

Pleased that she'd won the first battle, Deborah drew a deep breath. But even that had cost her. Her heart was already pounding. Raphi waited until there was a break in the traffic and pulled out. The ride took only ten minutes, to a wide street with palm trees in the Katamon neighborhood. The location of the GSS office off Our Mother Rachel Street was one of those state secrets everyone knew.

Her hands were sweating on the wheel despite the repaired air conditioning. Raphi leaned against the fender, watching her fumble with the new steering wheel lock included in the mechanics' guilt offering. To his credit, he didn't reach in to help. Deborah finally got it screwed in and locked the door.

In the nondescript apartment building, none of the door buzzers or mailboxes had names on them. Raphi pushed the third button and the door immediately buzzed open. He stepped back so she could precede him into a hall littered with cigarette butts and greasy food wrappings.

"Love the ambience," she said, as they waited for the elevator. He let her enter before getting in. There were no numbers listed near the buttons. Raphi pushed the highest button, the fifth. As the car rose, Deborah stared at the metal door scarred with graffiti. Was there an elevator in the world without "fuck you" engraved in the surface? Elevator manufacturers might as well have it printed alongside the maximum weight. She thought of Holden Caulfield in *Catcher in the Rye* and his futile efforts to erase *fuck you*s to protect his sister's sensibilities. She felt the same crushing helplessness at not being able to protect her children.

Raphi, dressed in jeans and still another white shirt, had on his "neutrally assessing" expression. It had to take effort to achieve such control that nothing he felt was visible in his chiseled face or cold, dark eyes. When she'd told him about her mother she thought she'd broken through to a different Raphi. How wrong she'd been. Every detail was stored for further exploitation. Defiantly, she wriggled her toes. Sparkling polish, make a note of that, asshole.

Why had she agreed to this meeting, anyhow? Partly curiosity, she had to admit. Who could resist a glimpse at the secret world?

How would they react when she turned them down?

"This is it," Raphi said. They were getting off at the fourth floor, which meant the button grid had been scrambled. Raphi pressed the second button four times, and the door opened. Deborah swallowed, the reality of this spy business sinking in.

"This way," Raphi said, tilting his head for her to follow him down a hall painted gray. He opened the first door with a key on his car key chain. Deborah followed him into an apartment. Two men and one woman were sitting in what looked like a regular living room—a tweed couch and two matching easy chairs around a tiled coffee table. The windows had been opened, but the room was still smoky and uncomfortably warm. Everyone was in civilian clothes. One of the men, thin and haggard-looking, stood quickly in what looked like a reflex of politeness. The GSS all around her, Deborah's confidence slipped a notch. As if he sensed it, Raphi stood closer to her and made the introductions. "Deborah Stern, this is an old friend of mine, Gil Regev."

Gil shook her hand. "A pleasure. I've been looking forward to meeting you." Then Gil smiled, a self-doubting half smile that transformed his tired face. A third man sat in the other armchair. He was enormous, with arms like a butcher and a neck so thick Deborah wondered if his shirts were specially ordered. His gray hair was slicked back with pomade. He was her image of a prison warden. "Moshe Cohen," Raphi introduced.

Deborah almost laughed. Moshe Cohen was the Hebrew equivalent of John Doe. He slightly nodded to her.

The woman on the couch was studying her.

"Deborah, you remember Anat," Raphi said.

Here was the sleek brunette from the party. So that had been a setup, too. Deborah felt nauseous as she glared at Raphi, then turned back to Anat, who showed off long, shapely crossed legs under a straight black skirt. Her red tank top was tight and low-cut. Deborah's dowdy gray suit would be in the charity bin by nightfall. She turned to Raphi, her voice flat. "I guess you weren't taking any chances at the party."

Raphi's answer was cut off by Gil's friendly laugh. "Raphi prefers teamwork. You'll see, I hope." He pulled out an armchair. "Have a seat, please."

Raphi scowled as he took his place on the couch near Anat, dragging the coffee table nearer in a motion intended to call the meeting to order. They all quieted.

"Deborah, everyone here knows I've already presented the outlines of our plan to you," Raphi said in a professor's voice. "We also know you aren't keen, to put it mildly. But we ask you to hear us through before you give an answer."

She heard a tinkling of glasses and turned as a woman soldier brought in a tray of soft drinks and glasses, then left. "Something to drink?" Gil asked solicitously.

Deborah shook her head. "Please, let's keep this short. I want to go grocery shopping."

Gil tilted his chair so he could look her in the eye. He swallowed hard, eliciting her sympathy. He spoke softly in British English. "Deborah, you do understand Hebrew well enough to know everything we're saying, don't you? These are matters of the utmost importance and it's essential that you grasp the nuances."

They'd heard her on television and knew her Hebrew was excellent. "I'll clarify any of the missing parameters," she answered, gargling the *r*s in an exaggerated Israeli accent.

"Excellent," Gil said, switching to Hebrew, blushing. "Excuse me if I sounded patronizing. I didn't mean to be. But lives depend on your decision."

She chided herself for answering archly. Gil seemed nice. He reached into a briefcase, pulled out notes and a pair of tortoiseshell glasses before launching into a monologue about the deteriorating security situation and the rise of Moslem extremist groups in light of the signed peace agreement. Then he revealed that trouble was brewing nearby, in the Bethlehem area.

Moshe Cohen fidgeted in his chair. "Get on with it."

Gil's Adam's apple moved up and down. He looked at Raphi.

"It will only take a few minutes to lay the foundations," Raphi said in a take-charge tone.

How much of this was orchestrated, she wondered, with one man playing good cop, another bad cop?

Gil finished his political analysis, took off his glasses, and then looked at her with a sheepish grin. "We'd like you to work for us. Technical matters, like being released from your night school contract, and getting a leave of absence, if necessary, from your job at Hadassah Hospital, would be handled at the highest level. Your salary will be doubled."

"What about health benefits, social security, summer camp discounts?" Deborah asked, wincing at her sarcastic tone, regretting once again her inability to remain detached.

No one laughed.

"Deborah, please. Spare us the self-deflective wit," Raphi said. "You've seen enough in recent weeks to know that terrorism is no joke."

Drop dead. Time to go home, she thought, reaching for her most professional voice and reciting the speech she'd practiced in her head. "Thank you for the offer. I admit you make it sound tempting, but the answer is no. Recently, I've done my share for national defense. I have important family and research commitments."

Did she imagine the uncomfortable look on Gil's face? The germ of a thought took hold in her mind. But surely it was too far-fetched.

Gil started to reassure her that she could continue her research. In fact, they would make sure she received the grant she'd applied for. It was government funding, after all.

Raphi interrupted, sounding pressed. "Deborah, we all know this isn't a normal job proposal. We need you. We're begging you to join us. In the long run, the peace process and thousands of lives will be affected. We don't know what precisely is being planned by the enemy, but our intelligence says it has to do with school children, somewhere in the Jerusalem or Bethlehem area. The lives of a bunch of little kids depend on you."

The words struck like a stiletto.

"Raphi!" The man they called Moshe Cohen leaped out of his chair toward Raphi. Deborah was surprised such a big man could move so fast. "She hasn't committed herself to us. How can you blab so much?" His fists were clenched as if he were holding himself back from violence. He was twice Raphi's size, but Raphi remained perfectly still. Gil stood up fast, rested his hand on Moshe's broad back, but Moshe fiercely shrugged it off. Deborah realized she'd been holding her breath.

"Raphi obviously believes we can trust Deborah," Gil said as the older man sat down, pulled a pack of cigarettes from his pocket, and lit one with yellowed, steady fingers. "Let's not escalate the drama, Moshe."

Comedy, not drama, was the right word, Deborah thought. When she'd practiced for this scene in her mind, she'd pictured a group of professional agents relentlessly trying to convince her of the worth of their mission. This sample reminded her of the Keystone Kops. Was it all camouflage, meant to deflect attention from what was really taking place here? Could these clowns be her country's vaunted secret weapon? As another of Israel's myths debunked itself before her, she felt more confident. "Gentlemen," she said, "I repeat. My answer was, is, and will be no. Don't you think I'd be somewhat conspicuous after the publicity my attack received? You're the intelligence experts, not me, but don't you think the enemy might catch on that my becoming the only Jewish teacher in an Arab college was a wee bit strange, especially after my picture was in all the papers for stopping an Arab terrorist? You know a second attack was made on me. How could you ask me to expose myself to a third?"

"That's exactly why we want you, Deborah," Gil went on, his voice soothing. "They'll think it's too obvious. Hotshot Israeli security would never choose anyone well known, making her an easy target."

"Now, why don't I find that reassuring?" Deborah asked through clenched teeth. "I'm curious. What would I teach in Bethlehem? Subversive biology? Maybe I'd list the wrong formula so all the students would blow up their little test tubes."

There was a slight easing of the tension around Gil's lips that made Deborah wonder how she'd blundered. "You'll teach the regular curriculum," he said. "The faculty and students will bend backward to accord a Jewish teacher hospitality."

Deborah looked at each of their faces. "Now, if

you'll excuse me. There's a sale on chicken breasts at the supermarket."

"Just a minute." Raphi said it softly, but she felt a knot of fear in her belly. "Please sit down."

She stared at him, furious at his treachery but vulnerable to his magnetism. There was something else. Raphi had saved her life. The image of Fu'ad's knife poised above her came to her mind. That was no act. The smoky room was suffocating. She shrugged and sat down.

Raphi focused all his attention on her. "Just think how you're going to feel when this blows up and you could have helped and didn't. What if it's your own children's school that's about to go up in smoke? How about the school next door? What makes you think you can cop out and sleep quietly? Doesn't responsibility go beyond the walls of your apartment? Do you think being a good mother only means tucking in Ben and Sarah at night?"

His mentioning her children's names in this room made her feel defiled. "Who the hell do you think you are, haranguing me about what a good mother is?" Deborah exploded at him.

The room was silent, and for a moment the others disappeared from her consciousness. Deborah felt as if she and Raphi were two magnets with opposite poles, a lethal electric current holding them in place.

Gil and Moshe Cohen shifted in their chairs. At last, Gil cleared his throat and looked toward Anat. She'd been inert. Now she leaned forward, exposing a Modigliani neck.

"We'll help you get custody of the children," Anat said in a syrupy voice.

Deborah turned to stare at her. Anat reached for a cigarette and lit it slowly, making a show of inhaling. No one else spoke. "When your husband tries to get custody of the children, we'll make sure you win—if you work with us."

Deborah felt a coldness in the pit of her stomach. "That's nonsense," she said, but her legs felt wobbly.

"We haven't decided on a divorce. My husband is counting on a reconciliation."

Anat smiled, as if Deborah had told a joke. Once again the room was silent except for a burst of Moshe Cohen's ragged smoker's cough.

Raphi spoke, using the authoritative voice she particularly disliked. "Do you know the Scroll of Esther, Deborah?"

"What did you say?" She squinted at him as if he might be mad.

He exhaled. "Esther. You know, from the Bible. The five scrolls: Lamentations, Ruth, Song of Songs, Job, Esther."

"Oh, *that* Esther," she said, covering her bewilderment with a mocking smile. Hadn't she just heard about the heroic Queen Esther, for whom her hospital was named, that very morning? It seemed so long ago.

Raphi went on with his lecture. "Esther, you recall, was chosen to become the queen of Persia. When her uncle Mordechai approached her to help save the Jewish people, she tried to put him off. 'Don't think that you'll escape the fate of all the other Jews because you live in the palace,' Mordechai warned her. 'Should you remain silent then relief and deliverance will arise elsewhere, but you and your father's house will perish.' "

He looked at her without apology. "Pretend you're Esther."

In a scientific process called magnetic reversal a complete shift of the earth's magnetic field takes place, making a compass needle point south instead of north. Sitting there, Deborah suddenly felt, as they say in Hebrew, as if she'd lost her north. Her face drained of its remaining color.

Gil poured a glass of water and handed it to her. His voice almost crooned. "We're not threatening you, Deborah, don't get the wrong impression. Raphi may be melodramatic, but as much as I hate to admit it he's usually right. We're going to keep the self-sacrifice to a minimum. This operation will cause a certain amount of inconvenience for you—we don't deny it.

But you'll be doing something important for your people."

Deborah hardly heard him. She wondered if she simply hadn't noticed it before. Anat's hand was resting possessively on Raphi's thigh. Deborah was horrified at just how much it bothered her.

"When's Daddy coming back?" her son asked later that night. Grandpa Stern had put the children to bed, but Ben was having trouble sleeping.

"I really don't know," she said. "We have some problems to work out. I know it's hard on you kids, but sometimes adults have troubles, too."

Ben stiffened and she tried to soothe his worries by pushing the hair off his forehead.

"Where were you tonight, Mommy?" Ben asked, his eyelids half closed now.

"A meeting," she sighed, tucking a summer blanket over him. The apartment was breezy despite the heat.

"Was that detective there?" he asked, looking up at her.

Her heart beat too fast. How could he know? Did kids absorb subliminal messages of what was going on in their parents' lives?

She didn't believe in lying to her children. They'd been told the truth about the separation. "No, honey." She kissed him and turned out the light. "Raphi wasn't there."

Raphi straddled Anat, his thigh muscles accentuated by the strain, disgusted with himself even as he turned to Anat's lean body. The unshaded bulb illuminated her dark nipples, and he wondered idly what color Deborah's were. At her demand, Anat's hands were tied with pantyhose to the bedpost. He came into her hard enough to make her gasp, and then withdrew, pausing, taunting her as she ran her tongue over her lips, letting it linger in the corner of her mouth.

He moved his fingers softly over the tumid flesh between her legs. She circled her hips, pressing her wetness into his hand. She looked up at him, her eyes dilated with lust. "Do it," she said through clenched teeth.

Her hands jerked on the bindings. He reached up and held her down as she struggled against him, writhing with her legs, so he'd have to push down her knees, his elbow cutting off her breath at her throat the way she liked it. Her eyes dilated as he filled her with hard, talkless thrusts, stopping only as she came, waiting to come himself, sweat dripping in his eyes, wishing she was someone else, pulling away and finally throwing himself on the other side of the double bed. He tore off her bindings.

Her voice was hoarse. "You really get off on this spy stuff, don't you?"

She lifted her face, asking for him to slap her. He was disgusted with himself, especially when he felt the beginnings of an erection as she ran her fingers around the inside of her vulva. He reached for his clothes on her vanity chair. "Time to go."

"Schmuck. Don't walk out on me like this. I'm not through with you. It's her, isn't it? I can't believe Gil makes her sound voluptuous. I find her mousy. Like her little science experiments." Anat sucked the two fingers that had been inside her in an imitation of oral sex.

He concentrated on dressing. "It's not her. I was against this operation from the beginning. I'm still against it." He pulled on his pants over his matted wetness, slipping the gun and his wallet inside his jacket.

"Since when do you carry a gun around Jerusalem?"

When he didn't answer, she threw the pillow at him.

"Damn it, Raphi. Don't play strong, silent schmuck with me."

"Your diction is charming."

"Sorry, Mr. Pristine Lips."

He was silent again. He pulled his leather belt tight, and then one notch tighter.

"Raphi. Don't go. Something's going on and you'd better let me in on it. I'm part of this operation. You requested it yourself. Fun to work together again and all that. Or am I being used, too?"

It wasn't fun, he'd give her that, and her joining had been his idea. When two regular members of the unit had been borrowed by the air force, they were shorthanded, and since they were already sleeping together, it seemed convenient to have her join. He felt a wave of guilt at his lack of deep feeling for her. Coming closer, he brushed back her hair, kissing her lightly on her lips. Her tongue reached for him, but he pulled away. "Good night. I'll call you soon."

"Raphi."

"Yes, Anat."

"She wears sparkling toenail polish."

"Yes. I noticed."

"Yes I noticed," she mocked. She looked for something else to throw and found a hairbrush. He moved quickly to avoid it. The handle broke off as the brush clattered on the stone floor.

"How long can a man be on his own?" Isaiah asked Yocheved, who was gently snoring, her hand still lazily curled in his pajamas. Because of religious law, they only slept together seventeen days a month, so they made love every night they could.

She'd heard him. "Leave him alone. He's still married." She tucked her head deeper into the pillow. "Don't you dare mention seeing her with someone else. It's not our business, Isaiah. You don't even know her. 'Don't look at a jar, but what's inside.' "

"Ah." He hugged her. "From *The Wisdom of the Fathers.*"

She gently disengaged his arm, but pecked his lips, waiting until he went back to his own twin bed. "Maybe it should have been called *The Wisdom of the Mothers.*"

10

On Wednesday afternoon, following a morning of gazing blankly at bank investment portfolios, Abed drove to the Dead Sea. He hid the car in a low embankment and climbed the sandy mountain path that led to one of the thousands of caves, home of ancient breakaway religious sects and seekers of solitude. The likelihood of running into an archaeologist searching for a new set of ancient scrolls was greater than being caught by an Israeli intelligence officer. Nonetheless, he'd come armed.

In Europe, terrorist leaders led rich, decadent lives. Here in Palestine, the revolutionary had little glamour, Abed reflected sourly, as he kicked aside ibex turds and sat down. He ran his hands over his favorite possession, an Israeli-made Galil rifle. In the Six-Day War, Israeli officers had complained of the "bang-bang-jam" mechanism of their local rifle, while the Arabs used the superior AK-47, *automat kalashnikova*. Israeli engineers had developed the Galil with a folding steel stock and a bipod that folded between the hand-guards when not in use. It also had a grenade launcher at the end of the barrel and, curiously, a can opener. Abed loved the guns, particularly when he turned it back on its clever inventors.

Although the successful attack on Ali Alhassan had raised his prestige with Moslem fringe groups, it had angered the fund-raisers, who garnered funds from upper-class Arabs like the Alhassans. Another thorn in his side was Raba's continued unwillingness to work for him in Bethlehem. She was at home nursing her husband, and refused his phone calls. Operation Man-

ger was built around her. There was no time for sub-
tlety. Abed needed to do something dramatic, and to
do it soon. Again he'd have to take an active role
himself. This time he'd chosen the necessary accom-
plice with care.

A long-tailed jerboa scurried by his desert boot,
startling him seconds before he heard shuffling at the
cave entrance. Abed braced the Galil against his side
and cocked it, knowing he could pick off anyone who
came in. A youthful voice called out their password:
"Deir Yassin," an Arab village where Jews had once
massacred Palestinian women and children. Still clutching the rifle, Abed slipped the mask over his square
bearded chin, his silky black mustache, his wide forehead, the distinctive beauty mark on his neck. There
was always wild speculation among the men about his
identity. None of them had seen his face or could
recognize him as the handsome foreign currency clerk.

Sami's face appeared in the opening as he bent to
accommodate himself to the low passageway. The scar
on his right cheek stood out even in the dimness, con-
trasting with his overwhite skin and the look of childlike innocence in his wide-set eyes. His guileless looks,
red hair, and light skin had fooled the infamous Israeli
instinct for picking out terrorists. Sami's father had
also underestimated him. Family resources had been
invested in Sami's older brother, who'd been sent to
college while Sami had earned the family living by
working in the dolomite quarries since he was seventeen. A mistake. Sami, only twenty-two, was the
smartest young man Abed had ever recruited. He'd
carried out his assignment with creativity in the animal
market. Most important, Sami had golden hands with
explosives. So talented was he that the Israelis had
overlooked his being a Palestinian and put him in
charge of blasting at the quarries.

"Marhabah," Abed greeted him.

"Ahlan wasahlan," Sami answered back, his voice
deferential.

Money business first, Abed thought. Sami was pay-
master for the Gaza squadrons. Abed squatted over a

blue plastic market basket filled with crumpled plastic bags and garlic bulbs, pulling neat stacks of Jordanian dinars from the basket. His long dexterous fingers flipped the bills as Sami watched carefully. Without warning, Abed lurched up, knocking Sami backward, his head snapping back.

"Remember the lesson of the battle of Uhud. Never be caught off guard," Abed said. In the seventh-century battle, archers had left their posts in disobedience, causing a terrible setback to the Moslems. Sami looked stunned and insulted. Abed reached out to help him up. "Money distracts even a brave man."

Sami rubbed his hands over his hip, looking warily at Abed. The scar twitched.

"Relax your guard and you'll be dead, Sami. Today's lesson."

Abed nodded for him to sit, and lowered himself gracefully to the cave floor, sitting cross-legged. In front of him, a crack stretched upward in the cave, and a plant was mysteriously growing where almost no rain fell. He began dividing the money in piles. Abed recited the names and sums without looking at the list. His memory was legendary. He handed Sami a large stack of bills. "Distribute it quickly. We keep our promises."

Sami just nodded.

Abed asked, "What have you heard of Ibrahim?"

"The other prisoners think he's crazy, but I don't. He's a good actor. He played Hamlet in tenth grade. I was Horatio."

Were Palestinian high schools the last in the world to force children to memorize Shakespeare in the original? Abed wondered briefly. Sami and Ibrahim went back a long way together, had stayed friends even after Sami had dropped out of school. Sometimes friends were closer than brothers. How would he get Sami to take his newest assignment? Abed paused to find the right tone, firm and commanding, for what he had to say next.

"Sami, there's a problem. Someone is revealing our

plans to the Israelis, and the Islamic Council will not abide it.''

In the silence a lizard's tail swished against the cave wall. Sami's skin turned paler, his twitch worsened as he made the connection. "God's mercy. You don't suspect Ibrahim, do you?"

Abed walked to a part of the cave where he could stand full height. "It devastates me to tell you that our brother-in-arms has cooperated with the enemy. Don't blame him. There are drugs, brought by Russian Jews from the KGB. Even the strongest fall."

"But he knew next to nothing!" Sami protested.

Sami's chest heaved, as if surprised at his own outburst. He'd never dared to question Abed before. Sami started backward, his eyes focused on Abed's gun. Sami looked cornered, but he wasn't going to give in. This time he changed his tone and whispered like a supplicant. "Ibrahim grew up with me. He was my closest friend. He was low down on the chain of command. Surely he couldn't have told the Israelis anything they didn't know."

"Evidently, Ibrahim is a better actor than either of us gave him credit for. He knew a great deal of our plan, and the entire operation is in jeopardy with Ibrahim in Israeli hands."

Sami's head hung in dejection and Abed was worried. Old ties ran deep. Abed needed an explosives expert both for this job and for Operation Manger. Abed's voice softened "And you will come with me, Sami. The two of us will work together."

"With you?" He blinked in astonishment.

No other recruit had worked with Abed. It would catapult Sami up the ranks of the terrorist hierarchy. "Just the two of us," Abed said.

Sami paced, running his fingers through his wavy hair. He hadn't come to terms with it yet. Wanting to force a decision, Abed lied. "I understand if you can't face it. I'll ask a different sapper."

Sami looked at him in panic. On intuition, Abed aimed for another weak spot. Sami had talked with a mixture of pride and jealousy of his Nazareth cousin, a so-called Israeli Arab who'd been chosen for an electronics program in Haifa. "I'll understand if you don't want to do this, but I do need an expert in explosives. Do you think your cousin would work for us?"

"No!" Sami's head jerked up. Sweat was running down his face. "He's a Jew lover. A spy. How can you think of it?"

Sami needed to be bound. Now.

Abed reached into the basket once more and pulled out a curved Bedouin knife. Sami's eyes grew wider, and he stepped back. Abed hiked up his trousers. With the younger man mesmerized, he cut a thin line on his thigh with the tip.

Sami gasped, staring at the blood dripping down Abed's leg. Abed reached forward, circled Sami's wrist with his fingers, and pressed Sami's palm into the free-flowing blood.

"Swear," he commanded, his breath on Sami's neck. "Swear your loyalty. Swear you'll submit to the will of Allah."

Sami swallowed hard but said nothing.

"Swear," Abed ordered, turning Sami's wrist to coat his fingers in blood.

Pale and trembling, at last Sami responded. "I swear," he said. "By Allah, I swear."

Gil called Deborah at seven Thursday morning. "Sorry it's so early. I wanted to catch you before you left for work."

Holding the receiver between her shoulder and ear, she put on the kettle, pulling the long cord across the kitchen. She'd been up since five, too nervous to sleep. "I'm not going in today. There's a problem in my lab."

"Oh?" Gil said with sympathy. "I'm sorry to hear that, but does that mean you have time for lunch?"

She had promised herself she'd collate data for a report today. If she interrupted her work, she'd be up half the night finishing it. "Okay. Where?"

"How about the King David Hotel? I like the terrace."

"At the King David I like even the bathrooms."

She did need someone to talk to about that GSS meeting, and Gil was the most likable of the bunch. When Rachel had phoned last night, Deborah had felt ridiculous making light conversation when she was weighing such a serious decision. Gil suggested they meet on the patio at one o'clock.

Deborah saw her children off to school, knowing the GSS was still guarding them. One side of Sarah's blouse hung below the other by two inches. Deborah squatted to button it. "We have to be extra careful after what happened," she said. "Remember, don't talk to strangers and don't go anywhere without telling me."

Ben made an annoyed sound. "Do you think we're stupid?"

"Come here, you," she said, teasing him, and catching his forehead in a kiss.

When they left, she spread her notes on the kitchen table, but concentrating came hard. She sipped ice water, used a facial mask that had been in the cabinet for years, and tried to convince herself that staying home had its advantages. At noon, she got out of her nightgown and put on a straight skirt with a yellow cotton blazer. The King David was Israel's most aristocratic hotel. She brushed her hair until it gleamed and chose heeled sandals that made her slender feet look delicate. She'd removed the polish last night. "Keep them on their toes," she said to herself, and then groaned at her own joke.

The day's mail hadn't arrived, but sticking out of her mailbox was an envelope with a caricature of a weight lifter and the words COLOSSEUM GYM decorating one corner. Deborah opened it with a finger, and only when it was half open did she realize how careless she was. It might be a letter bomb. She dropped it and waited, feeling foolish. When nothing happen she picked it up again and pulled out a gift certificate in her name for six weeks of free workouts. Had she filled out an entry form in a supermarket lottery? Nothing came to mind. Ben might have filled in one for her while she was packing up. She stuck it in her pocketbook and drove across town to King David Street. The King David Hotel's rose-tinged stone facade looked down on a Jerusalem street of the same name. The entrance had a gracious semicircle driveway, and a doorman in a gray uniform. The wide lobby was decorated with Persian carpets and deep sofas.

Gil rose quickly when she entered the garden veranda and stared at Deborah, his warm gaze missing no detail, from her sun-streaked blond hair to the flattering cut of the skirt. A look of warm appreciation rose to his face, and then yielded to a more sedate expression of greeting, as if he'd suddenly remembered his British manners. He stepped forward to pull out a chair for her. She was charmed. He was about Raphi's age, maybe mid-thirties, but he had tinges of gray in his sideburns and his thin shoulders were slightly stooped. The British formality, out of place last night, fit in here, on the white terrace surrounded by sweet-smelling geraniums and roses. The hotel had housed the British authorities during the Mandate and still felt like an outpost of colonialism. Jewish resistance had blown up the King David on July 22, 1946. The date was easy to remember because July 22 was Sarah's birthday.

Gil held the chair. "If you please?" he said, treating her to another appreciative look.

Deborah slid into the wide rattan chair, tugging down her skirt. He waited for her to get comfortable, and then eased her chair closer to the table, his hand touching her arm. He took his own seat across from her. Hers was the seat with the stupendous Old City view and no sun in her eyes. "Thank you," she said.

"What for specifically?" Gil asked, smiling into her eyes.

"The view, your invitation, your being human last night."

"I can't take credit for the view. The invitation is my pleasure. As for last night, well, it's never hard not to look good contrasted to Moshe Cohen. Have you recovered from your first scintillating session with the famous Israeli security services?"

His soft voice wouldn't carry to the nearby table where tourists were conversing loudly in German. "It was a surprise. You know how everyone has fantasies—James Bond types exchanging terse confidences. Are your sessions always such a farce?"

Gil had a way of paying undivided attention, making her feel valued and important. Deborah crossed her legs under the table and leaned back in her chair.

He laughed easily. "I don't think I'd call them a farce. Loud, overserious, tacky, you Americans say. What you saw last night was relatively civilized. Our sessions are worse when the two permanent members are there. Anat's not a regular. She was brought in for this assignment. I've always hated the meetings. Bloody waste of time if you ask me. But then they don't ask me."

Butterflies were feasting on the blossoms. On the flowered walks below the balcony two well-known journalists were walking to the tennis court. A woman was swimming laps in the pool. Deborah envied their relaxed life. "What exactly is your role?"

"Mostly administrative. Every now and then I take on an investigative assignment, but less so lately. I used to do fieldwork like Raphi. We worked together for years, but now I leave that to the younger at heart."

"Is he? Younger?" She hadn't planned to gossip about Raphi, but she was curious.

"We're actually the same age, Raphi and I, thirty-four, but he's not as cynical. And while I've slowed down, he's still quite remarkable in the field, a sort of intelligence wizard, the last of a breed of field officers who can do everything by themselves. He uses the gadgets, but doesn't depend on them. Still, even Raphi should know when it's time to retire."

She couldn't resist a desire to learn more. "He's got other work to fall back on."

"The university teaching, you mean. And other things. Investments. You don't have to worry about

Raphi. When he decides he's through, he can sit back and write a best-selling book about Middle Eastern economy—what does the foreign minister call it?—economic Zionism. He'll get married and raise a pack of kids."

Deborah wasn't sure why she felt a stab of painful disappointment at this last piece of news. Her mood was dampened. "Anat's a beautiful woman."

"Yes, a diamond of the first water, as we Brits would say. I'm not really British, of course, just my father's half. My mother was Czech, a Jew in the anti-British resistance. My father, a peer of the realm, came to Palestine to do his patriotic duty, arrested my mother, then fell in love with her, and threw in with the Zionists."

Deborah was touched. "What a lovely, romantic story."

"Isn't it? But that's neither here nor there. Raphi insists he'll retire after this current operation, which, unfortunately, everyone at the GSS believes you are indispensable for."

The words were scarcely out of his mouth when Raphi himself appeared at Deborah's right elbow, as if they'd conjured him there by mentioning his name.

"Gil, Deborah," he said, nodding to each. He pulled out a chair and sat down as if they'd been expecting him. Speak of the devil.

"As my husband would say, 'It's a shame we weren't talking about the Messiah,' " Deborah said, her face flushed. She drew lines on her napkin with her knife as she tried to deny the flash of joy she'd felt at seeing him. Nonetheless, she had a premonition that her pleasant afternoon would be spoiled. Her world seemed to collapse when she was around Raphi.

"Your secretary told me you were here," he said, the pilot's sunglasses hiding his expression.

A waiter was bringing the wine, and Gil sighed in resignation and asked for a third goblet. They sat in silence for a full minute. She felt herself stiffen.

"Don't let me disturb your tête-à-tête," Raphi said.

He took off his glasses and put them on the table, rubbing his eyes.

"Bad night's sleep?" Deborah asked in mock concern.

"Short." He shrugged.

Gil's fingers fisted around the bottle. Evidently he was surprised by Raphi's appearance. "Damn it, Raphi. You might as well tell us why you're here." He poured Deborah's glass first and then his own.

"Deborah left us last night without making a commitment. Today is Thursday. We have to get started immediately. I know you'd like to spend a week wining and dining, but that doesn't jibe with the local terrorist schedule."

He unsnapped an attaché case and pulled out the *Jerusalem Post,* turning to the classified. His finger stabbed at a box. "I brought you the English version. You don't read Arabic, do you? By the way, how good is your high school French?"

He was showing off that they'd obtained her school records. So she wouldn't give him the satisfaction of an answer. The waiter brought the third goblet, and Raphi poured himself a glass of white wine. "*Lehayim,*" he said, raising his glass in a toast to Deborah. "*Salut,*" she answered back, straining for her best accent. In truth, her French stank.

Manger College was advertising for a biology teacher with at least a master's degree, practical experience, teaching experience, and a good knowledge of English or French. It looked as if someone was advertising for her. "How did you manage this? Knock off the old teacher in a dark alley?"

"A small car accident, actually," Raphi said. "Whiplash of the minor kind. The examining physician happened to be on the scene, and insisted the teacher rest for at least six weeks with a nice insurance settlement. I suspect the dean, who is keen to upgrade the school, will prefer the new teacher. Certainly the students will. Unlike the old, she may have heard of DNA. In fact, I'm sure she has."

"And I suppose you expect me to apply?"

"Oh, nothing so time-consuming. I wouldn't want

to disturb your luncheon here with Gentleman Gil. His secretary called and made you an appointment for Monday. It's a Christian college, so Sunday is out. Gil's secretary is always *obliging*."

He said the last word with emphasis. There was an undercurrent of meaning, she was sure, and Gil's face was flushed and angry.

The waiter came for their orders. Deborah ordered salad nicoise. Raphi probably spoke French like de Gaulle.

"By the way, Gil," Raphi looked up from the menu, "are we eating on the company account?"

Gil's neck turned red. "I thought so," Raphi said. "In that case I'll take the fresh salmon. Gil, why don't you order Turkish salad for an appetizer?"

Gil's look turned so deadly that the image of the debonair aristocrat was nearly erased. It seemed so out of character that Deborah would have been equally surprised had a shark leaped out of the King David swimming pool.

Raphi took a bread stick from the basket and bit off an end. He turned to Deborah. "You *have* decided to join our cheerful little spy club, haven't you?"

"No, I haven't decided anything." She pretended to be concentrating on buttering her sesame roll.

Gil had regained his manners. He poured Deborah more wine. "Good for you. You don't have to do this, you know. Don't let him pressure you. Once you're in you won't be able to get out so easily." He blotted the tablecloth where wine had spilled.

"He's right, of course," Raphi said. "You don't have to do anything. Your agreement, if you decide to grant it, has to be unequivocal. And instant. Unfortunately, there isn't time for contemplation in our business."

"Don't feel pressured," broke in Gil. "There's no one waiting in the wings for your part."

"Unfortunately, Gil is right again. It's you or no one. Without you the operation goes on indefinite hold."

Deborah put down the roll and took a long drink

of water. A sense of doom settled over her like a shroud. Raphi made her feel guilty. Israel was the land of ultimate guilt. You felt guilty if you didn't help build the country, so you uprooted yourself and settled here. You felt guilty if you weren't nice to tourists so they would want to live here. You felt guilty if you didn't do anything heroic in the army. You felt guilty, for God's sake, if you enjoyed a sunny day in the winter when you were supposed to be praying for rain. And here she was, at least temporarily a single mother, feeling guilty because she refused to endanger herself after twice nearly being killed. They were waiting for her to speak. "The answer is no."

Raphi acted as if he hadn't heard her. "Let's see what's really involved here, so you can make a better decision," he said. His tone had changed. He was speaking softly, as if she were already his fellow conspirator. "You'll have to go to Bethlehem and be accepted on your own credentials. But we have no doubt you'll be hired immediately. No one has credentials like yours. Nor do we have to fake what a great teacher you are."

Flattery. They must want her badly. "If you're not careful I'll take that as a compliment."

"Actually," Raphi said, "lest you get a swelled head, you weren't my choice. I want you to know that. Gil here spotted you." He nodded to Gil, who gave an exaggerated smile. "Don't take it personally. I didn't think a nonprofessional could take this work. I still have my doubts."

"How comforting. Then why are you asking me?"

"The organization is somewhat democratic, despite its despotic image. I was outvoted. But with Gil out of fieldwork, I'm the only one available to work with you, that is, if you accept."

She looked at Gil, waiting for him to deny it. "I'm afraid he's telling the truth, Deborah."

Suddenly she realized that she was at the threshold of making the most important decision of her life. Through her wineglass she looked down at Raphi's hands, the same fingers that had twisted Fu'ad's neck like a chicken's. They were more like a concert pianist's, with neat, straight nails. She sipped from her own glass. "Go on, Raphi. Tell me exactly what I would do if I signed up."

"You'll take part in faculty meetings, listen in at student meetings, and plant a few microphones. That's all it will take for us to figure out what is happening inside. Not much of an investment on your part—for which you'll be well paid. Then there are the children."

Deborah bristled. "Which children are you referring to?"

"The victims of the attack. We're sure, now, that this organization is going to attack children."

"Like Maalot?" Deborah thought of the school full of children taken prisoner in the northern city in 1974. The IDF had been unable to rescue them without killing the children.

"This may make Maalot look like a picnic."

Deborah shivered, despite the hot sunshine. A sparrow flew onto the balcony and searched for bread crumbs. A little girl's voice rose from the pool below, "My turn, my turn, my turn." The German from the other table now grated on her ears. Both Gil and Raphi were looking at her, silent, waiting. What will it be, Deborah? They didn't have to say it. The question was in the air.

The waiter was bringing their dishes on a large, round tray. They sat in silence while he arranged the salad dressings in small china pitchers in front of them. As he reached for Raphi's salmon, the bang of a large explosion startled him and sent the olives spilling. Gil and Raphi were on their feet, apologizing that they had to leave just as a second explosion tore through the air. The beeper at Gil's waist buzzed, and his eyes sought out a phone. "Let's just go," ordered Raphi. He nodded to her briefly and they disappeared. Deborah remained alone with the two salads, the boned fish, a terrible headache, and the bill.

11

Abed chose a white Ford Sierra with the thin red lines decorating the chassis because so many policemen drove that model. There was a wide choice of cars in the parking lot at French Hill, a Jewish neighborhood so close to the Arab neighborhood of Issawiya that Jews and Arabs could look into each other's houses. Abed and Sami would escape to Issawiya if they needed to.

Breaking into the car took Sami less than thirty seconds. What wise hands he has, Abed thought, complimenting himself on his choice of protégé. He let Sami drive and took the passenger seat. *"Allah karim,"* God is great, Abed said, feeling marvelous.

Sami was fidgeting and twisting. "Is this your first stolen car?" Abed asked.

"Second," Sami said, a hand raking his hair, dyed black for today. Once he and a friend had stolen a car and driven to the Dead Sea. They were floating in the buoyant water and dreaming aloud about the future when they met two English girls. The one called Elizabeth like the queen had rubbed Dead Sea mud on herself. When she couldn't reach her back, she'd asked Sami to do it. He'd never touched a girl that way before. Elizabeth noticed how aroused he was and giggled, but not meanly. She'd flipped her muddy hair to the side, then reached behind and dropped the bikini top. Her breasts with thin blue veins looked so white against the black mud. "If I live to be one hundred twenty," Sami said, his voice strained, "I'll never forget her."

Sami's story embarrassed and titillated Abed. "Turn

in here," he ordered gruffly. They'd arrived at Wadi Jose, a strip of Arab car-repair shops.

The wiring took Sami an hour. In the middle he got hungry and ate a box of lemon wafers they'd found in the backseat.

Abed had no appetite. He took the driver's seat and brushed off the black Hasidic coat he was wearing. He drove carefully and parked the Sierra in a lot behind the police station.

Abed checked Sami's appearance: a brown-and-beige synthetic shirt with three neck buttons and slightly bowed brown pants. Jews expected Palestinians to look as if they've been dressed from a charity hamper. Sami picked up the box of chewy, sugared candies called Turkish Delights in which a bomb had been planted. Sami had molded the light new plastic explosives into the lower level of sweets. The top layer held real candies.

Abed blessed Sami: Allah would be with him. They'd meet at the Dead Sea cave in the evening.

Sami held the Turkish Delights close to his chest and walked, head slightly forward, toward the barracks. His top shirt button was really a microphone, and Abed would follow the action from the car. Abed picked up a copy of a religious Hebrew newspaper, *Yated Ne'eman,* to cover his face and listened.

Abed thought of the jail security as three concentric rings. Getting past the first guard was ridiculously easy. Abed heard a guard jawing to his partner about the relative merits of different wedding halls. He barely paused to read Sami's identity card.

Sami was inside the first ring. Now he'd stand in a slow-moving line of visitors for "minorities prisoners" who'd committed light offenses. Only one visitor at a time could approach the screened window. To see more dangerous suspects, visitors had to obtain a pass from the office and present it to an additional gate guard. Abed had advised Sami to linger at this point. The guard at the inner gate drank coffee all day and frequently needed to piss. When he did, Sami could slip into the corridor. The third ring of guards should by rights demand the pass, but they were infamously lazy, and might assume the others had checked it. Most security systems had a hole. Abed had studied dozens of reports by security prisoners who'd been in that jail to find this one. If Sami *was* checked and found lacking the right pass, he'd feign confusion and then leave. They'd go home and try getting to Ibrahim on a different day.

Ten minutes after Sami waited in line he whispered that the guard had left. He entered the inner courtyard. Abed held his breath as Sami approached the guards, but they only asked for Sami's identity card. A stroke of luck! The sounds faded as Sami went into a booth and removed his shirt for the body search. He would have to bend over so a guard could see up his ass. Abed knew he'd never be able to passively endure such humiliation.

The sound improved as Sami got dressed. "A minute," the guard was saying. "What is that under your arm?"

The Turkish Delights!

The Russian-made microphone was so good Abed could hear the guard open the box and run his finger over the powdered sugar.

Sami's voice sounded high as he got talkative in Hebrew that Abed realized was much better than his own. Sami offered the guard a candy!

What if the guard took the wrong candy and chewed into the explosives? Again, Abed held his breath.

Abed could hear the rustle of the paper.

It was all right. Sami was ordered to wait on a bench until a guard could escort him inside.

Time dragged. Now Abed was getting thirsty and hungry and regretted not eating. To cope with the thirst, he pretended he was back training in Libya, the hottest place on earth. Ironically, in a land of desert, for the first part of their test they'd nearly died in water. All the cadets were dumped into a pool, blindfolded. They had to fight for space, pushing each other down when that was over. Then they were left in the desert with only one bottle for two of them. He strangled his partner. At first he'd felt terrible about this, but the training commander had heaped praise on him and taught him that sacrifices were sometimes necessary for the greater cause. Guilt had been lifted, and from that moment forward Abed was willing to take whatever steps were needed to further *jihad*.

The microphone was waking up. A youthful-sounding policeman was speaking Arabic to Sami. "Are you here to visit Ibrahim Masri? I'm Yoram. I'll take you there. Usually we have to get GSS approval, but the boss is out to lunch and I don't see why you have to wait."

Abed was shocked at how open and naive the young guard sounded.

"The truth is that I feel sorry for Ibrahim. He hardly ever gets visitors," Yoram said in Arabic.

Abed could hear locks opening. Yoram urged Sami to hurry, the doors could only be left open for a fixed number of seconds before a buzzer rang. Abed jerked to attention. He didn't know the locks were timed! That must be new. There was more loud noise and echoes as the gate banged shut.

Seconds later Sami was greeting Ibrahim. He'd made it! Abed felt a surge of triumph. Allah was with them.

Abed heard the guard caution Sami that he had only five minutes for this visit. He would have to work fast. Abed's tongue cleaved to his palate, but he begged Allah, *Let Ibrahim not have forgotten the codes.*

Sami's voice sounded unnaturally high. "I've brought you some sweets."

"Don't give me your poison candies." Ibrahim's voice was startlingly familiar. "I know you've come to poison me. You have betrayed our holy nation. Why, oh why, have you abandoned me to their torture? Get the poison candies out of here."

A loud noise filled the speaker, as if Ibrahim had thrown himself against metal bars.

"Would you take it?" Sami whispered to the guard. "Maybe he'll calm down."

"No problem," Yoram said.

A fatal mistake, Abed thought gleefully.

Sami's voice was high and strained, but he persevered, coaxing and making conversation with his former comrade-in-arms, telling him about his family, asking about prison food.

Good for you, Abed thought. Sami was innovative. Ibrahim grunted answers, also doing well. Perhaps he'd underestimated him, too. Well, it didn't matter anymore.

At last Yoram said, "I'm sorry. Your time is up."

Abed could imagine him looking down at his cheap digital watch and touching it ever so gently, but hard enough to send off the beam to the explosive in the box.

The seconds ticked by, one, two, three. At four, the explosion broke the speaker.

"*Allah karim!*" Abed shouted to the car roof.

He opened the door quickly. He had seconds to get out before the car exploded, creating a diversion so Sami could escape. His black coat caught on the door, and he swore under his breath. At last it came free.

"God is great," he said again under his breath. He heard the second explosion in the parking lot as he ducked into the alleyway on the Road of the Prophets, heading to the Damascus Gate. Behind a curtain in an Old City T-shirt shop, Abed shed the Hasidic clothing and wrapped his face in an Arab headdress.

Smoke was still rising when Gil and Raphi arrived at the Russian Compound. Sappers bent over the car. Raphi followed them, cursing quietly, making mental notes. The wires on the timer had been blue and white, the colors of the Israeli flag. A signature. The terrorist knew that the GSS would be looking for a "signature," so he'd thumbed his nose at the Israelis by being so obvious. Those insolent touches, like packaging Yusef's testicles in a shopping bag from the Shekem, a store connected to the military, were the style of the Seventh Century.

Raphi was glad he had never gotten around to

eating lunch when he examined Yoram's body. Born with only two fingers on each hand, Yoram wouldn't have been drafted, but he'd volunteered for the army. The fingers he did have had been blown off. Members of the chemical identification division were gathering residue, searching for minute quantities of unexploded materials that hadn't been contaminated. C-4, a light-brown odorless putty, would have been perfect for candy.

The terrorist had used papers of an Ahmed Hajaj, a dead man from Hebron. The outer-ring guard who'd waved the terrorist through was now chain-smoking cigarettes, waiting to be interrogated.

Another guard had apparently eaten a piece of candy from a box that had been the source of the bomb. "It couldn't have happened," the guard kept muttering to himself.

The terrorist had been both clever and lucky on his way in, but his luck had run out. Leaving the jail, he'd run into a patrol of border police and was now being treated for burns and what would be called tactfully "other injuries." Yoram had been well liked.

Raphi shook his head. The attack had taken place while he was behaving like an asshole at lunch with Deborah. What did he care if Gil seduced her, or that he was fucking his secretary, or if he kept a whole fucking harem? He turned to Gil's freckled, red faced weeping secretary. "Call the King David Hotel and find out how much our lunch cost. Then send a squad car with the money to Deborah Stern. I'll write out the exact address."

In the late afternoon Deborah was pouring conditioner over Sarah's snarled hair. Ben was in the living room practicing a game the boys played in school with gum wrappers. The player clapped his hands, creating a breeze with which he tried to make his opponent's wrapper flip over. The noise suddenly stopped. Ben told her someone was at the door claiming he was a policeman with a letter. Her anger flared at the audacity of someone coming openly to her home. She quickly rinsed out the suds and wiped her hands on her jeans. By the time she got to the living room Ben was holding the letter. "Don't open the door to strangers!" she shouted. Ben looked as stricken as if she'd slapped him, and slunk off to the living room where Sarah had escaped and was watching television.

The bills inside puzzled her until she added them up to the 410 shekels she'd shelled out for lunch. Raphi. Only he would remember, even though he was coping with the bloodshed at the police station. Maybe if he and Gil hadn't been wining and dining me, they could have prevented the bombing, she thought guiltily.

She wept through the long, tearful TV interviews with Yoram's classmates. The news that Ibrahim Masri had been killed spooked her. Again she saw his eyes suffused in hate and heard him cursing her.

Now he was dead. Relief swept over her.

She hadn't been next. He had.

Ali was still recovering at home. Raba hovered over him, fluffing the pillows and bringing tea and cold drinks until empty cups were lined up like tin soldiers on his night table.

"So what's this devoted wifely treatment really about?" Ali asked her, reaching for her hand and pulling her to his side of the old-fashioned starched white sheets. She sat at the edge, afraid to hurt him. "I appreciate it, but we both know I'm not going to expire from my injuries. What is worrying you, Raba?"

Raba released herself from his grip, closed the door, paused, and then locked it. She sat down near Ali again and rested her hand on his thick hairy wrist. "Your injury is partly my fault." He respected her enough to hear her out without protesting or contradicting. She told him about the threat and how she'd refused employment in Bethlehem. "I had a phone call this morning insisting I take the job. I hung up."

Ali turned over her palm and pressed it to his lips. "You did right. It wouldn't be very gallant of me to let you risk your life or that of our baby to protect me, would it? In Egypt I also made contact with friends. We'll be hearing from them soon. I was assured we can translate our family's contribution to the liberation movement into money. Funds are running low for the Moslem groups right now."

She leaned over and pressed a quick kiss on his lips. He pulled her forward again, coaxing her mouth open, deepening the kiss, pressing her down against him so she could feel his tumescence under the sheet.

A loud knocking at the door made her sit up fast, her face flushed, her lips reddened. Suhella apologized for disturbing, but the servants had been watching CNN in the kitchen. There was an explosion at the Jerusalem police barracks. According to the newscaster, Madame's brother was dead.

12

Give an Arab a beating and he'll respect you. Compromise and he'll take it as a sign of weakness. He'll offer you coffee and knife you when you turn your back to drink it. Everyone in the police lounge had advice for Raphi. Those who'd served with Yoram were so riled they would gladly tear the Palestinian apart, if the law allowed them. The law didn't. Raphi filled a glass cup first with coffee and sugar, then added boiling water. Mud, they called this brew. He carried the glass to the observation room, where he'd direct Gil's investigation through one-way glass.

He and Gil had their own investigative routine, developed over years working together. They belonged to the generation of the elite Shin Bet officers who had absorbed the old GSS reluctance to use brute force. In recent years standards had been relaxed. Under the pressure of chronic terrorism, speed was more important than refinement in extracting information. Under a "ticking clock" clause, violence was allowed. The clock was certainly ticking for them, Raphi thought grimly. The eleventh hour had long passed, and they might go straight to the thirteenth.

Gil and Raphi's method, which they called "lethal suggestion," allowed a suspect to cave in with grace and let them sleep at night. Gil would conduct today's interview, since Raphi was working undercover. Raphi would observe through a one-way mirror; Gil would wear an ear wire.

The Arab, who still hadn't been identified, was huddling in a corner. One of his eyes and his upper lip were swollen from the encounter with the border policemen. Gil came in whistling and squatted near him to examine the bruises. He barked into a wall speaker and ordered an ice pack and cold drinks. Then, using an old test of theirs, Gil tossed the prisoner keys to the handcuffs. Every prisoner was keen on freeing his hands, but if a prisoner was as badly injured as this one pretended to be, removing the old lock would be a struggle.

Today's terrorist was free in seconds, already rubbing his wrists. A good actor. Raphi watched intently. This was an important minute. Once a prisoner whose hands had been freed had been foolish enough to attack Gil, mistaking his politeness for weakness. Gil had broken both his legs.

The Arab wisely contented himself with pursing his mouth in hate. Gil set up a small folding picnic table, with a bench on each side. The prisoner shook his head when Gil offered him a seat across the table from him on one of the benches, remaining in the corner. "Sorry about the rough treatment," Gil apologized, brushing a fly off his arm. Raphi smiled at Gil's Arabic, which was university-learned and formal, unlike his own colloquial speech. His father had insisted that Raphi and his sister speak Arabic and Hebrew from the cradle.

"I had a hell of a time keeping Yoram's friends out today. You killed a very popular young man. Is your eye all right?"

The Arab, a Semitic Cyclops, glared at Gil through his single unimpaired eye. The closed eye twitched as Raphi got his first clear look at him and nearly dropped his coffee. This was the Palestinian who'd met Raba in the animal market! His hair had been dyed black. Excited, he whispered the information to Gil.

Gil turned on the prisoner. "Don't look so outraged. I understand you completely. If a childhood buddy of mine were in jail I'd do whatever I could to release him."

"And smash his head with a metal pipe? Like hell you would," Raphi whispered into the mike.

They'd decided to pretend Ibrahim had been killed accidentally by the bomb. The prisoner couldn't know they'd noticed Ibrahim's collapsed cranium. Gil rubbed his ear, making the machine buzz back at Raphi, then leaned back in the chair.

"Where are you from?"

All he got was the expected grunt and a curse.

"Don't be an idiot. We're checking your fingerprints. The computer will have an answer in an hour. You might as well be cooperative on the little things. Shows goodwill. Then you can tell us to go to hell about the big things."

"Never!" The prisoner let out a string of curses. "You have stolen our homeland. You will be washed into the sea. Allah guides not those who do wrong. Those who believe, and strive in his cause, will achieve salvation."

"Bravo," Raphi whispered into the mike. He'd recognized the slight accent. "He's quoting, albeit not word for word, the Koran, and he's from Gaza, like his dead friend, Ibrahim."

Gil kept his tone even and light. "Cooperation is a matter of degree. No one would expect you to betray your own people. We just want to fill a few gaps."

"We'll fill your belly with a rifle. Says the Prophet, 'Slay those who reject the faith.'"

Gil wrinkled his brow. His voice got even softer. "Perhaps I should explain the advantages of cooperation. He wasn't a prophet, but as that American colonial Benjamin Franklin put it neatly: God helps those who help themselves. God in this case means Allah."

"Wherever you are, death will overtake you. Save your threats for cowards, Zionist dog."

Gil went on, as if Sami hadn't spoken. "We'll start simply. If you don't cooperate, we blow up your family home. All the neighborhood children will come around to watch. A pity, but your family will be on the street. Not so bad now, in summer, but winter isn't nice. Are you taking drugs? No? Well, nearly everyone does in prison. Once you have a habit, it's hard to quit. You should know. Devout Moslems have run supposed drug-rehabilitation centers as covers for seditious activity for years."

Gil paced, his hands behind his back, as if thinking aloud. "Won't your mother enjoy sharing another woman's kitchen? But then she'll be grateful for a roof over her head, won't she?"

The terrorist had steel in him, Raphi thought. No telltale eye movements showed Gil that he'd touched a sensitive nerve.

Gil touched his eyes. "Then there's the question of your brothers and sisters. First, those precious work permits that allow them jobs in Israel—we deny them with a stroke of a pen."

"Keep your fucking permits. We don't want to clean your shitty toilets anymore."

"Tsk, tsk. You haven't heard me through. Of course you're sick of menial jobs, a clever fellow like you who can penetrate the police lockup. That's why cooperation helps. We reward friends. Nothing obvious at first. That wouldn't do, would it? Get you in trouble with the masked boys. Not just your family gets permits, but the neighbors, too. Your brother is sent abroad, a representative of Gaza Youth. Your sister wins a scholarship."

Raphi noted the sudden interest at the mention of a sister.

"Your name?" Gil asked. "We know you're from Gaza and that you're not Ahmed Hajaj. This is Israeli intelligence."

A choked laugh, then the prisoner spat on the floor. "That I broke into. You Jews think you're smarter than everyone. But the time of Jewish arrogance and supremacy is over. The new Moslem era has begun. Israeli intelligence sucks."

"Cut it short," Raphi ordered in the earphones. "Let's not forget he killed Yoram Cohen, not to mention Ibrahim Masri. Tell him his sister will be working in a brothel at the end of the week servicing border guards."

"Speaking of sucks," said Gil. Raphi was impressed, but not really surprised, that Gil's academic Arabic included the words to explain in lurid detail how a sister might pay for lack of cooperation.

By the evening the GSS had data from the computer and their contacts in Gaza. "Sami Hamad, twenty-two," Gil said. "Typical Gaza family except that there are just three children. An older brother is college-educated and unemployed. And there's a sister Noha, twenty-three, still unmarried, bright and pretty, working as a secretary for the UN relief organization and studying part-time. Our Sami is an electricity prodigy, earned extra money for years siphoning off juice for private homes. At seventeen, his father made him quit school and work in a quarry. The boss spotted his talent and put him in charge of explosives. He was a childhood friend and classmate of Ibrahim Masri's. Why doesn't that surprise me?"

"Killing Ibrahim doesn't make sense," said Raphi. "They must have realized he would have given up all his secrets by now."

"Maybe they wanted to humiliate us by breaking into the police headquarters."

"Well, they succeeded in that," Raphi said. "There'll be a commission of inquiry and dozens of clever articles attacking the GSS in the Friday newspapers."

The computer department called to say the graphics for the next phase of their investigation were ready.

"Amazing what technology can do," Raphi said, looking at the sharp color images of a slightly older Noha studying at university. The artist had added a stylish haircut. A nice touch. Photos of Noha with a briefcase and car keys followed. The fruits of cooperation. Another group of pictures showed Noha providing sexual services for generously endowed Israeli soldiers. One showed her in a threesome with another woman.

"Make it like a slide show," Raphi said, staring into space with cold eyes. "Bring popcorn. Arab coffee with cardamom. Start with photos of Gaza, the school, the family, old friends. Then introduce the first series. With no transition, move to the others. Wake him at night for it. A rat running across his bed should disturb his sleep. After the slide show, let him stew for a day in solitary. Make him wait and wonder."

Her students were discussing the terrorist attack when Deborah entered her night school class. The police barracks had been blown up, and they had to concentrate on mitosis. If you stopped for every crisis in Israel, you'd never get anything done.

Deborah had an additional reason for her restlessness. Joshua was meeting her after class. He'd called right before class, not mentioning their fight but insisting there was something urgent to discuss. She dreaded another round of pointless accusations.

He was sitting in the teachers' room, dressed in a black suit and hat, looking defiantly handsome despite the sober garb. Take it slow, she reminded herself.

Pressed on his lap was a volume of the Babylonian Talmud. He felt her presence and closed his book. "It asks," he said, "what you should do if you are meditating and a person comes into the room. Are you obligated to interrupt your thoughts to be polite?" Without answering his own question, he stood up, "Let's go talk. Is the King David Hotel all right?"

"The King David?" she choked.

"Hotel lobbies have the right neutrality for conversation."

Deborah recalled seeing religious couples courting in the lobbies of the major hotels, which were public enough to ensure modest behavior for unchaperoned couples. Still, she felt silly going there again. "It's terribly pricey."

His jaw tightened. *Why did I say that?* Deborah berated herself. Any reminder of his lack of salary could only get this off on the wrong foot.

"I think we can cope," he said as they walked down the stairs together.

Joshua made an appropriate whistling sound and gestured in appreciation at the old Subaru's transformation. Deborah felt ridiculously proud, as if the shining paint, the racing stripe, and upholstery were proof of how well she could cope without him.

She and Joshua settled in two thick armchairs in the lobby. "How did you spend your day?" he asked her.

At least this isn't going to be a frontal attack, she thought with some relief. Still, she wouldn't relax.

"First I worked on an article for a journal." He didn't know about the lab. When she told him about its being contaminated, he got a strange light in his eye. "What is it?" she asked.

"Just the thought that nothing happens by chance," Joshua said. "When something happens, you might ask yourself if it's pointing a way to you."

Anger was already bubbling near the surface, but she held it back. "So how's life in the yeshiva?"

"Tranquil. Intellectually stimulating. Healing. Spiritual."

She toyed with the straw of her drink.

"That doesn't seem to make you too pleased, Deborah."

"Was it supposed to?"

"Deborah, I don't want to spend another evening fighting. I'm sorry I overreacted the other night. The thought of you with someone else drove me crazy. The facts are that we've been apart for six long months. Too long for me. We have two beautiful children. We share most of the same values. I still love you."

The words made her heart leap. When would she stop wanting to throw herself in his arms? Her fingers gripped the chair to hold her down. "Aren't you forgetting something?" she asked in a thin voice.

"My interest in religion?"

"Interest? Obsession. I'm willing to live a traditional life, but I can't live behind closed doors following orders because the rebbe says so."

Joshua pursed his lips. "You know as well as I do there are no closed doors. The rebbe doesn't direct every move. He's a consultant, just more experienced and more brilliant than a psychiatrist. How many times have you quoted experts to me?"

"The people you live with have such closed minds."

She picked up the hotel matchbook from the table and began flicking the matches with her thumbnail.

"What makes you think yours is so open? You won't even give it a try. You know nothing about the world I'm living in now. Do you realize there are six different free loan societies—one for dishes, one for baby equipment, one for extra tables and chairs, and three for money—right in my building."

"But I don't want to live in that world. I like my world, my career, the choices our children will have."

"You were nearly killed. Our children have guards following them to school—don't look surprised, remember that one of your police friends came to see me—and your lab is a mess. Don't you think it's time to wake up and see you have trouble in your life?"

You should only know. His pointing out her troubles was unfair. How many of them were because they'd split up? "So you're offering the Promised Land. Who do you think you are—Moses?"

"Joshua."

She couldn't help smiling. Joshua had always told her she had a short fuse but never stayed angry long. Maybe he was thinking of it, too, because her laughter was suddenly mirrored in his eyes. For that moment, life seemed brighter.

"Deborah. Give it a chance. Spend a Saturday with me—no, not with me, really, although you know I'd like nothing better. With the children. See what it's like."

She'd refused him so many times, but he was humbling himself to try again. She wondered what had brought this on. Jealousy over Raphi entering her life? Somewhere at the edge of her consciousness, she was beginning to crave a retreat from reality. She weighed the price in ill-feeling of the refusal against the possible gain that spending the weekend with him might achieve. Perhaps she could even confide in him about her assignment in Bethlehem. What a relief it would be.

She nodded her head and felt something loosen inside her. "Yes. I'll come. I'd like to."

* * *

Raphi drove to Deborah's night school so he could make a final successful plea for her to work for the GSS. He was amused to have a man dressed in religious garb precede him up the narrow stairs and ask for Deborah. Then it dawned on him that this might be the husband, the former lawyer, former army officer, current yeshiva student. Joshua was tall, dashing-looking, with broad shoulders and a confident walk. He'd been hoping Joshua was ugly or effeminate, or both. Damn! It hadn't occurred to him that Deborah might be seeing her husband.

She was doing the driving, Raphi noted with satisfaction.

Trailing the car was trivial. Why was she going back to the King David? Raphi always had disguises with him, and he wore a beard, a blond wig, and thick glasses before positioning himself at a table across the lobby. He had a transmitter in his professor's briefcase, and he focused it on the glass vase on the table where Deborah and Joshua were drinking ice tea. He could hear every word, and his anxiety grew. Deborah disappearing into the religious world would be convenient at the *end* of her assignment, but it would spell disaster for the GSS plans if she did it now.

Yoram's funeral was scheduled for Friday at 9:00 A.M. Hundreds of extra police were called up to prevent the possible outbreak of violence from mourners demanding revenge.

At 6:30 A.M., from behind the one-way mirror, Raphi watched two barrel-chested border policemen break into Sami's cell and wake him up. While one of them held him tightly, the other grabbed his hand and held it on a table. A mallet was brought down on each of his fingers, one at a time. Plastic handcuffs with small razor blades bound his wrists. His body was pressed backward over a stool, and his hands were strapped to his feet, cutting off circulation. One of the guards reached into Sami's pants, pulled Sami's penis and laughed. Another placed a cloth sack over his head.

"We're going to break your prick next," they told him, grabbing it in a fist.

Gil burst into the room, pulled the border policemen off him, and cursed them both.

"You're finished—the both of you. You'll be lucky if you find a job guarding a warehouse in Givat Olga." He called for the duty officer and a doctor and an ambulance.

Sami's pants were soiled and he moaned in pain. Gil pulled the sack off his head. Sami looked at Gil in a mixture of gratitude and fear.

"So sorry about this," Gil said, bending to put his arm over his shoulder. "Friends of Yoram's. I'll get you taken care of."

Yoram was being buried at Mount Herzl military cemetery, a short walk uphill from Deborah's house. National tragedies were open to the public, and Deborah decided to go. Joshua would approve of her decision to attend, she knew. In Judaism, attending a funeral was valued as the ultimate selfless deed because the deceased could never repay the favor.

Deborah was out of breath by the time she got to the entrance, where long lines of cars waited to pull into the cemetery parking lot. As each car emptied, the passengers joined the silent crowd of plain citizens, friends, classmates, and soldiers. Everyone stood with perfect discipline, eyes down, not a voice raised in the park entrance until Yoram's family arrived. Yoram's casket was carried by four soldiers past rows and rows of dead soldiers. No coffins were allowed in Jerusalem burials except for soldiers, whose bodies were often too mutilated to be carried under a shroud.

On cue, the crowd walked silently behind the family from the park to the grave site, up a path lined with rough stones like skulls piled up and covered with ivy. The piquant smell of marjoram, growing among the stones, seemed out of place. Yoram's mother, a black scarf tied below her chin, leaned on his weeping girl-friend. Yoram's friends, bleary-eyed teenagers, filled the hole, evening out the top. The quiet was rent by

the rhythm of scraping shovels, soil making dark arcs
as it fell into place. A friend of Yoram's read the
eulogy, his voice hoarse and reedy.

"Deborah."

She jumped.

Raphi took her arm. "Sorry I scared you."

She drew a calming breath. "I was lost in my thoughts."

He leaned against a pine tree and stretched his neck
back to get rid of a kink. "It's easy to get lost today."

"Did you know him personally? From everything I
read he was a wonderful guy."

"He was. A mensch. I've even had the honor of
being trounced by him at the chessboard. We talked
a lot. He was applying to study economics when he
got out of the army."

"I'm sorry. I know how much it hurts."

Raphi sighed and looked around. "There are rabbis
who insist the best way to gain a proper perspective
about life is to visit a cemetery. When you compare
your own troubles to the experience of being buried,
they seem smaller. I've picked out my own spot, with
a forest view. Want to see it?"

If she hadn't lived here so long, the black humor
would have shocked her. "Thanks, I'll pass."

"What were you thinking about when I startled you?"

"Don't laugh. A poem we memorized in elementary
school keeps going through my head. 'In Flanders
fields, the poppies blow, between the crosses, row on
row.' There aren't any crosses or poppies here. I guess
the stuff you memorize when you're a kid sticks."

"I know that poem," Raphi said. He picked up
where she'd left off:

> *"We are the Dead. Short days ago*
> *We lived, felt dawn, saw sunset glow,*
> *Loved and were loved,*
> *and now we lie*
> *In Flanders fields."*

Deborah shook her head. "I can't believe you
know it."

"I went to American schools, remember? Everyone learns it. Add to that my being hospitalized in France where John McCrae, the poet, served as a doctor in World War I. It was in a frame in my room. Do you know the last stanza?"

Deborah nodded, and said the words slowly, her voice thick with emotion:

> *"Take up our quarrel with the foe:*
> *To you from failing hands we throw*
> *The Torch; be yours to hold it high.*
> *If ye break faith with us who die*
> *We shall not sleep, though poppies grow*
> *In Flanders fields."*

A lump blocked her throat. "Too much, Raphi. I can't stand it." Tears ran down her cheek. She swiped at them with the back of her hand.

"You have to make a decision, Deborah. There's a school of children involved, enough to fill up rows and rows of a cemetery. I promise that your work will be as safe as we can make it."

Her eyes rested on the fresh grave. "Is there a possibility of saying no?"

Raphi shook his head. "I don't think so, unless I'm wrong about you. Not for you. Not for me." He paused and kicked a stone. "Sorry. Gil says I'm melodramatic." He put his hands on her shoulders, as if sensing her need to be steadied. "Deborah," he said, "I'll be there."

What was he talking about? "You'll be where?"

"In Bethlehem. In the college. Don't look for me. Just be yourself. Stay alert. Avoid any commotion. And if you feel you're in danger, get out immediately. No heroism."

His eyes closed briefly. "And watch for details. In the end, everything is determined by details—an extra chimney, a missing box of chalk, a stone out of place. If you need to contact me, call the wholesale paint store on Agrippas Street. Say you're painting stars on your child's room. I know it sounds corny—stars for

Bethlehem—but it's easy to remember. You'll also be getting an alarm watch you can press if you're in trouble."

Her head was pounding with the start of a headache. Her throat was dry, but she heard herself say, "Okay. I'll go to the interview, but if it's more than I can handle, I'm pulling out."

He reached into his back pocket and withdrew a wad of Jordanian dinars, the currency of choice in Bethlehem. She didn't even know how much one was worth.

"Keep these with you. I always do. Some cab drivers won't take shekels. If you have to get out, walk to the center of town and find a taxi."

Deborah stared at the crumpled, oil-stained notes in her hand. They seemed to seal her contract. She stuffed them in a zippered compartment of her handbag.

"Got to go." Raphi touched both her shoulders and looked into her eyes. "I'll meet you Monday after the meeting. Remember—"

"I know," she cut him off. "No heroism."

Raba watched her brother's funeral on TV from her bed. She'd fainted again at the news of her brother's murder, and Ali had insisted on bed rest. Arguing seemed futile and exhaustion sapped her strength. Ibrahim's body had been transported by the army to Gaza. Extra troops were brought in to quell possible riots. The family would be allowed to mourn, despite the curfew, as was their custom, in an outdoor hut. Alone, Raba tried to comfort herself with the bits of the Koran she remembered from her youth: "It is Allah who gives you life, then gives you death; then He will gather you together for the Day of Judgment." But the words felt like dust in her mouth.

A phone call in the middle of the night had awakened her. At first there was only silence. Then breathing. She was about to hang up when the familiar voice from the night she was blindfolded told her Ibrahim hadn't been killed in a rescue attempt. He'd been killed because he was a collaborator.

Out of respect to her new position, the voice went on, that information was being suppressed, so that his family could have a proper funeral and mourning period. No such courtesy would be paid when her husband was killed.

Raba had sat up all night thinking, and then watching the morning dawn shimmer on the dew of the garden.

Now she was wide awake as she recognized the streets of her childhood on the television screen. The sandy, crowded, garbage-littered alleys never changed. A mob shouted threats and slogans. Soldiers with metal shields patrolled the huge, chanting crowd, which was hailing Ibrahim as a hero. The camera suddenly focused on her father raising an angry fist. She wiped away tears as a high school photo blown up to poster size was held aloft by two little boys, their faces masked like terrorists'. The cameras were diverted to a struggle between a gang of masked young people trying to hoist the Palestinian flag and Israeli soldiers. The screen filled with the film of tear gas, the camera turning to the burning of the Israeli flag, and then back to the coffin.

Ali was everything to her. Her husband, her mentor, her gentle lover, the person who shared her dreams. She prayed the baby would be a boy just like his father.

Raba's face was soaked with tears. Her chest heaved with silent sobs. Her life as she knew it was over. There was no chance to stay out of the conflict now. Only she could save her husband. She uttered her own prayer to Allah for help.

13

The guards at the military checkpoint on the winding road that led to Bethlehem waved Deborah's Subaru through. On the other side of the barrier, Palestinian cars entering Jerusalem were being inspected for guns, hatchets, butcher knives, and hammers that could be used to maul Israelis. The hillsides lined with olive trees and grapevines seemed an inconceivable setting for terror. A gentle wind ruffled the leaves of the olive trees, making the white side of each leaf glisten in the sun. Tiny white flowers had fallen from the trees and made halos on the soil. A boy shepherd, no older than Ben, watched over the sheep, while an older sister herded the goats.

Tranquillity was often an illusion, she reminded herself. She parked near Rachel's Tomb, a small white-domed stone building where the biblical matriarch was thought to be buried. After years of childlessness, Rachel had given birth to Joseph, and then died while having his brother Benjamin, Deborah recalled bleakly. Her sister Leah was buried with their mutual husband Jacob down the road in Hebron. According to tradition, Rachel cried perpetually for the return of her exiled children. Women came here to pray for good health and fertility, winding red threads around the tomb marker and carrying snippets of thread home as talismans to cure ills.

A beige Peugeot station wagon with the Manger College emblem on both sides and a slim, dark-haired driver was waiting just past the tomb. The driver nodded to her as she got in. Deborah forced herself to lean back in the seat into a relaxed pose. Her heart was beating hard as the car wove through the narrow streets of Bethlehem. No flowers here. The narrow alleys smelled of blocked sewers. She felt the nervous anticipation of the Yeats sonnet:

And what rough beast, its hour come round at last,
Slouches towards Bethlehem to be born?

Except for a few extravagantly large houses under construction along the roadside, the town looked more dilapidated than Deborah remembered it from before the intifada when she frequently drove visiting Christian colleagues there. She'd lend them plastic baskets to help her shop for sleek zucchini and plump tomatoes at Bethlehem's open-air market. A tailor on Star Street used to alter her clothes while she waited, drinking strong coffee nearby. Now anti-Israel political graffiti in black paint scarred the shops and fences. One was in English: "We will knock on the doors of Paradise with the skulls of Jews." Weary-looking Jewish soldiers toted submachine guns and heavy packs as they patrolled the roads.

The silent driver stopped at a worn wooden sign that proclaimed Manger College. Deborah checked her new alarm watch. She was on time. Two young women with their heads wrapped in kerchiefs stood by the gate and stared at her so intently that Deborah reviewed her appearance: hair twisted in a chignon, pale-green summer suit, closed-toe shoes. It wasn't her clothing they noticed but her essence. The students could already sense she was a foreigner: a Jew in Manger College.

She drew a deep breath. "Can you tell me where the administration building is?"

The two Arab women looked at each other, puzzled.

"The *headmaster's* office," she tried. For some reason, every child in the region, Arab or Jewish, knew the antiquated word "headmaster" while far more common words were enigmas.

One of the young women perked up. "Yes. Of course. Come with us. We'll take you." Deborah thought she heard the word "Jew" in Arabic as the two of them whispered to each other.

"Are you the new teacher?" the companion asked. "Are you Jewish?"

In America no one *ever* thought she looked Jewish. No one would *ever* ask if she was Jewish. "Yes. I may be teaching here. And yes, I am a Jew. Is that a problem?"

"Oh, no. Jews are our cousins." Arabs used to say that a lot. Deborah hadn't heard it in years.

The signs on the buildings and posters on bulletin boards were nearly all in Arabic. Deborah regretted never learning their alphabet. It was written right to left like Hebrew but was more decorative because it was used extensively in Arabic art. Groups of students were standing in circles, engaged in arguments. Under a tree a piously draped woman was teaching a dozen disciples. Posters on a board depicted struggling Palestinians. "I wish you good luck here," one of the girls said, showing her to the door.

"Shukran." Deborah thanked them in primitive Arabic and watched them smile as they walked away. Behind a desk in an anteroom, a secretary was typing on a noisy electric typewriter. "I'm Deborah Stern. I have an appointment with Dr. George Barguth."

The secretary rose quickly, upsetting papers on the desk. "One minute please. He is not here yet."

A leaden sensation replaced Deborah's nervousness. She felt as if she'd crossed the desert to get here, and Barguth wasn't even around. The secretary made a phone call in Arabic that Deborah couldn't get the gist of. Again she cursed her lack of knowledge. She walked around the anteroom, passing time. On the wall was a map of the Middle East. Familiar cities were penned in in an old-fashioned scrawl: Damascus, Amman, Jerusalem, Lod. No mention of a country called Israel. Angry tension coiled in her gut. The secretary returned, her heels clicking on the tiled floor. "I'm very sorry," she said without eye contact, "Dr. Barguth apologizes. He'll be late. Would you like tea in the meantime?"

Deborah masked her annoyance. "Thank you. I'll wander the campus."

Once outside, she tried to concentrate on details. Unmatched buildings clustered around a central courtyard. Barguth's office was in a converted private home, the nicest building. A half dozen one-floor barracks held classrooms. The largest building was two stories and faced with stone. Deborah walked in. To her left, she found a large library and a computer room. She climbed stairs to a second floor. Closed off by fire doors were two science laboratories. She was pleased. If she got the job, she might be able to run an experimental program there. The counters were dusty. She guessed that the current science programs didn't include lab work.

Deborah came down the stairs. In the opposite direction of the library was a small cafeteria. Kitchen workers were chopping salads. There was a strong smell of roasting lamb.

The secretary's smile seemed genuine when Deborah returned. The dean had arrived. Deborah was ushered into an inner office.

Barguth was a large man, overweight, wearing a gray three-piece suit tailored in London or Hong Kong. He dominated the office, casting off a masculine scent of tobacco and expensive aftershave. His hair was thinning but neatly combed over a broad forehead shiny with sweat. He leaned forward to shake her hand with a warm, damp grip. "I beg your pardon for my lateness."

The office was spacious, with high ceilings. It was shaded by overhanging red-tiled eaves. Dark wood bookcases were built on two sides, and a TV, VCR, and audio disc player were set in recessed boxes. Barguth's large desk, also in dark wood, was orderly. The blotter, note holder, and his personal diary were made of tooled brown leather that matched his chair. Only the bank of three red digital telephones seemed out of place in the old-fashioned elegance. Two smaller rooms opened off the far side of the office.

Barguth sat down. "We're so pleased to have you

come. You may have heard that our biology professor was the victim of an unfortunate automobile accident. Did my secretary offer you something to drink? Well done. Please, tell me about yourself." Barguth spoke Regency English with grammatical precision and a heavy accent Deborah found charming.

She provided a résumé of her background, noting the highlights of the CV that was on his desk, supposing it was a convention to open interviews like this even though he'd read her file. He nodded appreciatively at her accomplishments and lifted his thick brows when she mentioned the grants she'd been awarded. "Rose of Jericho," he said after she summarized her research. "Excuse my ignorance. I knew it as a flower, but not a disease."

Deborah took a sip of the sweet tea the secretary had brought in porcelain cups. A test, she thought. "Yes, rose of Jericho is a plant, too, of course. *Anastatica hierochuntica.* I believe you call it *kaff alrahman,* 'the hand of the merciful,' or *kaff alnabbi,* 'the hand of the prophet,' in Arabic, because it blooms with the rains. You've seen it near the Dead Sea, like a crushed spider at the base of the sandstone outcrops. It's what botanists call a winter annual."

"You know we're Christians here," said the dean, tipping a pack of cigarettes toward her, waiting for her refusal before he lit up himself. "And the rose of Jericho is a symbol of resurrection for us. Interesting, isn't it, how we all, Christians, Jews, Moslems, believe in the resurrection of the dead, yet we spend our lifetimes fighting each other? This rose of Jericho, we always point it out to our donors when we take them on tours, but I have never understood how a plant can stay alive with so little water. Could you kindly explain? It would help me answer questions."

"I'm not a botanist," Deborah said, "but I believe that the seeds are stored inside, and are literally dislodged by raindrops. They germinate in hours. The plant has little flowers but they're nothing special. The stem is the uncommon part, curving inward and closing in the fruit, which has, if I remember, four seeds."

She curved her right arm to show him. "The taproot can anchor the dead plant to the ground for dozens, maybe even hundreds of years. Because of the arid habitat, it doesn't seem to be decomposed by fungi or bacteria. Some think a chemical in the stem inhibits microbial activity." She paused, squinting to focus her thinking. "Desert rats can't get at them either. But water makes the stem straighten out and the cellulose walls tear enough for the seeds to be released."

He was making notes inside his desk diary with a gold Cross pen, meticulously rolling the point away when he finished. "Thank you so much. I never knew that about the stem. Fascinating. I must remember it, as I'm expecting American visitors at the end of the week."

He leaned back in his chair and sighed as if a burden had been lifted from his broad shoulders. His smile gleamed large and white, making her feel relieved. "Mrs. Stern. Our students will enjoy your lucid explanations. You have a rare gift, one a teacher is born with, to communicate ideas in science and make them interesting. Welcome to our staff. When can you start?" He paused and frowned, a line creasing his broad forehead. "The sooner the better. In four weeks our students must sit for the rigid Jordanian examinations. I fear they're not fully prepared. Our critics, of which we have many, will be pleased if they fail, and they must not. This Wednesday? Too soon? Then next Monday. I'll call a staff meeting so you can meet everyone. We have another new teacher joining us, and I can introduce you both."

"Oh?" Deborah half expected him to mention an economics professor, someone slim and muscular with frozen black eyes.

"A psychologist," said Barguth. "Like you, a woman educated in America, and like your rose, she is from Jericho." He grinned, closed-mouthed, at his witticism.

She laughed back. "I look forward to meeting her."

They agreed on her starting on Wednesday. The college would provide transportation from Gilo, the closest Jewish neighborhood, where it would be convenient to leave her car.

Deborah was tucking away her date book when Dr. Barguth motioned her to wait. "Just one last matter," he said. "We recognized your name from the newspapers. You're the woman who fought back against a terrorist in a Jerusalem muffler shop. We were surprised you'd be willing to work in an Arab college with all Palestinian students."

He spoke matter-of-factly, but Deborah felt nervous. "Frankly, I was surprised you would hire a Jewish teacher. Don't *you* have any reservations?"

A wide smile crossed his face again, so she went on. "Many more Arabs than Jews suffer from the disease I study. I don't think most Arabs are terrorists, any more than I think Jews are. I went to public school and have no trouble teaching Christians or Moslems or Hindus, for that matter. This is an ideal opportunity to move up a step to college teaching. I'm sorry for your teacher, but his accident came at a fortuitous time for me. That is, if you have no objection to hiring a Jew."

He looked in her eyes like a priest seeking out her soul. Raphi had cautioned her to stick as close to the truth as possible. "As they say in Arabic," he'd said, " 'The liar forgets.' "

Finally, Dr. Barguth looked away. "If you have any problems whatsoever, please come directly to me. The former teacher prepared an outline of the curriculum, but feel free to change it as you deem necessary. Thank you for coming to our aid."

"The pleasure is mine." This time she stuck out her hand and gave his a firm shake.

Success always made her cocky. She decided to wander into town in the half hour before the driver returned. From a blind peddler, she bought black, country grapes, eating them one at a time, wiping them with her fingers and sucking out the sweet juice, making black stains on the corners of her lips. Three men sat smoking under an awning. The smell of hashish scented the air. She took a deep breath of it and turned back toward the college by a different alley, shady and less traveled. A sudden noise, like some following her, jolted her out of her equanimity. She spun around, only to see a whorl of plastic bags catching the breeze in an alley corner. Mocking laughter echoed from above, where two girls in blue school dresses dangled their feet from a balcony. Deborah took another breath, straightened her back, and walked back to the campus, where the driver waited.

Only on the way home did she put her finger on what was still troubling her about the interview with Dr. Barguth. Details, Raphi had said. Pay attention to them. One detail didn't jibe. *You're the woman who fought back against a terrorist in a Jerusalem muffler shop.* For the sake of security, none of the papers mentioned that the garage where she was attacked was a muffler shop. How could he have known?

"You see it's not so bad," Raba said when she and Ali were settled in the back of the Mercedes. Ali usually drove when they were together, but since his injury, Wassim had insisted on going everywhere with them, as much bodyguard as chauffeur.

Her decision to consider the job in Bethlehem prompted the worst fight Raba had ever had with Ali. She'd hit below the belt, reminding him of his vow never to take the Arab male's position of authority over his wife. "When will you realize that you're the one who is vulnerable, not me?" he'd shouted in a rare moment of exasperation. Only when she told him that the job was at Manger College did he seem to relent. "Oh, Manger College," he'd said. "Maybe that is less problematic." In the end they'd compromised, agreeing to meet the dean and evaluate the dangers together. It turned out that Ali recognized George Barguth from the Rotary. The dean had introduced her to the head of the psychology department, who had only a master's degree in counseling. No wonder Barguth was so eager for her to join the staff. His enthusiasm was contagious, even to Ali. Such a highly qualified teacher who also spoke Arabic was rare to come by, he'd said. Donors would also be thrilled that he was adding a woman to the staff.

Wassim swerved to avoid a pickup truck that had tried to overtake them. Raba nearly fell into Ali's lap. "Careful, I'll give you another concussion."

"Wassim, keep your eyes on the road." His voice was chiding, but his hands were massaging the back of her neck. Raba kissed him lightly on the mouth. He was still angry, she could tell. "The secretary mentioned that there's another new teacher. A Jewish woman. A biologist. Don't you find that strange?"

Ali shrugged. "We always had Jewish teachers in medical school. Barguth is an odd sort, keeps a low profile but he's a brilliant tactician. I've heard he raises a lot of money in America. I would like Jewish doctors in our hospital, but we can't hire any."

"I can't imagine too many Jews applying for jobs in Gaza. Not since the Jewish woman was axed to death near Khan Yunis, and the lawyer was shot in Gaza City."

"I wouldn't say Bethlehem was the ideal location from that point of view, either." Ali looked thoughtfully out the window at a donkey loaded down with brush. "Your new colleague must be someone hard up for work or else she's very gutsy."

Raba slipped her arms around Ali and suggested another possibility. "She could always be a spy."

Every Sunday through Friday, a shiny white Mercedes bus of the style used for tourists passed through Bethlehem and then turned left on a little-used side road on its way to the experimental girls' high school in Kibbutz Zayit Ra'anan near Hebron. Abed had learned a little about the school. Except for the matriculation exams at the end of eleventh and twelfth grades, there were no grades. The curriculum included courses no other school offered: Japanese, stock market analysis, and opera, all from a feminist point of view. Some of the brightest girls from important Jerusalem families were therefore willing to tolerate the forty-minute ride every day. The curriculum might be flexible, but the bus timetable was exact. Abed watched them go by, as they did every day, between 7:38 and 7:45, even in the summer when there were examinations and special courses.

That's when his plan would go into action.

Operation Manger was three-pronged. Riots would start in Bethlehem, and students would take over the campus. Abed would capture the bus of teenagers and imprison them there. The worst fear of all Israelis was that terrorists would kidnap their children. The Church of the Nativity would be wired with explosives, sending the Vatican into chaos. Jewish-Christian relations would be strained, because the Jews would only be interested in the children, and the Vatican would only want its relics. One teenager would be sent home dead the first day to concretize the threat. Abed would demand that all political prisoners be freed, and the Seventh Century would be recognized as a force on a par with the PLO. No more compromises would be made without their consent. Unlike the PLO, the Seventh Century would never settle until the last Jew was subjugated.

His technical problem had been his organization's inability to penetrate the campus. Barguth was beloved by his students and seemed to have an iron grip on the faculty. Unfortunately, Manger College was the only large Palestinian campus between Jerusalem and Hebron, and Abed needed a base for his standoff with the GSS. Besides, Manger College had the lowest military presence of any West Bank institution. Abed assumed that because Barguth had been such a weakling in opposing the Israelis, the army left him alone. In his own kingdom, Barguth had demonstrated a wily ability to foresee trouble and stave it off. Now with Raba on the inside, Abed would have advanced warning of any campus plans.

The thought of working with her thrilled him.

The only remaining snag was locating Sami. Abed hadn't heard from him since the attack on the jail. He doubted if Sami had been captured. The police, under the pressure of a public commission, would have boasted of catching him. Israeli journalists were aggressive at ferreting out stories, and no one had hinted about a captured terrorist. Abed had no replacement for Sami. The best explosive experts had been hired by the PLO.

Abed drove toward Gaza, where someone might know about Sami. There was also badly needed money to be picked up. If enough funds hadn't arrived from Iran, he'd tap Palestinian merchants. Outside crowded camps lived Arab millionaires in magnificent villas. For years wealthy Gazans had supported the PLO. Now their good health depended on donations to fundamentalist Islamic causes.

Abed waited in traffic as always at the Erez checkpoint. In his mirror he watched the soldier harassing a Palestinian. Abed felt sickening rage. He drove away, clutching the steering wheel.

He wouldn't have been so angry if he'd realized the Palestinian being questioned was really a Jew named Raphi Lahav.

The Gaza Strip. Raphi got a rush every time he came here—365 square kilometers of trouble, one for each day of the year.

His head was cloudy as the truck he was riding in pulled up to the checkpoint. For an hour and a half he'd been breathing perspiration, flatulence, and fried Moroccan meat rolls. One of his fellow travelers worked as a night cleaner in a Jerusalem restaurant and was bringing home leftovers.

There were 700,000 residents of the Gaza Strip, and little employment. Moslem propaganda castigated the "Jewish economy" but it provided paying jobs. Just as the Palestinians had become dependent on the Israelis, the Israeli economy had become dependent on cheap labor. Raphi had argued against it at every economic conference. There was no such thing as cheap labor. In the end, Israelis paid billions in security and in lives while greedy contractors exploited day laborers.

Raphi sipped tepid water from an old plastic cola bottle, blinking to fight off the mental fog. Sweat soaked the collar of his cotton shirt and the beltless waistband of his pants. There were dark stains under his arms. Antiperspirants weren't part of this role. He enviously pictured Gil puzzling over files in an air-conditioned office, fussing over the coffee, and pinching his freckled secretary's fat behind.

Each passenger had to be checked and Raphi dawdled, letting the other six men go ahead of him. The sun was scorching.

"What is your name?" asked the soldier, barely looking up from a clipboard.

"Daud Mustafa Bahar."

The soldier's hand jerked. "Mustafa" inserted before a surname was the day's code word to alert the guard to the presence of an undercover officer.

The guard recovered, resuming a bored, condescending scowl. He kept Raphi longer than the others, examining his papers so slowly Raphi didn't have to fake his irritation. All the same, Raphi thought, it was too damn hot for these theatrics.

The traffic had built up on the Gaza side of the checkpoint by the time Raphi got back in his seat. He cursed under his breath. His fellow travelers mumbled in sympathy, and their vehicle moved slowly on the clogged roads. The land was sandy with occasional palm trees, as they made their way past small family huts with long lines of faded laundry strung out in the sun.

Twenty minutes later they reached Gaza City, where the traffic was further slowed by dirt-smeared children playing amid the moving vehicles. A little boy with a broken hand drill slung on his shoulder like a machine gun kicked a can under a dump truck and barely escaped being run over by a motorcycle. More than half the population of the Gaza Strip was under eighteen. Raphi taught a seminar in Middle East economics and could tick off the statistics. In the past twenty-five years under the Israelis the per-person GNP had risen more than anywhere else in the Middle East, including Israel. Still, it was a study in ugly squalor. Iz Alddin Alkassam battalions like the Seventh Century, which were the military arm of Moslem fundamentalists, flourished in the discontent and planned attacks into Israel.

Raphi walked the familiar streets of Gaza City. Hopping over the scraps of barbed wire and rusted oil barrels, he recalled grimly that one of his childhood heroes, the biblical Samson, died in Gaza, blind and humiliated. The smell of garbage rotting in the heat was everywhere. Little boys were gathering aluminum pop cans from a pile of garbage for resale by the kilo. Near a school, a vendor pushed a wooden cart heaped with sugar-coated candy apples, already covered with flies. Girls in faded blue dresses with scarves on their heads giggled in the school yards. The boys, no matter how young, played Arabs and Israelis in the dusty fields.

Raphi found the secretary and introduced himself as a veterinary student just back from Sweden, looking for tutoring jobs. Education was the most common dream out of this squalor, even though university graduates had to scramble for work, too. Despite the poverty, private lessons were a Gaza obsession. Few students could pass the towjeehee exams needed for college admission in Arab countries without help. Raphi's English, biology, and mathematics were particularly good, he told the school secretary. He could also teach martial arts. She nodded and took down the information without enthusiasm. Student tutors were as common as dented tin cans in Gaza.

After leaving his name with five schools, Raphi entered one of the ubiquitous coffee houses where frustrated, unemployed Gaza men played backgammon and cooked up plans of revenge against the Israelis. Ceiling fans did little to disperse the cigarette smoke and the smell of cardamom-flavored coffee.

His every instinct said Deborah was going to get killed in Bethlehem unless he found out enough in Gaza to head off the attack.

It was time to use bolder methods to attract attention.

Raphi sat at one of the low tables and took out

imported cigarettes, offering them around. "Might as well enjoy these. They're my last."

A few young men at the table looked at him passively, politely Raphi spoke louder. "Back from school in Sweden. Looking for a job. Anyone have a brother who needs to learn algebra or karate?"

Everyone had a brother who needed to learn algebra, but no one could afford to hire him. Like the man he was pretending to be, they were out of work. "Do you know anything about judo?" a short man, nearly a midget, asked, as if anything to pass the time would be better than the boredom of this café. "Why don't you challenge him, Fawzi?"

The midget nudged a barrel-chested man sitting on a stool that looked too small to support him. Fawzi scowled at the nudging, then smiled and puffed his chest as he rose, tipping the stool behind him. "Do you know judo?"

"Some," Raphi said, his voice quiet. "Karate is what I know best, though."

"What belt do you have?" asked one of the young men.

Nonprofessionals were always talking about belts.

Black as your heart, he thought. "What does the color matter?" Raphi asked.

Fawzi's chin was in the air, taunting him. In his early twenties, the street fighter outweighed Raphi by fifty pounds. He was squat and thick-necked, the right physique for judo. Raphi was too lean and narrow to be a great judoist. He'd more or less given up judo since tearing his ligament.

A slow smile spread across Fawzi's broad face. Raphi kept his own face motionless as he took off his sneakers and socks, and lined them up under his chair. He rose slowly, sighing once, crushing his cigarette in the coffee dregs.

Raphi positioned himself across the café, moving tables out of the way. Fawzi imitated him, pushing tables and chairs. The two men faced each other approximating the distance in a judo match. The café hadn't seemed jam-packed before. Now dozens of young men appeared from nowhere and crowded around them. Fawzi shouted for them to move back. He stepped side to side.

Raphi stood still, then took one step forward with his left foot to signal that the match had begun. He always fought with his right side forward, but Fawzi wouldn't know that.

"Get ready to wipe up the floor," Fawzi bragged to a friend on the sidelines.

A braggart.

Fawzi had been badly taught, Raphi saw almost at once. Students typically rushed from one level to the next without perfecting stance or technique. Heavy judoists had to learn to compensate for their weight against a lighter, faster opponent.

Raphi kept the smile of satisfaction off his face. Fawzi made a beginner's error of looking at his collar and losing eye contact. His eye movements gave away the next move, and he was way too slow. Raphi stood still, body relaxed, and waited for his opponent to make a first lunge. Fawzi reached to get a grip with two hands on Raphi's shirt, just below the collar. As Raphi expected, Fawzi tried to turn and throw him.

When in doubt, resort to basics, Raphi thought, stepping forward with his right foot, at the same time pressing his right hand into Fawzi's face. One finger covered Fawzi's nose and another his eye while his thumb put pressure under Fawzi's chin. He pulled him back, over his right knee, using it as a fulcrum. Doubtless Fawzi had been trained to fall on his side, so Raphi twisted him facedown, making sure he couldn't roll out.

Dust lifted from the floor.

Fawzi was stunned by his quick defeat. His face darkened in fury.

Raphi leaned forward and stretched out an arm to help him up. Fawzi looked as if he might try to pull Raphi down until he noticed Raphi's foot poised near his neck. Raphi dusted him off and waited for the final bow.

"He's not even sweating," Raphi heard someone in the crowd whisper. "He's amazing."

Raphi's back and his leg hurt, but he smiled wide and offered Fawzi a cigarette. Fawzi took it with shaking, thick fingers. The young men crowded closer now, begging to hear all about martial arts. Raphi could teach a course, one suggested. The crowd pushed around him, everyone smoking, ordering more coffee. Raphi maneuvered the conversation, weaving in anecdotes of his training and his life as a veterinary student in Sweden. The young men told exaggerated stories of their revenge on the Jews. Amid the tales, Raphi picked up enough local detail to fill a security dossier, yet there was nothing directly pertinent to the Seventh Century.

"What about you, Fawzi?" Raphi asked, acting on instinct. "Have you been involved in anything exciting?" Until then Fawzi had been too quiet, but now, as if to save face, he bragged about a recent attack where they'd picked off a young farmer from the Jewish settlements of Gush Katif. The room became silent. The farmer had been stabbed in the back while adjusting a drip irrigation system. Raphi smiled to hide his wrath.

Raphi's voice dropped. "I heard a rumor there's something big underway. Any chance I could get in? I'd love to see some real action, something like what Ibrahim Masri did, may Allah have mercy on his soul."

The silence deepened. No one answered. Fawzi's chin quivered. He looked down and shrugged.

The men drifted off. Raphi ordered humus and *ful,* the broad beans that were a Gaza specialty and something he'd always liked. He sat at the window and watched a stunning young woman, probably no more than seventeen, baking pita on the roof of the building across the street. She was modestly dressed, in a long white dress, but he could see her breasts straining against the thin fabric as she worked, unpegging laundry on the rooftop clothesline while each of the pitas baked. He had a brief fantasy of taking an afternoon

nap with this woman pressed naked by his side. She
felt his eyes on her, and looked up from her task,
holding the hot pita in her hands a fraction too long,
dropping it on a tray, sucking a burned thumb. She
shyly smiled at him. He didn't smile back. Some of his
colleagues believed that the way to achieve security
breakthroughs was to seduce innocent young Arab
women and men and then blackmail them. Raphi
scorned their approach, but he didn't kid himself.
What he did was just another variation on a theme.
When you went into the cesspool you came out
stinking.

Abed cursed the smell of garbage that seemed to
permeate his skin. He parked outside the largest bank
in Khan Yunis and for an hour acted the role of the
knowing investment banker. Twenty-five new factories
had already been approved. His bank in Hebron was
playing a major role in financing them.

By the time he went to his headquarters later, he'd
changed from a business suit to jeans and a T-shirt, a
black-and-white keffiyah wrapped around his face. He
was fully masked.

The inner cell of the Seventh Century met in the
home of one of Gaza's wealthiest families. The widow
Alfouri had created a comfortable hiding place below
her marble floors with access cleverly hidden beneath
her kitchen sink.

The widow served dinner. Abed ate slowly, wiping
bits of chicken and olives from the sides of his mask.
His men were no punks. Their names were already on
the Israeli wanted lists. Each had taken part in successful hits. Yet none of them could say who Abed
was. Only the operational commanders in Lebanon
knew his true identity, because of the ever-present
fear of informers penetrating the cell. Today's conversation was serious, first about Sami, whom no one had
found, and then about the impressive performance of
this stranger, Daud Bahar, who'd mentioned Ibrahim
and who studied in Sweden.

Sweden! Abed had studied in Stockholm, and had

often visited the large campus in Uppsala, an easy forty kilometers along the E4. Abed flipped a mental catalog of the leading Arabs in Sweden and came up with nothing. He hated surprises. Could Bahar be from a competing Palestinian cell with a separate chain of command? He might be a higher-up sent to monitor funds. Or Bahar could be a GSS agent. But even the condescending GSS would be more discreet than to send someone to the heart of Gaza City to make a spectacle of himself, wouldn't they? *"Jag vet inte,"* I don't know, he said out loud in Swedish. "I want to meet this Daud Bahar," Abed said. "How is it best arranged?"

After lunch Raphi returned to the schools, asking if anyone had left him a message.

A secretary nodded and handed him a tiny slip of crumpled paper torn from a cigarette pack. On it was an address and a time. He was to meet a potential student in a refugee camp just outside of town, just after dark.

14

Deborah would be arriving soon, an hour before sunset on Friday, and Joshua felt as nervous as a blind date. Six months of separation had driven a wedge between them, making the closeness of the past seem an illusion. So much depended on this weekend.

Neighbors down the hall were away and had offered Joshua their apartment so Deborah could have privacy. The dilapidated building was on one of the crowded apartment blocks in the Prophet Samuel neighborhood, which before 1967 was the border dividing east and west Jerusalem. The original tenants in the 1950s had been the city's poorest Sephardic Jews, porters and washerwomen with large, unruly families. They'd sold out to young, religious couples living on modest stipends from the area's many yeshivas.

Joshua's poverty was a matter of choice. He could, if he wished, return to a lucrative law practice, buy a new car, replace the black suit he was rapidly wearing into shabbiness. Living poor, he believed, was a goad toward repentance, just as the long hours he studied religious texts as a beginner humbled him. He was ashamed of the arrogance of his former life. The elite private high school, officer training, high-profile law practice had all pumped up his ego. At the first test of his humanity, he'd failed miserably.

The only person who'd looked beyond his surface was Deborah. Losing her permanently terrified him.

Joshua arranged Deborah's favorite yellow roses in a vase, then turned to the Sabbath candles. He dripped pale drops of wax on the bottom of each holder so the candle would stand straight, lit the wicks and then blew them out again to make the lighting easier. Deborah would appreciate it. Unlike him, she valued even the tiniest acts of kindness. He looked around the apartment, satisfied. He'd washed the floors and made up one of the twin beds in the parents' bedroom, regretting for the hundredth time that she wouldn't be sleeping in his. Six months was the longest he'd gone without sex since he was seventeen, and celibacy would be harder with her down the hall.

Once again he asked himself if the easiest way to get her back would be to confess what had happened three years ago. He still felt sure she'd despise him.

As he despised himself.

In Jewish law, sins couldn't be wished or prayed away. Repentance required a change of heart. True repentance, wrote the medieval philosopher Maimonides, whom Joshua read every day, meant that your personality was so altered that, if you could turn back the clock and return to the same dilemma, you would make a different moral choice.

If only he could turn back the clock.

He'd been called up for a month of reserve duty with his infantry unit. Like most Israeli men, he grumbled about it, but the camping out, camaraderie, and military talk was a happy part of the rhythm of life. There was little actual mortar practice. Mostly they did routine patrols in the North, keeping out the rare infiltrator over the Syrian and Jordanian borders. Joshua had served with the same men for seventeen years, but he was closest with Oren, an assistant research director with a drug company in Haifa. The only fight they'd ever had was when they were twenty-one and both fell in love with the division secretary, a Yemenite woman named Nina with a tiny waist and wild black hair. Oren had won and married her.

Their month of reserve duty ended the first week in June, which included June 5, the anniversary of the Six-Day War. Looking back, they should have been more alert that weekend. But there had been few infiltrators in recent months, and he and Oren were talking politics and finances and, for the first time, babies.

Both of their wives were pregnant, Deborah for the second time and Nina for the first.

They always arranged to do night duty together. That meant patrolling in a jeep equipped with infrared viewers. It was nearly dawn and the only movement they'd spotted was field mice and deer. The smell of burning eucalyptus roots and the hot grease of their jeep was strong. A jackal howled in the hillsides. Joshua drove. To their distress, the jeep kept stalling. At last, they stopped on a hillside to watch dawn breaking, the first rays of pink light shining from Jordan.

"Let's call it a night," Oren said, yawning. Joshua was a major, Oren a captain. "I'd like to eat a good meal and eat a good woman. Pregnancy makes Nina sexier than ever." He made an obscene slurping sound. "Let's go. At least we can fry potatoes."

"One more swing around," Joshua said, knowing he was being perverse. He was tired, cranky, and now he felt annoyed. Even after all these years, Joshua suspected Oren's too frequent talk of his torrid sex life was a reminder of who had won Nina. "We haven't inspected the security road yet." He pointed at the sandy path running on Israel's side of no-man's-land. Before dusk, the road was brushed by a half-track equipped with minesweepers so that even a footstep would be visible by day.

"Asshole," Oren said. "We're in a jeep, remember? What are you going to minesweep with, your hairy dick?"

Joshua pulled rank. "We're going. I have an intuition that there's something out there."

Five minutes along the dirt road, they sighted footprints on the trail. "Well, well, well, fancy that," Joshua said, driving the jeep closer to investigate.

Just then he spotted a thin wire where the road sloped downward, jammed the gear into reverse, and stepped on the gas.

The jeep stalled

"Jump," he ordered Oren, leaping for the side.

The sound deafened him. The side charge exploded

as Joshua was halfway out of the jeep. He woke up briefly in the helicopter that flew him to Rambam Hospital in Haifa. "Oren," he'd said. "Everything will be all right," a medic had answered, hovering over him. Even in his stupor Joshua realized that was a euphemism for saying Oren was dead.

The terrorists from Syria who'd laid the side charge had never been found. Oren's death was a total waste. Joshua was badly injured, with internal bleeding, broken legs, and a concussion. From the hospital, he phoned Nina many times. "Thank you so much for calling," she'd sobbed the first time. "I know Oren loved and respected you. It means a lot to me to know you were with him when he died." On the third or fourth call he could already feel her impatience. "Of course I don't blame you, Joshua. We've talked about this. I wake up in the morning and try to get through the day. I have to for the baby's sake." Later, when he called her every day, she advised him to seek help. Finally, she refused to take his calls.

Feeling desperately guilty, he'd begun his investigation of religion. The religious soldiers who served with him seemed happier and more content than the others. They were workingmen who believed in God and observed the commandments. But just celebrating the Sabbath and keeping kosher wasn't enough to ease the plain of his guilt. He found himself drawn to the extremely religious world, men who never served in the army but who studied the ancient texts all day long. He'd immersed himself, too, and the pain was numbing at last. Somewhere along, he'd also grown to love the material he was studying. The more he studied the intricacies of tradition, the more fascinating he found them.

His conscience pricked him whenever he thought of the unfair burden his choice placed on Deborah and the children. His original plan had been to reclaim his wife and children once he "found himself." The flaw was that finding himself was taking too long, and he missed Deborah too much. Now he also worried that she would find someone new, like that detective, and replace him. That's why he'd urged her to spend Saturday with him.

Joshua took one more look around the apartment and closed the door. Outside in the hall, he noticed the chipped paint and wondered if Deborah would be repelled. Nearly every family had small children who left trails of crunchy snacks and gum wrappers during the week. Today at least the hallway smelled of chicken soup and baking cinnamon rolls. The floors had been mopped down for Shabbat, Joshua realized with relief.

Friday night dinner would be at the Teittlers'. Deborah had to be impressed by the big, loving family that had accepted him so warmly. Yocheved, who was energetic and intelligent, would show her that devout women were not robots blindly following divine dictates, but intelligent, spiritual beings. She could provide a new role model for Deborah.

"Daddy! Daddy!" Joshua was brought back to the present by Ben and Sarah racing up the halls, grabbing him by the knees. They were dressed in Sabbath clothes. Ben's hair was wet and slicked down. "Mommy's down below. Your building smells nice. Mommy will like it."

Suddenly Joshua realized how much the children were counting on this weekend and he froze, unsure it had been a good idea to invite Deborah here after all. What if she rejected him outright?

Deborah was outside, a jaunty straw hat covering most of her blond hair, a crisp, white, long-sleeved blouse rolled till just below the elbow, her effort to conform to the neighborhood standards of modesty. She looked beautiful, but anyone could spot her as an outsider. The skirt wasn't long enough. Too much hair showed. She asked him to take the bags because the car was blocking a driveway. "I'll park it," he offered on impulse.

"Just be careful," she shrugged. "I'm not sure it's still insured for you."

The words remained between them like an unforeseen roadblock. He sat in the driver's seat for the first time since the separation. The car smelled of pine and Deborah's floral perfume. He drew a deep breath. His hands automatically moved to the gears. He shifted into reverse and pulled away.

Deborah watched Joshua maneuver the car into a tight alleyway. She scolded herself for bringing up the insurance. What the hell did it matter? She'd promised herself to be on her best behavior and to give this a real chance. She'd come to the study hall a few times when Joshua first came, but never to his apartment. Ben and Sarah, who'd been here before, led her up the stairs to her weekend apartment. Then, jittery with excitement, they ran to go to synagogue with their father. He was a devoted dad, she reminded herself.

Fresh sheets covered one of the beds. She felt guilty that a mother with three cribs in the children's room had taken time to get ready for her. No, the corners were too squared off for a mother of small children. Joshua had done it. She pictured his hands running over the sheets and, unpredictably, a chill went up her spine. He'd also set up the Sabbath candles and bought her favorite roses. She felt tenderness for him as she lit the candles and chanted the blessing, adding her private prayers for help in making her difficult decisions. Not only her body ached for him, but she longed to unburden herself to Joshua, whom she'd been so attracted to ever since she first set eyes on him in London, on her way to Israel.

Soon he and the children came up the stairs, returning from synagogue, their voices warm and laughing. They retrieved her and began the hike to the Teittlers'. Joshua paused to scoop up Sarah, making Deborah's heart contract in nostalgia.

Maybe I can adjust to this world, Deborah thought, walking beside him. The quiet was a balm. No radios or televisions blasted from apartment windows with tragic news reports and rock music. No cars polluted the roads. The only sounds were human, a baby crying, a mother calling out instructions, a family singing in harmony. Best of all, no terrorists were leaping out of garbage cans.

They reached the Teittlers' building. A boy with long side curls answered the door and directed them to his mother in the kitchen. Another boy, his hair in a ponytail, was sitting on a high plastic stool sucking a bottle. A robust, smiling woman with warm brown eyes was arranging chopped fish patties around a fish head. Her hair was covered with a white snood, but one long auburn strand escaped, and she brushed it away with her arm. "I'm Yocheved," she said, wiping her hands on an apron. "I'm so glad you could join us. Yisrael Mayer, take Benjamin to play. Tell Yehudis to play with Sarah. Joshua, why don't you sit in the living room until Isaiah comes? He accompanies an old man home after synagogue so it will take a while."

She went back to arranging the platter. "Joshua tells us you're a biologist. I guess a fish head won't shock you."

"No, I've seen worse," Deborah said. "Can't I help?"

"Nothing left to do," Yocheved said, licking her wrist where the fish jelly had dripped. A baby cried from a rear bedroom, and a girl of about nine emerged carrying an infant. Yocheved reached for the baby and nuzzled her. "Our youngest—Rivkee."

"How many children do you have?" Deborah asked.

"We're lucky. We have a lot of blessings," said Yocheved. "I don't like to mention the number. To fool the evil eye." She smiled, as if she'd thought of a private joke, and Deborah wasn't sure if Yocheved was serious or pulling her leg.

There was a short knock. Yocheved's face lit up as the door opened, and a bald, portly man walked in. *"Gut Shabbos,"* Isaiah said, smiling to his wife, hanging his black hat on a peg near the door and sliding a shiny black skullcap onto his bald pate. Deborah had the feeling she'd seen him before. Suddenly she felt impossibly closed in. She leaned back against the crowded kitchen counter, upsetting a half-filled glass of apple juice. The onions and the smell of the chicken soup were overpowering. Her head was spinning.

Joshua was standing over her. "What's wrong? You're so white. Are you okay?"

Deborah took a deep breath and apologized for making a mess. "I was just warm, I guess. It's a hot day."

She tried to hide her lingering queasiness as they gathered at the table, the men on one side, the women on the other, of a long table with a clear sheet of plastic covering a white cloth below. Joshua had always abhorred plastic tablecloths. Evidently, he'd overcome his aversion. An elderly widow and an attractive young woman student from a religious seminary were also guests. Yocheved introduced Deborah to them. The family sang the Sabbath song "Shalom Aleichem," a sweet melody bidding angels to enter, in practiced harmony, and Isaiah serenaded Yocheved with a proverb praising women. From the oldest to the youngest, the children stood before their father with a bowed head and received a blessing. Isaiah put his hands on each of the children in turn. "May the Lord bless you and keep you. May He cause His countenance to shine upon you and grant you peace." There seemed to be eight, counting the baby.

When Joshua blessed Ben and Sarah, Deborah felt teary. She and Joshua had always talked about having four children. She wondered if she would ever have another child.

Isaiah said the blessing over the wine, pouring from his cup for everyone at the table, and handling the silver goblet to Yocheved, who drank from where his lips had been. Then they all rose for ceremonial handwashing. No talking was allowed between saying a blessing while drying hands and eating bread. With such a long table, the silence lasted five minutes. Deborah had forgotten to prompt the children, but they seemed to know this already. Of course, they had been here before, and Joshua must have primed them long ago. Deborah felt left out. Isaiah cut the bread, took a piece, and passed it around.

Yocheved served chicken, carrots, coleslaw, roast potatoes, and potato pudding. Ben and Sarah picked at the food, but Joshua wolfed it down and even took seconds of potatoes. Was this the man who'd loved chili so hot it burned his mouth? Between courses, Isaiah and the children discoursed on the Bible portion and sang wonderful melodies.

Across the table, Deborah watched Yocheved, who glowed in the light of her family. She and Deborah were about the same age. Yocheved wasn't a plastic saint spouting aphorisms; she'd lost her temper when Yisrael Mayer spilled the soup. Isaiah didn't offer help in the kitchen and he talked with his mouth full, yet they appeared to have achieved an easy harmony.

Deborah helped clear the dishes over Yocheved's protest. "You have company every week, don't you?" Deborah asked, as she scraped plates into the garbage. "Don't you get weary?"

"Sometimes," she said. "Then I take a week off. I keep myself going by remembering that each day is another opportunity to develop the trait of giving. Before we were married, Isaiah and I decided we wanted to offer Sabbath hospitality."

"Did you really discuss that while you were dating?"

"Of course. Don't you think it's more important than finding out which movies you like? Marriage isn't just a vehicle to satisfy personal needs. Why bother unless there are higher goals?"

Deborah eyed her carefully. Something about her encouraged frank talk. "That doesn't sound very romantic," Deborah said softly, testing the waters of just how candid Yocheved would be.

"True, if you see marriage as a consequence of romantic love," Yocheved said with an alacrity that showed she'd thought about this a lot. "Romantic love goes back to Lancelot and Guinevere, and look what happened to them! To me, love is an appreciation of another person's virtues. I see myself as part of a two-person team. I believe Isaiah and I can only reach half our potential on our own. Together we're creating something bigger than the sum of two parts." She blushed. "I don't have to lecture you. You and Joshua have been married for seven years."

"And we've lived apart for the last six months. It's not exactly a secret that we're having problems."

Yocheved stacked the last dishes and brought out tea cups. "Sometimes you have to rethink your goals in life. Compromise. Make changes. Are you really so happy in the world you occupy that you can't exchange it for his new one?"

Deborah didn't answer. In the living room a song was starting up. Yocheved cut honey cake onto a tray, releasing a wonderful smell of cinnamon and cloves.

"I don't really know," said Deborah, taking the tray from Yocheved. "I wish I did. It's not only the religious world I'd have to come to terms with. Joshua has changed, too."

Yocheved looked thoughtful. "Ideally, a marriage is able to absorb changes. I wish you good luck with yours."

Deborah carried in the tray. Isaiah cleared his throat. "The week's Bible portion, called *nasoh*, discusses the question of an errant wife."

The tray nearly fell from her hand. "Errant" was a euphemism for unfaithful.

Isaiah went on. "We learn that in the days of the Temple a wife whose husband suspected her of indiscreet behavior went through a ceremony in which a section of the Torah scroll was dissolved in a drinking potion. If she was innocent, the husband had to pay amends. If she was guilty, she would shrivel and die."

Deborah knew the choice of subject was aimed at her. The portion of the Bible read in the synagogue that week also included the service of the Temple priests, sacrifices, and Nazerites, any of which Isaiah could have chosen to speak about. She couldn't stop herself: "I've always wondered why there is no discussion of an errant husband."

The table grew silent. Joshua looked annoyed. Ben stared at his plate.

Isaiah spoke without making eye contact with her.

"Men and women have different roles. If I'm not mistaken, even your world of biology has shown difference between men and women. Thus the laws regarding men and women are different. Anyone who thinks they're not is hopelessly naive."

"Men are commanded to be faithful," Deborah said. "Surely there should be a divine punishment if they're not."

Joshua spoke for the first time. "There is divine punishment," Joshua said, sounding like the lawyer he used to be. "Isaiah is not implying that men aren't judged. He'd be the first to claim they are. Men and women both are held equally accountable for everything they do."

Deborah felt grateful that Joshua had supported her. Nonetheless, the atmosphere was still tense. One of the Teittler children began crying loudly. Deborah wondered if Yocheved had pinched him as a distraction.

"I'm sorry," Yocheved said afterward. "Isaiah offended you."

"I suppose I saw it as a personal attack," Deborah said, feeling ungracious to have caused controversy at the table of people who had opened their home to her and her family. "I admit I'm touchy. I'm not so naive as to suppose that only religious men have a double standard. Most men in the secular world agree with your husband, although it's unfashionable to admit it."

Deborah and Joshua walked back in silence because Sarah had fallen asleep. Joshua carried her and put the children to bed on his couch.

He walked her to her room. "I knew you'd find a reason to start an argument," Joshua said, shaking his head. Deborah was stunned. He'd stood by her in public, but in his heart he'd condemned her. "Can't you get along with people even for an evening?"

She was outraged at his unfairness but tried not to lash out. "I don't think you would have spoken to me like that in the old days."

"The old days are over."

"What does that mean?"

"We have to start anew. I love you. I want you to be here with me. I know you'll have to make some adjustment, but think of what we'll gain." His seductive lawyer's voice was smooth and persuasive now. His profession of love, as always, confused her.

"How could I live here being as I am, thinking as I do? I would feel like a hypocrite. I like a traditional lifestyle, but my work is also important to me."

"You wouldn't have to give up your career."

Deborah narrowed her eyes. "I don't understand."

"Many of the women here work, they're just not so career-driven. You said there's a problem in the laboratory. Right here in the neighborhood there's a medical lab."

"You're not suggesting I prick fingers all day?"

"I forgot you'd consider that beneath you."

She was a research scientist, not a lab technician, and he knew it. Joshua might be stubborn, but he was nobody's fool. "What's really happening here, Joshua?"

"Isaiah feels we should decide immediately, not even wait a month, on getting together or getting divorced."

His words startled her, like a slap on the cheek. "Isaiah feels? I suppose Isaiah already has someone new in mind for you?" She thought of the attractive graduate student at the table. Joshua's face was flushed. "He *has* mentioned someone to you."

"Deborah, don't be childish. It's you I asked to come for a weekend. It's you I dream about. The kids are happier here. Ben doesn't get into playground fights and Sarah has dozens of friends. You think I don't see how depressed they are over our separation? We can make our marriage work. I know we can."

He was trying to make her feel guilty, and he was succeeding. "Both sides have to work at a marriage," she said. "When was the last time you did something for me, and showed you were willing? So far, I've done all the bending and adjusting, even though you changed the ground rules."

Joshua shook his head. "I forgot how much you like formulas. Life isn't a petri dish."

"*I* like formulas? You're the one who thinks religion is a set of unbending rules."

"The Bible's eternal."

"Unlike certain marriages."

Joshua's eyes turned icy, then dull, and he gave her an exaggerated shrug. "This is getting us nowhere. All I'm asking is that we give ourselves a chance. Leave your mind open, and don't poison the children against this way of life."

Deborah had *never* criticized him in front of the children. That idea must have come from Isaiah.

She felt limp with exhaustion. Her shoulders slumped. "I'm tired," she said. "I don't want to fight either. Why don't we talk about it in the morning?"

A disoriented look came into his eyes. Religious couples made love on Friday night. Maybe it would heal. Traitorously, despite her anger, her hands itched to reach up to his shoulders and lose herself in sensation. But no, she felt too resentful to make love.

"Good night, Joshua," she managed to say. "Pleasant dreams."

He shut the door and his footsteps faded in the hall. From the narrow window, Deborah looked out on the empty street and thought of the day she'd first met Joshua in Hyde Park. Soapbox speakers were pontificating on different issues, but the largest crowd had formed where an Arab speaker was being challenged by a tall, handsome young man with piercing blue eyes. The name Joshua Stern was inked on his knapsack, and he was calmly debunking the speaker's claims that Jews were colonialists and interlopers. The air was charged, and Deborah was attracted by Joshua's confidence and charisma. "Open the Bible. You'll find Jews in Jerusalem two thousand four hundred years before Mohammed was born," he said, the corners of his sensual lips turning upward.

The speaker paled. "I'm a Communist. Your biblical mythology doesn't move me. Where were your values at Deir Yassin?"

Deborah knew Deir Yassin was an Arab village near Jerusalem where the Jewish underground killed families in 1948.

Joshua made eye contact with the speaker and spoke calmly. "Do you know where Deir Yassin was or why the village was so strategically important? When the residents were warned to leave, why didn't they? Do you even know when the battle took place?"

When the Arab didn't answer, nervous giggles were heard in the crowd. "I'll help you out. It was 1948, and Jerusalem was in danger of being cut off. All the fighters had to use was dynamite, a sloppy but effective tool. If you don't believe me, I can refer you to an Arab friend who lived there."

The crowd drifted away. An hour later, Deborah had seen Joshua examining postcards at a kiosk and spoke to him. "I wanted to tell you that I was glad you spoke up in the park. What you said about Deir Yassin surprised me. Even at campus debates I'd never heard anyone defend the Jews' actions at Deir Yassin."

He answered without looking up. "Let's say I expressed the minority opinion. Deir Yassin was a mess. The whole argument was an exercise in futility, one of those lofty scenes acted over in states unknown."

"Unborn."

"I beg your pardon?" He turned to look at her, and his eyes registered appreciative surprise.

"Unborn. 'In states unborn and accents yet unknown,' " she corrected his Shakespeare.

They'd wound up having dinner together. She liked his intelligence and honesty, and was drawn by his good looks and the challenge of breaking through his frosty shell. They'd argued Middle Eastern politics. "I can't wait to see how your views hold up to reality when you reach Israel," he'd said at dinner.

Here she was, eight years later, carrying out a spy mission on a Palestinian campus and she couldn't even tell him about it.

The only person she could talk to was Raphi. She wondered how he was spending Shabbat.

*   *   *

Decades of martial arts experience had made Raphi ambivalent about weapons: he respected them, but never relied on them. A gun could give you a false sense of security. And getting caught with one when you were pretending to be, say, a math tutor would be suicide. He removed the stiletto strapped to his arm and left it with a woman hawking eggs. She'd been on their payroll for twenty years and would hand it over to the soldiers patrolling the market. At the end of the stiletto, marked for Gil, was a floater, a microfilm with an enciphered note that had to be immersed in water. He smiled, picturing Gil dropping it in a glass of water and reading it with a magnifying glass. It included the address where Raphi was heading and the message: "If I'm not back by ten, come and bury me."

The address was inside a refugee camp. Supposedly, a fourteen-year old boy needed a tutor in both English and martial arts. Raphi recognized the address from his maps. Nonetheless, in case someone was trailing him, he feigned ignorance, pausing frequently to ask for directions. His body reeked. Sweat stained his shirt and ran down his forehead, sharpening his vision. He stopped before the crooked door of a cement shanty. Dead flowers rotted in a window box, a failed attempt to brighten the pathetic environment. A single scrawny chicken was penned in the yard.

Raphi whistled an Arabic tune and rapped his knuckles against the door. The scrape of a chair was followed by heavy steps. The scratchy voice asked, *"Min albab?"* Who is it?

"Almualim." The teacher.

An aged, toothless Arab woman opened the door a crack. She looked him over and then let him in. The door creaked. One lightbulb lit both halves of the room. A tattered armchair was positioned across from a black-and-white television emitting music from Egypt. The room stank of kerosene cooking and mold although it had been swept clean. The old woman sat back down in the chair. On the other side of a long room, two men in their twenties and a gaunt teenager sat at a chipped wooden table. They looked alike, and were probably brothers or cousins. The Strip was clannish, and cousins often married each other, joined the same terrorist gangs, and shared acts of violence. The men rose.

Raphi scanned the house for an escape route. The back door was closed with cement blocks. The riskiness of his plan hit him like an unexpected blow to the chin. *What was I thinking?* "Good evening," he said.

"Good evening. Thank you for coming," one of the men answered, launching into an improbable tale about how the boy and his friends wanted to pass their exams and apply to study in Egypt. Arab universities didn't easily admit students from Gaza because they weren't as well qualified. The young men believed that was Israel's fault, too. Everything was Israel's fault.

Raphi listened, wondering when they would get down to the real business. "Could you possibly combine martial arts and English in one lesson to reduce the costs? Could you give a group lesson to approximately ten boys?"

Raphi approached the boy, placed both hands on the youth's narrow shoulders and felt him tremble. "What is your name?" Raphi asked in English, reaching forward to tilt the boy's chin up so he could look in his face. The boy's eyes widened in terror. "My name is Fadhel," he answered in the heaviest Arabic accent Raphi had ever heard outside of films. Fadhel bit his lip and looked at his pigeon-toed feet clad in dusty sandals. His frightened gaze shifted to one of the men standing nearby.

Raphi switched back to Arabic. "We'll start from the very beginning. Have you any training in either judo or karate? Neither? Then in martial arts, too, we'll start from fundamentals."

Fundamentals for fundamentalists, he thought.

The elderly woman excused herself and sent Fadhel on an errand. The moment she and the boy left, the door creaked open again.

A tall man, his face swathed by his mask and a

keffiyah, stepped inside, aiming the thin barrel of a Galil submachine gun at Raphi's heart. He nodded to the other two, and one of them reached forward, and searched Raphi, feeling his sides and between his legs. Raphi stood still.

"He's clean," his searcher said, in an unconscious parody of cop movies. Then they too left.

"Who are you?" Abed asked him in West Bank Arabic.

"Daud Mustafa Bahar."

The pointed gun was held with easy confidence. No amateur, this terrorist. *Iza ana amir, uninte amir, min yisuk alhamir?* If I'm a prince and you're a prince, who will lead the donkey? Perhaps he'd found a prince at last. One who might kill him. Raphi's lips cracked in an obsequious smile. "Is tutoring a crime now in Gaza? Manners of greeting must have changed."

For a long time, the masked terrorist only stared at him. "I have heard you studied in Sweden. Where? From Göteborg?" He pronounced the last like a Swede, "yotebory."

"No," Raphi shook his head. Was there even a university in Göteborg? "Lund," he said. The brother of a GSS researcher had studied medicine in Lund, which was how the university was chosen.

"Why have you come to us?"

At this distance the Galil could blow his face away. Raphi knew his next words would determine his fate. "Sami sent me."

The gunman shifted, held the gun closer to his shoulder. "Which Sami? There are so many."

"Elizabeth's Sami."

In the quiet Raphi heard a baby crying from the next house. A dog barked in the distance.

"How did you meet this Sami?" Abed's voice sounded hollow.

"He was wounded in the blast. Friends in the Old City revived him. He had spoken enough in delirium for them to be alarmed. They summoned me."

"Ah, by chance."

"There is no chance, only divine purpose."

Again there was silence. Raphi broke it first: "I've been back for a few weeks. I've come to volunteer. Sami begged me to seek out his command unit in Gaza, for myself and for him as well. He was sure you'd be eager to have my help." Sweat was running into Raphi's collar. An unconscious gesture would get him killed. Likewise, if Sami's information contained a clue that Raphi was a spy, he'd be dead in a minute. Raphi wondered if he could kick the gun away.

Abed looked thoughtful. "Why would Sami say that?"

"Because he knows that in Sweden I studied under the Teacher, may his name be blessed."

The Teacher, Radwan abu Tarif, a fundamentalist Gaza terrorist from the early eighties, had entered local folklore for his daring acts against Israelis. He had shamed Palestinians working for Israeli intelligence to repent and join him. One daring act had been capturing an Israeli engineering team and forcing them to abandon plans to bulldoze the refugee camps. The Teacher had suddenly disappeared in 1984, just before the American elections. At first it had been assumed that the Israelis had killed him. They had. Nonetheless, rumors, spread by the GSS, still circulated about the Teacher living secretly abroad, training a tiny cadre of Arab students to strike back at Israeli targets abroad. No one could ever check out the disinformation. The ID department liked to layer a false identity by linking it to facts that couldn't be checked. Being one of the Teacher's secret trainees explained Raphi's mastery of martial arts and his anonymity. Recruiting one the Teacher's men would raise the status of any of the competing groups. Raphi was counting on this as he faced Abed. Raphi repeated a passage, part of the code he'd learned from Sami. "Settling of accounts will continue until judgment day, as long as the stones and the trees say: 'Here is a Jew hiding. Kill him.' "

Raphi watched his enemy carefully, but not even a twitch of his arm muscle revealed his thoughts. The gun pressed painfully into Raphi's cheekbone. *Was he bluffing?* Abed's voice was icy. "Is that *all* you have to say?"

There must be an additional coded password that Sami, damn him, had failed to provide! Raphi hated double agents. They always made mistakes, often on purpose. He played his last card. "I can lead you to Sami."

The masked man pulled back the magazine bolt.

"You are an impostor. Sami is dead."

Speed was all Raphi had. His right hand struck a knife hand block against Abed's arm, knocking the gun aside. Bullets shot into the floor. Raphi's right hand hit Abed's nose, shifted to his groin, slid down Abed's right leg, and tugged at his trousers. At the same time he swept Abed's left leg with his right foot, dislodging him, making him fall back. It took less than two seconds—all of it. Abed was no amateur. He caught himself and came forward to counterpunch. Raphi struck with a hook kick. Abed's head snapped back.

There was less than a second for Raphi to grab the Galil. He snatched it and pressed it to the man's head.

"You've spent too much time on worthless codes and too little on training. In Sweden we don't even use codes anymore, just straight talk. Tell your leader, whoever he is, to meet Sami this week at the usual place at the usual time."

Raphi shoved the gun under the mask, enough to reveal tight curled hair of a black beard. "You must have a reason for hiding your face. To show good faith, I respect it. I will forget your insult. Tell your leader I wish to join you. I'll find you again when you least expect it."

Raphi's fingers itched to pull the trigger, but he was forced to play this game out. He was sure this man was a member of Seventh Century. If Raphi killed him, the message would never get to the leader to meet Sami. If this *was* the leader, of course, it would be a grave mistake to let him go.

There were noises outside. Someone who had heard the gun blast would return. Raphi unlatched the back door and looked into the dark. His leg hurt as he ran around the corner. He forced himself to slow and catch his breath. If he ran into an Israeli patrol while holding a Galil they would shoot on sight and ask questions later.

15

On Tuesday morning Deborah got into the Manger College van with the same silent, dark-haired driver at the wheel. She opened the window, and the van filled with the sweet, cloying smell of almond trees. Since Saturday night, when she came home from Joshua, she couldn't shake her melancholy. The children were already talking about "when Mommy and Daddy get back together," but she felt more distant from him than ever. She wondered if the GSS really could help her win a custody battle.

Surrounding the campus was a tall, metal security fence.

Deborah was sure it hadn't been there eight days earlier when she had come for her interview. Jewish campuses had been guarded for decades—ever since the Hebrew University cafeteria had been blown up. Why should Manger College be fenced on the very week the GSS had sent her here to spy?

On the day of her interview, the campus had been eerily quiet. Now shouting voices startled her. She walked briskly, trying to show confidence and to use the noise as a buffer against her fear. In one hand she carried an oxblood leather briefcase, and under her arm were poster-sized color enlargements of cells. She was already sweating. In the crowded courtyard young people stood in tight knots gesticulating at each other. Several of the young men were wearing the long cotton white dress of traditional Moslems. The largest group maybe twenty-five young men, huddled under a pine tree marked with a black-and-white sign THE SMITH GROVE.

What could be the subject of such fierce debate?
She was.

She picked up a few words, and the anger distorting
their faces told her the rest. The news must have
passed like a brushfire that there was going to be a
Jewish teacher on campus. They might have even recognized her from TV as the killer of a Palestinian
fighter.

She could be slaughtered her first day on campus.
What were Raphi and the others thinking when they
sent her here?

I'll be there, Raphi had promised. But where was
he? Where was Dr. Barguth, who'd been so friendly?
She glanced behind her. The driver had left.

She held her shoulders back, forced a smile, and
walked purposefully toward the low building where
she prayed to God her classroom was. That meant
walking past the most vocal students. She commanded
herself forward. Her face was wet, but she ignored it.
No one was going to see her wiping her brow!

The armful of enlargements slid down to the
ground. *Shit.* Once again she fought the urge to turn
around and run.

With their eyes on her, Deborah squatted to pick
up the papers, shaking her head as if annoyed with
herself. She gasped when a shadow fell over her. "You
need help?" a voice asked with sarcasm. Three young
men leaned over her. One reached down and picked
up her enlargements, holding them up to the light,
turning them upside down while the others laughed.

With supreme effort she faced them, smiled, and
reached out her hand. "Thank you," Deborah said.
"I'll take those now."

The student holding the enlargements laughed again
and handed the papers over. One of the others turned
suddenly and glared at her with cold brown eyes. Then
he winked.

Raphi! She nearly dropped the enlargements again.
Her heart beat even harder than it had before. Remembering his instructions, she shifted her eyes
toward the terraced hills in the distance.

The prickle of fear made the back of her neck stiff while she resisted turning to see if anyone was following her. Only when she got to the front of her building did she allow herself a look. The entire group had become quiet again and was watching her. Her heart slammed against her ribs as she yanked open the door and went inside. When the door closed behind her she drew a second breath, long and ragged. There was only one classroom on the corridor. *This is it,* Deborah thought. Her stomach ached with tension. Students were already sitting inside. The door was open. She took a few more deep breaths and walked in.

Suddenly the whole class leaped to its feet. Color drained from her face. She looked frantically for an exit, only to realize, in a flash of understanding, that the students were simply standing in an old fashioned gesture of courtesy. Her face turned red. Deborah swallowed hard. "Thank you. Please be seated."

She introduced herself, gauging how she looked in their eyes. Choosing the right clothes had taken a long time. Her hair was twisted up in a simple chignon, and she was wearing a yellow summer suit that had felt right for a traditional setting. The thirty students were taking in every detail. Twenty-four of them were women. A few wore attractive slacks and French blouses, but the majority were wearing long, unfashionable cotton dresses and the traditional Islamic headdress, a white scarf draped around the head and neck, and ending in a bib. There were even a number who combined new and old: a smart pants suit and a scarf. The number of devout Moslems was a surprise. Manger College was supposed to be a Christian institution, supported by churchgoers in the United States and Europe. Raphi had said the campus was considered moderate. If this was moderate, what did the extreme campuses look like?

Deborah paused and looked at the class again. Every eye was on her. *You can do this,* she prompted herself. *Be a teacher.*

This was the moment when a teacher, anywhere in the world, had to impose authority on a classroom or be forever doomed. If Arab students were anything like Israelis, they needed to be shown instantly who the boss was. She cleared her throat and waited a minute, making eye contact with a handsome woman in the back row. Deborah asked her name. "Jehan," Deborah began, "ever since you were a little girl you've been taught that the body is made up of cells. When you cut yourself, new skin cells replace the old ones. When you grow, you get more cells. But how do the cells really reproduce?"

Again, silence. Jehan's face turned red.

"Anyone else? That's the sort of question we're going to investigate in this course. Frankly, I'm not interested in having you recite my lectures. I want you to confront the basic questions of biology. Our goal in today's lesson is to examine the mechanics of cell reproduction. Open your notebooks. There will be a lot to write."

Deborah used the half minute of scrambling for paper to assess her classroom. It was bare of decoration, but the white board she'd requested was propped on an easel behind her, and an overhead projector for color transparencies waited in the back of the room. From her briefcase Deborah ostentatiously removed the set of expensive colored markers she'd splurged on to impress them. Standing sideways so as not to turn her back to the class, she wrote "How do cells reproduce?" on the white board, thinking as she wrote, *I could be stabbed right now.*

She smiled to cover her nervousness. "Biologists usually divide the cell cycle into mitosis, the act of cell division, and interphase, the period between mitosis."

She wrote "mitosis" and "interphase" in neon purple, then walked the aisles and looked into their notebooks, pointing at the mistakes where blushing students had copied it incorrectly. An old schoolmarm's trick. You could always count on students copying incorrectly, and exert your authority by correcting them.

"Don't let the term 'interphase' fool you. It's not time-out. That's when the DNA, this tiny but important code, is copied." Deborah reached for the enlargements which contained micrographs in which fluorescent dyes stained the DNA orange. She passed them around the class. The students looked surprised and pleased and, more important, impressed by their new teacher. She wrote Watson, Wilkins, and Crick on the blackboard. The students dutifully copied the names; no one had heard of the discoverers of DNA. She handed out a reading list and asked the students to report back to her about which bookstores and libraries carried them. "I can order books but let's see what's already available. I saw that you had a large library."

After a pause, she went back to the lesson. "The three phases of cell growth are customarily called G one, S, and G two. No, they're not stages in the British Secret Service—or our own General Security Services." She waited for them to laugh, and they at last did. "Nor, by the way, is Dr. Watson the famous partner of Sherlock Holmes."

Discussing the color transparencies covered the last fifteen minutes of class. Caught up in the lesson, her audience seemed ready to suspend judgment on her. They leaned forward in their seats. She might be new at intelligence, but she realized with relief that she didn't have to fake the teaching. The students were taking down every word, every line, afraid to ask a question. Her mind raced ahead with ideas for waking them up as students. She mentally shook herself: *Remember why you're here.*

After fifty-five minutes, the bell rang, an old-fashioned touch for a college. Deborah gave a challenging assignment. Students might complain about hard teachers, but that's what they really wanted.

"We have no time to spare, but if we work together you should be ready for your examinations," she said. In another gesture of politeness, her students waited for her to leave the room before leaving themselves. This time she was prepared.

She let out her breath. That had gone well enough, but had she learned anything useful? There was no time to write notes or process her thoughts. She tried to fix details in her memory. The impressions would be crowded by those from the faculty meeting, which began in ten minutes.

A dozen teachers had already gathered in a room that smelled oddly of mint and cumin, the source of which seemed to be trays on a marble counter in a small kitchen area. Dr. Barguth wasn't there yet, so she introduced herself to several of the men and women, trying to focus on each person's face and repeating his or her name to herself. Memorizing the names was harder than she'd expected, because many began with vowels, or sounded too similar for a foreign ear to distinguish between Abu Yusef and Abu Yasif, Riyad or Rayid. Most of the teachers were men in their forties to sixties. They spoke to her in English and seemed to know who she was even before she introduced herself. "Oh, yes, Mrs. Stern, so nice to meet you."

A breathtakingly attractive woman who managed to look petite despite being pregnant was introduced. "This is Raba Alhassan, our other new teacher," one of the teachers said. Deborah was instantly alert. Raphi had said to pay particular attention to the other new teacher. She was wearing a gray tailored maternity suit and fabulous shoes. Deborah could swear they were Stuart Weizmann pumps, by an American Jewish designer. Wrong information, she chided herself.

"Nice to meet you," Raba said. "I guess we're the two new curiosities here."

Raba's English was American Midwestern, but her name was Arabic and she had been speaking Arabic when Deborah came in.

"Dean Barguth told me there was another new teacher. I guess you're American like me."

"Not by birth," Raba said dryly. "I'm a Palestinian who grew up in Detroit. And you?" Raba's large dark eyes focused on her.

Deborah met her gaze. "I'm a Jew who grew up in Connecticut."

Raba nodded. "Where did you go to school?"

"I'm doing my graduate work here at the Hadassah Medical Center, but undergraduate I went to Brandeis University. It's a small liberal arts college in Massachusetts."

"I've heard of it," Raba said. "They have a good graduate school in psychology. One of my professors suggested I apply, but I didn't think I'd feel comfortable. A Palestinian on a Jewish campus."

Deborah laughed. "I know what you mean. Just imagine being the only Jewish teacher on a Palestinian campus."

Deborah looked for a faint trace of a smile on Raba's face but didn't find one. Her own smile felt frozen, and she thought she sounded too loud and overeager. Unlike her, Raba evidently wasn't the sort of person who wasted smiles. Deborah felt gauche and unsophisticated. Raba opened her mouth to ask something when Dr. Barguth appeared. He walked in like a politician, smiling to them all, expecting instant attention as he began to talk. Speaking in English, obviously for Deborah's sake, he expressed his pleasure in having two new faculty members, both women. Then he apologized for having to bring up a serious topic right away.

Deborah felt nervous anticipation. An inner voice warned her it was too easy.

Dr. Barguth cleared his throat. "Let us speak frankly. Manger College has maintained a policy of political neutrality. That means while we fully support Palestinian independence, we won't let this campus become a battleground against the occupation. You know that I believe with all my heart in a Palestinian state. But someone has to prepare a generation of educated Palestinians to take over the reins of government when that time comes. And it will come. Those who turn their classrooms into political rostrums defeat their own purpose. I'm sorry to inform you that we've had both formal and informal warnings that the relative quiet we've enjoyed in Bethlehem, particularly at Manger College, will be coming to an abrupt end. Forces would like to disrupt what we have achieved.

I'm taking precautions by increasing campus security. You've all undoubtedly noticed the new fence. It took a large portion of our funds earmarked for development, and frankly, I resent that. By next week we'll have a guard checking bags for weapons, like the Israelis. Students and faculty will be receiving new identification cards that will be checked electronically. You can imagine the toll this will take on the atmosphere of our campus. Likewise, I find it a bitter pill to swallow that Manger College is using the same checking system employed at the Erez checkpoint in Gaza."

There were a few nervous coughs. Barguth's hands were balled into fists. "As you know, gadgets are never enough. I expect you to cooperate. Be alert for irregularities—anyone who doesn't appear to be a student or campus gatherings that feel out of the ordinary. Report to my office immediately. As of tomorrow, political meetings will be limited to no more than eight persons."

He paused and took a drink of water. "Vigilance can prevent a disaster. As Horace said, 'The man who is tenacious of purpose in a rightful cause is not shaken from his firm resolve by the frenzy of his fellow citizens clamoring for what is wrong, or by the tyrant's threatening countenance.'

"I hope I've made myself clear."

There was a burst of sound in Arabic. He tapped his water glass. "At least we can end on a more pleasant note. I congratulate Mr. Naif Barakat, our philosophy teacher and a member of my church, on the birth of his first grandchild. Mrs. Barakat has sent us refreshments. There is no pork, Naif has assured me, in deference to our Moslem and Jewish faculty members. It will give you a chance, also, to meet our new teachers, Mrs. Stern and Dr. Alhassan, whom I again welcome. We are proud to have teachers with such accomplishments on our faculty. Enjoy."

Once again the meeting broke up in noisy conversation Deborah couldn't understand. The men lit cigarettes, while the handful of women teachers moved to the back of the room, presumably to deal with the food. Deborah followed their lead.

Set on the counter were salads and honey pastries. A woman teacher was trying to light a gas cooking burner to heat up coffee. The flame rose so high and fast that she jumped back. Deborah reached over and shut it off. "It's not getting enough air. Please allow me. I work with Bunsen burners."

Deborah tilted the cooker and saw that the air hole in the gas tube was blocked by coffee grounds. She poked out the hole with a fruit knife. "Most people assume that the air for cooking comes only from where you light the flame, but air is drawn in along with the gas. If not, it burns straight upward like a torch." She lit the burner and a smooth blue flame appeared. The other woman flushed and thanked her. Deborah put down the matches, feeling embarrassed talking too much. The teacher wanted a flame, not a lecture. Deborah picked up a dessert tray and carried it to a table.

"Mrs. Stern," Dr. Barguth greeted her. "How did you enjoy your first class with us? Your students were very impressed."

"Already?" Deborah forced a laugh. With ten minutes between the end of the class and the beginning of the faculty meeting, how could he have received a report? Were the classrooms bugged? "I had no idea feedback could get to you so fast."

"Nothing is a secret on this campus. We're one big family. Several students came into my office just before the meeting and asked to transfer to biology. That's quite a compliment since the biology exam is so soon."

Deborah watched his face for irony. There was none. She felt cheerful. "I hope they won't be disappointed," she said, taking a plate.

Barguth gently took it from her, and piled up carrot salad, seasoned with garlic, cumin, parsley, and olive oil. This was a familiar Moroccan specialty her neighbor Ramonde often made. "I hope you won't find our Arabic food too spicy," Dr. Barguth said.

Deborah shook her head. "On the contrary. I must have been born in Marrakesh or Baghdad in a previous incarnation. Until I moved to Israel I couldn't understand the Bible passages in which the newly liberated Israelites pined for the garlic they'd left behind, but now I'm afraid I sympathize."

"Somehow I never pictured our great Egyptian pharaohs as garlic eaters," Barguth said conversationally.

"But they were," Deborah said. "Garlic bulbs are pictured in the pharaonic tombs three thousand year old."

Only then did she realize that the room had become quiet because everyone was listening. To fill the silence she went on. "An ancient Egyptian medical papyrus lists dozens of garlic cures. Have you ever heard of the Akbar Clinic and Research Center in Panama City, Florida?"

The faces weren't smiling. She sounded preachy, garrulous, and condescending. In addition she must have stumbled on an unknown sensitivity. Unfortunately, she couldn't think of a way out except to finish what she was saying.

"A researcher there named Tarig Abdullah, a physician, showed that raw garlic boosted the immune system's natural killer cells. The staff, including Dr. Abdullah, ate twelve or fifteen cloves a day, extracted their immune cells, and put them in the ring, so to speak, against cancer cells. They destroyed more cancer cells than normal immune cells." Unable to stop the smile that twisted her wide mouth upward, she concluded, "The results aren't conclusive, but Dr. Abdullah hasn't had a cold since 1973."

It was a good punch line, and Deborah expected everyone to laugh, but no one did. The silence got depressingly deeper. At last Raba Alhassan spoke, her voice cold. "Yes, 1973 was a good year for *Arab* cures."

One of the teachers gasped. Nineteen seventy-three was the year of the October War, the one the Jews called the Yom Kippur War because Arab armies at-

tacked on the holiest day of the Jewish calendar.
Catching Israel by surprise was a source of Arab pride.

Deborah suddenly recalled that "garlic-eaters" was
an insulting term to Orientals and Asians. Maybe
she'd insulted the Arab teachers. Raba wasn't finished
with her. She moved closer to Deborah and gave her
an appraising stare. "Don't you have any *Jewish* research on garlic?"

Deborah felt like an ass, but anger and self-respect
kept her from caving in. She spoke slowly and carefully, trying to keep her voice from shaking. "In fact,
Dr. Alhassan, there is. The same year, a certain Dr.
Benjamin Lau and colleagues at Loma Linda University in California used garlic against cholesterol and
got very good results."

Dr. Barguth chuckled, his belly conspicuously rising
above a low-slung belt. "Well, I've learned more
about garlic today than in the last fifty-six years. If
your husband wants to experiment with anyone, tell
him I'll be glad to be his guinea pig." Then he turned
to Deborah. "Dr. Ali Alhassan is one of our most
renowned heart surgeons." Reaching into the dish of
carrot salad with a spoon, he pulled out a large piece
of garlic and conspicuously swallowed it, diffusing the
charged atmosphere with laughter.

Deborah was grateful for the bell announcing
classes. The teachers dispersed. Raba walked away
without looking back. A pulse of anger was beating
inside Deborah's head as she thought of cleverer re-
plies she should have made. The driver was waiting
for her. He wove recklessly from one line of traffic to
another, pulling past a flour delivery truck, cutting off
a motorcyclist. Ten minutes later she was standing in
front of her own car in Jewish Jerusalem.

Deborah had arranged to meet Raphi late, insisting
on putting her children to bed first. She was unhappy
about their spending so much time with baby-sitters,
and the nighttime ritual was a reassurance for her as
well. Sarah asked for *Good Night Moon,* which Deborah had read the kids hundreds of times. Somehow

the "good night clocks and good night socks" seemed unbearably poignant and she felt a stupid rush of tears.

They agreed to meet in an all-night grocery in her neighborhood. Raphi was already in the back of the store, where the milk counter was cut off by boxes of cereal. He was wearing a boyish baseball cap and holding a container of yogurt.

"No live cultures in that one. Take the one marked 'bio,' " Deborah said.

"Viva lactobacillus," Raphi laughed. "How did the rest of your day go, Teacher? I heard you were brilliant in class."

His eyes were soft and attentive as she spoke. Nothing was too small, and he often asked the same question twice, phrasing it differently to make sure he had it right. He seemed to know when to probe and when to back off. When she got to the part about the faculty meeting his reaction stunned her.

"Excellent," he said when she was finished. "I can hear from your tone that you're disappointed in yourself, but you shouldn't be. You couldn't wish for a better cover. Do you think anyone would imagine intelligence had sent someone as explosive and impulsive as you as a spy? Garlic!" He shook his head in amazement. "Who would have thought of it? You've done very well."

"Now that's a backhanded compliment if I've ever heard one," Deborah said. Nonetheless, she was delighted by his praise. "Will you be on campus every day?"

His forehead wrinkled. "I'd like to say yes, but it depends on how fast Barguth's new security arrangements are in place. Fake electronic IDs are expensive, and the department sometimes drags its feet. I'll do my damnedest to get there."

He thrust a folded brown envelope into her hand. "Whether I'm there or not, keep teaching this week. Nothing unusual is expected. Here are instructions for next week. They're a little different and more challenging. Read them, and then burn them."

Deborah went to pay for milk. When she turned around Raphi was gone.

Joshua Stern held Isaiah by both elbows and looked him in the eye. "You're not listening. I'm sure she's from a wonderful family, that she's devout, that she writes poetry—but I told you, I have a wife. Deborah was very impressed with Shabbat here. It will take her a while to overcome her stubbornness, but she'll come back to me. I could feel her yielding last week and I'm not going to mess it up by getting involved with another woman. Frankly I'm surprised that Yocheved would suggest it."

Isaiah blushed. "She didn't. This is my idea. What harm can it do? For a man to meet an unmarried woman is not the same by law as for a married woman to meet a man. There are cases, of course, when husbands and wives get together again after separation, but they are very rare. Whatever happens, I think you should already be planning to get child custody."

"Why are you bringing this up again?" Joshua wished his friend and study partner would mind his own business. Recently he'd begun to wonder how such a diligent scholar could also be a gossip. Idle talk was a grave sin.

"There's something I haven't told you."

Joshua stood still, his hands clenched against his side, reminding himself what a patient teacher Isaiah had been when he started his studies. "Let's hear it."

"When I was at the Wall I saw Deborah with a man."

Joshua's jaw tightened. "Before or after last weekend?"

"I really couldn't say." Isaiah scratched his bald spot. "You know we go there so often."

Allah particularly welcomed the voice of the supplicant in the morning hours. Abed knelt on his prayer rug, pressing his brow toward Mecca, asking for understanding. The sun was just beginning to shine on the purple grapes of his family vines when he finished praying. Bees buzzed around their flowers. From the kitchen came the smell of fresh bread. Laila was baking pita and singing. When his mother had been distressed and suspicious about the bruises on his face, he'd claimed to have tripped on a box of papers at the bank and banged his head on a computer. Laila had teased him. "I thought I was the blind one in the family," she'd said.

There was no need to panic. Despite his personal setback, if he made contact with Sami the humiliation would have been worthwhile. Even if the supposed disciple of the Teacher had been a GSS agent, there was no way he could connect the masked man in Gaza to him. By the fifth year of the intifada, nearly every other important Palestinian activist had a police record, but he'd never been arrested. As far as Israeli security knew, he was a middle-class banker for whom all unrest was abhorrent because it hurt investments.

Foremost on his mind was Deborah Stern. Why was that same woman showing up again like a bad penny, as the British would say? Could the GSS think so little of them that they'd send the same woman as a plant and think no one would notice? On one hand, he couldn't take a chance that she was connected to the secret service. On the other hand, he couldn't kill her at Manger College without bringing unwanted attention to Bethlehem. He'd have to kill her somewhere other than the campus.

Abed ate his breakfast, dipping the fresh pita into olive oil and *za'atar,* and drinking tea. He felt better. Using the Mitsubishi provided him by the bank, he drove twenty minutes southeast to the Dead Sea. He climbed up the hills, wary of snakes. The Arabs called the local viper "Two Step," because it was so lethal you could only move one foot before collapsing. In one hand he carried a gym bag marked Hapoel, a Jewish sports organization. Inside was a Kalashnikov, a gun inferior to his Galil.

The cave was totally obscured. He lowered himself down through a break in the rock. The cool of the cave was welcome in the 110 degrees of dry heat. He unzipped the bag, removed the gun and braced his back against the wall. If Sami had gone over to the enemy, Abed was ready for him.

Half an hour ticked by. Sami was late. He never had been before. At last, the words "Deir Yassin" echoed from above. Abed's fingers pressed back the bolt of the Kalashnikov.

Sami came alone. Even in the shadow, Abed could tell Sami had become thinner, and that he was favoring one leg. Under the white-and-black keffiyah, his hair had been cut short and stubbly. The old scar throbbed crimson. To his dismay, Abed saw that both of Sami's hands were wrapped in dirty bandages! The delicate wiring of demolition would require two good hands.

No more carelessness. Abed kept his fingers on the trigger.

Sami stopped and nodded his head in obeisance. Satisfied that he was alone, Abed approached him with a hug, holding the gun against Sami's back as they embraced, kissing both cheeks.

"Salem aleikum," Peace be with you, Abed said.

Sami weaved. "You don't mind if I sit, do you?"

The request was subtly different. Before the attack on the jail, Sami wouldn't have asked to sit; he would have waited for Abed's invitation. Sami had moved up in rank. He'd proven his worthiness and cunning by killing his best friend and penetrating Israeli defenses. Abed tightened his grip on the Kalashnikov.

"Tell me everything that happened," Abed said, pulling out a pack of French cigarettes and offering one to Sami. When it slipped from Sami's hands, Abed lit up in his own mouth and placed it in Sami's. "Can you manage?"

Sami held the butt between the two bandaged paws to exhale. "They were singed in the blast," he said, desolately.

They sat cross-legged across from each other. Abed lay the Kalashnikov over his knees as Sami retraced his actions at the police station. The recitation confirmed the details Abed already knew from listening to the microphone. Sami became emotional as he described the explosion. The words escaped in short phrases. ". . . pinned by the wall . . . Ibrahim lifted me . . . cement chips . . . my eyebrows . . . brought down a metal bar on his head."

Abed gave an impatient shake of his head. The story didn't gibe. "How could you manage it with your injured hands?"

"There was no pain then. The burns were too fresh."

Abed nodded for Sami to continue. "Ibrahim was very strong, but surprise was on my side," Sami said, tears running down his cheeks. "He didn't die right away. He looked at me with horror and disbelief. There was so much blood. I heard running, and turned to leave." Sami's cheeks were streaked with tears, grotesquely rolling over his scar.

Abed waited for Sami to regain control. "Tell me the rest," he urged.

"The exit we'd planned on was blocked by the border police. I found another, on the side of the barracks. I remember walking the Street of Prophets, my hands tucked in my pockets to hide the blood, but I'm not sure what happened next. I felt very cold. When I woke up I thought I was dead. Pious women bathed me and wrapped my limbs. Then one afternoon they said someone important had come to visit me, a disciple of the great Teacher.

"I was desperate to get in touch with you. Perhaps I should have been more careful, but by then, my hands hurt so much I was nearly out of my mind with pain. I prayed to Allah and entrusted him with the message. I gave him only half the Koranic codes. I knew that you'd be a better judge than I if he was trustworthy."

Abed's mind buzzed with unanswered questions, but they would wait. "How are your hands?"

"Healed enough to butcher the enemy."

Abed smiled. "You won't have to do anything quite so bloody yet. Sami, have you ever thought of registering for college?"

16

Two weeks after she'd started teaching, Raba's students were ready to present their first papers. A young woman reported on autism with observations as keen as any field researcher's. Not all the students were as gifted, but on the whole they were intelligent women. Whenever the seminar touched on child psychology, class interest was particularly keen. Several students were mothers, and they all had younger siblings. Raba worried about her own baby, moving restlessly inside her. This week she'd had light bleeding and cramps. Going to the Jericho doctor was out of the question. He'd report to Ali and he'd insist she give up her job. She tried to reassure herself that some discomfort was normal. Aunt Fatima always said babies were like olives and didn't fall from the tree until they were ripe.

After class, Raba waited for Wassim in the courtyard where six women were studying the Koran in a circle around a beautiful, dark young woman with a melodious voice. Their leader hit her palm with a fist to make a point, quoting from the Koran: "He who has done an atom's weight of good shall see it; and he who has done an atom's weight of evil shall see it."

That was her aunt's creed. Fatima's religion was articulated through the kindness with which she treated people. She'd never refused a request for charity. Twice a week she dispatched Uncle Ziad to a shelter with home cooked food, claiming she simply couldn't adjust to cooking for a small family.

The Islamic instructor went on. "Outsiders don't understand. They think Moslem women are simpletons. They are obsessed with our veils. They laugh at com-

arriages, yet three-quarters of the men in the West cheat on their wives, while our husbands are faithful to us and the family. Western women slave for material objects, only to feel empty and dissatisfied.

"We Moslems are already one-fifth of the world's population and growing rapidly. When the Prophet revealed his message, there was only one true believer. In twenty-eight years, Islam spread through the ancient world. We are in a comparable position today, at the onset of an expanding Islamic universe. The same Americans who denigrate our culture will one day kneel in our mosques and beg Allah's forgiveness. The Prophet's word will soon reach every corner of the world. Not only in India and Russia, but in England and the United States. The Moslem woman is respected. She creates a harmonious home and is protected from the strife of the outside world. Read Western magazines. Can we *have* it all, woman ask, not can we *give* all. Only in submission to Allah can both man and woman rise to full stature as perfect human beings. Never has a properly dressed Moslem woman been treated as a sex object."

The students giggled nervously. Except for the married ones, sex was taboo. Their virginity was guarded carefully, as Raba's had been.

To her surprise, she was inspired. Her knowledge of Islam had always been more intellectual than a doctrine she considered applying to herself. Hearing Islam extolled made her feel proud. As a child, her mother's religious fatalism had repelled her. In Detroit, except for the Christmas pageant, from which Raba had excused herself like the Jewish kids, she'd felt American. Oddly, only since returning to the Middle East did she realize the degree to which she'd been an outsider in America. Raba thought of the time she and Aunt Fatima had slunk out of a movie theater after watching a story of an American woman escaping a Moslem husband in Iran. Only recently Raba had learned the movie was filmed in Israel.

In the years she'd been in America, being devoutly Moslem had become fashionable among educated Pal-

estinians. The simplicity was appealing. How pleasant
it would be to see life as black and white instead of
shades of gray that demanded constant moral reckoning.
The longer she was back, the better Raba understood
her brother's plunge into the new Islamic movements.
In Gaza he would have been inspired by the many
fundamentalists who rounded up drug dealers and
provided religious nursery schools. Ibrahim's ability to
suspend other values to pursue the Holy War against
the Jews had a logical consistency, even if she abhorred his tactics.

"Raba." Sami's voice interrupted her thoughts and
startled her. Sami always seemed to emerge from nowhere to find her on campus. She still had trouble
getting used to his transformation. No longer was he
the mangy young man at the animal market. His red
hair was neatly trimmed, even too short. He was wearing an expensive rugby shirt and pants that showed
off a slim masculine figure, overdressed the way Arabs
on American campuses looked when they aped the
preppies. He seemed so much older and more confident.

Raba handed Sami a folder as if she were returning
an assignment. Inside were today's details about the
views of faculty members and copies of memoranda
Barguth had distributed. It wasn't much, but it represented her feeble attempt to save Ali.

Sami took the folder and handed Raba a note. To
anyone looking on, they seemed like any teacher and
student on a college campus. Sami thanked her and
joined men students under the trees.

Raba opened the note. It was in English. "You are
doing fine so far, dear Raba. Remember that your
husband's continued good health depends on your
continued performance."

Her hands shook. The words were clear enough, the
syntax correct, the style educated. The neat, precise
handwriting, pressed with a very heavy hand, showed
the tails of letters long and overly pointed: the handwriting of a pathological murderer. Whose writing was
it? She'd compared it to Sami's and knew it wasn't his.

Raba felt a compelling urge to phone Ali. She dialed from a public phone, feeding in metal tokens, watching them drop as he was paged. "Raba. What's wrong?" She could hear that he was short of breath from running. She felt asinine. "Nothing. Nothing really. I'm sorry I had them page you. I just wanted to hear your voice. Maybe it's my hormones making me crazy." He surprised her when he said tenderly, "I've been thinking about you all day. Worrying about you. Are you okay? I'll come home early. We'll have dinner on the patio and go for a walk. Maybe a movie. What do you say?"

She pictured him spreading the entertainment section of the newspaper on the low table, marking movies with a highlighter pen, and waiting for her to make the final choice.

She paused, the anxiety weighing down her chest again. "Let's just stay home. I love you, Ali Alhassan. Please take care of yourself."

One of Abed's hideouts was near Bethlehem in the Dehaishe refugee camp, a hodgepodge of homes that ranged from shanties to villas. The camp was separated from the road by a high mesh fence, built by Jews to protect their cars from the rocks hurled by Palestinians. The cage effect made it easy to spread resistance, particularly among the young, who supported violent groups like Abed's. He tore apart a white sheet from his mother's trousseau. She'd used a sheet like this as a white flag in 1967. He felt a grim satisfaction as he fashioned a sling out of his family's symbol of surrender. That was all the disguise he would need to make himself invisible on Bus 19, filled with sick and disabled, going to Hadassah Hospital clinics.

He took an Arab bus to Jerusalem, and waited for the 19 on Herzog Street. The hot breeze carried a smell of pizza, typical of the misguided Westernization of the Middle East. Even worse, next to the pizza parlor was a video library, the kind Moslems were closing down in Gaza. He'd seen enough pornographic films in Sweden to know how addictive and destructive they were. After a diet of sex videos, he couldn't get hard unless he slept with two women at once.

The bus arrived. The right-hand window, immediately behind the rear door, was always his first choice. Security was almost nonexistent on Israeli buses. Bus drivers were supposed to check the seats at the end of each run, searching for explosives. Many didn't bother. Abed breathed deeply and enjoyed the intoxicated feeling he always got when he was on a mission. He scrutinized the bus. The front seats were taken by a fat woman, her leg in a cast, and two elderly persons. Around him were college students, a pregnant woman, an old rabbi, and two grandmothers talking loudly in Russian. Two seats ahead a soldier slept. He had a Galil, identical to the one Abed had lost. The rifle had slipped from his lap, pointing downward to his feet!

Abed told himself not to be idiotic. He wasn't on the bus to steal a gun. His goal was to kill Deborah Stern.

He got off near the emergency room and ambulance parking and took the elevator to the seventh floor. The halls were nearly deserted. Many Israelis left work early in the hot summer. One of the cleaners had supplied a detailed map of the hospital. Palestinians did the blue-collar work inside Israeli institutions, and the Seventh Century possessed interior maps of them all. The diagrams were so good that Abed had been able to determine which window of the men's room could look across the inner courtyard into the seventh-floor animal house where Deborah worked. If he focused on the window, his acoustic surveillance device could even pick up whispered voices. Carefully, he opened it like a telescope. The Israelis had warehouses full of such gadgets, but for Palestinians they were expensive and hard to acquire.

The number pad on the door into the animal house worked like a Touch-Tone telephone. Each button gave off a distinct beeping sound, which it sent to the lock. A middle-aged man in a faded blue shirt approached the door and began tapping numbers.

Abed took a few seconds to focus, so he wasn't sure if the first number was a 5 or a 6. The others were 3 and 8—maybe the phone code for his name, and then 9,4,9,1—a birth year backward. Abed removed a black skullcap from his pocket and threw away the sling. He waited ten minutes for the researcher to leave.

A corridor connected the animal house to the main building. He kept his pace slow, though he was edgy and impatient. He pushed open the outer door to the animal house and found himself in an antechamber. He went to work immediately, tapping in the numbers: 6,3,8. Nothing happened. He tried 5,3,8 and the door snapped open. Inside were piles of lab coats, gloves, and shoe covers. He put them on, pleased at the additional disguise.

Off a main chamber were dozens of different rooms. Which could be Deborah's? If the names were written only in Hebrew, he'd be in trouble because he couldn't read the letters.

Again, he was lucky. The Jews were always impressed by foreign titles: under the Hebrew their names were written in English. He blessed Allah and his good fortune.

Deborah's room was the first one.

On the door was another electronic pad! No one had mentioned a second one.

Arab cleaning staff were not allowed in this part of the building, Abed realized in frustration. He studied the electronic pad. He could dismantle it, but there might be a backup security system. The door might not open or, even worse, destroying the lock might block the others from opening, including the exit.

He hated to admit defeat.

There were footsteps coming down the hall.

A young woman with a clipboard was going into each room in order. Deborah's room was next.

Abed pretended to be having trouble with his rubber shoe covers. The technician gave him a sympathetic smile and looked at her watch as if, sorry, she was too busy to help. He was so close he caught the code she punched in: 2,4,3,2,5. He smiled. He was a whiz at math puzzles. The letter combination came to him: C-H-E-C-K—that's how someone would dial the letters C-H-E-C-K on a phone.

Abed was inside seconds later.

He memorized the electric, gas, and water systems. He moved the cages around looking for additional outlets.

Abed heard someone in the outdoor entrance, and quickly put the cages back in order. A loud click echoed in the hall.

Deborah was walking in! She'd come earlier than usual.

Abed's heart hammered. He'd seen her only once, on TV. The photographs they'd taken on campus had always shown her with her hair pulled up like an Austrian nanny. He was surprised it was so long. She was better looking than her photos, almost as blond as Kirsten, but more serious-looking, despite the casual dress. She was wearing jeans and a pale green T-shirt.

His first idea was to hide in the cabinet and strangle her. He flexed his fingers. The thought of the green eyes bulging excited him. He'd need an escape route. Each researcher's room had a black door. Abed pushed it open, feeling the whoosh of air behind him. At first the sound puzzled him. Then he realized the system was set up to let air in only through a single filter that kept the lab free of contaminants. And he got a better idea.

Deborah checked her mice every Thursday. Even if she couldn't officially report the results, she was observing their growth, making rough measurements, and keeping anecdotal notes for herself. She preferred late afternoons when most of the researchers had already left, so she wouldn't have to explain how she was keeping herself busy these days. She stopped briefly in her office, where contamination signs were still taped all over. They reminded her of the black and white death notices Israelis posted outside the homes of the deceased. Often three or four were plastered on a wall, one next to the other, as if the bad news had to be confirmed again and again. For months afterward, fragments of the posters clung to the stone walls—leaving eerie, unsightly traces of death.

At the animal house she tapped in her numbers and got into the lab clothes, tucking her hair in the cap. Joshua had always admired her long hair, and she had indulged him rather than cut it. What was the point now? She might as well get something short and sophisticated like Raba.

The mice stirred when she opened the door. "How are you today?" she asked aloud before checking. BALB/C, the white ones, had thick fur and had grown. They'd been injected with her trial vaccine. It was working! Her mind raced to the next stage of research, trial runs, local testing on volunteers, and eventually FDA approval. In the midst of her reverie, Deborah halted. Something was wrong. The single cage left uncovered as a monitor of airborne infections was covered. Deborah checked the pad where the technician recorded her visits. She'd been there half an hour earlier.

No technician would ever make that mistake. It was a unthinkable as a violist leaving his case unsnapped or a mechanic not closing the bolt that held the power steering in place. A mechanic! Her thoughts flew back to the muffler repair shop. No! No one could have penetrated the lab, could they?

A bad smell filled the room. Deborah recognized it as gas. Odd. Her gas line was closed, and all the air coming into her room passed through a filter. She sniffed again. The smell was getting stronger. Something was definitely wrong. She put the cage back on the shelf and reached for the door handle.

The exit door was locked.

She tried to open the front door, but it was also locked.

She was already breathing fast, and her head was pounding. The smell was making her clumsy. She had to get out! She banged an empty cage against the door. Maybe someone would hear her. But the reinforced walls hid all sound.

The mice moved restlessly in their cages.

I can't die here, Deborah thought, pushing the door again. She blinked her eyes to stay awake. Her throat was raw from gasping. Her voice squeaked for help.

The animal house rooms had acoustic paneling. No one would hear her. Why hadn't phones been installed?

She looked at her watch. It was nearly six. No one would come until the morning. Her shoulders sagged in weariness. For a brief moment her mind was clear. The alarm! Each time she pressed the button of her Seiko she called his name: Raphi, Raphi, Raphi.

Raphi parked the red sport car in the ambulance zone, ignoring shouted protest from the guard. He pushed aside the crowds in the hospital lobby, running the stairs to her laboratory. Empty.

Where could she be? The electronics had led him to the hospital.

The animal house. He ran to the seventh floor.

The outer door was locked.

He found a chair in the hall. It fell apart as he smashed the glass, setting off a series of loud alarms. Good, a security team would be here. He prayed they'd come on time.

The inner door to Deborah's room was also locked. Damn! He could smell the gas. How long had she been in there? Through the wire-reinforced windows he saw her slumped on the floor.

The doors were made of thick wooden panels. Raphi had seen Zacharia, his martial arts mentor, break wood this thick, but he'd never done it himself. He drew in his breath and called on his years of martial arts training, focusing all his inner energy on a spot three inches above the lock. In one blow, exhaling with all his might, he smashed his hand through the wood. His fingers were slick with blood when he forced the lock open.

Deborah was gasping. He drew her outside and

tried to get her walking. She collapsed on the first try and he caught her arm. "Don't die. Please don't die," he begged her.

Her eyes opened. He drew his first breath. Again he tried to make her walk. She wobbled on her legs. He held her like a rag doll. "Deborah, Deborah," he called over the alarms. "I've got to get you oxygen." She shook her head. Hospital alarms were ringing. She whispered so softly that he pressed his ear to her mouth. "Back door," she gasped. He wrapped his bleeding hand in the back of her T-shirt, bent his knees, and lifted her.

Outside, a security guard was writing down the number of his car. "Shin Bet," Raphi hissed, knocking the pad out of his hand. He put Deborah in the passenger's seat. Her eyes started to close and he shook her roughly.

"Are you okay?" he asked, glancing at her, as he accelerated. "Fight the urge to sleep." She looked dusky and was shivering, but he was afraid to shut the windows. Fresh air was good. He flicked on the car heat.

He called her name again. She trembled and tried to sit up, then slumped back. Her hands pressed her fingers into the side of her head. Another tremor ran through her body. He turned up the heat.

Raphi's legs were shaking with repressed terror. What if he'd come a minute later? He had been at Anat's apartment, not far from the hospital, when the buzzer went off. If he'd been across town at the university she'd be dead.

He stopped at a pub and ran around the side of the car, helping Deborah out of the car and walking her around. "Stay here," he ordered, propping her at an outdoor table. He was back in a minute with a tall glass of coffee. "Drink it slowly. It's got brandy."

He held the glass while she wrapped her fingers around it. Her eyes closed, but she forced them open. She took a long sip and screwed up her face. "Lucky it wasn't carbon monoxide," she said. "It bonds to the hemoglobin."

A laugh of relief and pride in her bubbled up inside of him.

She held the coffee away. "I'm glad you find it funny."

"Oh, Deborah, Deborah, did I ever tell you how wonderful you are?" he asked, pulling up a chair, putting his arm around her. She was the most resilient woman he'd ever met. He squeezed her shoulder as they sat quietly, listening to the crickets and the far off hum of traffic, smelling the beer from the pub.

She took another sip of the coffee. "What now?" she asked.

"When you finish the coffee we're going to go for a walk."

She met his eyes. "No. I meant what about the fucking terrorists. We're not going to let them get away with this, are we?"

She's not walking out on us, he realized, thrilled and guilty as hell. "I think not," he said, his mouth tight.

Deborah rested the glass on her lap and put her head back. "We're not doing too well. I hope you have something up your sleeve I don't know about."

Raphi smiled. "Could be."

Feeling marvelous, Abed took the stairs two at a time to where Laila was collecting pigeons' eggs. Everything was falling into place. Raba was filing regular reports. Deborah was dead. In a week, he'd take over the campus.

The carrier pigeons were an easy communication system. He delighted in watching them soar under the noses of the mighty GSS, who were lulled by their faith in high tech. One box of pigeons had been trained to fly to Manger College. Abed had made Laila swear that if the army ever entered their house she would find a way to free the pigeons.

"Anything for me?" Abed asked.

"Yes," Laila said, her voice high with excitement at his presence. "I took it off already."

He kissed her forehead and unwrapped the note from Sami.

His jaw tightened as he read it. A complication. The students were having second thoughts about carrying through the plan. Manger College had never been involved in demonstrations, and they were contemptuous of campuses where students had drawn in soldiers to put down riots and therefore lost their autonomy. Sami had tried to convince them that Deborah's presence was a sign that their college was infiltrated, but they insisted on proof, arguing that she was the best teacher on campus, simply too talented to be a GSS plant. Besides, everyone knew about her killing a terrorist. Who would believe the GSS would use her as a spy?

Abed was livid. He'd never had trouble recruiting students before. It was bad luck that he'd had to use the most reactionary campus in Palestine.

Now that Deborah was dead, he would have to work harder to convince the students that their campus was in the process of a GSS takeover.

"Is something wrong?" Laila asked. She could sense his mood better than anyone else.

"No, nothing, sweet one," Abed said, controlling his fury.

Abed's mind was already plotting. He needed evidence that Deborah had been a GSS agent. If he couldn't find any, he'd simply manufacture some.

17

Raphi was back in Sweden. He was shoveling snow in Göteborg. The more he shoveled, the faster it came down. Soon he would be buried. He forced himself to wake, soaked not with snow but with perspiration. His first reaction was surprise that he'd begun remembering his dreams. His second reaction made him sit up straight.

"Yotebory," the terrorist had said. Only Swedes called Göteborg that. Everyone else pronounced it "Gothenberg." The masked man had spent time in Europe, probably Scandinavia. Raphi was sure of it.

His right hand hurt like hell. To pick up the phone with his left hand he rolled over in what Anat mocked as his "monk's bed." The description was apt: beige cotton sheets pulled taut over a hard foam-rubber mattress. His neck pillow was wrapped in a towel. Anat had never slept the night there. Sex was one thing, his privacy another. He tapped in Gil's phone number. Gil could check the list of West Bank Arabs who'd studied abroad. There could be 10,000 names. It could take weeks. Gil had been asleep and cursed like a sailor. "Could we have it by tomorrow?" Raphi asked.

Then Raphi called Deborah. His heart lifted at her whispered hello. "I have the worst headache of my life. You don't think it could be stress, do you?"

Raphi laughed.

"Ow—not into the phone, please," Deborah whispered.

"Call me when you feel up to it. I've got a few tricks that will appeal to the scientist in you."

"I can hardly wait," she groaned. "How's your hand?"

He was oddly touched that she'd asked. "Sore, but functional, as long as I'm not playing Liszt."

"I didn't know you played the piano."

"I don't. But I'm thinking of learning. Anything beats my present job."

He was smiling when he hung up. Whistling a gypsy tune from the "Hungarian Rhapsodies," he went to make coffee. The kitchen in his apartment was part of an open space that included a dining nook and the living room, where his desk was. It was compact and modern, the counters in gleaming granite, the kettle and sink stainless steel, the chrome of the bread box shiny, and not a spoon out of place. For a year he'd sailed on an intelligence yacht in the Mediterranean, and in the toss of a storm's waves a casually discarded fork had lodged itself in the bulkhead. He'd become compulsively neat ever since.

Raphi measured out an Italian blend into the cappuccino maker Tamar, his sister, had given him. He loved to cook. His daydream of happiness was a laughter-filled evening cooking with a woman he loved. Once he'd suggested an evening like that to Anat, but she'd mocked him and made a coarse comment. Scrambled eggs had turned out to be the extent of her kitchen repertoire.

He wondered if Deborah liked to cook, or if she opened cans and microwaved prepared foods.

He showered while the coffee brewed. The only time he ever took a relaxed bath was in the family vacation house in Herziliya-on-the-Sea where they'd all indulged themselves. Tamar had insisted on the double whirlpool bathtub when their mother had a pear-shaped swimming pool built in the magnificent gardens. Their father installed a dish satellite that received broadcasts in the dozens of languages he spoke. Raphi had joined in the camaraderie by ordering a professional massage table. The family got together rarely, but when they did, they wanted to feel they were fulfilling their personal fantasies of luxury.

The holiday house seemed far away as Raphi concentrated on getting dressed. His closet contained dozens of disguises hidden behind a false drawer. He chose a gray, long-sleeved dress with a broad back that covered him down to the shoes: Palestinian drag, they called it at GSS. "For what God has forgotten, He's supplied cotton," he thought, fashioning prominent breasts to go with his unfeminine shoulders. Shoes weren't such a problem anymore, since both sexes wore sneakers. Raphi chose a brand manufactured in Jordan. He shaved twice, then put on makeup. In a deep pocket he stuffed his Glock 9mm, partly rubber, seventeen-shot. Small and compact. A scarf drooped over his forehead and covered his neck. He was arranging it artfully when Gil phoned back.

The bad news was that 5000 names of male West Bank students who'd studied in Europe had come up on the computer. Worse news was that the head of intelligence had been called into the prime minister's office. The PM wanted to be reassured that Deborah Stern *really* wasn't working for them. The chief had used their standard line—would they be so stupid as to use anybody as obvious as Deborah? The prime minister was no dolt and told the chief to fuck himself. If Deborah was working for the GSS, he promised to personally halve their operating budget. "What if the prime minister knew that not only was Deborah working for us, but that our most valuable field officer was risking being unmasked in Bethlehem?" Gil asked. "When the electronic system is set up, *no one* is going to put his ass on the line by authorizing your false identity card."

Raphi asked, "Is there any good news?"

"Yes. The system hasn't been installed yet. The electricians didn't turn up for work yesterday."

Raphi relaxed. Thank God for Middle Eastern inefficiency.

Deborah was crossing the line from passive to active espionage and it scared the hell out of her. She couldn't eat or drink. She put her cold toast out for the birds. Why am I doing this? Deborah mused. Maybe Joshua is right and I'm not reading the signs right. Yocheved was probably home baking cookies. I, on the other hand, was nearly gassed in my laboratory a few days ago. Nonetheless, today, instead of hiding, I'm planting electronic devices on a Palestinian campus.

Last year at a conference, she'd met a biologist who'd led women up perilous mountain climbs. At lunch, Deborah had asked her why making the ascent was so important. The explorer had talked about confirming powerful internal drives. Deborah too knew that something beyond guilt and duty was pushing her to persevere. If she put it grandly, she was motivated by her unfulfilled destiny, a quest that went beyond logic and that she'd never been in touch with before. A struggle to prove herself.

Since this was the first week of July, the beginning of school vacation, Ben and Sarah would be going to Joshua's later today so they could attend the yeshiva's free day camp. If they liked it, they might stay as long as three weeks with their father. July 22 was Sarah's fourth birthday. Dr. Stern insisted they make the party in his rose garden. By then Deborah would be finished with her assignment. With the extra money, she could afford to take the children to a beach holiday. She'd have to make the decision about her marriage. Not today. She had enough on her mind.

Deborah kept her hands busy packing their bags, sorting last year's summer clothes, which looked tiny because the children had grown so much. Religious girls wore skirts and T-shirts with sleeves that came down to their elbows. The boys could wear T-shirts and long pants. She started to pack the bathing suits, then remembered that Joshua had said there was no swimming.

She gave Inbal last-minute instructions, glad not to have to see Joshua. Deborah kissed the children good-bye. The dark-haired driver was already waiting in the Manger College van, its radio playing rock music. He seemed absorbed in the beat and ignored her. On campus, too, her presence was tolerated without the antagonism of her first day. The campus was quieter since Barguth had banned large political meetings. Deborah went through the gate as the bell rang. A single caucus of students dispersed from the pine copse called Smith Grove.

The bugging devices, tiny tape recorders, were no larger than an American dime but they contained components that could beam conversation to a satellite. Deborah's bugs would store the information, then transmit it at odd intervals to a receiver in a phone booth outside the campus. From there, the broadcast would be beamed for analysis to a listening station a few miles away in the town of Efrat. Deborah had to place four microphones: in a tree, the faculty club, the women's bathroom, and the cafeteria.

Bugging a tree would be the hardest but, in the end, the safest. Even a cautious, experienced terrorist would tell you bugging trees was nearly impossible because they had little resonating surface. "A work of art," Raphi had called the listening device put together by a retired missile engineer who created personalized electronics as a hobby. "He was crawling the walls after three months of retirement," Raphi had told her. "Until he found his niche with us." A pine cone had been taken apart and fitted with a resonator that would amplify voice vibrations.

Deborah was wearing a wide Indian-print skirt and a dark purple blouse so that she could move unimpeded. She sat on the grass under the tree in conscious imitation of American leftist professors who liked to fraternize with their students. Brandeis had had its share of bearded gurus. Their talk, which had fascinated her then, seemed unbearably pompous now. What had they known about war and peace? Even Ben and Sarah, who'd been through the Gulf War in gas masks, knew more than these so-called experts, who were just looking for an easy way to get laid.

Deborah shifted uncomfortably, pine needles itching her sticky thighs. The temperature was in the low hundreds again. Get this done and you can go inside, she encouraged herself. She waited until the entire quad was deserted. The end of the pine cone contained a new synthetic glue that could attach the listening devices anywhere, "even on an elephant's behind," Raphi had said.

The lowest branch was too high to reach without climbing.

Too much time was passing. Deborah slipped off her sandals. She was in good shape because she'd been working out in the gym, making use of the free membership. Climbing wouldn't be hard. She squinted into the tree. The sun was in her eyes. Still barefoot, she gathered a handful of pine cones from the ground, and stealthily removed her bugged one from her briefcase, keeping it to one side so she could tell which was which. Holding it in her left hand, she hiked up her skirt and braced her knees against tree bark. One, two, three—and she was up. The goal was only eighteen inches away. Her skirt snagged on the tree, and she worked at detaching it.

Footsteps along the path! At last, the thread came loose. She jumped off and waited. No one.

Her knees hugged the tree again, and she inched up, moving the skirt almost to her thighs. She had to remove the tape from the cone and wipe the surface clean with one hand before attaching it. The cone slipped and fell. Deborah cursed and dropped to the ground again, counting her blessings that the cone hadn't fallen on the sticky side and attached itself to the ground.

Raphi hadn't covered the possibility of her dropping it.

She hoped the mechanisms hadn't broken. On the next trip up the trunk, she got the cone bonded crookedly but firmly to the apex of two branches. She let out her breath.

"Mrs. Stern!" Dean Barguth's voice almost shook her from the tree. How long had he been standing there? Deborah held on tight, screwing up her face in consideration.

He sounded worried, incredulous. "May I help you? Shall I call a gardener?"

Deborah shook her head and jumped down, her face scarlet. With an effort, her voice stayed calm. "Oh, no. I thought of taking one more pine cone for class today, but those I have already will suffice."

She brushed her hands together and pulled down her skirt. "We're considering the question of how dying cells are replaced, and these pine cones will make an interesting analogy. You must know that pine trees stay green all year because they grow new leaves before shedding the old ones. This tree is called the Aleppo pine. I believe you call it *snobber*."

I am getting good at this. What a liar I've become. And what nonsense I spout at will.

"I'm impressed with your resourcefulness. I can't imagine our former teacher going to such lengths." Barguth laughed. "Sorry. The thought of him in that tree is ludicrous."

"The thought of me in the tree is ludicrous, too. I'm afraid I've gone a little over the top with this class. But they're so enthusiastic, I want to push them," Deborah said. "Do you know the expression 'tomboy' in English?"

Barguth nodded.

"My mother was horrified to find she'd given birth to one. She was European and elegant. Her image of a little girl was in starched white blouses and organza party dresses." Deborah pushed back stray tendrils of her hair and put on her sandals. "I was always looking for tadpoles and bringing home injured pigeons." She bent to gather the pine cones, all under the X-ray vision of the dean. He looked up at the tree, staring hard. Her heart felt as if it had stopped beating.

"May I help you, Mrs. Stern?" Dr. Barguth leaned forward and put out his hand. She breathed an inward sigh of relief.

"That would be nice," Deborah said, brightly smiling. *Why won't he go back to his office?*

She dumped pine cones into his thick arms. "Careful. Once you're stained with pine sap, nothing will get it out."

The dean threw his head back and laughed. "Now you sound like *my* mother. She's a stickler for neatness and cleanliness, boils shirts white and irons underwear. She still tells me off if I've got a crumb on my jacket."

Fifty meters away in the classroom, the bell was just ringing.

"Just put them on my desk," Deborah said, pointing to the classroom and expecting Dr. Barguth to walk ahead.

He insisted on accompanying her and talking. Since she'd mentioned pigeons, did she know an environmentally safe way to get rid of them? "I don't want to hurt birds, but my wife insists they bring mites."

"She's right," Deborah said. "Try hanging toy snakes or a plastic owl outside the window."

When will he leave?

Deborah straightened the books on her desk and took out markers. Barguth sat down. The class looked at her with expectation.

"You don't mind, do you?" he asked. "I've heard so much about your class I'd like to listen for a while."

Shit, she thought, forcing herself to smile. Shit, shit, shit. She held up the pine cone. "Now, who can guess why I've brought one of these to class today?"

For a pleasant change, a barrage of hands flew up. They were showing off for the dean. Deborah called on a young woman. *"Talita, min fadlek."* The students loved it when she used a few common Arabic words. Suddenly inspiration hit. *"Snobbera fi alid ahsan min ashareh fi sajira.* A pine cone in hand is better than ten in the tree," she said. Her first Arabic joke. The real maxim was with birds, of course. The class roared in approval. Dr. Barguth's laugh was loudest.

When the laughter quieted, a student made a good guess about pine cones and cell structure. Deborah was delighted with her ingenuity and how well the class was going when she realized the only student who looked indifferent was a stocky woman in a gray dress, her head modestly covered, a bandage on her hand. Oh, my God! The pine cone flew from her hand and hit one of the students in the arm.

"I'm so sorry." Deborah stepped forward to retrieve it. Dr. Barguth was there ahead of her. *Had he followed her eyes?* Deborah swallowed hard.

Dr. Barguth handed it back to her. "Please, madam," he said, and then, glancing at his Rolex as if an appointment had just been recalled, he got up to leave. "I've enjoyed every minute. We're very privileged to have you at Manger College."

She glowed at his public endorsement. If only he knew. After class, she hurried to the women's bathroom and closed the door. The sink was leaking. Her father had always said that at least one faucet was dripping in every home. She had no idea if chronic noise would affect the listening device.

The microphone to plant here was inside a lightbulb. Standing on the toilet, she lifted herself to the top of the stall, unscrewed the lightbulb, replaced it, and then threw the old one in the garbage. How many Jewish biologists does it take to place a bugged lightbulb in a Palestinian campus? she asked herself. Just one. There couldn't be two that crazy.

Bugging the faculty room was easy. Deborah slid a tiny microphone under the shelf where the coffee cups were stored.

Three down, one to go. The Manger College cafeteria opened for lunch, when most students ate their main meal. The food, she'd heard, was good and cheap. The room was small and crowded, no more than twenty formica-topped tables. Behind a counter, a rack of roast lamb was turning slowly. Her adherence to Jewish dietary laws ruled out eating it, but she liked the gamy smell, tempered by the scent of coffee and cigarette smoke. Everyone was eating plates of rice and lamb, drinking coffee, smoking and talking. Deborah realized how little she knew about her students' lives. The dozen students fell silent for a moment when she entered, and then the buzz of their conversation started again. Deborah ordered a Coke.

She carried the can back to an unoccupied table. When she popped open the top, the cola ran out the top and over the table. She tried to wipe it, but the napkins were as thin as wax paper.

"Try these." The voice startled her. It was Raba Alhassan, offering a thick handful of tissues. Deborah was flabbergasted. They hadn't spoken since that fight the first day.

"May I join you?" Raba asked. She was holding a tray with rice and lamb, and a cup filled with tea and a sprig of mint.

"At your own risk," Deborah said. "Let me get rid of these." She crossed the room to throw out the tissues.

"It's hard to get used to nonabsorbent napkins when you've grown up with Scotties, isn't it?" Raba said, putting down her tray and sitting across from Deborah.

"You're right. That and no ice in the soft drinks. After eight years in this country I still hate warm soda."

"You've been here eight years! I had no idea. You're almost a native. Mrs. Stern, I've been wanting to apologize since our first encounter," Raba said. "I totally overreacted to what you said."

Deborah appraised her but the woman seemed sincere. "My name is Deborah. Thank you for apologizing, but I understand. My presence makes people nervous. I'm starting to think teaching here wasn't such a good idea."

"Excuse me for asking, but why did you take this job? You're obviously such a popular teacher you could have worked anywhere."

A warning light went on. Something told Deborah she was having a two-track conversation: one conversational, the second probing. She sipped the warm Coke and grimaced. "I'm a *novelty* here, don't forget. That explains my popularity. The Jewish job market is tight. If I taught Japanese or business I could probably get a job. Anyway, I went to public school and my teachers were all races and religions, so teaching

Palestinians doesn't faze me." She heard herself running on and switched gears. "You're also new. What made you start so late in the year?"

"Someone told me about the school, and it turned out that my husband knew George Barguth from the Rotary." Raba lowered her voice conspiratorially. "The word is that there are only a handful of women teachers on the staff, and they're mostly first-year tutors or education majors. Barguth's donors are Christians, not Moslems, and he's under pressure to increase the number of women so Manger College doesn't look like a fundamentalist Moslem institution. I'm a token hiree. I'm only teaching seminars this year, not lecture courses like yours."

Deborah rubbed her forehead where the headache was coming back. "Seminars are as important as the introductory courses. Who knows? I may have been hired for the same reason. I also heard that he wanted more women on the staff," she said, pushing the soda away.

Raba didn't miss a beat. "Oh, really? Where does one hear such information in Jewish circles?"

Deborah had to think fast. "I also work at Hadassah Hospital, and we sometimes get funding from Christian sources."

Raba's gaze was level, unfathomable. "Barguth was bragging the other day about your biology class. Are the students all really going to pass their exams?"

Deborah folded her hands and sat back slightly. "Most will. There are some excellent students, and others who don't know vertebra from a Wonderbra. Biology is the only science taught here, other than computers, and I think there's a greater interest than anyone realized. One of the students mentioned that there used to be a chemistry major, but the labs have been closed for years. What a shame."

"Perhaps you could coordinate a whole science program." Raba looked uncomfortable, maybe even resentful. "Will you be staying on next semester?"

By then I hope Manger College will be a faded mem-

ory. "I'm not sure. I'd like to, but Dean Barguth hasn't said anything. How about you?"

"Yes. We're already planning for next semester, after I have the baby, of course." Raba's face tensed, as if she was physically uncomfortable.

Deborah hesitated. "Are you feeling okay?"

"Actually, I've been a little queasy. Do you have children?"

"Two, a boy and a girl. I was queasy for nine months, couldn't drink coffee or eat zucchini, and survived on baked potatoes. Frankly, you look a little more than seasick. Are you sure you're okay?"

Raba nodded. "I'm sure it's nothing. Every now and then I get these strong cramps."

"How far along are you—fourth or fifth month? I'm no doctor, but in the middle months you have to take pains seriously. They might be early contractions, and you could dilate too early. Sometimes a hormone—progesterone—is released too soon." Raba had gone white. "I don't want to scare you. It's probably nothing. Ask your doctor."

"The doctors are more old-fashioned in Jericho than Detroit."

"There are some excellent people at Hadassah Hospital where I work," Deborah said. "If you wanted, I could arrange for you to see someone."

As soon as she said it, she realized she'd overstepped polite bounds and sounded patronizing again. Raba Alhassan wasn't a friend, but a woman who had shown nothing but hostility toward her until today. This was the sort of blunder she'd made about the garlic.

Raba seemed more embarrassed than angry this time. She blushed. "Thank you. I'll discuss it with my husband."

"That's right, he's a doctor, isn't he? Well, ask him." When Deborah realized that sounded condescending, too, she backtracked. "I'm sure there are excellent Palestinian doctors."

The muscles around Raba's jaw were flexed. She looked down as if she wanted to hide her expression.

"Yes. Of course." She glanced at her small gold watch. "I'm afraid you'll have to excuse me. My driver will be here shortly to collect me. Nice talking to you and thanks for the advice."

Raba walked away, looking more pregnant from behind than from the front. Her hips had taken on the looser swing of pregnancy.

Deborah felt nervous. *I trusted her more when she was being hostile,* she thought. *Why was she asking me all these questions?*

Raba's tray was still full. She hadn't eaten anything.

Deborah had nearly forgotten about planting the bug. The tables provided a good surface for the vibrations needed for listening devices, but they were so light, they were probably piled up when the floor was mopped at night. That would expose the device. She ran her fingers underneath the table. Wads of gum were stuck on the bottom. Raphi said the transmitter could work through concrete. Gum wouldn't be a problem, but the thought of wedging it into someone's chewed gum went beyond the call of duty. There was always a pack of gum for the kids in her briefcase. She chewed two pieces at once, to make sure it would cover.

When no one was looking, Deborah slipped the gum from her mouth and wadded it around the tiny transistorized listening device. It stuck easily to the bottom of the table. Done! Deborah felt an unexpected rush of triumph at having planted all the bugs successfully. She walked briskly to the gate, hoping her driver had come early. The red van was nowhere in sight.

She needed to walk off her nervous energy. Next to the campus was a cluster of nearly identical small houses. On one porch an elderly woman leaned over a round aluminum tray, picking stones and boll weevils from rice. Arab businessmen in three-piece suits were standing in front of the grocery store, smoking and talking. Bethlehem was such a hodgepodge that amid the homes and stores crops were planted. Summer vegetables—zucchini, corn, and tomatoes—reminded her of her own family's backyard garden in Connecticut. Deborah laughed at a scarecrow, head wrapped in a red-and-white checked keffiyah, the same color King Hussein wore.

Ahead was the intersection to the Jerusalem-Hebron road. It was time to turn back.

As soon as Deborah changed directions she saw the familiar red van driving toward her. She assumed the driver had been looking for her and was told that she'd walked ahead. She waved to him. How fast he's driving, Deborah thought, her forehead wrinkled. As the van got closer she could see red hair and realized that her usual driver wasn't behind the wheel. This man *was* driving awfully fast. Didn't he see her? She waved back and forth vigorously, but this only made him increase his speed.

Her feet seemed to understand before her brain did. She had already swung around and started to run when the words came into her head: he wants to hit me.

To her right was the field, but the fence was so low he could easily follow her.

No one could outrun a car.

Where were all those Israeli soldiers she'd seen patrolling the territories? Where was Raphi?

Farther up the road was another cluster of houses and stores. Deborah ran, lifting her skirt. Her sides ached. She tripped on a root, pulled herself back up, and only then realized she was still clutching her briefcase. To gain speed she threw it into the bushes, knowing even that was futile. The motor roared behind her. She turned to see how close as the edge of the van's fender slammed her hip just before the outside mirror on the passenger's side smashed her lips. Deborah landed face up on the rough cement of the sidewalk.

Anger replaced terror. They'd try to stab her and gas her and now someone was running her down. Defying every rule Raphi had taught her, she reached for a hoe resting in the front yard and hoisted it above her head. The van was turning around. Deborah leaped forward and smashed the back window, jumping back as the glass shattered in every direction. "Get the hell away from me," she shouted, shaking her fist.

The main highway was only 300 meters away. Gasping for air, she reached it just as an army jeep covered with stone-protecting iron mesh was pulling up. Once again she waved her hands high in the air, this time shouting for help. Two soldiers carrying M-16s jumped off the jeep.

She gulped for breath and got out the important details. The soldiers raced up the hill. A third offered her a canteen of water. She bent over and leaned her head between her knees.

"Wait here," one of the soldiers told her. "We want to know what you were doing in Bethlehem."

Fuck you, Deborah thought. She wasn't waiting for anyone or anything. She was going home.

Out of the corner of her eye, she saw Bus 161 stopping on the road to pick up passengers. She summoned her remaining strength and ran to catch it before the door closed. The driver gave her a strange look. She caught her image in the mirror: disheveled hair, cheeks smudged with dirt, bleeding lip. She took the closest seat to obscure her torn skirt. Only then did she realize that her briefcase, with her money, her house key, and all her teaching notes, was abandoned by the field. She started to explain, but he smiled and told her it was all right, she could pay next time. She looked at her watch, and realized everything had taken place so fast, she hadn't even pressed the emergency button. There was no point now.

Her keys were in the briefcase. She hoped Inbal hadn't gone out. Rachel also had a key. If Deborah couldn't get into her house, she'd take a flight to Nepal. The one place she never wanted to see again was Manger College in Bethlehem.

Striking at Deborah on campus had been a desperate move, Abed realized. He'd been shocked that she was still alive, and he'd ordered Sami to scare her enough so she'd never come back to campus. Sami would send a report by pigeon about how it had gone.

In the meantime, Abed had important details to take care of.

He entered Manger Square through the back alleys. Unlike Jerusalem, where old, dark passageways had been transformed from "dingy" to "quaint" by new signs, lights, and a bevy of shops and cafés, the tourist section of Bethlehem looked unplanned and neglected. A plastics factory stood next to once-stately private homes built with picture windows onto Shepherds' Fields. Hot winds spread the acrid smell of decay over the town. Municipal facilities were so primitive that residents could run out of water for a week at a time. Israelis taxed Palestinians, but little was poured back into the town, Abed thought bitterly. He felt equally resentful toward Christian store owners who earned fortunes selling olive wood and mother-of-pearl souvenirs, and then returned to their garden homes in Beit Jalla and Beit Sahur.

Using an alley entrance, Abed entered a large shop called Holyland Treasures. The business had been handed down from father to son. The present owner, John Shafi, sixty-seven, expected his own sons and grandsons to go into the business. He was greatly disturbed, Abed knew, that three of his five children were living abroad; two in Los Angeles and one in Melbourne. He blamed the Israeli occupation. For a Christian, Shafi held strong nationalist views and had been a faithful supporter of the Palestinian rebellion, both by contributing money and by illegally importing arms. Of course, he'd also earned a fortune in arms deals.

Holyland Treasures had an enormous inventory of crosses and rosary beads, plaster statues and mother-of-pearl-covered Bibles. Abed knew from his work at the bank that the Shafi family also controlled a large construction company. Abed was expected. The door to the inner office had been left ajar for him. He tucked in the edge of the keffiyah to cover his face. John Shafi was sitting in a chair, not behind, but in front of his desk, drinking coffee and watching customers. He nodded to Abed. Abed recognized John's handsome grandson Anwar, one of the activists at Manger College, waiting on tourists. The store was air-conditioned to chilliness, and free orange juice was served, putting customers in the mood to spend. Shafi ordered more coffee on the intercom and begged Abed to sit. Almost immediately they were joined by Anwar carrying a tiny porcelain cup of coffee and a tall glass of water to clear the palate. He excused himself and went back to his customers.

"Now what is it I can do for you?" Shafi asked, handing Abed a cigarette.

Abed presented him with a shopping list that contained plastic explosives, detonating cord, blasting caps, and motion detectors. Shafi sighed, "It will be difficult." Abed knew what he was going to hear: a complaint that the Israelis were making his business harder, a declaration that Shafi was taking impossible risks even though he wasn't a Moslem, and finally a request for more money. They went through the preliminaries, arriving at a price.

Shafi put down his coffee cup, seeming to assess its contents. "Why is it that I sense you want more from me?"

The old crow was crafty. One thing Abed had learned in the bank was that no one got as rich as Shafi by being stupid. "You're very perceptive. You see, this action will be different from the explosions in Tel Aviv and Netanya. It will take place right here in Bethlehem."

Shafi gasped and his eyes widened, but Abed knew he was faking. Rumors that action was shifting to enclaves of passive resistance like Bethlehem had been circulating for weeks. Shafi had superb connections. Abed might as well lay it out for him.

"Putting it simply," Abed said softly, "I need your store."

The older man's veined hands pressed into his cheeks, his forefinger resting on the bridge of his hawk nose, as he listened to how the explosives would be placed at the low entrance to the Nativity Church, along the nave of the Catholic chapel, behind the ornate brass decorations of the Orthodox chapel, and in the Grotto itself where the baby Jesus was born.

"It will be a disaster for business," Shafi said.

"On the contrary," Abed said. "Bethlehem will be on every television screen and magazine cover. When the Vatican and the Orthodox churches throw their weight behind the preservation, every Christian in the world will feel obligated to visit."

"And if the church is destroyed?"

"It won't be, and even if it is, think of the pilgrimages for its renovation. But it is not for your profit that I urge you to cooperate with us. Even though we are of different faiths, you have been like a father to us. Just as your own grandson Anwar is a brother to me. He has joined us and shares our battle."

Shafi was no twig to be snapped in the wind. The old man was the current patriarch of a large, wealthy family. As Abed left, Shafi's eyes narrowed and there was warning in his voice. "Just remember, young man. You don't need additional enemies."

On the way home, Abed could see the streets to Manger Square filling with tourist buses. Look at the church now, he thought. It may not be here long.

At home, the message had arrived. Abed's hands shook as he read the first sentence. Evidently Sami's attack had been successful. Deborah literally had been run off campus. Barguth had responded with stunning fury. Within an hour of the incident, a message had been relayed to Iranian groups in Lebanon, fundamentalist groups in Syria, and, more important, to Barguth's network of Palestinian fund-raisers in the United States. Whoever was *pestering* him on his campus should call off his pit bulls immediately. Not another penny was to move their way.

Abed read the note again. The typical PLO rhetoric galled him: The Palestine people hadn't suffered to achieve its goals only to have success spoiled by hotheads. The armed struggle would lead to a systematic, just society.

In short, he was being ordered to call off Operation Manger.

Abed's fingers fisted, crushing the paper. Barguth represented everything that had gone wrong with the Palestinian revolt. At this critical moment when the Jews were on the run, Barguth was willing to sell out to the enemy.

Abed took out his pocket lighter and burned the message, kicking the ashes around the floor.

There were moments in a man's life when he had to act on his own and strive for greatness.

Operation Manger was Abed's destiny, which could not be denied.

Funding would be cut off, but that would be temporary. As soon as the brilliance of his plan was recognized, Abed would be showered with funds. Groups in Michigan and Virginia would be vying to become the top supporters of the Seventh Century.

In the seventh century, Islam had conquered half the world with the sword. In the twentieth century, they would conquer the other half. A thousand mosques had been built in the United States in the last decade. Ten thousand would be built in the next.

He quickly calculated. Enough money remained in his coffers for five days. He'd have to act immediately, pushing up the attack by a week.

George Barguth, like his namesake Saint George, would be a martyr for a cause. Abed would personally assassinate him.

18

Raba felt restless and disappointed. After the incredible tension of the last two weeks, she and Ali had planned to spend a quiet day together. Then one of Ali's patients had gone into shock and needed him nearby. Raba tried to correct papers, but her mind wandered. As she puttered about, she remembered Ali's idea that she take up Aunt Juni's offer of a cooking lesson. "She's not going to let up until you agree. She has a reputation for getting what she wants." Ali's relatives had been so friendly that turning down Juni's outstretched hand seemed mean-spirited. The enthusiasm in Juni's voice when Raba phoned made her feel guilty that she'd put off the visit so long.

Aunt Juni lived across town in a two-story pink limestone house Raba entered through the large curved porch, into a central hall that served as a living room. Juni took Raba's hands, looked her over, and kissed her. "Oh, come in, come in, little one. You're looking better. More color in your cheeks. The weight becomes you. A cup of coffee before we start? Oh, that's right, you Americans don't drink coffee while pregnant. Then mint tea it will be. I have fresh pastries."

Unlike the elder Alhassans' home or her own uncluttered rooms, Aunt Juni's house was full of knickknacks—flamenco dancers with knit skirts, china dolphins, and glass bowls in pastel colors. Juni would have been puzzled if anyone had denigrated her collection as "dust collectors." She loved every piece, touching and straightening them as she passed.

The smells of frying onion and rose-scented pastry

came invitingly from the kitchen as they entered it. The counter was covered with a dozen glass bowls in wonderful shades of blue, green, and yellow. Juni pushed aside dishes and magazines cluttering the table and poured boiling water from a thermos over fresh mint leaves. Raba listened as Aunt Juni mixed details about cousins with cooking talk—"Did you know that if you blanch garlic three times it will turn sweet and won't overpower a sauce?"—declarations on how Syrian rice was inferior to Egyptian because margarine instead of oil was used, promises that she would take Raba to Jaffa to buy shoes.

She's the only one who's noticed that I love shoes, Raba thought.

Juni stood up, wiping her forehead on her apron. "May his soul be blessed, I am making my dead husband's favorite dish. I will show you how."

Raba moved up closer, peering into an enormous cooking pot, "What is it?"

"Kawareh bi humus."

Calf's foot with chick peas. Raba paled. "Aunt Fatima never made it."

"Marvelous woman, your Aunt Fatima. She saved your life. And I understand that she's a wonderful businesswoman. Cooking was probably not her interest, or perhaps the American butchers only do steaks and hamburgers. Did you get sheep's head in America—it is so difficult to get the butcher to remove the nose properly—and then there's all that singeing of the hair and removal of the brain—I always rub a little rose water on it after it boils. You don't know how? Never mind, I'll show you next time."

Raba felt herself pale.

Juni stirred a great aluminum pot with a wooden spoon. "Get me the bowl from the refrigerator, little one, and we will get started. I am so pleased you have visited me today. We have so much to share."

From anyone else, Raba might have been offended by the constant "little one," but Aunt Juni always sounded so warm and sincere it didn't matter. Raba obediently opened the refrigerator and took out a ce-

ramic bowl containing calf's feet, split hoof turned up.
She nearly gagged.

"Good, good," Aunt Juni said, examining each foot,
rinsing it under the faucet, scraping the sides with the
back of a paring knife. "I give them a hot bath." She
dropped the feet into a large saucepan and waited for
the water to boil. Raba shifted in place, uncomfortable
in the quiet after the constant stream of chatter. Juni
pursed her lips as if she were concentrating, then at
the first bubble lifted the feet with metal tongs and
dropped them into a transparent dish of cold water.
"Good, nice and firm."

She poured olive oil in a metal pan. "These are good,
but nothing compares with pig's feet, you know."

"No, I don't," Raba managed to get out. "I've never
eaten pig."

"We don't usually eat it either, but once we did."
Juni's voice had become quiet and conspiratorial.
"Uncle Ahmed was having important guests. He'd
bragged about my calf's feet, but the Moslem butcher
didn't have any, so I bought pig's feet from the Christian. The guests licked their fingers. The women asked
for my recipe, but I was coy. You'd be surprised how
you can control people through their stomachs."

Raba tried to hide her shock. She watched Juni
cook. When the oil was hot, Juni dropped in the calf's
feet one at a time, stepping back as the fat and water
sizzled. From two smudged containers she reached for
a liberal pinch of salt and pepper, then a tablespoon
of bright orange turmeric. She asked Raba to drain
the chickpeas and drop them in before she covered
the meat with water and brought it to a boil.

To Raba's surprise and delight, the cooking feet
smelled wonderful, like roasting beef. Juni took off
her apron and insisted on serving tea with date-filled
cookies.

"I don't approve of you working so hard," Juni said,
pouring tea. "Not that I haven't worked myself, mind
you, but you are frailer, and you haven't yet read-
justed to life here. Uncle Ahmed, bless his soul, was
a gambler. He would gamble away the money from

the hardware store until there was nothing to pay suppliers. I had to make ends meet. He sold copper wires and tube cutters. What could Juni sell? Information." Her voice dropped again, although for all Raba could tell they were alone in the house. "I've worked for them all, you know. The Israelis, the Jordanians, the PLO, Hamas. Information in Jericho, call Juni."

The news was harder to absorb than the cooking. She wanted to believe Juni was exaggerating. Raba had the dizzying feeling she was way over her head in this espionage business.

Raba swallowed hard. "Didn't you feel disloyal?"

"Hah! They're not family. Fools, all of them, little boys fighting private wars. We suckle them when they're born. We suckle them when they're grown, lucky to get our own pleasure from time to time. Your Ali is as rich as Croesus, so he can dabble in medicine. His family owns trucks, metal factories, half of Jericho. I got none of that, but I've done okay. My children don't have to worry, about money or about getting arrested."

It was true that Juni's children seemed to have passed unscathed through the intifada. Then Raba recalled a family story about a son getting in trouble, and Juni sending him abroad dressed as a girl.

She shook her head as if to clear her thoughts. "Aren't you afraid you'll be caught or killed if you work both sides?"

"I've always been able to get away with things," said Juni, her fingers massaging her double chin. "It's a talent. In school I was the one who took the teacher's chalk and someone else would be blamed. Some people understand schoolbooks, like your husband Ali, and some know how to get on in life, like me."

"Why are you telling me this?"

Juni smiled in approval. "To see if you're loyal. And because you'd never have believed what I want to tell you if I hadn't been candid with you. Raba, my dear, you're family now. Besides, I like you. For a change there's someone original and bright. We're getting dissolute marrying our own cousins.

"You're caught in a knot tangling tighter every day. You can bring destruction to yourself and the whole family. You'll be all right for a week, ten days maybe— but then get out of Bethlehem. Play sick, go on a vacation with Ali or pretend to visit your aunt in Detroit. Whatever you do, don't go to Manger College.

"You'll think you can outsmart them—but 'He who digs a hole for his brother will fall inside himself.' " She wiped her forehead again and took a deep breath. "And I wanted to tell you that, whether you listen or not, wherever you are, I'll do what I can to help you."

Raba's head was pounding with questions. How did Juni know so much? What could be happening? But Juni's manner made it clear that the subject was closed. She was already refilling Raba's cup.

After she'd dropped her letter of resignation to Raphi at the paint store, Deborah expected relief or even exultation. Instead, she just felt exhausted and depressed. She went home to lie down. Her body ached. Purple and black tracks crossed her hip where the van had hit her. She missed her children.

The doorbell rang. *Damn.* No one was expected. She froze.

The phone rang.

A test. If she answered, whoever was outside would hear.

The answering machine, which recorded the numbers of in-coming and out-going calls, had only been installed recently, at Raphi's insistence. After four rings it picked up the line. To her great annoyance, Deborah heard Raphi's voice. "I'm outside your door with a cellular phone. I think you're inside. Please answer. I have a key. Please. I need to talk to you, Deborah."

"Get out of my life," she shouted, storming to the door. She didn't want to see him because she might weaken. "You got my note. How much clearer could I be? I can't see you anymore. You always get the better of me. I've quit. Get it? Take your spy world and shove it up your ass."

Raphi laughed. That made her madder.

"Open the door," he pleaded. "Pretty please. I've got a surprise for you."

He'd never leave until he saw her. But as soon as she turned the key she knew she'd made a mistake. He gave her his crooked smile and she melted. In his hand was her briefcase.

She tried to toughen up, and jerked it away from him. "How did you get this? Where were you yesterday? I'm sick of people trying to kill me."

"Do you mind if I come in?"

"Would it help me if I did?"

He walked in and sat down on the couch. "I followed you yesterday. I didn't shoot because, if I had, the van would have fishtailed. Besides, I knew the driver was just trying to frighten you and would not hit you." He leaned his head back and looked at the ceiling.

She stalked him. "I suppose you won't deign to tell me *how* you knew that."

"It doesn't matter now. The good news is that I've convinced everyone you've done your job and we shouldn't pressure you to keep on."

Her mouth formed an O.

The last thing she expected was for him to accept her resignation without a fight. "What's the catch?"

He shrugged and looked impatient. "None that I can think of. Contrary to what you're implying, we're not monsters. I'm on *your* side, remember?" He held up a hand scraped raw from her rescue at the laboratory.

She regretted flying off the handle. He'd saved her life, and not for the first time. She'd hurt his feelings, she could tell because the scowl was gone and he was wearing his inscrutable face: neutral eyes, mouth slightly open but neither smiling nor frowning. "So why are you here?" she asked.

"I came today with carrots, not sticks. The GSS thinks, and I agree, that you deserve a few days' vacation."

"Sorry. Rio is out of my budget."

"Also lousy weather this time of year," Raphi said, smiling rakishly, as if recalling a private memory. "No need to travel abroad. We're offering you a few days at a seaside villa. Sunshine. Sand. Quiet. You can bring the kids."

She pictured Ben and Sarah building castles on the shore, then remembered that they were going to day camp.

"Go on. Tell me more. The kids don't have to come. They're with their father for the week."

Did she imagine the tinge of relief in his face? He'd been well named for his late actor uncle. She decided to call his bluff. "Well, when can I leave?"

"Now." Raphi smiled and sat down on the couch. "Go pack."

Deborah was still waiting for the punch line as she threw a bag together. When she came out of the bedroom he was lying down on the couch in a rare moment of unguarded repose. He looked transformed. The harsh lines of his face and sharp body language were replaced by a relaxed sensuality. She caught her breath, and wondered what sort of person he would have been if he'd grown up in a country that didn't make soldiers out of their young. "Where will I be staying?" she asked quietly.

He jerked up and rubbed his face, instantly alert. He recited the phone number. The area code was 09. Herzliya-on-the-Sea. She left a note for Rachel, who was coming by to borrow a couple of novels.

Still holding the notepad, she said, "I know how to get to the Sharon Hotel in Herzliya. Give me directions from there."

"No need. The boss insists I drive you," Raphi said.

Ah, the plot thickens, she thought. "You GSS boys think of everything."

His Alfa Romeo was outside. She remembered it was wired and waited for him to open the door. He started the tape deck, and the car was filled with "parsley, sage, rosemary, and thyme." He'd probably put some thought into what an American-born Israeli would like. Then she remembered he'd gone to Yale.

The air-conditioning was on, but the sunshine warmed her face. Outside the temperature was 95.

To her amazement, she dozed off. When she snapped awake they were already passing the Arab village of Abu Gosh, out of Jerusalem. She was embarrassed, but so unbelievably sleepy that if she'd had anything to drink she'd have sworn he'd drugged her. She fought for wakefulness, and finally asked if he minded her sleeping. Joshua always hated her snoozing while he drove.

"Of course not," Raphi said. "As you've probably surmised from my macho personality, I enjoy driving. I'll wake you up when we get there."

Deborah curled into the bucket seat. Her dreams were full of anxiety. The mice from her laboratory had gotten loose. They were running around her living room, hiding behind the sofa and in the bookshelves, while she was helpless to catch them. Each time her fingers reached out, they slipped from her grasp. She woke with a start. The car was slowing. She smelled the sea. Before her was a seaside villa, the outside covered in white stucco, with a red roof. A swimming pool protruded from behind the house. Roses in a dozen shades wound along a mosaic path that led to a dark wooden front door. There had to be a catch. Where was the wicked witch? she wondered sleepily. Raphi reached for her bag, and opened the villa door.

She followed him into an interior that was even more charming than the outside. Someone in the GSS must have exquisite taste. She thought back to the man they'd called Moshe Cohen and knew it wasn't him. *It's not Anat either. She'd have picked purple plastic bar stools.*

On one side of the entrance was a modern, pine kitchen, decorated with blue and white Dutch tiles with windmills and blond children. Deborah was surprised that there were the two sinks of a kosher kitchen, marked in the same blue tiles "Milk" and "Meat." She would never have guessed that the GSS kept kosher. The kitchen led to a sunporch, where a blue-tiled table formed the center of a cozy dining area. Beyond glass doors was a veranda with a white deck table, an umbrella in the middle, leading on to the pool, which looked at least forty meters long. Across from the kitchen, on the other side of the entrance hall, was a living-dining room, with a fireplace in a far corner and a table large enough to seat sixteen for a formal dinner party. A section jutted out in a sitting area, where there were two padded armchairs near a low Moroccan table with a hammered-brass top.

Raphi got busy pulling up shades and opening windows.

"No one has been here for a while," he said. "The mustiness will pass. There are four bedrooms, four bathrooms," Raphi said. "Not counting the shower near the pool. I suggest you take the one on the right with a whirlpool bath. I'll go out and get some lunch while you unpack."

He paused on the way to the door, picking up a fruit bowl with the names of fruit in Italian. Something about the way he did it was too familiar.

"Whose home is this?" Deborah asked on instinct.

"Let's say it belongs to the greater family."

"Whose family specifically?"

He looked surprised. "Mine, if you really want to know. Does it matter?"

"You don't get it, do you?" Deborah shook her head angrily. "Or maybe you do and are just pretending you don't. There's a problem Raphi. It *matters* because nothing you say is ever exactly as it is. A celebration party turns out to be a recruiting session and the GSS vacation resort turns out to be the Lahav palace."

To her surprise, he looked hurt. "Stop being so cranky. I promise to stay out of your way. You won't even see me." Before she could reply, he closed the door.

Deborah kicked her suitcase and went to her bedroom. What had Gil said about Raphi having other sources of income? He had to be some kind of raja. She stood at the bedroom door and let the sight se-

duce her. A round canopy bed echoed the shape of
the room with curved mirrors. Through glass doors,
the swimming pool beckoned. The bathroom looked
like something out of an Italian movie: two sinks, large
mirrors, a shower, plus a whirlpool bath for two.
Champagne glasses and an ice bucket were stored on
a recessed shelf.

It could be worse, she laughed to herself. I'm here
already, I might as well enjoy it.

Her undressed body looked pale except for the
enormous bruise, which had darkened blue and yellow
and orange. Her bathing suit, a once-beloved tur-
quoise stretch, had looked all right at home. In the
ceiling-to-floor mirror it looked faded and baggy. I'm
too shabby for Herzliya-on-the-Sea, she thought.

Hanging on pegs behind the bathroom door was a
stunning gold and brown Gottex bikini in a Moroccan
design, and the most beautiful burgundy velour robe
Deborah had ever seen. On impulse she put it on,
releasing the scent of Shalimar perfume. It probably
belonged to a woman of Raphi's, or maybe he kept it
here for sybaritic breaks. The medicine cabinets were
filled with the kind of expensive French cosmetics sold
in duty-free shops.

Deborah slid open the glass door to the pool and
breathed in the combination of flowers and sea. It was
impossible to be indifferent to the beauty: a rock garden dotted with terra-cotta flowerpots, each species
separate and labeled. Someone had nurtured wild-
flowers, purple dwarf chicory and bright pink spiked
thymbra. She slipped off the robe, turned toward the
pool, and dove in flawlessly.

Too bad Raphi can't see me swim, she thought aimlessly. At least that would impress him. Swimming was
her best sport. There was a lake nearby in Connecticut, and she'd been on the swimming team in college.
She'd taught both Ben and Sarah how to swim. Their
new camp didn't have a swimming program, Deborah
remembered regretfully. Maybe she could bring them
here sometime. Her arms curved over her head as
her crawl sliced through the water, swimming almost

without a breath for the first two lengths, getting the kinks out of her neck, and then striking a rhythm that she felt she could hold forever. The sky above was cloudless blue, the sun hot. Birds sang. The breeze carried the scent of honeysuckle. Out of habit, she counted laps. Then she forced herself to stop counting and swim for pure pleasure.

She tried to concentrate on the future. Sooner or later Raphi would catch his terrorists. Joshua would stop being so stubborn and come back to her. He could be religious and a lawyer. Why not? Half the lawyers in Jerusalem, like Rachel's husband Dan, were religious. Deborah was already keeping the Sabbath, the house was kosher, and she'd gone to the ritual bath when she and Joshua lived together.

Then reality intruded. In her heart she knew Joshua would never compromise. What she used to value as high principles had become rigidity. Their strong physical attraction and their devotion to the children might not be enough to build a future.

As Deborah shifted to her side, she was startled to see a face looking down at her. Raphi. She hadn't heard the car. How long had he been standing there? He wore a dark blue bathing suit, low on the hip but not obscene. The hair on his chest made a-V, thicker down the middle, disappearing into his suit. His body was lean and tanned, despite living in Jerusalem. He stretched, then went on to slow body movements, as if isolating and stretching quadriceps, biceps, then abductors. It was fascinating to watch. Although he didn't look like a bodybuilder, the muscles seemed enormous when he flexed them. He had terrific legs. In fact, he had a fabulous body, even though he wasn't tall and broad like Joshua. The unwished-for thought came unbidden to her mind: he's probably dynamite in bed. Guiltily, she pushed the image away.

Raphi dove in from the far end of the pool. His dive was good, but not quite perfect, she thought smugly. In the water, women had a slight advantage because of the distribution of fat cells, which kept them buoyant. Her students would find that interesting. With a pang of guilt she realized she no longer taught a class of hopeful students at Manger College. They'd fail the test without her.

Raphi hadn't surfaced. Why was he staying under-water so long? A minute passed. Where could he be?

Could he have hit his head on the shallow end? This was his pool. He had to know the depth. This was his damned house. Sometimes young athletes had heart attacks, but that seemed far fetched. Still he didn't surface. Deborah swam looking for him. He was close to the bottom in the far corner.

Shit, she thought. This can't be happening.

"Raphi, Raphi," she called, and dove down to reach him. His body looked slumped over.

Deborah had taken water-safety instruction in high school but never had to do an actual rescue. She reached down and tried to pull him up by his arms. His eyes flew open and he pushed up to the top, laughing.

She struck his shoulder with her fists. No words could contain her wrath. Deborah swam to the far end of the pool, panting from indignation. *I hate you,* she thought.

Then all the tears she'd suppressed over the last horrible weeks started. She held on to the side of the pool, her shoulders wrenching up and down.

Raphi swam up behind her. He tried to comfort her, but she shrugged his hands away.

His voice was thick with remorse. "It was a joke. I promised to stay out of your way. I'm sorry. I didn't mean to scare you."

"Can't you ever, ever be real?" she asked, gasping out the words. "Everything is an act for you. A manip-ulation. Don't you ever think of anyone's feelings?"

He'd edged over to the side so that he could see her face. Deborah turned away from him, but not be-fore seeing his eyes, soft and repentant. She was re-minded of his tears when he'd held Rachel's baby at the circumcision. She shook her head. Don't feel sorry for him, she warned herself. He's a snake.

Raphi's voice was low. "I don't tune in too well

even to my own feelings. It's hard to live with, believe me."

"Sorry, I'm fresh out of sympathy. I've got my own problems." Deborah pressed her hands onto the inner ridge and lifted herself out of the pool. She shook water out of her hair, opened the gate at the end of the property and began walking to the beach. She half expected him to follow her, and was disappointed he didn't. She wanted to strafe him with insults.

Near the sea she could breathe better. The public beach in Herzliya was always crowded, but here among the private villas there were only a handful of people: a young mother in a bikini with a blond baby, two teenagers playing paddle ball near the water, and an elderly couple holding hands, which made her feel sorry for herself. Deborah took off her sandals and sank in her toes where the warm water reached the sand. A crab crawled from behind a rock. An abandoned sand castle dissolved with each gentle wave. She walked for an hour, dipping from time to time to cool down from the heat, bending to pick up pretty shells for Sarah. The wonderful smell of fried fish wafted from a beachside restaurant and reminded her that she hadn't eaten since breakfast many hours ago. Her money was back in the villa. She sighed in resignation. There was no choice but to go back.

Her anger had eased. He wasn't trying to scare her, she realized. He was simply infantile. It astounded her that someone who was an esteemed intelligence officer and university lecturer could be so thickheaded.

She was getting closer to the villa and had to decide on her immediate plans. If he's bought food, I'll eat. I'm too hungry and tired to go home. I'll spend the night here, and then go back in the morning.

The back gate had been left open. The smell of simmering butter drew her to the kitchen. Raphi had his back to her. An apron was tied around his waist. He spoke without turning his head to look at her. "I know I'm an asshole. I'd like to make it up to you. At least have something to eat."

The table was set. He'd opened a bottle of Carmel

Semillon. On a long wooden board was a French baguette and two kinds of cheese—brie and a milder yellow. He'd made a salad, Israeli style with the pieces of tomatoes and cucumbers cut geometrically small and pickles diced in. Rich-smelling coffee was brewing, and two places had been set with hand-painted cups and dessert plates on straw mats. A delicate glass vase in the middle of the table held fragrant roses from the garden.

He turned, carrying a frying pan with hot crêpes.

"Cooking is a hobby I rarely indulge," Raphi said in answer to her lifted brows. He poured her wine. "I like this one."

"So do I. It's one of my favorites."

"At last we agree on something. Now that we know we can drink together, can we make up and be friends?"

He held out his pinky, the way Israeli children made peace after a fight.

Her first impulse was to laugh, but she stopped herself. She realized that she was getting a rare view of this complex, mysterious man. She put out her pinky. "Peace," she said, following the kindergarten formula for making up.

He hooked his pinky around hers and squeezed it. They shook pinkies and recited the ditty: "Peace, peace to the world, anger, anger, nevermore." They stood frozen, pinkies gripped, until he cleared his throat and nodded to her chair.

Lighten up, she warned herself. "How do you happen to own a villa like this? Teaching economics must pay well."

"It belongs to my family. My maternal grandparents owned a tea empire in Russia. Grandma and Grandpa were early Zionists. Every tea chest included pamphlets about establishing the Jewish state. When they got here, out of a combination of idealism and business sense, they bought property all over the country. Downtown Tel Aviv, which they owned a chunk of, wasn't too expensive when it was still a sand pile. Without too much effort we Lahavs seem to get wealthier by the generation, mostly in commodities, which makes sense since the original money was in tea. It's allowed us to take up dissolute professions."

"Is that why you went into economics?"

"That's part of it—a family inclination. There was that or diplomacy, and as you've noticed, I don't have the knack."

She'd been thirsty, and finished the wine fast. He poured a second glass and she was halfway through with that before touching the crêpes. The wine after the sun on an empty stomach was giving her a buzz. His voice reached her beyond the haze. "Actually, I was hoping to remake the fucking Middle East with economic ideas. I thought economics could buy peace. Ask any economist, he'll tell you they can." Raphi swished the wine in his glass. "Just don't ask him to fit Khomeini or Saddam Hussein or the Seventh Century into the balance sheet."

The afternoon was cooling, and a sea breeze from the porch blew in her face. Deborah leaned back, the crêpe melting on her tongue. Briefly, she closed her eyes to savor it. "Why do you do intelligence work?"

"A childhood habit I could never break."

Deborah didn't know if he was getting drunk or being condescending. "Why do you always talk like that?" she asked.

"Like what?"

"In ready-made phrases as smooth as pâté. 'A childhood habit I could never break.' You talk about your grandparents fluently enough, but when anything gets personal you close down. Why would anyone who cared about you be satisfied with that?"

His face colored. "Okay, try this. I had the benighted idea that my country needed me. Don't teach your kids Arabic and karate if you want to keep them safe. Everything goes into a file. By seventeen you have to be registered with the Israel Defense Forces, and it seems that Middle Eastern languages and martial arms made me too desirable."

Her anger had disappeared completely. I bet you were desirable, Deborah thought. The wine was making her feel heated and dangerously relaxed. She tilted her head back and looked at the ceiling. "So they recruited you, too. Like me."

He finished his wine and poured a third glass. "I suppose. My family was back in Jerusalem for my last two years of high school. By my senior year I was already working for intelligence.

"I'd been out of the country so many times growing up that I was eager to prove to my classmates that I was still a real Israeli. I wanted to be in *sayeret matkal,* the chief of staff's personal unit. I ran to the Dead Sea on Saturdays to stay in shape. No problem with being in an elite unit, I was told, as long as I could be borrowed for special assignments."

"You must have wowed the girls."

"Yeah," he grinned. "Magic. Girls who wouldn't let me copy their homework before started inviting me to small parties." Then he looked serious. "It doesn't take long until you start wishing that someone will like you for yourself and not to find out if commandos have longer dicks than paratroopers."

Do they? Deborah wondered, realizing she was drunk. She was suddenly aware that her emotions were shifting too fast, and that she felt far too much sympathy for Raphi. She pushed back her chair and excused herself. "Thanks for dinner," she said. "I'm going take advantage of that fancy bathtub now."

She filled her glass one more time and left him finishing the bottle. In the bathroom, she got undressed and turned on the water in the cognac-colored tub. It had to fill enough for the water level to pass the spouts on the side so water could be circulated by the air passing through. Shalimar bath lotion was on the shelf, and Deborah poured in a capful, filling the room with luxurious scent. When the water level got high enough, she pressed the knob and turned the pressure level to maximum. The water jerked into motion. She sipped the wine and put her glass on the shelf near the empty champagne glasses, then slid into the tub. It was noisy and wonderful, and the water pounded on her breasts and belly, and up her thighs. The tub was made for two, and she allowed herself the fantasy of Raphi joining her in it.

When she got out, he was in the living room reading. Bach was playing in the background. A brandy glass was on the low brass table. He poured one for her and she drank it.

"That was wonderful," she said. "Now all I need is a massage and I can go to heaven content."

He put down the book, grinning like a Cheshire cat. "I'd be only too happy to oblige."

She gave him a wary look from the side of her eyes.

"Seriously. Think of me as a eunuch. Massage was part of my martial arts training. We had to give massages every day."

He got up and came back carrying a plastic bottle and handed it to her. European Lavender Formula Massage Oil. She read the ingredients: almond oil, lavender, grape-seed oil, avocado oil, and lecithin. The last was waxy hygroscopic phosphatides used to form colloidal solutions, with emulsifying, wetting, and antioxidant properties. I am drunk, she thought, pouring a few fragrant drops on her fingers and rubbing them together.

"Come see," Raphi called from another room. "Will I convince you if you see we even have a professional table here? I give everyone massages. I'd like to make up to you for acting like a schmuck. If your bathing suit is wet, I'm sure you'll find something in one of the drawers."

The golden bikini beckoned. It was one size too small, pushing up her bust in the front and lying low on her hips. In her inebriated state, her belly managed to look sexy sticking out of the bikini bottom. She moved her hips like a belly dancer in front of the mirror, then slipped into the velour robe.

He was spreading a sheet and setting up an electric space heater. "Sometimes people feel cold after massage."

He really *had* done this before, she reasoned. The room was bare except for a large collection of antique-looking swords. Feeling shy, she slipped off her robe

and lay facedown on the table. There was a click of
a tape deck. The Bach was gone and then Indian sitar
music engulfed her. "Conditioning. I can't massage to
Renaissance music," he said. "Try to relax."

The oil was cool on her back. His hands pressed
into her lower back, just holding there. In slow circles
he moved between the two parts of the bathing suit.
"How does that feel?"

"Good," she whispered. The understatement of the
year.

Raphi moved to her calves and feet, stroking and
kneading, so that when he moved up to the thighs, it
felt natural and wonderful. She'd had massages by
women several times, but his hands were defter and
stronger, and they penetrated the muscles but didn't
hurt. She tried to relax and not to be turned on, but
there were tiny darts of pleasure between her legs. Six
months was too long to go without sex. Shame filled
her as she fantasied his fingers moving up over the
soft flesh between her legs. Her head pressed deeper
into the table to hide her flushed face. Once she
thought she felt his fingers brush by, but the touch
was so light she might have been imagining it. Could
he feel how damp and swollen she was?

When he got to the top of the thighs, he moved
back to her shoulders, working first on one and then
the other and finally kneading the tension between the
shoulder blades. Tingling spikes of desire ran through
her body, and her vagina and breasts never felt more
alive. And when he whispered for her to turn over, she
ached for his hands to come down onto her breasts. If
he even touched them, she thought she'd come. Sum-
moning more willpower than ever before in her life,
she evened out her breathing and pretended to sleep.
After a few seconds, he covered her with a blanket,
and she heard the door close.

Raphi went back to the living room and finished the
bottle of brandy. If he were honest with himself, the
idea of seducing her in order to get her to go back to
Manger College *had* gone through his mind. But he

had always despised operants who had used sex to reach their objectives, and she made him feel guilty for far less serious crimes. He wasn't thinking of espionage when he'd massaged her. He'd felt an awakening of tenderness, lust, and the desire to care for her.

Staying in the same house with Deborah hadn't been a good idea. It was the only thing he could think of when he got her resignation note and realized he'd have to act immediately.

They'd gone too far for her to back out.

He'd talked too much about himself over dinner. He always felt vulnerable, like Samson, when he revealed too much of himself. How could he explain the lapse? The wine? She'd disarmed him in the pool with her tears. He was getting too involved, he knew. Maybe it was just sex. He thought of her again lying there in his sister's old bikini and his prick throbbed. Shit. He was supposed to be running her, not falling in love with her.

Maybe he should phone Gil and ask him to come out. That would neutralize things. Then he thought of Gil lounging at the pool with her and wanted to rip out his best friend's throat.

Raphi looked outside. The waves were lapping against the beach, the moon lighting the sandy cliffs. A run along the beach was what he needed, but according to GSS orders he wasn't supposed to leave her alone at night.

The phone rang twice. The first caller slammed down the receiver when he heard his voice. Raphi regretted not having a machine that automatically identified the numbers of incoming calls. He'd have to get it from the service later. Within seconds the phone rang again. There was a secretary saying she was calling from the paint store, and then Gil was on the line. "We haven't turned up your European terrorist yet, but we're down from thousands to hundreds. And I did some snooping into a file on Dean Barguth. *Tres* classified, but I'm sure you'll repay me for taking such a risk. How about lending me your car for a year? It seems Barguth is very tight—are you ready for this?—with the prime minister himself. Hence the ban on penetrating the campus. Barguth is someone very important in the negotiations.

"Then there are those microphones your lady installed. They confirm that an attack involving the campus will take place within ten days. How are you doing at charming her into returning?"

Raphi sighed into the phone. "The score's not in yet. Keep working on that terrorist. If we unmask him, their entire action will unravel. I'm sure of it."

"Barguth's been phoning Deborah on the hour, offering her the moon if she returns. I suggest you let her listen to the tapes. He's a persuasive guy. Maybe you can learn something."

"Thanks, schmuck head," Raphi said.

"Love to you, too," Gil shot back before he hung up.

Raphi dialed Deborah's number, and entered the answering machine code to play her messages.

"My dear Mrs. Stern. I cannot express adequately my shock and sorrow at your experience at our campus yesterday. As soon as we determine who the perpetrator was, we will bring him to justice. Our new security system is in place, and we will provide personal escorts for you on campus. Our students could not sustain your loss as their guiding teacher at this time."

"Dear Mrs. Stern. You have not responded yet to my calls. Perhaps you are not home, because the flowers we sent you were delivered to your neighbor Mrs. Tzabah and await you. Again, we hope you are well and express our sincere apologies for the horrifying incident yesterday. In addition to any medical expenses you have incurred, Manger College is eager to pay you compensation as a token of our self-recriminations in not foreseeing the threat to you and somehow preventing it."

There were six calls. Variations on a theme.

He'd play them for Deborah first thing in the morning.

*   *   *

Joshua read the notice from the day camp: there had been a change in the program. Swimming had been arranged at a pool with separate hours for boys and girls. Ben and Sarah hadn't brought bathing suits, and he had no idea where to buy them. Deborah had always done the kids' shopping.

The thought of everyone swimming except for his kids galled him, especially since Ben and Sarah loved to swim. Deborah had taught them how as babies. Reluctantly, Joshua called her, but no one was home. He felt funny going in without telling her, even though it was still legally his home.

He knocked. No answer. He opened the door. The apartment was neat and still. Out of habit, he opened the refrigerator, and saw leftovers from Shabbat packed away in containers, labeled like science experiments. One pickling jar said "Cucumbers in NaCl." He took a pickle and walked through the house, going into their bedroom. It smelled of Deborah's floral body lotion. He ran his hand over the bed, and then struck it with an angry fist. When had Deborah gotten so stubborn?

The children's room already reflected subtle changes. Ben had taken the stuffed animals off his bed. In a jar on his bureau was a collection of apricot pits that kids used in a tossing game called *ajuim*. He'd played it himself as a boy growing up in Jerusalem, before Legos made their way over the sea.

Summer clothes were always put away in the bottom drawer and Joshua found the small bathing suits. He held up Sarah's. It was a match to a blue one of Deborah's, bought on a mother-daughter sale at a local boutique. In a drawer above it he found his own abandoned sport clothes. He picked up a T-shirt stained with paint and held it to his nose. A smell of kerosene had clung to it despite washing. Joshua thought of all the house painting he'd done with Deborah. They always wound up making love. For no good reason, he added the shirt to his pile of clothing.

The only thing out of place in the house was a stack of books on the dining room table: the long, historical romance novels Deborah read late into the night. Next to them was a note to Rachel: "Went out of town for a few days. Take whatever looks good to you. Here's my number if there's an emergency."

The first digits were 09. Herzliya-on-the-Sea. They didn't know anyone there. Could it be a biology convention at one of the hotels? She hadn't mentioned anything.

On impulse, he dialed the number.

When the man's voice answered at the other end, Joshua slammed down the receiver.

It all fit. Previously, Deborah had been reluctant to leave the children, even for a day. All of a sudden she was willing to let him take care of them to attend day camp. She'd left the children with him and gone away with a man, he thought, knocking the books to the floor.

Who could it be? He stomped around the apartment in a fury. The only candidate could be that intelligence man, Rachel's cousin. Joshua tried to recall him from Rachel's family parties. Short. A professional spook. Not Deborah's type.

The lawyer in Joshua asserted itself. She'd gone off with a man. She'd left the kids with their father. Well, she'd have to work hard to get them back. No court would force a nonabusive father to bring back his children from a summer vacation. Joshua knew that on a scale of fathers' sins, his would be considered trivial to any court, religious or secular. He'd given himself a break from family pressures after a traumatic military injury. His wife had refused to support him through it.

He'd file for divorce and demand custody. If he filed in the religious courts, he could count on the judges' being sympathetic for a religious husband whose wife had cuckolded him.

Let her deny she'd gone away with a man! He put the note in his pocket and went out, slamming the metal door.

Raphi had been dreaming of Deborah all night, so when the real Deborah appeared wearing a robe in the morning he couldn't stop himself. He pulled her into his arms and kissed her hair. He put his hand on her chin and leaned her head back to kiss her mouth, but she shook herself and pulled away.

"No," she said, closing her eyes and drawing a breath. "It will be too complicated."

"It's already too complicated," Raphi said. She was probably right, but he couldn't remember feeling so moved by a woman. He kissed her warm neck that smelled of the massage oil.

She was adamant. "There are issues you don't know about."

She was probably worried that if she made love with him she couldn't ever go back to Joshua. He wondered if oral sex counted. It wasn't the sort of question you could ask a rabbi.

He took a deep breath. "Okay. We can leave it for the time being. As long as you don't say never. I have something for you to listen to."

He played Deborah the answering machine tape.

"I feel embarrassed," Deborah said, drinking coffee. "Here I am sitting by the sea and everything seems out of proportion. Maybe I was too hasty in quitting. He's offering me double pay and to provide security. With what he's paying me and what you're paying me, I could take the kids for a real vacation next month. It's tempting. I'm surprised to hear myself asking this, but do you think I'd be crazy to go back?"

He shrugged. "Not crazy. There is a risk involved. I can't deny that. Sitting in Herzliya, risk always feels remote. The sound of the sea against the shore, the sunshine on the patio—it makes you feel very safe. That's the way it is. The moment the threat is over, denial kicks in, and you think you were just imagining the danger. I once came back from an action in Lebanon where we had to identify a Fatah leader's hideout and get out fast. I tripped on a garden hose, and set off an alarm. I barely escaped. By noon the next day I was running on the beach here, and I overheard a radio broadcast about our planes bombing the hideout. I couldn't believe I had anything to do with it. A week from now the bruises will have faded, and you'll be asking yourself if you imagined the whole incident.

"Barguth is offering you protection from inside—which, unfortunately, is more than I could really offer you. Those examinations really do seem to mean a lot to him. Also, he's stubborn, and you seem to have made quite an impression on him. From our point of view, I wish I could say that what you're doing is no longer important and that we don't care if you go back or not. But that would be a lie."

Deborah was thoughtful. "My kids won't be back for another week. He'll have to give me protection and schedule double classes so I can finish the material fast," she said. "I'm going for a swim. Then can you drive me back to Jerusalem?"

19

Joshua forced himself out of bed while it was still dark, following the strictest religious routine. Morning prayers could be said as soon as there was enough light to tell one shade of blue from another. He'd slept poorly. His dream last night had been that he was cutting his own throat.

Five clerks were processing divorce requests when Joshua arrived at the Jerusalem religious court. With a lawyer's precision, he filled in his request for child custody and hired a religious court advocate to get him immediate temporary custody. The children were already staying with him, and Deborah would have to fight to get them back. A date for a hearing was set for two weeks away. The whole business had taken fifteen minutes and his life was changed forever.

When he got back to the yeshiva, to his astonishment there was a message for him that the head of the yeshiva wanted to meet with him. Getting a private audience with the rebbe was an honor equivalent to having a supreme court judge invite an articles clerk for coffee.

The rebbe's study had the tinge of mustiness of a library, and the shelves literally sagged under the weight of tall books. "Come in. Sit down please," the rebbe said warmly. His soft blue eyes were always a surprise in the worn face of a small man nearly eighty. Joshua felt like throwing himself on the bony shoulders. The rebbe smiled. "Tell me how your studies are going and what is happening in your personal life."

The rebbe's eyes glowed as Joshua described his adventures with the complex texts. "Very good," he said, nodding. "I've heard you have a wonderful legal mind, and that you can appreciate the fine points of an argument. Now, what is happening between you and your wife?"

Joshua struggled to swallow. His voice became thick and sad. The rebbe listened as Joshua told him about Deborah spending a night in Herzliya with a man. "I'm sorry if I've shocked the rebbe," Joshua said, remembering not to call the rebbe "you".

The rebbe smiled. "People always think they're shocking me. Believe me, I've heard it all before." He sighed and leaned back. A glass of tea long ago gone cold stood on his desk. "I'm sure you've learned that it's a mitzvah to judge people favorably. You know that in theory, but are you practicing? Frequently our assumptions are wrong. Imagine, for instance, that someone took your favorite hat from a rack. You'd be very angry. Later you learn that the man was blind. Suddenly, you're not so angry. You're a lawyer. Imagine this case. A famous rabbi is accused of eating coffee and cake on the fast of Yom Kippur."

Joshua smiled. So did the rebbe. "It really happened," the rebbe said. "Two witnesses swore they'd seen him with the food in his hand. But what was the real story? The rabbi's daughter-in-law had just had a baby. Although she was exempt from the fast, she wanted to be stricter than the law and refused to eat *unless the rabbi himself brought her food.* You can imagine the rest.

"Perhaps your wife had a good reason for being in Herzliya and for not telling you. You must resist the urge to judge. Joshua, my son, that means judging yourself as well as others."

Those eyes seemed to see into Joshua's soul. He felt a moment of panic. Could the rebbe have guessed about his killing Oren? He swallowed hard. "I've not only judged Deborah, but I've handed down her sentence."

The rebbe shook his head. "The Talmud says that the holy altar itself weeps when a man divorces his first wife," the rebbe said. "This is a very serious decision. You have a tendency to act impulsively. But divorce is a process, and the wheels of our courts turn slowly on purpose. Nothing is irrevocable because you've filed a few papers."

Joshua felt foolish. "Even if I've threatened to take away the children?"

"Women are often forgiving. Our Torah says they are greater prophets than we men. Every time men have lost faith, they have been inspired by righteous women. Call her immediately and apologize. Bring back the children to show good faith."

The rebbe was telling him to give up his trump card. Joshua panicked. "But what if she *has* slept with another man? She is prohibited to me forever."

The rebbe looked stern. "Joshua, our laws are not made for self-flagellation. Do you have witnesses? We are instructed to *live* by the Torah, and to emulate divine love. Anger distorts our thinking and is a sin."

Joshua didn't like the idea of returning the children, but he felt obligated now to call Deborah and give her a chance to explain. He used the pay phone in the hall. As the phone rang lascivious pictures came to mind of her at the beach with Raphi. She loved the water. Despite the rebbe's caution against anger, the veins in his neck bulged. When the answering machine tone sounded, he slammed down the receiver.

The new electronic college gate was locked and a guard was on duty when Raba arrived. Her ID was checked with a magnetic scanner. Barguth's gloomy prediction was right: the feeling of being locked in detracted from the campus atmosphere and made everyone apprehensive. The students' body language reflected the new strain. The young men who usually sat in a wide circle under the pine trees were hunched together, as if in a football huddle, their backs stiff, their knees folded beneath them.

"What's going on?" Raba asked one of her students.

"It's the fence. An agitator is claiming that the Israelis are behind it, that the campus has been infiltrated by the GSS and we should strike in protest. Others have been arguing back that we should wait for the dean before taking any action."

"Where is Dr. Barguth?" Raba asked.

"At a meeting in Jerusalem. He won't be back until late afternoon."

So that was why Barguth had asked her to stay late today. Raba would be meeting with him at five o'clock. She heard the angry voices. "Is there any proof?"

"No. Just the fence, of course, and the presence of Mrs. Stern on campus. That redhead is claiming she's a spy and that the school is already bugged."

A redhead!

Raba moved around the circle of students and saw what had been obscured before: Sami was in the middle. Dear God, he isn't even a real student, Raba thought. He looks as natural here as he did on the animal wagon. She had to admire his spunk and versatility. He was so young, just like her brother.

The debate had evidently been going on for some time. Sami's voice was hoarse. "The campus has already been infiltrated by GSS agents. Why should we sit on our hands when the battle is here?" He was holding up a machine the size of a briefcase. "You'll see, I'll find proof."

One of the other students laughed. "That machine is good if you're bugging your bedroom to see if your wife has a secret lover. You can throw the machine under the bed and see if someone hollers." The others joined in the laughter. "Who are you trying to fool? Didn't anyone ever teach you that a sweeper is nearly useless on a campus even as small as ours? It can only pick up a transmission if it's pointed directly at the broadcast. Listening devices are tiny. Your chances of finding one are infinitesimal."

The laughter was louder now. Sami's face flushed. His scar was throbbing. Raba was relieved when someone came to his defense. "You're a newcomer," a student said. "This isn't Bir Zeit with its violent demonstrations.

We've kept it quiet here and we like it. Leave well enough alone."

Despite the students' disparaging comments, Sami's words had exacerbated tension. In her seminar, Raba's usually serious and quick-minded students seemed to be daydreaming. She too felt uneasy, and recalled Aunt Juni's warning. To make matters worse, Raba was feeling physically ill. The cramps came more often and she was more nauseous than she had been in the early months, when everybody expected morning sickness. After class, she walked as fast as she could without being conspicuous to the women's bathroom. She retched out her breakfast. Her knees were shaking. She tried to put her head between her knees, but it was easier to sit on the floor, her back propped against the stall divider, staring at the pale green tiles in the too bright incandescent light. She would have gone home, but she had that meeting with Barguth. He wanted her help on a grant to expand the psychology program, and the deadline was looming.

Her thoughts shifted to Sami and his claim that Barguth's beloved campus was bugged. It was hard to believe Deborah would be so foolhardy as to spy for the GSS on a Bethlehem campus. Her teaching talents had been demonstrated, and the reasons she'd given for working here were sound.

Maybe too sound.

Raba had been impressed that Deborah hadn't given idealistic reasons for coming to Bethlehem. She mistrusted all those Jews eager for "Arab-Jewish dialogue." Deborah had claimed her prime consideration for taking the job was career advancement. On the other hand, maybe Deborah realized that claims of "creating bridges" would sound self-righteous. Raba sighed. That was the kind of double guessing she and Ali had decided was pointless.

"If Deborah Stern were a spy, where would she plant a microphone?" Raba asked herself, talking out loud in English to clarify her thinking. "In places where students gathered. Like a student cafeteria."

She pulled herself up, brushed her hair, and put on

lipstick. Everyone ate at the cafeteria because it had the cheapest hot lunch in town. Her hand stopped in midair. Deborah hadn't been eating. Why would Deborah Stern go to the student cafeteria just for a cola? There was a soda machine near the faculty room. Raba hadn't thought of it before.

Deborah hated soft drinks without ice.

Raba's heart beat fast. Still queasy, she walked slowly across campus. A student stopped her and wanted to talk about an assignment. Raba put her off.

Sami's red hair was easy enough to spot. Raba came up behind him. "Could I speak to you for a minute?" she whispered.

Sami looked surprised but pleased, and walked with her to the arch of the building. She whispered, "If there were a bugging device, how *would* you tell?"

Sami grinned, looking boyish. "There are devices that pick up the current, but you have to point the sweeper at the exact spot. The broadcasting frequency is usually very high. To tell you the truth, I was supposed to plant one and find it later, but now the students would never believe me."

"That might not be necessary," Raba said. "Do you have that detector with you?"

"Right here," he said, lifting a briefcase.

Raba frowned. "How did you ever sneak it past the guard?"

"Baksheesh," said Sami, using the Middle Eastern word for a bribe. "It's amazing what a carton of Marlboros will do."

Well, so much for Barguth's high-tech system, she thought. Technology is only as high as the level of integrity. She explained about meeting Deborah in the lunchroom.

Sami gave a shout of triumph. He waved one arm, palm up. "After you, *aldocktora.*"

All the tables were taken in the noisy cafeteria. The aroma that had smelled so wonderful in the past now made Raba feel sick. She pointed to the table she'd shared with Deborah, and Sami got out the machine. Several students holding food trays gathered around.

The dial didn't move. Raba's stomach ached.

Sami's face was mottled with embarrassment. Raba felt mortified too. "I'm sure it was this table," she said. "I ate here with Deborah."

Sami's face lit up. "My dear Raba. The tables are moved every night when the floor is mopped."

She felt hopeful. "I hadn't thought of it."

There were only six tables. Sami pointed his sweeper at each of them. Nothing happened. Several of the students snickered. She was about to leave in defeat when Sami touched her arm. "Wait," Sami said. "Over there." He pointed at a corner where two additional tables were folded.

He aimed the sweeper.

Clearly and sweetly, it beeped.

Carefully, he brought it closer to the table. The sound got louder. Wedged into the chewing gum was a tiny listening device.

There was loud noise in the dining room, as curious students pressed closer. Sami waved them back as he squatted by the table. When his hand was an inch away from the device he stopped.

He touched his forehead to show he was thinking, then moved his two forefingers back and forth, crisscrossing in a gesture that meant no. Everyone understood. If he took the bug away they'd know for sure it had been discovered. As if directing traffic, he gestured for them to go back to lunch and continue talking. The students nodded and silently made the victory sign.

The news spread of Sami and Raba finding the device. Out in the courtyard, students gathered around them. "You have your proof," Sami said. He sounded cocky, but he deserved to after his humiliation. "What more do you need before you fight back against the occupation and take control of your own campus?"

Raba's role was being passed mouth to mouth. The students smiled at her in complicity. Oddly, she had rarely felt so depressed. When she was a senior in high school she'd been awarded the Betty Crocker Prize for cooking. She was the worst cook in the class,

but the award was based on a standardized test and
not kitchen skills. The other girls, who could turn out
perfect dumplings, rightfully resented her. But she had
no choice other than to accept the award at gradua-
tion. The same feeling of unworthiness came back now
as students made victory Vs with their fingers to her.
They all assumed falsely that she was devoted to
their cause.

She retreated to the library and tried, fruitlessly, to
write the grant proposal. She sat back, reflecting. On
one hand, despite the evidence, it seemed hard to believe Deborah would risk her life to spy in Manger
College. She had children. Even with an enormous
financial payoff, it sounded far-fetched. On the other
hand, the more she thought of Deborah playing them
all for fools, the angrier she got. Raba read what she'd
written, decided it was nonsense, and crumpled the
paper. In the slowly passing minutes she nursed her
anger while she waited for Barguth.

As Raphi was driving Deborah back to Jerusalem,
Private Naomi, monitoring the listening devices in
Manger College from the mobile station in the hillside
city of Efrat, heard a message alarming enough for
her to report it to the GSS duty officer in Jerusalem.

"Is there any way you can shut off the bugs from
outside the campus?" Anat asked.

Naomi hesitated. "No. That's one of their short-
comings."

"Well, then, if there isn't anything we can do about
it, there's no use worrying, is there?"

Anat recorded the message in the log book and
went for lunch.

When a very frantic Naomi called back a half hour
later, there was no answer.

Abed believed Raba's discovery of the listening device was a divine sign. If Sami alone had found it,
students would have suspected a plant. But no one
would question Raba.

The moment for action had arrived. Abed gave Sami firm instructions to be in Bethlehem at 5:00 P.M.

The timing couldn't be better. Sami had said the student organization was meeting in an emergency session. Violent campus protests were scheduled for that evening. Out of respect, the students were waiting for Dr. Barguth.

Abed would make sure he wouldn't arrive.

Barguth had returned home after his morning meeting in Jerusalem. According to his housekeeper, whose brother was on Abed's payroll, Mrs. Barguth always had a hearty lunch prepared on days like today when he didn't go to campus in the morning. The dean never rushed this meal, taking time for a cigarette and coffee. Often he took a short nap and made love to his wife. He was a lusty man. According to the housekeeper, Mrs. Barguth's bathroom had a disgraceful collection of flavored douches the dean had bought on a fund-raising trip to Paris.

Abed hid behind an almond tree. Barguth's Volvo was in the driveway. Ever since he'd decided to kill George Barguth, Abed had been thinking of an efficient way to do it. A car bomb was out of the question. Barguth checked under his car with a periscope ever since an Arab mayor had his legs blown off by a Jewish reactionary group. He might also notice the slight rise in a seat indicating a pressure bomb. Shooting, even if he used a silencer, could be noisy. It would be hard to keep a bullet from hitting the windshield. The dean was thick-necked. Abed looked at his fingers. Even for him, strangling would be difficult.

Abed's hands ran over his *jambiya*, an Arabian dagger with a dual-edged, curved blade. He waited patiently, reciting portions of the Koran to pass the time.

At last, at 4:15, Barguth left the house, patting his wife playfully on the behind. A beep came from the car. Abed's heart skipped a beat, until he realized it was only a remote-control mechanism for the car door. The dean looked under the car with a periscope, opened the door and sat down, placing the remote control on the seat.

Abed stepped forward. "Dr. Barguth," Abed said in his most obsequious voice. Barguth was startled, but then took on a forbearing look. He sneaked a look at the car clock. Abed knew he was in a hurry and wouldn't be paying full attention.

Abed approached the car. "Excuse me. Could I have a minute of your time?"

Barguth rolled down the window all the way and cleared his throat. "Yes, certainly."

"I studied business administration in Sweden and wondered if you were looking for staff in your college."

Barguth looked vaguely interested and volunteered to take his name and information to set up an appointment. He reached for a pen, but Abed stopped him. "Here, let me," he said.

Abed leaned in the window. He reached into his shirt. Barguth's eyes widened as he saw the knife. Abed was too quick for him. Even at this difficult angle, the knife cut easily through Barguth's thick skin. Abed sliced a smile line from the back of Barguth's neck in one motion. After a spatter, blood came spurting from the carotid artery. Abed was ready for it and jumped back. Barguth's cry for help was stifled by the blood being sucked in and out of his severed trachea. A curious scent of talcum powder came rushing up with the blood, as if Barguth had heavily powdered his neck after a shower. Abed waited for the blood flow to slow to a spray then pushed Barguth over to the passenger seat. His body slid to the floor, staining it red.

Abed reached in the back to look for something to cover the driver's seat. He jerked back in dread. The backseat was covered with twisting snakes! He reached for his knife, then realized the snakes were plastic. Chiding himself for foolishness but still shaken, Abed took a tartan blanket from the backseat.

Abed's fingers closed around the steering wheel. The Volvo felt familiar; he'd often driven Kirsten's in Sweden. Abed drove to a cliff not far from Shepherds' Fields. He dragged the body from the car and tumbled it down the hill. The snakes puzzled him and made him feel unlucky, so he threw them away, too.

He stopped at a well and washed his hands, face, and neck. Then he went to meet Sami in Manger Square.

Deborah could hardly believe she was on her way back to Bethlehem. She reprimanded herself for being fickle.

Last night she'd spoken at length with Barguth. He suggested the rescheduling of her class to late afternoon, so he could personally be on campus when she returned. The campus would be quiet in the late afternoon, he reminded her, because most of the faculty went home by then. There would only be her own students and whoever stayed on to use the library or computers. Since she was reluctant to take the campus van, he'd sent a cab for her. He promised to wait for her just inside the new gate to show her his support. The arrangements seemed adequate.

She was learning that one crisis could simply overshadow another. When she'd come home from Herzliya she'd received a phone call from a rabbinical court advocate hired by her husband. Joshua wanted to divorce her. He had the children and the advocate vowed to help Joshua keep them permanently.

Deborah had told him to fuck himself, knowing that childish behavior had to work against her but was simply unable to control herself. When she got off the phone she was short of breath, terrified and angry.

She would never forgive Joshua for threatening her with her children!

In a panic she'd called Raphi, got his answering machine, and asked if the GSS could really exert influence on the courts. Then she'd called Rachel, who'd paged her husband in court. Dan was a patent lawyer, but he might know someone who could help. When he heard that a rabbinical advocate would be her adversary, he suggested she hire one herself—but a woman. There was a new school for women rabbinical advocates, gaining an excellent reputation. Deborah liked the idea of a woman defending her. No, correct that. She didn't like the idea of anyone having to defend her. What a fool she'd been to let Joshua take the children! How could he twist that against her in court? He had been a vicious and manipulative lawyer against those he'd considered his enemies. She thought of all the ways he would try to make her seem like an unfit mother. What if he found out about her job in Bethlehem? Exposing herself and the children to danger wouldn't endear her to a family-centered court. The heaviness in her chest felt like a millstone.

As the taxi approached the gate she pulled herself together. It couldn't be worse than her first day and she'd survived that. She checked her Seiko. 5:05.

At the guard's booth she showed her pass. The handsome young guard with a mustache was new.

Deborah was prepared for anything but the stony silence that greeted her.

Her eyes flitted around the campus, and then back to her watch. 5:07. There was no sign of Dr. Barguth. Only about twenty students were in the wide space between the buildings. Oddly, they were wearing Arab headdresses—the men with keffiyahs and the women in white scarves. They were all staring at her.

Could the listening devices have been found? Raphi had assured her there was an instant-warning system. A team was listening twenty-four hours a day and would notify Jerusalem within seconds if there was even a suspicion that the bugs were located. Where the hell was Barguth?

If they hadn't found the devices, there was nothing they could hold against her. All she could do was act as if nothing was wrong. She started walking to her classroom. The several dozen men and women gathered together into a mob. It moved toward her, from every direction, as in the worst of her nightmares. Jehan, one of her own women students, broke the silence. "Stinking Zionist whore," Jehan yelled, shoving her. "We invite you here and you bug our campus." The crowd tightened around Deborah like a noose.

Another woman kicked her. "Filthy, lying Jew."

Panic turned to a fighting rage for survival. Every childhood Holocaust image forged with her current reality. She whirled around and slammed her briefcase into the woman's face. With her left arm, she elbowed another. A man stepped forward, and Deborah smashed down his toes with her heels on his open sandals. Her knee connected with another man's groin and she felt the soft squash of his penis. Surprise had given her the initial advantage, but when it was gone, she was hopelessly outnumbered. In self-defense class they'd practiced fighting a crowd. Raphi had said to concentrate on the leader, and to attack him first. The problem was that she couldn't identify the leader. She dropped to the ground, and spun in a circle, kicking outward as she turned. For a moment her foot kept them at bay, then three men attacked her from different directions. Hands pressed her throat, and her breath was being cut off. Her scalp burned from hair being pulled. Someone knocked her feet from under her. Then a heavy object came down on her head. The pain was excruciating before everything went mercifully black.

20

Abed locked Barguth's car in a back alley of Bethlehem, slipping the remote control into his pocket. He held strips of Bethlehem postcards: scenes of the church, a Bedouin in a flowing robe, statues of the Prince of Peace. The words "shepherd" and "Bethlehem" were misspelled, and the faded colors reminded him of paint-by-numbers sets sold in his mother's grocery store. Still, like Shafi's trinkets, gullible tourists bought them.

Sami was in the square selling postcards, too. His were a yard long, showing golden views of Jerusalem and Bethlehem.

Abed came up close and whispered for Sami to follow. "What's happening on campus?"

"Our people have taken over, but they're stalling about more drastic action before Barguth returns. They're loyal, and since there's proof that the GSS infiltrated their campus, they believe he'll come over to their side."

"What makes them so sure he'll go along?"

"They say he's levelheaded and protective of his campus, but a passionate Palestinian patriot in his own way. I don't think he'll have a choice. The students are already piling up tires to burn outside the gate. The campus will be fully radicalized by next week, when we act."

Abed's voice dropped. "Circumstances have changed. The attack will take place tomorrow morning."

Sami looked startled. "Why so soon?"

Abed felt a lurking suspicion that there was something behind Sami's concern. "Why not?"

Sami took short puffs on his cigarette. "No reason. I was surprised, that's all. I assumed we'd have all week to plan."

Or you'd have time to tell my enemies, Abed thought. He'd keep his eye on Sami. Unfortunately, Sami's knowledge of explosives was indispensable.

Motioning for Sami to follow, Abed went around the back to Holyland Treasures. He opened the door without knocking. Inside, John Shafi was counting profits. Stacks of dollars, yen, deutschemarks, francs, and pounds were on the table. Sami's eyes widened.

"Didn't you know the merchants of Bethlehem were the best robbers in the world?" Abed asked derisively.

Without looking up, Shafi scowled and gestured to a room to the right. "Everything you ordered and more is in the back room. Take what you need." He picked up the money and left.

Abed called after him. "Regards from your grandson." Shafi didn't even turn. Arrogant Christian bastard, Abed thought.

As insurance against Shafi selling him to the GSS, Anwar had been appointed to the resistance steering committee. Money could buy anything, except when family was concerned.

Inside the storage room, an entire wall was stacked with boxes marked "Madonna and Child" and "Singing Jesus." They were brought in by the thousand from Poland, where former KGB officials sold stolen Soviet ordnance.

Abed's hands were shaking so badly that he had to concentrate so he didn't drop the boxes. He hadn't realized how excited he was. It wasn't surprising. The biggest event of his life had begun.

He put a box down on the table and ordered Sami to open it. Sami's fingers were still swollen from his injuries in the jail, but he deftly pulled out a plaster statue. The Madonna was smiling wide, holding a blond, blue-eyed Jesus. Not your typical Palestinian boy, Abed thought, as Sami turned the statue over. "There's definitely something in it," Sami said, his voice high. The bottom had been glued in place. He pried it off with a rusty nail file he kept in his pocket.

Sami's face was radiant.

"What did he get?" Abed asked.

"PETN and RDX."

"RDX?"

"Cyclonite. It's in the blasting cap, too. That and lead azide for a priming charge. We used it at the quarry when we could get it."

"Singing Jesus" featured a crêche with microphone and remote control so a family could make it sound as if the three wise men were singing over the baby. "Contains all you need, including batteries, extension cord" was printed on the box in red and green. Brilliant, Abed thought. No one would check the strength of the remote control or that the insulated wire was a cheap detonator cord nearly identical to reinforced Primacord. In another box was a motion sensor to activate the charge.

Sami prepared his charges, talking almost constantly. He'd learned a lot in the quarry, he said. A short-delay technique was used in which a number of charges were detonated at very short intervals to produce a ripple of explosives along the quarry face. He wanted to do something similar in the Church of the Nativity. Abed listened, increasingly impressed with Sami's knowledge. Sami bragged that he'd stolen textbooks on explosives from the Hebrew University's Harman Science Library in Jerusalem. "Now their books on explosives are locked up," he smirked.

Through the slit window near the ceiling, Abed saw the sky fade from blue to gray. The peddlers and priests went home. Manger Square became quiet. Except for Christmas Eve, when an elaborate noisy show was broadcast from here to the whole world, tourists avoided Bethlehem after dark. An Australian tourist had recently been stabbed to death while kneeling in prayer.

The square was dark when Sami finished. A cool breeze rustled paper litter. The homey smell of meat soup came from a nearby apartment. Abed's stomach rumbled, and he wondered what his mother had prepared for dinner.

First they had to break into the church. No one had ever broken in before, so security was relaxed. Army patrols with spotlights came by the square several times a night. A Palestinian night watchman passed only on the half hour, but Abed was cautious and wanted him out of the way before they started.

Sami, holding the explosives, went to reconnoiter. Abed had a spool of rope from the storeroom. He could cut it with his knife. He also had filled his sports bag with tools. He waited behind the protrusion of rock wall that separated the parking lot from the church courtyard for the night watchman to walk by. Only recently had the Israelis agreed to the Palestinians' having a Tourist Police Force in Bethlehem. Abed considered anyone who joined it a traitor and therefore deserving of death.

Abed saw the watchman coming, an M-1 rifle slung on his shoulder. He was at least fifty-five. That's how old my father would have been if he'd lived, Abed thought. He felt the usual welling of sadness that came whenever he thought of his father. He wished his father were here now to share in his triumph.

When the watchman approached, Abed stepped forward and grabbed him by the neck, squeezing hard. The man's eyes popped outward. Abed heard a gasp behind him. Sami. "Allah's mercy. It's Mohammed Aziz. He's a friend's father," Sami said. "A devout Moslem with fourteen children. Spare him."

Abed loosened his grip, glad that the night hid his embarrassment. Sami handed him rope and they gagged and tied up the man. I'll make this work for me, Abed thought. "When the Israelis come, tell them the church is wired. If they don't follow our instructions it will be reduced to rubble. Do you understand?"

The elderly watchman nodded, a tear rolling from one eye.

Abed and Sami approached the church. The door was secured with an old-fashioned lock and chain. It was soft iron so Abed cut it with an ordinary hand file.

They closed the door behind them.

The first charge would be set in the low entrance. There was more than one way to encourage a person to bow, Abed thought.

The second bomb would be placed on the ancient mosaic floor, sunken below today's floor level in the basilica. The biggest blast would be in the Grotto of the Nativity. The Catholic chapel was to the left of the Orthodox. That would be wired, too, as a special gesture to the Vatican.

Sami laid his charges: a series of radio-controlled detonators, backed up by trip wires and a motion detector. If somehow the Jews overrode their communications, they would trip the wires as they came into the church and blow themselves up. If they found the trip wires, the motion detector would find them. Sami told him it would take a genius to take it apart without knowing in which of the hanging lanterns the motion detector was.

Abed walked around the church as Sami worked. He couldn't help admiring the 1600-year-old building and hoped he wouldn't have to destroy it. In Damour, Lebanon, Moslems had turned Christian churches into shooting ranges. He paced as Sami knelt on the mosaic floor, laying out his battery, the blasting caps, and the explosives. Again he prayed Sami could be trusted. Feeling he was being scrutinized, Sami looked up and signaled.

Now it was Abed's turn. He took the wire that would serve as an antenna out the window and climbed onto the roof. Dew had made the stones slippery and there was little moon to see by. The night wind blew cold on his neck.

Over the centuries the church had been added to many times, making the roof a dozen different heights, with at least three bell towers with crosses on top. Abed tripped on electric wires that must have been left from last Christmas, but he caught himself. He edged up the side of a tall bell tower.

A breeze made the bell sway. Abed held the wire in his teeth, and in one movement he grasped the crown of the bell, put his legs around the bell waist, and held the clapper between his feet. It was damp, and when he tried to rise, his body slid down toward the sound bow. He was afraid that if he moved the clapper would strike. Moving inch by inch, he raised himself to the roof of the bell tower, carefully releasing the clapper.

No sound. He was high off the ground. Don't look down, he ordered himself. He reached up and wound the wire around the traverse beams.

When Abed got down, Sami was finishing off. His face glowed with the excitement of a pyromaniac at a fire. They checked the watchman, who was still securely tied.

Abed felt exuberant. It had gone so easily. Sami started to talk, but Abed put his finger to his lips.

Part one was done. Now for part two. It was nearly midnight and Sami had to set the charges on the road from Bethlehem.

Sami smoked a cigarette and then opened the next box. He pulled out the Madonna. "This one's empty," he shrugged. "Must have forgotten to load it, or maybe it's a decoy."

He opened the next box. It, too, was empty, and then two more. Sami's voice cracked. "We're out of explosives."

Abed didn't want to believe it. He tore through the rest of the boxes. Only empty statues remained. Abed smashed a Madonna, her foolishly smiling head rolling across the floor. "That fucking swindler!"

Shafi lived in the village of Beit Sahur. There was no time to go find him. Besides, Abed suspected he might not be home.

"Never mind," Sami said. "We can always steal explosives."

That was a new thought. Abed's spirits rose. "Can we really?"

"There are quarries all around Bethlehem. We don't need anything fancy. TNT will do."

Abed didn't like being so dependent on Sami, but there was no choice. He directed Sami to the car.

"Isn't this Barguth's car you're using?" Sami asked. "Did he lend it to you?"

"Something like that," Abed said. He put the tools and extra rope on the floor of the passenger seat. Even in the dark he could see them absorb bloodstains.

Sami must have noticed the blood. He gave Abed the directions and lapsed into uncharacteristic silence. "There it is," Sami said, pointing at a prefab building amid slabs of unfinished dolomite. "The equipment is locked inside each night."

Abed broke the lock and followed Sami over electric saws, chisels, and shovels to a supply room lined with metal shelves.

In Libya, Abed had taken a rudimentary course in explosives and had enjoyed the mathematics—calculating the speed of burning detonator cord against the speed of oncoming vehicles. But he'd never had practical experience beyond a few training exercises when they blew up abandoned warehouses. Watching Sami work today, he understood why other terrorists called Sami "the engineer." Sami opened boxes and bags like a lad in a candy store, nodding his head and talking about what he'd found. The bottom shelf had boxes of TNT, packed in five-kilo sacks. Sami stuck in his finger, expressing satisfaction that no dampness had invaded. On the middle shelf were bricks of pentolite, a mixture of TNT and pentaerythritol tetranitrate. He opened a second cabinet and took blasting caps. Just to be sure, he took what was left on a spool of black detonator cord, adhesive tape, and, because Sami was cautious, a handful of precut white blasting fuses. He opened a deep drawer and smiled: inside was a detonating battery.

When Abed tried to take the blasting cap from him, Sami shook his head. "You take the dynamite. These are sensitive."

Abed opened one of the heavy sacks. The material inside looked as innocuous as whole-grain flour. He loaded the Volvo, then went back for pickaxes, shovels, and, as a last-minute inspiration, two orange vests of construction workers. Abed looped the detonator cord around his arm.

Sami baby-sat the blasting caps in the backseat where the snakes had been. He'd become talkative again, and his chatter was getting on Abed's nerves. "These big sacks are nearly harmless without the detonators. Now one of these," he said, holding up a blasting cap and smiling, "could send us to heaven. They're a good kind, with the wires meeting in a piece of fuse initiated at both ends. The effect is cumulative."

Abed drove carefully and was glad the Volvo was well sprung. The road between the checkpoint and Bethlehem curved over a field planted in pumpkins. Only the rare car taking the turn off to Kibbutz Zayit Ra'anan would go this way. To their right was a stone memorial for an Israeli woman whose car had been hijacked near French Hill. Near it, the asphalt of the road had buckled and a patch of dirt waited for new paving. In the rearview mirror, he and Sami looked at each other and shared a smile. They both believed in signs. This was the perfect spot.

They worked without torches. One car passed, but since construction work was often done at night no one took notice of Arabs digging ditches. Sami stuffed each hole with TNT. The white Mercedes school bus was a model used for tourists, high off the ground with a thick box for luggage underneath. Even if it was empty the box would protect the chassis from real damage. The explosion would damage the box and blow out the tires. The driver would have to stop. Other charges were set to damage the back of the bus. Sami explained that he was using a ring main system, a circular arrangement that meant the fire would burn from both sides to the TNT buried in the ground. He ran the wires into an olive tree, and then camouflaged the battery with olive leaves.

Sami's forehead creased with worry.

"What now?" Abed asked.

"I need to find a way to activate the solenoid without setting us off, too." Sami rubbed his face, his thumb moving over his scar. At last his face lit up.

He sprinted to Barguth's car, reached onto the seat and took the remote-control unit for the car's lock. "It transmits infrared waves. The same system that switches the power to the solenoids of the car's central locking system can power our detonator." He cut out the receiver and solenoid from under the hood, wires still hanging, and attached. Then, before finally connecting the detonator wires, he fired the remote control to the solenoids a dozen times. With each test he stepped several feet farther from the battery, testing the activator time. When finally the detonator no longer fired, he moved three yards closer and set the remote control down. This was its safe range. From there they would fire the charge.

Sami worked for a half hour. A tank could go over the TNT and nothing would happen, he said, until the detonators were lit. He pronounced the system perfect. Abed felt something loosen inside him. The first light of day shone pink in the distance. Islam declared this the peaceful hour, when special influences acted on the soul. During the month of Ramadan, fasting commenced from the moment a Moslem could tell the difference between a white and black thread.

Abed and Sami turned toward Mecca, fell on their faces, and prayed.

> *"Show us the straight way,*
> *The way of those on whom*
> *Thou has bestowed Thy Grace,*
> *Those whose portion*
> *Is not wrath*
> *And who go not astray."*

A rooster crowed in the distance. Dew covered the plowed fields, glowing in the dawn. Abed, as was his custom, added his own *ayat* from the Koran:

> *"Follow thou the inspiration*
> *Sent unto thee and be*
> *Patient and constant, till Allah,*

> *Does decide: for He
> Is the Best to decide."*

He and Sami rose together, as if they'd synchronized their motion. Our hearts are bent to the same purpose and we will have Allah's blessing, Abed thought.

Sami moved to the hillside, fifty yards away where he'd left the remote control, idly picking the weeds. He placed the remote-control device beside him.

Abed climbed up a hill behind the olive trees and went over the calculations. Sami had estimated that it would take a quarter to a half second for the solenoid at the battery to read the message and transfer the spark to the TNT. Abed wished it was more exact. He calculated that the bus would be coming along the old road about thirty miles per hour, or forty-four feet a second. The quarter-second uncertainty meant an eleven-foot potential error. He'd set the charge when the bus was fifteen feet before the explosion. The side blast would smooth out the error. He marked the roadside with a stone fifteen feet before the charge.

His eyes squinted past the rock terraces to see the cars traveling toward Bethlehem from Jerusalem. Most were private cars, carrying teachers and businessmen to jobs in the area. A few were Arab women taking driver-education courses in cars marked with a learner's tag. At 7:37, Abed saw a white tourist bus turning the bend from Jerusalem. The sun caught its roof and glared in his eyes. As it came closer, he could see it was half empty and that some of the girls were standing in the aisles, talking to their friends. His pulse accelerated.

The bus turned right off the main road. It drove onto the patch of dirt road at exactly 7:40.

Abed signaled Sami with the uplifted fighter's fist of victory. He saw Sami pick up the remote-control device and press. Then his eyes shifted back to the roadside. He held his breath and counted.

At first Raphi wasn't alarmed when he hadn't heard from Deborah. She'd said that after Bethlehem she was going to the gym. The gym closed late. He wondered if she'd realized the GSS had arranged her membership. Nonetheless, by midnight he started to worry. He tried to work off his mounting tension. In his routine, he stood absolutely still, holding his right fist in front of his chest. Slowly he raised a left hammer fist high in front of his forehead, then struck down from his shoulder level, gradually increasing power. He did this over and over for twenty minutes, fighting the urge to speed up. For the next hour he practiced kicking, stabbing from every angle until his T-shirt and jeans were drenched with sweat.

Still no call. Could Barguth have double-crossed Deborah? It seemed unlikely. Maybe she was just being difficult again. No, she had a temper, but when Deborah promised she'd do something she came through. At 2:00 A.M. he phoned her house. The answering machine picked up. "Deborah, please phone immediately, no matter what hour," he said. Then he monitored her phone machine. He heard his own message first. He sounded tense and peremptory. There were calls from Rachel, a call from her boss at Hadassah Hospital, and finally from Joshua's rabbinical court advocate. Raphi's visceral reaction that she was getting divorced was joy, but he worried about her having to wage a messy custody battle.

If she was still alive.

The phone jolted him. Deborah, he thought, with relief. Raphi grabbed the phone. "Hello."

"Raphi, bad news." It was Gil. *My God. Had she been killed?*

"What is it? Deborah?"

Gil seemed confused. "Why, no. Has anything happened to Deborah?"

"I don't know. I haven't heard from her."

"I'm calling with other bad news. But since you mention Deborah, I did want to tell you that I was reading over the log book and saw a strange notation during the day from the noontime duty officer. It appears that a "female woman's voice—American—in the faculty bathroom—said something about finding microphones—maybe in the cafeteria. I checked with the listening team. After that, the mike picked up noise and shouting in the cafeteria, then the voices stopped, and, when the students began talking again, the conversation was nonsensical, as if they knew they were being listened to."

"When was the report made?" Raphi asked, holding his breath.

"Wait a minute. Between one and two p.m."

"Deborah went to Bethlehem at five. If there was a problem, we could have stopped her! Who the hell was on duty?"

But Raphi knew the answer before Gil told him it was Anat.

"Goddamn her!" Raphi shouted. "Deborah's out there alone. They might kill her. I'm going out!"

"In the middle of the night? According to you, she got there nine hours ago. You're a little late. And we've got a bigger problem: Barguth's missing. Evidently he was doing some fancy negotiations with the government yesterday, but he didn't call the prime minister's office at 10:00 P.M. as he'd promised. He went home for lunch and never showed up at school."

No wonder Deborah hadn't called. Barguth hadn't shown up himself, let alone offered her protection.

Gil was still talking. "The prime minister has made finding Barguth top priority. Cohen is calling an emergency meeting."

Raphi drove like a madman. His face was twisted with rage when five minutes later he slammed the door of the GSS office. *This is the room where we conspired to convince Deborah to spy for us,* he thought bleakly. The GSS psychologist had suggested they create an exaggerated, farcical scene where Deborah would feel like the only sane one in the room. When the scene turned ridiculous Raphi would become very serious and make Deborah feel guilty. Their custom-tailored psychological recruitment had worked perfectly.

The GSS had used her, and Raphi had played the

largest role. Deep down, he knew his anger was at himself.

The living room stank from too many stale cigarettes and too much black coffee. Raphi remembered how, also at the psychologist's suggestion, they'd aired it out the night of Deborah's recruitment. Tonight the bulletproof windows were tightly shut and an air conditioner thudded in the background. It reminded Raphi of a closed wing in a mental hospital. Moshe Cohen was leaning back in an armchair watching his own smoke rings rise to the ceiling. Gil was drinking coffee, in short, tense sips. Uzi—like the gun—and Jacques, the two other men who formed the original core of their unit, were sitting on the couch, conversing quietly in French. Today was their first day back after a special assignment. *You were here to vote against me last time,* Raphi thought bitterly, remembering the painful four-to-one vote that had pressured him to begin the search for a nonprofessional woman to go undercover. *Are you here to vote against me today?* Uzi and Jacques were partners, and also homosexual lovers. Brilliant undercover agents, they had been on loan to the air force to investigate a bribery charge against a gay aeronautical engineer. Ironically, if they'd been on duty Anat wouldn't have been imported to round out the team. Uzi and Jacques were professionals, and would never have allowed personal jealousies to influence them. Deborah would be sleeping in her bed, her blond hair spread on a pile of pillows.

"Where's Anat?" Raphi asked, pushing aside a metal chair.

"We had Uzi and Jacques back, so we didn't call her in tonight," Moshe Cohen said, watching his face.

Raphi knew it was a lie. Cohen had sent Anat away until Raphi cooled down.

"Why are we here anyway? Let the Palestinians look for Barguth. Who the fuck cares what happened to him?" Raphi asked, his voice dropping low. He picked up Cohen's pack of Marlboros, took the last cigarette, and lit it, inhaling in an exaggerated European way. Raphi hardly ever smoked, they all knew. It was a signal that his lethal temper was just barely leashed.

Cohen refused to be hooked. "Who cares about Barguth? The prime minister, that's who cares. And Yasser fucking Arafat. And the president of Russia. And the president of the United States. Maybe Mrs. Barguth." Cohen made a mirthless smile showing tobacco-stained teeth. "It seems that at yesterday's meeting Barguth had initialed an agreement for the Palestinians. All of you political sophisticates are aware that there have been long-standing complaints among rank-and-file Palestinians against PLO officials. After years of sacrifice for the intifada, the locals resent their foreign-based fat cats boozing and womanizing in Europe. They've insisted on being part of the final agreement. Barguth is accepted by everyone. He's old-guard PLO—was a supporter since the organization was founded in 1964. On the other hand, he watched his fanny and didn't get expelled from the country and subsequently murdered by his own Palestinians like Kawasmeh of Hebron. And if that weren't enough, he has another feather in his hat. While other educators were calling strikes, South African style, Barguth was educating a generation for leadership. Half the potential Palestinian bureaucrats in a future Palestinian government will be graduates of his college, owing personal loyalty to him. If George Barguth goes along with the agreements, the local gangs with the rocks go along. The local leaders go along. The PLO in Tunisia goes along."

"What precisely is being signed?" Gil asked, putting down his coffee cup.

"A peace treaty. Between Israel and the PLO. Somewhere in Norway. It's being negotiated so secretly even we don't officially know about it."

Raphi heard the biting anger in his own voice. "If I understand you correctly, you mean Deborah walked into the campus of a top leader in the territories despite an explicit order from the prime minister to stay away—and bugged his bathroom?"

"Something like that," Cohen said, reaching for a cigarette and remembering they were all gone. His voice took on an exaggerated patience like a kindergarten teacher's. "As you recall, it was more complicated. We still think something is going to happen in Bethlehem, and all the arrows point to Manger College. It could be that fundamentalists have chosen it to embarrass Barguth, or it might just be one of those horrible coincidences. They were looking for an unlikely site and may have been as ignorant as we were of Barguth's importance. Without realizing they were stepping on big feet, they targeted Manger College, maybe because security was relaxed there. Ironically, by placing the microphones, we may have precipitated an action."

"You mean we fucked up royally," Gil said.

"That remains to be seen," Moshe said.

Raphi silently cursed himself a hundredth time for being part of this. The phone rang.

With a butcher's thick fist, Cohen picked up one of the dozen smudged phones in the room. His lined face tightened and his hand went to his chest. He'd had a coronary bypass last year. To Raphi, the room felt like a graveyard when Cohen daintily put down the receiver. "Barguth's body has been found in Shepherds' Fields."

Cohen took a ragged breath. Raphi could smell his perspiration across the room. "It gets worse. A bus of students has been blown up near Bethlehem. The survivors have been taken hostage to . . ." he paused, "Manger College.

"There's one last item. The guard at the Church of the Nativity was found tied up and gagged. He claims two Palestinians did it, and that they told him the church was wired to blow up if the Israelis didn't agree to terms. He didn't recognize the terrorists, but one was very tall and the other had red hair."

21

Abed released his pent-up breath as the explosion went off on time. The bus lurched forward, spraying dust and gravel.

It was magnificent. Allah be praised! Abed had to stop himself from shouting a battle cry.

The driver reacted instinctively to the blowout and jammed on the brakes. Long rubber shreds fell off the massive front tires. Then magically, the rest of the rubber unpeeled. The metal rims dug into the dirt, and the bus tipped forward and slammed to a stop into the dirt road. From behind the olive tree Abed could see the girls tumble from their seats like dolls. One of them who'd been standing smashed against the windshield, breaking it into a million tiny pieces of glass. Abed was surprised it hadn't been replaced by the layered sandwich glass used for protection against stones. The driver's nose was bloodied. He stood up and went to help the injured students. From the back of the bus, another man righted himself.

An alarm went off in Abed's head. Why was there another man? A teacher or a guard? Word of a possible attack must have leaked out. He hadn't counted on armed guards!

Still, he had the advantage of surprise and camouflage. No one could see him from behind the olive trees.

Abed estimated that there were ten girls on the bus. The front door folded open. Everyone was getting out. A few of the girls seemed frightened. Others acted with calm efficiency, lifting out injured classmates, issuing orders, and taking charge. The driver, a middle-aged man with an overhanging belly, carried a gun in a back-pocket holster. Abed guessed it was an Eagle, an Israeli-made magnum with an air-cooling system. Only one student and the second man were left on the bus.

The driver squatted to look at the wheel.

Abed stepped forward. "This is an armed action of the Seventh Century. Raise your hands!" he shouted in English.

The driver's eyes shifted to the girls, then he complied.

"Get off the bus!" Abed shouted.

A girl in flowered leggings stood as if frozen on the bus steps, and shrieked for her mother. "*Immele . . . immele . . . immele . . .*" The guard put his left arm under her shoulder to lift her down. He had a pistol in his right hand. Abed sprayed him with bullets from the Kalashnikov. The staccato discharges of the submachine gun made the girls scream louder. The guard looked stunned for a minute. Red stains began spreading on his blue T-shirt as he toppled from the step of the bus into the dirt, knocking the teenager with him. They both slid into the dusty roadside and were silent. Abed felt triumphant.

In the flurry, the driver had shouted something to the girls that Abed couldn't understand. He assumed it was a command to take refuge behind the bus, because that's what they were doing.

A burst of fire came close to Abed's head. The driver was a good shot.

Abed signaled to Sami and pressed his hands to his ears.

Sami had buried the second charge near where he expected the rear wheels to stop after the first explosion had halted the bus. It exploded, making a loud roar and throwing dirt, stones, glass, and rubber in all directions. The olive trees shook, their leaves making a crazy pitter-patter. Despite his covered ears, Abed heard the screams. When the dust cleared, he saw that another of the girls was bleeding from the chest.

Is another one dead? Abed worried. He hadn't

planned to kill anyone before getting to Manger College and making his demands. He thought hard. It didn't matter. He had planned to kill one girl later today, anyway. Now he wouldn't have to bother. The deaths would raise the stakes and bring the Israelis around fast.

"Surrender or the rest of you will die!" he shouted.

The driver shouted back: "Do you make war against children? Let the girls go! Take me as a hostage."

He was brave, Abed thought, and foolish.

"There is a third explosion that will maim you all. Come out with your hands up. Drop the gun, driver, or you will be responsible for the death of all the students."

Abed gave him a minute to decide. Jews always underestimated Arabs. He expected the driver to pretend to give up, and then make a mad rush for him.

Seven of the eight remaining girls walked forward. One, a slim dark-skinned girl, hovered over her fallen classmate.

"You, too," he said.

"She's not dead," the girl said.

"You will be if you don't move," Abed shouted back. Reluctantly, the girl joined the others.

Now only the driver was hiding. "Driver. Throw out your gun. I collect Israeli firearms. And balls, if you've got any."

The driver predictably leaped from behind the bus, the Eagle at shoulder level.

Abed bombarded him, but the driver managed to get in one good shot, nearly hitting him. Abed pressed on the trigger again. The driver fell to his knees, then tumbled forward. A few of the girls whimpered. The others were crying silently.

He had eight teenage girls to deal with. "Does anyone speak Arabic?" he asked.

No one volunteered, but all eyes fixed on the dark-skinned girl who looked startlingly like his sister Laila.

Laila was blind because of Israelis like these.

The girl spoke Palestinian Arabic with a Moroccan accent. Abed was annoyed with how quickly she'd re-

covered. Why wasn't she crying and cowering? He
raised his left hand and slapped her face, knocking
her backward.

"You have stolen my land and oppressed my people," he said, pinching her cheek until tears filled her
eyes. "Get moving."

They walked ahead of him like a captured harem.
The thought made him feel strangely excited.

He called to Sami to retrieve the driver's Eagle and
join them. "If anyone moves, pull the trigger."

The campus was ten minutes away by foot. The girls
walked forward in a tight knot. At first they whispered, but he shouted for silence and pushed one of
them from behind. Several were tall and good-looking,
one had bad acne. Abed wondered what was going on
in their minds. When one tried to escape, he shot near
her and she quickly got into line.

Cheers greeted him when he got to the campus.
Students raised their fists in the gesture of defiance.
One of the Jewish girls fell to her knees and cried
hysterically. Sami started moving toward her, but
friends took her arm and led her forward. The cheering stopped. The Palestinian students grew sober, as
if realizing for the first time the deeper implications
of what they had done. Abed reminded himself that
only a handful of them were radicals committed to
violence. The rest were middle-class, kids who'd accidentally become part of a historic action. Nonetheless,
he couldn't abide dissension on campus.

He would assert himself before they got cold feet.

He'd fantasized about this for years: the day he revealed his identity and became a star among Palestinians. Since returning from Sweden, he'd kept a low
profile. With great patience he'd cultivated the image
of a wimpish banker, a weekend storekeeper. Only a
handful of the villagers he'd recruited guessed his
power. Soon everyone in the world would know his
name. They would speak of Abed as they spoke of
Carlos, who had masterminded the killing of Israelis
at the Munich Olympics.

"Ismi Abed," my name is Abed, he said.

Slowly and deliberately, Abed began to remove his mask. He had the absolute attention of the twenty-five or so students left on campus. The Jewish girls, too, were watching, mesmerized. To his great pleasure, in the back of the crowd he saw Raba Alhassan.

The sun was shining in his eyes. He moved back to the shade of the pine grove. The others gathered around him.

"My name is Abed, and I am the head of the Seventh Century." He paused, letting them look their fill. "Our name was carefully chosen. We are bound to bringing back the time of Islam's greatest glory and to destroy Israel. Allah has chosen us to return the crown of honor to the Arab people. That is a grave responsibility.

"For those of you who are concerned about our intentions, let me assure you that we do not plan to hurt these eight girls unless their government refuses to listen to us. We will demand the release of our Palestinian brethren. Some of you are Christians. We are brothers. Unless we protect each other, there will be tumult and oppression on earth. The evil government of America backs the Zionist infidels. Our young people rot in jails. Today the Zionists penetrate our campus; tomorrow they will enter our hearts. Do not fear. Says Allah: 'It is only Satan that suggests to you the fear of his followers. Be not afraid of them, but fear Me, if you have Faith.' "

Students raised their fists, and the whisper *"Idbah alyahud"* rose to a chant. Those with guns lifted them up and down to the rhythm. Abed smiled and held up his arms to receive the glory. He nodded for Sami to herd the girls upstairs. They'd decided on the old chemistry laboratories on the second floor to keep the hostages. The laboratory rooms had been built with reinforced fire doors like the kitchen. The only access was a single staircase beyond the library.

Other students were dispatched to block the entrance with burning tires. Nails were sprinkled over the ground. Barguth's gate guard had been replaced by Anwar Shafi. Before long TV crews would pick up his image and Israeli snipers would shoot him. That would pay back the Bethlehem Shylock.

Abed sprinted up the stairs where Sami had taken the students. He'd put them all in one of the two old laboratories. "Why haven't you divided them?" Abed asked.

"The students wanted to ask you first," Sami answered, nodding to two Moslem activists. "You see, in our absence, the students have already taken one prisoner." Sami paused, milking the drama. "They've locked up Deborah Stern."

Delight sluiced through him. He raised his fist in triumph. It was almost too good to be true. "Some faces that day will be humiliated, and other faces that day will be joyful." Here was another sign from Allah.

"Allah bless you," Abed said. "Let me see her."

The door creaked open. Deborah huddled in a corner on the stone floor. Defeated. She was either sleeping or unconscious. The noise made her stir. Abed stepped forward, feeling an irresistible urge to make her pay for the humiliation she'd caused him. He leaned over and slapped her face. He was about to kick her when a student ran into the room. "Quick, quick, sir," he said. "Someone important from the Israeli army is on the phone, asking for you."

Abed was giddy with happiness. He forced himself to think. How was it, he wondered, that the Israelis already knew his name?

Raba had been near the gatehouse when Deborah stepped out of her cab.

You deceitful bitch, Raba thought. What are you doing here now? Even as she thought it, she realized that Deborah was walking into a lions' den by coming to the campus and had an impulse to warn her. She stopped herself. If Deborah was foolish enough to return, she'd have to face the consequences. When the students had attacked Deborah, Raba felt as if she'd been flipping channels on TV and against her better judgment had become engrossed in a violent movie. When it was over, she tasted the saltiness of blood, and realized she'd bitten her lips. She wiped them on the back of her hand, feeling guilty that she'd stood there doing nothing.

It was nearly 6:00 P.M. Wassim should be outside waiting.

The middle-aged guard who'd checked her bag in the morning had been replaced by a student. The campus was sealed off, he told her, and no one could come in or leave. Sheepishly, he apologized that the rule included her. "Please understand, it's not that we don't trust you. Imagine what would happen if the GSS interrogated you."

Raba shivered. "But my husband will worry."

Anwar twirled his mustache. "A message has been left at your house that you won't be home tonight."

A cot had been set up for Raba in the teachers' room. There were containers of labene cheese and cola in the refrigerator, stacks of sliced turkey, bread, and olive oil. She picked up the phone to call Ali, and realized the line had been disconnected. In her briefcase was a cellular phone, but instinct told her not to use it yet.

Raba slumped onto the bed. She felt like a prisoner. The campus had grown quiet. Ali was operating tonight and wouldn't come home until dawn. As soon as he did, he'd put two and two together and work his contacts to get her out. There was no sign of Barguth. Would he make the students release Deborah when he came, or had the campus slipped from his capable hands?

Raba couldn't sleep. The cot was narrow and lumpy. It had been a long time since she'd slept on anything but a comfortable bed. She got up and looked out the window. There was no moon. The Big Dipper shone in the north. Stars of Bethlehem, she thought. A verse from a song stuck in her head: "O little town of Bethlehem, How still we see thee lie; Above thy deep and dreamless sleep, The silent stars go by." She didn't even know where she'd learned it. Her soul was fettered with Christian images. I'm a Moslem, not a Christian, she shouted to the walls.

A frightening notion made her heart skip a beat. Perhaps her return to Palestine had been ordained. Ali had been sent like a divine messenger to marry her and bring her back to Palestine. In America she had been the archobserver, viewing her people's struggle from afar. She had become a psychologist, analyzing other people's conflicts. But since coming back to Palestine she had become an insider. Perhaps her being here on campus had been ordained.

The baby moved within her. The thought of her child growing up a Palestinian in an independent state thrilled her. And she could say: your mother took a small part in making this happen.

She must have dozed off toward dawn. The room was inundated with bright sunshine when she woke. There was cheering from the school yard. She ran a brush through her hair and went out. The first person she saw was Sami, holding a gun on a group of teenage girls.

No, no, no, no, no.

Her belly roiled.

She ran outside. In front of the pathetic children walked a tall Arab, his face swathed. This must be the leader, Raba thought. The students, ill-kempt from a night in their clothes, hailed him like a returning Caesar. Who was he?

She watched with fascination as the man called Abed revealed himself. Like everyone else, she was spellbound. He was one of the best-looking men she'd ever seen: quintessential Semitic high cheekbones with a regal curved nose, deep brown eyes, and a red mouth. He was tall and muscular. The beard probably made him look older than he was, and gave strength to his chin. The slight imperfection of a mark on his long neck somehow enhanced his beauty. His charisma transcended his looks. He held himself proudly like a sheik. His speech was untrammeled, educated, and emotional. When he spoke she felt as if she were hearing the prophet Mohammed, *al'yhi asalat walassalam,* address them.

Abed seemed to have the attack in control. When

he assured them the girls wouldn't be hurt, Raba felt herself relax. She wondered if he'd let her go home.

She went to Dr. Barguth's office, but he wasn't there. A woman student had replaced Barguth's secretary. "You might as well wait," the student told her. "Abed wants to speak to you."

A mixture of terror and excitement filled her. How did Abed even know who she was? She paced, then sat in an armchair, her back to the wall map. Twenty minutes later he came striding through the office, unaware of her presence. He reached for a telephone, his brow furrowed in concentration. Their eyes met in the reflection of the window, and he turned, surprised, and then nodded to her. His expression was curious, half friendly, half searching. Never had she felt so lost.

He talked into the mouthpiece. "You'll have to do better than that." He put down the phone and smiled at her again, his eyes probing hers. She couldn't breathe.

"Please, let's go into the office," Abed said, meaning Barguth's study. He waited for her to rise and precede him, then closed the door. Raba felt alarm and a growing lack of unreality as he leaned back in Barguth's chair. She sat at the edge of the visitor's chair, avoiding his eyes by watching the pigeons strut in the eaves.

"Excuse me one minute. I have one call to make," Abed said. His hands on the phone were well groomed, with hair sprouting from under the cuffs. The fiery orator's gleam in his eyes from the school yard was replaced by a sensual warmth, and his smile was devastating. His dark, curly hair was wet. He must have showered and changed clothes.

The only sign of tension was in his hands, which stroked his beard. He dialed Gaza, she could tell by the area code, and instructed someone there to go through with a discussed plan. Then he turned to her. "Dr. Alhassan, may I call you Raba? I am honored to meet you. I knew your brother, Allah be merciful. I am deeply grateful for your assistance."

She tried to conceal her trembling. "How long are

we going to stay here? I would really like to go home."

Laughter shone in his eyes. "I'm afraid we don't have a timetable. That was the Israelis calling before. Can you imagine, they have offered to lower the charges against us if we let the students go. You're a psychologist. Do you think they really think we're imbeciles, or that they act as if we are fools to convince us we are?"

"Both, I think," Raba said, surprised at how emotional she was getting. "You know that when someone treats you like an idiot, it *is* easy to believe you are one. Negative thoughts are always easier to believe. And we have been fools, playing their game. Now it's time to reclaim our history."

His face lit up. "I'm glad you feel that way. Let me confide in you," Abed said, getting up from the desk, sitting on the corner so that he was directly in front of her chair. "We're involved in something big. Some of our leaders have been ready to sign away our future. Now they won't be able to. We've gained the upper hand." His voice thickened. "You understand what we're doing. There can be no compromise in jihad. We want Jews out of our villages and cities, now. Think of it. Bethlehem is just the start. Jericho, Hebron, Nablus, Gaza will be next. Then Jaffa, Haifa, and Jerusalem. Let the Jews go back to Poland. They have no right to Palestinian land."

The fiery look disappeared and his voice sounded sensuous. "I'm thrilled that Allah has sent you to be my partner."

He put out his hand to shake hers. It was an odd gesture for a Moslem man to offer a woman, but she was afraid to refuse. His fingers were uncallused but strong. Inside her, she felt a throb of sexual response. Her face turned scarlet with shame.

The phone rang. "Like clockwork," Abed said, letting go of her hand. "Don't go away. I need you to do a favor for me." To whomever was on the phone, he said his first deadline was 6:00 P.M. Either they released Palestinian prisoners and moved troops out of the villages, or he would kill a girl each hour and blow up a church.

When he'd finished, Abed turned back to her, smiling at his own success. "Do you mind doing one small favor for me?" It was a command, not a request, she realized. He put one hand on her shoulder.

"Sami says the prisoners aren't doing well even though we haven't lifted a hand against them. We don't want them to get ill or die on us. We need someone to talk to them. You're a psychologist, and you know English. Check them out for me, won't you? See if any of them need medical care.

"Later, there's a rare treat. I'm going to interrogate Deborah Stern. I'd like you to come along."

22

After a sleepless night, Moshe Cohen and company were given a one-hour deadline to prepare a plan for the chief of staff. Raphi half listened while Uzi and Jacques, their voices hoarse from smoke and exhaustion, presented a sophisticated outline that would involve negotiations and an air rescue using new helicopter techniques they'd learned on their last assignment. "Remember, despite all the pressure, we can't rush in," Jacques was saying. He didn't have to say why. A hostage and a young officer had recently been killed in a similar rescue when explosives had failed to blast through a heavy door.

Cohen summarized the diplomatic developments. Raphi yawned. He was a diplomat's son and knew too well how today's enemies were tomorrow's partners and vice versa. Cohen's report contained no surprises: peace talks had been suspended. The pope was praying, and the cardinals were meeting in an urgent session. Fundamentalist Christians in the United States were pressuring the White House: the attack was the actualization of worldwide Christian fear that Bethlehem's churches would be trashed by Moslems, as the churches had been in Lebanon.

Jacques had an update on what was happening locally. Social workers had been dispatched to the homes of the two dead students so the families would hear of their personal tragedy before it was broadcast on TV and radio. Raphi imagined the parents who'd waved good-bye to smiling daughters in the morning regretting their last pointless fight about messy rooms and curfews.

By ten o'clock the networks would be carrying the story and sending reporters to the scene. No other city of its size in the whole world had as large a foreign press corps as Jerusalem. Raphi thought of the reporters as jackals, waiting for more dead Jews. The government and army radio stations could be counted on to hold the news on the kidnapping for another hour, but there was always a chance that someone would get wind of what was happening and ignore the government's request to hold the news until the army could get into place. Ambulance sirens had been heard, and private citizens would soon be piecing together an early version.

The army was moving at unprecedented speed to encircle Manger College. Reserve units had been called up because older soldiers could be counted on to keep their fingers off the trigger better than the teenagers of the standing army. As soon as the news was out, civilians would rush to the site. Jacques expected demonstrations and riots in every city, and the army would have to deal with outraged Israelis as well as terrorists.

Jacques raised the problem of their double agent. Sami hadn't warned them of the attack, nor had they heard from him since. No doubt Sami was responsible for setting the explosives on Bethlehem Road and in the church. Had he defected? Gil, who was running him, didn't think so. He believed Sami would get in touch and offer help as soon as he was able to. As a precaution, Gil had rounded up all the members of Sami's family. They were in administrative detention, and could stay there without trial for up to six months. "So what else is new?" Raphi asked, yawning again. "Was there ever a double agent who didn't sell us out?"

Gil's jaw tightened. His report was next. He had the only slim good tidings to report: three of the listening devices on campus were still working. The one in the teachers' room had picked up Raba Alhassan's voice. She had spent the night there. More important, just a few minutes ago, the Efrat station had picked up a

speech. Gil turned to Raphi and faked an exaggerated yawn back to him.

Raphi, suddenly alert, gave him the finger. The room was silent as Gil played the tape.

Their terrorist's name was Abed. No one had heard of him. His voice was cultured and charismatic.

I know that voice, Raphi thought.

At 9:30 the five members of the team parted ways. No one mentioned Deborah, alive or dead. They're such cold-blooded bastards that she's not even important; well, she matters to me, Raphi thought. Gil promised to go to the yeshiva to inform Joshua of her disappearance and to find out if he'd heard from her. As soon as Gil returned, he'd take over the monitoring of the office. Moshe Cohen went to pacify the prime minister and get authorization to make fake offers to the terrorists while Jacques and Uzi polished the helicopter rescue. Raphi, the only one who'd been on campus, was assigned to mapping out the entrance route.

Raphi usually avoided elevators, but he purposely took one to the basement map room, in case his colleagues were tracking him. Once there, he walked back up one floor to where the personal lockers were. Unemployed terrorists didn't wear French designer jeans like his. He needed cheap, generic, polyester pants, but there was no time to go home for his own supply. Gil kept clothes ready for the rare occasions on which he ventured into the field. Raphi knew Gil's locker combination. He took underpants with elastic stitched crookedly in Ramallah, dusty sandals made in the Old City, and a keffiyah from Amman. An operative had been killed because he was wearing Israeli briefs.

Moshe Cohen would be furious, but Raphi was beyond caring. By the time they worked out a foolproof plan, Deborah and the eight remaining teenagers would be dead.

The Thirteenth Hour had arrived.

His own chances of saving them were slim. But he had one long shot: his identity as Daud Mustafa Bahar had never been blown. If Abed was who Raphi suspected he was, he'd have a good reason to allow "Bahar" into his fiefdom: Abed wanted to kill him.

Raphi rolled up the clothes and left through the garage.

At 10 A.M. Dr. Ali Alhassan glanced at the digital clock on his dashboard. He'd been in Gaza all night, operating on a patient who needed a triple bypass. If there were complications, the only option would be a heart transplant. He saw a road worker signal ahead, and slowed his silver-gray BMW. A bulldozer was lifting dirt on the roadside. The delay annoyed him. Raba hadn't come home last night and he was worried. He'd tried the cellular phone, but it didn't ring. She must have turned it off.

Ali stopped so his car wouldn't get dirtied. That's when he heard the click of his back door. He reached for the Smith and Wesson .44 below his seat. The quick movement made it impossible for the masked man to grab his throat. His assailant was lunging forward when Ali shot him at close range, lodging a bullet in his larynx.

Ali pulled off the man's hood. He was young: maybe twenty. His heart was still beating, but it would stop by the time Ali drove back to the hospital. He hoped the heart would be a good match.

Joshua was spending the morning reviewing rabbinic laws of divorce. He was eager to discuss certain points with his advocate. He hadn't told the rebbe about engaging an advocate. The rebbe had mandated Joshua to forgive, but his heart was frozen in hatred. Joshua had phoned Deborah again in the early morning. Flaunting her indecent behavior, she hadn't come home all night. Joshua looked up from his book and recognized the thin, bareheaded man walking into the yeshiva. Didn't he even have the respect to put on a hat in the study hall? But when Gil came closer and Joshua saw the grim line of his mouth, he knew something terrible had happened.

Gil suggested they go outside. Joshua told him to speak freely; no one eavesdropped at a yeshiva. The room was noisy with students arguing and reading aloud.

Gil's finger traced the gold letters on Joshua's book of Talmud. "Have you heard from Deborah?"

Joshua leaned closer. "No. Why?"

Gil ran his hands through his hair. "She's been doing some spying for us. Did she tell you?"

Joshua jerked back. "No. She might have surmised correctly that I wouldn't approve. How could you stomach soliciting a mother of two children?"

Gil's voice was tinged with anger. "For the same reason we ask fathers. Because the bloody country needs them." Gil looked around to see if anyone had been listening. His voice lowered. "She was supposed to go to Bethlehem yesterday. There's a chance she was captured and is being held as a hostage, but frankly we don't know. I'm here because we're required by law to tell you."

"Then tell me. Stick to the facts. Where. When. How. I'm a major in the infantry," Joshua said. "Don't patronize me."

As soon as Gil left, Joshua took a cab from the yeshiva to his father's house. For the first time in his life he felt awkward going there. His father had never approved of his leaving Deborah. Now she was gravely endangered because of it. His father would blame him instead of recognizing Deborah's culpability.

The bitter irony of his brooding over images of his wife in Herzliya-on-the-Sea with Raphi while she was risking her life for the country ate at his soul.

The cab rounded the corner and stopped in Rehavia, the gracious neighborhood where Joshua had grown up. It still had a mysterious tug on his heart. Children were going up and down on the seesaw, singing a rhyme—*Nad ned, nad ned, red, aleh, aleh v'red*— just as he had hundreds of times in the same park.

Joshua had a key to his father's house, but he knocked anyway. He understood the reason for the law: his sudden appearance might shock his father.

The door jerked open. "Joshua," his father said. He'd always been taller than everyone else's father, but now he was stooped and frail.

The TV was on, sounding loud and metallic. "Am I disturbing anything?"

"Of course not. What else is left to disturb in my life?"

Only then did Joshua realize that outside the yeshiva the whole country was glued to the drama in Bethlehem. "Come in," his father urged. "The news will be on in a few minutes."

Abed's stomach rumbled from hunger, but he was too nervous to eat. A tray of turkey sandwiches lay untouched on Barguth's desk. He paced, looking at the clock, as the minutes passed slowly. *Sabr,* the Moslem concept of patience, meant more than the Western. It required perseverance, constancy, self-restraint, and refusal to be cowed. The more patience, the greater was service to Allah. Abed needed to set an example for his followers.

Everyone in the world, from dignitaries to street cleaners, would watch him on television today. But how odd it was that most of all he waited to hear the praise of his fellow villagers. The store would be full of well-wishers. Those who had pitied him after his mother had remarried would congratulate her. His stepfather would be furious that Abed had risked their family security, but everyone in the village would laugh at him. "Burhan the lover," they called him behind his back.

At noon, Abed knelt and said the second of the five daily prayers. Then a journalist and a cameraman were admitted to the campus. Celia Black, formerly employed by the BBC, was so rabidly anti-Israel that she'd somehow twisted Israel's humanitarian rescue of Ethiopian Jews into "an exercise in racism." Abed had secretly admired Israeli willingness to spend a fortune sending illiterate Africans to school. He'd selected her from the anti-Israel journalists because women were always sympathetic to him. For balance,

Abed chose Helmut, a long-haired German freelance cameraman. They were both searched. Not long ago Algerian Moslems who brilliantly hijacked a plane to Marseilles had made the fatal error of allowing in food trays that turned out to be bugged.

Abed thought about listening devices as he showered again in Barguth's private bathroom. There had to be at least one more on campus, or the Israelis wouldn't know his name. Later, he'd extract that information from Deborah. He splashed on aftershave, combed his hair, and adjusted a keffiyah to show his whole face. He wanted to look romantic but not threatening.

Celia sat across from him in Barguth's office. She was wearing a short skirt and crossed her legs, so Abed had a peek up heavy, unshaven thighs. Her immodesty was repulsive, but he gave her his best smile and thanked her for coming.

The conference would be videotaped and then played back. Helmut indicated that the camera was on. Abed tilted his face slightly so that his profile would show.

"Good afternoon. I am Abed, the leader of the Seventh Century, an *Iz alddin alkassam* unit of the Islamic freedom movement. For those of you who are unfamiliar with our cause, let me say that Iz alddin alkassam was a Moslem leader who fought against Jewish colonization of Palestine." *Speak slowly and look at the camera,* he reminded himself.

"Today, we Palestinians are fighting the same battle. This week we were forced to take action against our oppressors. They pretend to accord us new rights and to be on the verge of making peace. But secretly they appropriate more of our land for their settlements and penetrate our schools. Even in the heart of this quiet town of Bethlehem, holy to Christian people all over the world, they make war on us. Soon we will show you evidence.

"They have assassinated the dean of this fine college. George Barguth is a martyr to the Palestinian revolution. We have vowed to avenge his death." He paused, so the shock of Barguth's death could pass through the Arab world. Meet the new leader, he wanted to shout. Instead, he lowered his voice.

"To stop their further abuses of power, we have taken the following steps:

"In our hands are nine Jewish hostages. We have ascertained that the eight high school students we captured near our campus are all spies, and would have joined Israeli military intelligence in the next few months. Therefore, we consider them our enemies. The other, as you will see, admits being a General Security Service agent.

"We have placed explosives in the Church of the Nativity in Bethlehem, not because of our antagonism to the principles of Christianity, but because of the lack of support of Christian leadership for our cause. That very manger where Mary spoke to Allah will be the site of Allah's just revenge."

Abed gazed into the camera. "None of this need come about. Our demands are reasonable. Saving both their spies and the Christian holy site is within the hands of the Zionist government. If the Israelis attempt subterfuge, all hostages will be killed, as they have been in the past."

He paused again so they could recall the bound Israeli soldier who had recently been shot in the head while commandos failed to free him. "One more thing," Abed said, anger seeping into his modulated tones, "a personal issue. If the occupying troops go near my family, all hostages will be killed instantly. I warn you. I have established a means of secret communication and will know if you as much as enter my village."

Abed made a cutting motion to the cameraman. "Cut," he ordered. "Part two is upstairs."

The cameraman stopped instantly. At Abed's instruction, Sami blindfolded him and Celia. There was no need for secrecy, but blindfolds made them feel important. Celia would become a darling of the media and get a book out of this. Helmut could use the story to get laid.

Abed held Celia's sweating hand and led her up the stairs. He took off her blindfold inside the chemistry lab.

"You can interview her now," Abed said.

The cameraman got his equipment together. He focused on Deborah. The reporter rubbed her eyes. She pressed her finger to her nose, making the nostrils spread. "Abed," the reporter asked, "I've seen this woman before. Isn't this Deborah Stern, who fought off the attacker in the car garage? What in the world is *she* doing here?"

Joshua gaped in horror at his wife's bruised and distorted face on the TV screen. Her eyes were dull, her head low as she read slowly from a paper. Joshua's eyes rose to their wedding portrait, a copy of the one at home. A laughing Deborah had flowers woven into long blond hair. His heart ached. "I was recruited by the General Security Services," Deborah began, her voice strained. She licked her split lips. "I became a biology teacher on campus in order to spy on the students and faculty. I planted a listening device in the cafeteria, but it was detected."

Deborah lifted hollow eyes as if trying to communicate her helplessness. "I urge the government to listen to the demands of the Palestinians," she said reluctantly, "so that we will be set free."

There was a final full-face shot of Abed. The cameraman, according to the CNN reporter, made porno films in Germany. He obscenely lingered on Abed's eyes and sensual mouth as Abed reminded Israel and the Vatican that his deadline was only five hours away.

Through the dismay and anguish, Joshua tried to decide what to do. He felt a shiver of shame at how he had abandoned her and left her vulnerable to GSS recruitment. His brain was sluggish. It took him a minute to realize that the camera had switched to the reserve army unit that was positioned around the campus. There were faces he recognized! "That's my unit!" Joshua shouted. It made sense. Infantry would be called up for a crisis like this. The men in his unit were just the right age to handle a confrontation with students: too old to be impulsive but still physically fit. Since his injury, he hadn't been called up for reserve duty, but he could volunteer for it.

He would rescue Deborah and bring her to a safer world where life was whole and not fragmented by a thousand pressures.

"Do you still have my spare uniform here?" Joshua asked. He felt more energized than he had in a long time.

Even after he'd married Deborah, his orderly, German born father had insisted on storing an extra complete set of army attire in Joshua's old bedroom. His father smiled, but his eyes were misty as he led Joshua to the wooden closet where a green uniform, perfectly ironed, was hanging under transparent plastic. Shining black boots were lined up below it. The smell of mothballs filled the room as Joshua took a brown wool beret from the shelf.

He felt odd as he buttoned the shirt and tucked it into his pants. The uniform still fit, but it felt borrowed after wearing nothing but black for so many months. Joshua looked in the mirror, hardly recognizing himself. This is what you'll go back to if you leave the yeshiva, he told himself. Could he take up life in the outside world again? No. That's no longer me. After rescuing his wife, he would destroy his uniform.

The phone was ringing. "It's for you," his father said. "Israel TV is sending over a reporter for you to make a statement. I suggest you leave through the back door. I'll pick up the children."

With acute embarrassment, Joshua realized he had forgotten all about his children. He hugged his father. "Thank you for everything. Wish me luck."

23

Something looked familiar about the soldier waiting at the bus stop. Raphi slowed down. Only when he'd driven by did he make the positive identification. It was Joshua Stern, wearing an IDF uniform. What the hell was he doing here?

Despite his hurry, Raphi backed up. He opened the door. "Where are you going?"

Joshua squinted at him. Raphi saw the recognition grow, and, with it a condescending sneer.

"Bethlehem," Joshua finally answered. "But not with you."

"The road is closed to buses. It's me or walking."

Joshua hesitated and then got in, carrying a smell of mothballs. Raphi regretted his offer as soon as the door was closed. His curiosity about Deborah's husband had outweighed common sense. Face to face for the first time, he had to admit Joshua looked compelling. He was very well-built and handsome, and his face had lost the befuddled look it had on the night Raphi had seen him with Deborah at the King David Hotel. With intelligent blue eyes Joshua glared at him like a scorpion he wanted to crush under his boot.

"Raphi Lahav," Raphi said. He put out his hand to shake, but Joshua scorned it.

Joshua turned his face away. "I know who you are and what you are." He curled his lip in distaste. "A vulture picking at people's lives."

As a verbal blow it was good, Raphi thought. "Don't pin your guilt trip on me. You're the one who left your wife so you could search for your eternal soul," Raphi said. "Do you think she would have worked for us if she'd been living with you and you were supporting her? What are you doing here anyway? Shouldn't you be praying? Yeshiva students don't usually do reserve duty."

"I'm an infantry officer, and I needed to be here."

Raphi revised his opinion: maybe Joshua wasn't so self-centered after all. That made him an even more formidable rival. They reached the checkpoint. The road to Bethlehem was officially closed in both directions, but no one questioned Raphi's GSS identification. He drove through before they could check Joshua.

"Thanks," Joshua said grudgingly. "I don't have the papers."

"Somehow I didn't think you did," Raphi said. He'd probably made a mistake. He had a suspicion that Joshua's presence was going to cause him trouble. He turned left to the area near the campus.

Soldiers lined the roads to the military camp, which had been set up around the campus. Raphi could smell it even before he saw it: the unique mix of grease, sweat, and smoke that went with the military. Was it his imagination, or had Joshua paled?

Raphi let Joshua out, presumably to join his unit. Raphi parked the car and left the keys with the camp commander, whom he recognized as a high school principal in civilian life. "I'm going in undercover. If I don't make it out, give them to Gil and tell him I said to drive carefully."

Through borrowed binoculars, Raphi could see the gatehouse. The mustached guard was armed but looked young and raw. Raphi had guessed correctly that Abed wouldn't waste trained manpower on preventing a frontal attack against a well-equipped Israeli battalion. Whoever this kid was, Abed was willing to risk him as cannon fodder. He probably had a few trained men, a backup flank of enthusiastic but unskilled Moslem students, and then a few dozen sympathetic but uncommitted students who happened to be on campus for the takeover. They would be worse than useless as a fighting force.

In contrast, in the Israeli camp, there were artillery,

tanks, infantry fighting vehicles with missile launchers, combat engineer vehicles equipped with heavy booms and winches, dozer blades, and 165mm demolition guns. Despite his general disillusionment with the military, Raphi felt a childlike excitement around so much modern military equipment. In the days when his own father was negotiating for Czech Mausers and Deborah's father was smuggling jeep radiators to Israel, a walkie-talkie was a luxury item. No one could dream that forty-odd years later Israeli soldiers would have computerized missiles and deluxe RPGs.

Despite the weaponry, Abed had the advantage. He knew that the army could easily plow through and take over the campus. He'd also know the army would hesitate to do anything that would endanger the hostages. Raphi thought of Deborah and the teenagers in Abed's grip, and his temper flared. Abed's sole protection was the knife at their throats, but it was an effective one. Statistically speaking, the children's chances were very poor. Terrorists weren't sentimental: children made up a large percentage of their victims.

About one hundred yards separated the Israeli first line and the campus gate. The area was littered with barrels, nails, broken wooden cartons, and the remains of tires. The smoke of burning rubber stung Raphi's eyes.

A figure appeared before him. Raphi rubbed his eyes, but the phantom didn't disappear. It was Joshua Stern.

"What the fuck do you think you're doing?" Raphi shouted.

"I'm going in after my wife."

"I was afraid you'd come here with a dumb-ass scheme." Raphi's words became daggers. "They'll slice your throat before you can even say Shema Yisrael."

"And what makes you think you'll get in? For all your bluster, I haven't been impressed with your achievements. Why is she inside and not you?"

Time was running out too fast for bickering. "What is it you propose to do?" Raphi asked, his voice taut.

"I'm going to run through the main gate and set off

an explosion. While I create a diversion, your people can come in with their helicopters."

Raphi was surprised Joshua knew about the helicopters. Jacques and Uzi must be moving fast. "Too risky," Raphi said.

"No one's asking you. She's my wife and it's my risk."

Raphi restrained his temper. "I'm not arguing conjugal rights here. Nor am I suggesting I have all the answers. But I know the campus and you don't. I speak colloquial Arabic and you don't. Most of all, I've already met Abed, and maybe he thinks I'm a terrorist like him. Let's look at your plan. According to what I've heard, Deborah is in the old chemistry labs on the second floor. Let's say you made it alive to the entrance. And let's say you managed to dump a mine on the doorstep. By the time you got to the second floor, the guards there would have pumped a magazine of lead into Deborah and the girls. The only chance we have is to get someone on the inside without alarming them."

Raphi held his breath. Joshua's idea was dangerous, but it wasn't stupid. Sometimes a rash action like blasting your way in could create enough of a diversion for a rescue to take place. Raphi knew there was no guarantee that his own plan would work either, but his well-honed military intuition said he had a better chance. However, Joshua was an officer and could cause delays in Raphi's plan. Under normal circumstances, Raphi could call on Moshe Cohen to override an objection from another branch of the military. The GSS had special authority. But Cohen wouldn't be inclined to back him up today.

Joshua looked undecided. Raphi tried a different tack. "Your plan isn't bad, but I have a better shot at getting her out alive. And if I fail, at least your children will have one parent."

Joshua was silent. A troubled light filled his eyes. Raphi played his last card. "You're right if you think I'm interested in your wife. She's a sensational woman. You're an asshole for leaving her. For reasons I don't understand, she's been faithful to you so far. But now you're holding back the children and she's furious at you. I'm going to help her and comfort her, just as I did when she was nearly killed."

Raphi took a deep breath, begging fate that Deborah's love for this man was dead. "On the other hand, if you let me do this, I'll back off, disappear for a while. She won't hear from me. That will give you time to get it together if you can. Apologize. Mend your fences. Be a family."

Raphi waited. At last Joshua nodded.

The relief he felt was wholly inappropriate, Raphi realized, as he changed clothes quickly in the medical tent. He nearly forgot to take off the Seiko watch. Why hadn't Deborah pushed the alarm if she was in trouble? He didn't want to draw the obvious conclusion.

Before he changed identities, there was a moment when he needed to be alone with himself. He tied down the tent flap and took a position in the middle of the room. He felt jittery. You're good at this, he told himself. Empty words were not enough. He had to feel the role in his body. Raphi stood perfectly still for a moment, relaxing his shoulders and knees and slowing his breathing. He tilted his pelvis into a fighting stance, finding his center of gravity. He drew another deep breath and said to himself: You are a Palestinian terrorist named Daud Mustafa Bahar.

Joshua, goddamn him, was waiting outside the tent.

Joshua blocked his way. "I want to clarify something. You'll disappear after the rescue?"

"That's right," Raphi said, controlling his temper. "But not forever. If you can't win her, I'll be there to pick up the pieces. Now, if you don't mind, I need to find someone to cover me. Major Stern, do you perhaps remember how to fire a gun?"

Joshua was anxious as he watched Raphi run toward the gate of Manger College. He was a fool to have agreed to cover him. He hadn't fired a gun for three years. Could he still do it? His hands trembled as he aimed the M16. What would Raphi tell Deborah if he succeeded in getting inside? They could engineer a plan where Raphi would appear to drop out of sight, but was really waiting in the wings until Joshua was neutralized. One inch to the right and he could stop that pompous bastard forever. Then the army would use Joshua's plan, which his renewed military instinct told him might work just as well as Raphi's. He felt confident that he could win Deborah back, but she'd become more self-confident and independent since he'd left her. His putting on a uniform to rescue her would clinch it. She was basically tenderhearted and romantic. She would feel compelled to match his level of commitment and return to him, forgiving him, as the rebbe had suggested.

He aimed his rifle. The smell of smoke and grease made him momentarily dizzy. For a second he was back in the jeep with Oren, insisting they do things his way. The parallel made his knees shaky. In a ray of clarity he remembered that true repentance meant returning to the scene of the crime and making a *different* decision.

Joshua said a prayer of thanks for the opportunity to reclaim his soul. Next he would reclaim his wife. He looked down at the gun in his hand, and, with the skill he'd once prized, calculated the angle and fired.

Raphi ran for the front gate, leaping over the barbed wire and throwing himself behind the barrels. He'd warned Joshua he'd be moving fast. *Fire, you fucking asshole,* Raphi thought. The shell landed perfectly, close enough to look serious but not too close. Sand blew in every direction and stung his eyes. Raphi zigzagged and dodged between barrels. He shouted in Arabic, "Deir Yassin, Deir Yassin," the password he'd learned from Sami. "Don't shoot. Let me in."

Raphi was less than ten feet from the gatehouse, hiding behind a barrel. Rushing forward was a possibility, but he couldn't take a chance. At this distance, the kid might get lucky and kill him. Raphi's loud voice startled the guard. "In my right hand I'm holding a Galil rifle that belongs to your leader. In my left hand I have a twenty-two caliber Beretta. To show good faith, you can have the Galil." He threw the Galil at the guard, aiming for his face. The guard leaped back, too startled to do anything but avoid the gun.

"Give that to Abed. Tell him I'm returning it as proof of my friendship." The guard looked confused. Raphi shouted, "Call him now, you mother's cunt, or I'll shoot you."

The guard picked up the phone. Raphi's guts felt watery. Long minutes ticked by. At last, a tall, well-built man approached the guard station and ran his hands lovingly over the Galil, checking the receiver markings to make sure it was his. Then he touched the magazine to make sure it was caught before pulling back the cocking handle as far as it could go. He pointed the gun at Raphi's chest.

"Is that the algebra tutor and Swedish veterinary student, Daud Mustafa Bahar?" Abed's voice was thick with sarcasm. "Sorry, no need for a tutor today. Thank you for returning my weapon. No unknowns. Very simply, X equals you surrender now or I'll shoot you dead."

Raphi cursed himself. Why hadn't he killed this man when he'd had the chance? This was indeed the same fucking terrorist he'd fought in Gaza. Abed was the sort of attractive, younger man about whom Yasser Arafat had nightmares—someone appealing enough to unite the fundamentalists and draw young people.

"Ahlan," Raphi greeted him. "So good to see you again . . . Abed. We weren't formally introduced in Gaza. You misjudge me. I promised I'd come to help you. As soon as I heard about the operation I figured you had a bunch of green recruits and could use some professional help."

"How did you find me here?"

"Let's just say I have excellent sources."

"How did you get past the Israelis?"

Raphi didn't answer.

Now, show him you have balls, Raphi commanded himself, realizing he could be dead in seconds. He stood up, guns aimed at him. Raphi hoped that Joshua wouldn't forget to cover him, and that his last shot wasn't just lucky. If Joshua was rusty and erred by an inch, Raphi would be dead.

As soon as Raphi reached full height, the gunfire rang behind him. He did what any terrorist would do under the circumstances: he ran at astonishing speed away from the Israelis to the shelter of the gate. *Let Abed be curious enough about me not to shoot me on sight.*

"Congratulations, Daud Bahar," Abed said. "You've made it."

"My congratulations to you. You've also 'made it,' so to speak."

Abed didn't smile. "Now, there is just the matter of the Beretta you spoke of."

Raphi grinned. "I was faking."

"Anwar, search him," Abed ordered.

Anwar's soft hands pressed over his body. Raphi could tell he was squeamish about touching his ass and crotch. Anwar's fingers slipped into the back pocket, and he shouted in triumph.

Oh shit, oh fuck, Raphi thought. In his hurry he'd forgotten to empty Gil's pockets. Possibilities flashed through his mind: lunch receipts, movie tickets, the address of a new secretary—any of which would identify him as a GSS operative and seal his coffin.

Anwar's embarrassed chuckle jolted him. In his manicured fingers he held a blue square wrapper holding an internationally known brand of condom, marked only in English: LUBRICATED, ELECTRONICALLY TESTED, ROLLED AND SEALED FOR YOUR CONVENIENCE AND PROTECTION. HIGHLY SENSITIVE.

If I survive, you'll never live this down, Gilly.

Contraception, but not sterilization, was permissible under Moslem law, but condoms weren't exactly spare gear for macho terrorists. Nonetheless, a sexually active terrorist *might* have one in his pocket. Everyone knew about AIDS. Raphi quoted the section from the Koran used as justification for contraception: "Allah desires ease for you, not hardship."

"Give it back to him," Abed sneered. "He probably needs it."

Abed was implying that Raphi was a faggot. Defending his virility was the least of his worries, as Abed lowered the Galil and tilted his head for Raphi to proceed him.

I'm inside and alive, Raphi thought. Like the man who'd fallen the top twenty floors of the Empire State Building, so far, so good.

Raphi squinted at the familiar campus as if he were there for the first time. He asked Abed appropriate questions about the weapons on campus and the line of defense in case of attack. Abed gave vague answers. "I'll fill you in as we go along," he said. "Come into my office. There's someone you know there."

It might be Deborah! If this was a test he hoped she'd have enough presence of mind not to give the game away.

But when Abed opened the door it was Sami squatting over a carton that held a pigeon with a band around its leg. What do you know, they're using carrier pigeons. Once again Raphi was impressed by how the Seventh Century had outsmarted the GSS.

In the cover story Sami was supposed to have told Abed, he'd met Daud Bahar while recuperating in the Old City. In fact, Sami had only met Gil, not Raphi, face-to-face. Would Sami make the connection? And if he did, would he reveal Raphi's true identity?

He smiled broadly at Sami. "How nice to see you, Sami. How are your injuries?"

Sami held up his hands to show they'd healed. The fingers looked scarred and crooked.

"Your sister Noha was an invaluable help in finding you and Abed," Raphi said. "In the way of women, Noha couldn't help boasting that you were studying in a prestigious college."

Sami's eyes enlarged at the implication of his sister. He hesitated. Raphi knew he was weighing his options.

"Daud Bahar," Sami finally said, inclining his head in a bow. "It is my honor to see you again."

Abed had been watching the interaction carefully.

He nodded toward the pigeon on the floor. "We're using carrier pigeons. This one seems sick. You're the veterinary student. Have a look."

Another test. Why did Gil have to make me a veterinary student? I could have specialized in art history! Raphi thought frantically of anything he might know about birds. The pigeon was dun-colored and larger than usual loft pigeons. Bulbous growths almost covered its big yellow eyes and long bill. He was about to point these out when a strange forewarning came to him: the obvious answer was wrong. Why did he think that most carrier pigeons developed facial growths? A picture of a columbary in an Italian art book flashed in his mind.

He reached into the carton and lifted it and ran his fingers over the bottom. He'd once had a parakeet with a tumor.

"Here it is," Raphi said, running his hand under the bird. "Your pigeon has cancer." He wanted Abed to feel the imagined lump, but the terrorist was oddly squeamish and declined. "Sorry. No cure. Birds do have surgery, but this one looks too old and crusty to survive it. Do you have others as a backup?"

Abed looked pensive, then nodded. The phone rang. He waited for the tenth ring to answer. Again, Raphi admired his simple but effective tactics. The Palestinians understood Israelis. Raphi imagined the Israeli on the other end turning black with impatience. When Abed finally put the receiver to his ear, he said nothing. Raphi wondered who was calling: a high-ranking soldier or someone political from the prime minister's office. Moshe Cohen? He was the only one in the unit who spoke Palestinian Arabic as well as Raphi. Abed talked as if he had all the time in the world. "These are our preconditions for negotiation. First, twenty-five leaders, whose names I'll fax you, will be released immediately. Second, Israeli troops will pull out of the Bethlehem area, from Rachel's Tomb to the Dehaisha refugee camp. Third, no further negotiations will take place without the Islamic parties, represented by the Seventh Century.

"It's noon. You have until six o'clock to meet these conditions. Two teenagers are already dead. The third will be executed. Subsequently one girl will be executed each hour. By morning there will be no hostages. The Church of the Nativity will be no more. The choice is yours."

Abed put down the receiver before anyone could answer. A broad smile made his face devilishly handsome.

He turned to Raphi. "You couldn't have come at a better time," he said, exuberant. "We've all heard stories of how the Teacher got reluctant captives to confess. You must have learned something of his methods. In a few minutes I'll be interrogating my first hostage. You can demonstrate for us. Leave me now. I'll join you shortly."

Abed closed the office door and fingered his Galil. He was excited to have it back, but he hated surprises. There were too many unanswered questions about Daud Bahar. How had he gotten past the Israelis? How had he known where to find him? A competing Moslem cell might have been tracking his actions. Abed had already infuriated the PLO and couldn't afford infighting with other like-thinking Palestinians. It could be that Teheran or Damascus, afraid of a humiliating failure by the Seventh Century, had asked another group to help him pull this off. Inquiries in the Old City had confirmed the story about Sami's recovery there. And there had been rumors, lots of rumors, about disciples of the Teacher returning to Palestine. On the other hand, rumors didn't mean much. Spreading them was a specialty of the GSS.

Could Bahar possibly be Israeli intelligence? He spoke perfect Arabic. There wasn't a vowel or a consonant that wasn't distinct. Arabic had to be his mother tongue, and his mannerisms were Arab as well.

It made no sense at all for Israeli intelligence to send a single agent into an armed campus. Moslems, not Jews, believed in suicide missions.

He forced himself to think this through. It paid to
be cautious. He had an excellent memory. Suddenly a
thought came to mind. Hadn't he heard something of
a particular GSS superman who sometimes worked
alone? In Libya at night in their tents the trainees had
described an old foe who spoke a dozen languages,
including every kind of Arabic—from Moroccan to
Iraqi—like a native. Abed had assumed it was a tall
tale. He'd been around for a while, so he would probably be older than this Bahar. On the other hand, age
was hard to guess. What had the trainees called this
superman? Lefty. A sort of joke, because he fought
from the right side.

Abed tried to remember. Which side had Bahar attacked him from?

For sure, it was the right.

That was too flimsy to draw conclusions from. Abed
had studied in Stockholm, and Bahar claimed to have
studied in Lund. It was possible that Abed hadn't met
or heard of a student there, but it was unlikely. He'd
been involved in politics on his own campus and
nearby in the large university in Uppsala. Abed had
a photographic memory for names. That's how he distributed the funds to his recruits without a written list.
Of course, he could have changed his name. It seemed
more inconceivable that the famous Teacher was operating in Scandinavia and he hadn't known. His arguments went back and forth in his mind, and Abed
felt frustrated.

Suddenly he knew what to do. He dialed the Swedish consulate general in Jerusalem. An Arabic-speak-
ing woman answered the phone. Abed asked her to
transfer him to the Swedish woman in charge of studies abroad. "I'm interested in studying veterinary science," said Abed. She gave him all the information
he needed in a sweet lilting voice that made him think
of Kerstin. He thanked her profusely.

There was a medical school but no vet school in
Lund. Daud Mustafa Bahar was an impostor. That was
for sure. But who was he? Was Sami involved in a

plot against him? Abed would have to put them both to a final test.

Deborah awoke to intense pain—a splitting headache, dizziness, nausea, and soreness in the back of her head as if it had been split in half. She ran her fingers over her hair, and felt a huge lump and clumps of blood. Through the haze she heard noises coming from the room behind the wall. She thought she heard girls' voices speaking in Hebrew. Her mouth was dry and she was thirsty. Her watch said 10:00. She pressed the alarm button, wondering if Raphi could pick up the alarm wherever he was. She tried to focus. She was in the chemistry laboratory. It was lined with cabinets and work surfaces. There were three porcelain sinks, and near each one was a gas outlet. The dust choked her throat. How many years ago had they taught chemistry here? She got herself up with great difficulty and turned on one of the taps. Nothing came out at first, then a rusty trickle. Evidently it had never been disconnected. She let the water run until the color turned yellow, beige, and finally clear. The water running over her hands and face revived her.

Her head aching, she squinted to survey the room. There were narrow windows on one side. The ceiling was high. It was at least twenty-five feet off the ground, too high to jump even if she could squeeze through the window. Her hands weren't tied. She opened all the cabinets. Under one of the sinks was something that looked like old, cruddy salt. The label had been blackened with mold. She scraped it away with her thumb: KPO. KPO_4, she guessed. Potassium phosphate. If I just had sodium nitrite and ammonia I could blow myself out, she thought. But there was nothing else, not even a container of ammonia cleanser. The chemical was useless.

She sat down again, her back to the wall. Please, God, she tried to bargain, if you get me out of this I'll never curse again. I'll take the children to synagogue every week. I'll light extra candles Friday night. The only thing she couldn't promise was to go back to Joshua. She didn't think she could forgive him for threatening to take her children away. "Somehow I'll bring them up to be moral, God-fearing persons even if I'm on my own," she promised God. She wondered what kind of stepfather Raphi could be. He was a good uncle. Her spirits lifted. Raphi had rescued her before. Maybe he could do it again.

Deborah heard voices again from next door. She listened harder. They were speaking Hebrew! There were other Israeli hostages! She had to contact them.

Trying to get their attention might bring the guard and more abuse. But resistance required communication. She tried to think of all the coded means of communicating she'd ever read about. How did one tap SOS? In the end she decided that the simpler the method the better. Here goes nothing, she thought. Using her knuckles, she tapped the most common Hebrew nursery rhyme: "Little Jonathan runs in the morning to nursery school, *Yon-a-ton, ha-ka-tan, razt-baboker-el ha-gan.*"

Immediately the rhythm of the second verse came back! "He climbed the tree and looked for baby birds." Her chest pounded. Only an Israeli would have recognized that! Who could it be?

Who was there? She tapped back the letters for "Shalom" using one tap for *aleph,* two for *bet.* Each of the twenty-two letters in the Hebrew alphabet also represented a number. In Deborah's code she simplified the numbering and hoped that whoever was there would be clever enough to decipher it. She heard a shout and a mix of voices. How many were there?

The letters for "Shalom" were tapped back to her. She tapped the words "Deborah Stern—hostage."

Then someone behind the wall began to tap back a long message. It was slow work. Her head hurt and she had to force her mind not to wander during the laborious tapping.

Her horror multiplied with each new word. There were eight girl hostages!

Their bus, which followed the same route at the same time each day, had been an easy target.

Her door was rattling. She banged three times against the wall and hoped the girls would understand it was a distress signal. Then she quickly edged away from the wall.

In walked the redheaded guard called Sami, a cigarette dangling from his lips. He handed her a plastic water bottle. Evidently no one had realized the sinks in the chemistry lab worked. Deborah wasn't sure why that pleased her. She pretended to drink greedily, watching her captor.

Sami had a babylike face marred by a large scar. It made him seem vulnerable. Don't be fooled, she counseled herself. He tried to kill you once in the van. He'll try to kill you again.

"I need to use the bathroom urgently," she said, emphasizing the Hebrew word *dahuf* for urgency, wondering if he'd understand.

Sami nodded. He pointed his gun and led her down the hall to the women's faculty room bathroom. She kept her eyes down until she was in the stall. The lightbulb with its hidden microphone was still there! She had to make contact.

Sami had understood her Hebrew and might understand English or her smattering of French. He was leaning against the door of her stall. She was so inhibited she could hardly urinate let alone give a cry for help. Her mind flipped furiously for an identifying sign. *Stick to the truth when you lie,* Raphi had taught her. "It's a little hard for me to function with you standing there. You don't mind if I sing, do you?"

"I don't care," Sami said, sounding embarrassed.

Deborah began to hum different tunes, and then broke into a children's song from the Purim holiday. Purim wasn't until March, but Deborah assumed the fine points of the Jewish holidays would be beyond Sami. In GSS headquarters, Raphi had compared her mission to that of Queen Esther, the Purim heroine. She hoped someone would make the connection.

She washed her hands and face. One cheek was bruised, and her lip was cut in two places and her eyes swollen. She looked like hell. But she'd look a lot worse, she thought grimly, once the real interrogation began.

None of that mattered. How could she get the girls out?

Deborah pressed her watch alarm for the twentieth time and wondered where Raphi was.

Sami brought her back to the room. Within minutes the door rattled again. Deborah threw herself on the floor, and tried to fake sleep.

A hand shook her shoulder. A man's voice said in Arabic, then in English, "Kick her in the ribs."

In a reflex she opened her eyes.

"I thought so," the voice with the Arabic accent said smugly. "She's not only a bitch, she's a liar."

Deborah sat up and leaned against the sink cabinet. There were four of them. The tall bearded man had slapped her before. Sami's face was twitching with excitement. The third was Raba. The fourth was an Arab man of medium height whose face was turned away. She tried to catch Raba's eye but couldn't.

"Who exactly were you working for? Which unit of the GSS?" the tall one asked.

"I don't know what you mean," Deborah said.

He slapped her face. His nails lacerated her cheek.

Abed turned to Raba. "Your turn. The success of our mission is dependent on her talking. Have no mercy, she is vermin."

Raba stared at Deborah. She was breathing hard. Deborah could see that Abed was watching Raba, his eyes commanding her to obey him.

Her body was trembling. She won't do it, Deborah thought. Then Raba's lips became taut and she slapped Deborah so hard her head snapped back.

Raba's voice was full of venom. "You've brought this on yourself by bugging the campus. Stop pretending you're on a mission of mercy. The children are here because of you. If they have anyone to blame, it's you. You are causing needless violence. Aren't these Jewish children and your own children more important than your egotistical desire to be some sort of hero? Confess and spare yourself the torture."

Raba's voice wavered. Despite the slap and lethal words, Deborah didn't think Raba's heart was in this. Maybe she was kidding herself, but there had to be *something* to base her hope on.

Abed was squeezing Raba's shoulder like a proud husband. "Very nice, Raba," he said. *Why, he desires her,* Deborah thought.

Deborah spoke slowly, choosing her words as she went along. "I got the job in Bethlehem by myself. After I started working the Foreign Ministry asked me if I would send in reports occasionally. There were no secrets. Anyone could see what was happening on campus."

Abed's mouth twisted in a mocking gesture. "We checked on the former biology teacher whom you replaced. He's cruising the oceans on the *Sagafjord*. Not within the usual budget of a teacher. He got quite a settlement from the insurance company, a GSS pension, to be precise. Let's get on with it." Abed put his hand fondly on Sami's back. "Sami, it's your turn."

Sami's smile looked boyish and eager, but there was nothing childlike in his blow. Lights flashed inside her head. Blood leaked out of her mouth and a tooth was loose. The pain was excruciating.

Sami shouted into Deborah's face, "Who gave you the microphone? Was it the GSS? Which agents? Where are the other listening devices?"

"I don't know his name," Deborah said, fishing for something that might be innocuous but that would stop the beating. "He had a British accent. You found the device I planted. What more do you want from me?"

Sami whispered something to Abed.

Abed nodded. He was ebullient, turning to the other man, whom Raba didn't know. "Daud!" Abed commanded. "Now you. Finish the job. Please make it clear to Mrs. Stern that she must give us more precise information."

The fourth Arab moved in closer. Abed halted him. "She's lying. I know there are more listening devices. This time, poke out her eyes."

When Daud didn't move, Abed called him again.

"*Now,* Daud. I want her to appear blind next time on TV to show that I'm serious about the threats." Then Abed said something about blotting out the eyes of the infidel.

Sami reached inside his pants and pulled out a rusty nail file. He held it out to Daud, who swung his arm to reach for it. His elbow was toward her. Oddly, the gesture looked familiar. Through her pain and fear she realized this was Raphi! Hope flared for a fraction of a second, and was as soon extinguished as she realized Abed was holding a Galil.

Raphi's fingers ran over the blade. Surely *he* wouldn't blind her to carry through a rescue plot. But if he didn't he would give himself away. He'd once said something about only survival being important. Maybe he'd sacrifice her eyes. Her terror escalated.

Raphi looked from Sami to Abed. "If she appears blind on TV, every ugly cliché about Moslems will be reinforced. She looks bad enough already."

Deborah held her breath.

Abed shook his head. "Is that what the Teacher taught you? To be squeamish? I have a particular debt to pay back to the Jews. If you won't do it, I'll do it myself."

Raphi grasped the blade in his left fist. Deborah closed her eyes and screamed.

They're going to blind me now.

She heard a bang and a moan. When her eyes opened, the butt-stock of the gun was coming down on the back of Raphi's head.

Abed chuckled, "Don't go anywhere. We'll be back in a few minutes."

His pitiless laughter echoed inside her head.

Raba had screamed too as Daud Bahar lifted the nail file in a closed fist. At the last moment, he turned in place and aimed at Abed's heart. Abed was ready for him and knocked the knife away with the rifle. It had been a diabolical test that Daud Bahar had failed.

Flecks of dust floated in front of her eyes and her heart was beating fast. She reached out to grab the counter, but it wasn't there. Abed put his arm around her, holding her protectively to him.

The dizziness lasted only a few seconds. Abed's arms made her feel protected and safe. They were long, lanky, and strong. They smelled fresh and citruslike, of her favorite scent: 4711.

When she placed the smell, the coincidence entered her fuzzy mind like an alarm clock into a deep sleep.

That was the scent of the man who'd taken her away blindfolded. She had been too distracted to recognize him before.

There was something else nagging at her mind, too. Up close, the mole on his neck was two-tone and irregular. *He had a melanoma on his neck. That's how I remembered him.* Ali had said that about the man who'd attacked him in Egypt.

It all fit too well. Raba felt sick to her stomach. She fought the urge to throw up.

The strength that had attracted her to Abed turned to revulsion. She tried to pull away, and Abed looked down at her, startled. "Are you okay?" She shook her head.

"I'm dizzy. I need to sit down." He insisted on taking her arm and leading her to the teachers' room. He brought her the last glass of cola from the refrigerator. It had gone dead and was treacle sweet. His fingers stroked her face, from cheekbone to lips, and he ordered the other students to call him at once if Professor Alhassan needed help. She kept her head down until his brisk footsteps disappeared.

Students were sitting on her cot, watching CNN. It was after twelve o'clock, stuffy and hot in the room. Spiced turkey and cheese sandwiches, made from the supplies in the refrigerator, were being passed around on a tray. They offered her a sandwich, and she nibbled it, hoping it would quell the growing nausea.

Around her, the students ate greedily. No one had eaten a real meal since yesterday, Raba realized, when the lunch staff had gone home before the campus takeover. There was no one to prepare the usual lamb and rice. A student was fiddling with the gas burner but couldn't get it started for coffee. Deborah could do it, Raba thought ironically.

On TV, clips of Abed and Deborah from the news conference were broadcast over and over. A school bus had been blown up. At least three Israelis had been killed, CNN reported. The driver was in serious condition at Hadassah Hospital. The remaining students were being held as hostages on a formerly quiet Christian campus in Bethlehem.

Two students and a guard were already dead! Raba felt very hot, then experienced palpitations, and then a buzzing in her ears. She put her head between her knees, brushing off the students' offers of help as she caught her breath and stopped herself from fainting. She heard the rest without watching the screen: the prime minister had reiterated that Israel would not negotiate with terrorists. Throughout the country high school students had gone on hunger strikes in solidarity with the kidnapped children. Prayer services were being held in every city, town, and kibbutz.

It all felt unreal, particularly that she, Raba Masri Alhassan, had taken part in a brutal interrogation.

With one slap she had negated the beliefs of a lifetime.

She'd always wondered how average citizens could turn into the beasts who tortured others. Experts who'd examined the Rorschach inkblots from Adolph Eichmann and other Nazi war criminals couldn't tell them apart from tests of well-adjusted personalities.

The trial of John Demjanjuk, accused of being the concentration camp executioner Ivan the Terrible, had been widely covered in Michigan. Could this nice old man have been the monster of Treblinka? she'd asked herself. She knew that obedience to what researchers called the "authority of violence" played a role in pushing ordinary people to commit cruel and violent acts. There were famous experiments in which, ordered to do so by men wearing lab coats, average Americans agreed to give victims dangerously high levels of shocks. When Raba had read the study as an undergraduate, she had been sure she would have been in the minority of persons who resisted.

Well, she hadn't been.

On TV, the broadcast switched to a dark-haired Jewish woman who begged the terrorists to release her daughter. Raba's throat clogged and she got tears in her eyes.

I'm helping the terrorists. No. I've become one of them.

As my brother was corrupted, so was I.

Is it too late for me? Is my eternal soul forfeit? Raba thought of her mother on the day she'd returned home after the futile attempt at leaving her husband. She wasn't much older then than Raba was now. Had she felt her soul die as she entered the house and watched Abdullah Masri smile in triumph? Twenty years fell away and Raba remembered her scream as her father lifted his thick hand to slap her mother. Raba's fear that her mother would leave again had overcome common sense, and she'd grabbed his hand, trying to stop the violence, and he had shaken her off. Raba had stopped speaking after that. Soon, Aunt Fatima had come for her.

Her mother had always told her that Aunt Fatima had wanted her because she was the best reader in the third grade.

Raba stroked the scar on her leg. Aunt Fatima had taken her because she'd stopped talking, Raba now realized. Her mother must have begged her sister to rescue Raba. And she had. Until today, Raba hadn't remembered the incident.

Raba was lost in her thoughts when someone tapped her on the shoulder, making her jump. She turned around quickly to see Sami.

"Sorry," he said, squinting at her through tired eyes. "She says she'll only tell you."

What was he talking about?

Sami sensed her confusion and gestured in the direction of the chemistry lab. "Deborah Stern. She'll only confess to you."

Raba felt herself stiffen.

"Me? Did she say why?"

"No. Only that she trusts you to get it down right."

Four messages of importance came into the GSS office between 10:00 A.M. and 1:00 P.M. The first was from the listening center in Efrat. Deborah's voice had been heard in the women's bathroom. She was alive, but her mental state was in question. Why should she sing a Purim song in July? Purim was in March. Was it some kind of code? The soldier on duty played Gil the tape.

The second call came from the computer room. Their terrorist was Abed Shahada, age thirty-three, from a village just outside Jerusalem. Gil read over his background, noticing that he might be Abu Lail, a terrorist trained in Libya the summer before last but never positively identified. Abed was unmarried, but he had a sister named Laila who'd been blinded by rubber bullets. It was conceivable that he'd taken his nom de guerre from her. He'd studied in Sweden and would know too much about the country, Gil realized. His woman friend, a Swede named Kerstin, had agreed to answer questions and was eager to visit Israel. Anat had already been dispatched to pick her up.

Since returning, Abed had kept a low profile, running the foreign investment division of a bank in Hebron. Ironically, his security portfolio was clean. The Ministry of Finance had once short-listed him as a liaison between Israeli investors and West Bank firms, but his Hebrew was not adequate. If he was indeed Abu Lail, he was crafty, strong, and ruthless, according to a Bedouin double agent in the Libya training camp. He had strangled a fellow cadet for his drinking water.

Gil was reading the report a second time when his secretary brought in the transcription of phone calls being made from Manger College. There were only two, both made by Abed. In one he phoned the home of a widow in Gaza, ordering the death of Ali Alhassan. She'd checked. Dr. Alhassan was okay but he couldn't speak because he was doing emergency surgery. The second call oddly was to the Swedish consulate in Jerusalem. About veterinary schools.

The phone rang for the fourth time. It was the commander of the military camp in Bethlehem complaining that his soldiers kept shocking themselves on a safety device in their man's Alfa Romeo. The commander had the keys and wanted the car out of the camp immediately. Where should it be delivered to?

Gil was about to say there had to be some mistake when he saw Moshe Cohen looking furious, standing at the door. "I'll get back to you," Gil said into the phone and hung up. Moshe wanted to know where the hell Raphi was with the maps.

Gil cursed in three languages.

Merde. Harah. Kusi'mak. Raphi was in Manger College and would be killed for sure unless Gil rescued him.

24

The previous blows were nothing compared to what she'd get now, Abed warned Deborah. He leaned in her face, his brown eyes diabolical. Before, he'd wanted her to be recognizable on TV but now he didn't care if her own mother wouldn't know her.

He doesn't know my mother is dead, Deborah thought, oddly pleased, feeling as if she had a secret weapon against him. He held bloodstained ropes. Beginning at the shoulder, Abed wrapped Deborah's arms, tightening each loop, until both her arms were encircled. Women survived Mengele, Deborah told herself. At last you can see how you would have withstood the torture. Abed flexed the rope Deborah saw her mother's face. *Mother, mother, mother,* she heard herself call out, as the pain worsened. Abed tied her arms together behind her and pulled the rope toward her ankles, bending her into a circle. Everything stung at once—her wrists, elbows, legs, hips, back, as if they were breaking and being pulled out of their sockets. She knew she was dying. Let it come quickly, she prayed. Deborah passed out, then came to and blacked out again. She heard herself giving nonsensical answers to the questions, about her laboratory mice and the day she'd had lunch with King David.

Abed untied the rope between her hands and legs, and loosened the bonds so that only her wrists and ankles were tied.

He slapped her face. She was so numb it meant nothing.

"Who sent you here? Where does he live?"

Flies gathered on her bloody mouth.

"How did they recruit you? What were you supposed to do? Who exactly were you working for?"

She couldn't speak, wouldn't answer. Now her mother's face was angry. *Survive, Deborah,* she said. *You are not exempt from serving. In each generation there will be enemies who rise-up-to-destroy us.*

Abed grasped the nail of her pinky finger with a pair of pliers. Her soul spun from her body in a delirium of anguish.

I'm free, she thought, looking at the bloody pulp. Sand fly wings were growing from her arms. She was flying over the campus like the pigeons, bearing testimony. *Survive, survive,* Raphi called from afar.

King David was strumming his harp and singing to her. The Lord is my shepherd, the Lord is my shepherd.

Having her fingernail pulled off had set her free. She had withstood the torturer's tools.

Again she heard King David singing. From the straits I called to You. And You answered me in you greatness . . . God is with me I have no fear. I shall not die but live. . . . In the name of God I cut them down. . . . They encircle me like bees, but they are extinguished like a fire does thorns.

Little Jonathan ran to nursery school . . . hole in his trousers . . . hole in your head . . . Amid the buzz there was sudden clarity, like a sunbeam through a cloud on her kitchen balcony.

The children had to be saved, no matter the cost.

"Bring me Raba and I will confess. Only Raba," she gasped.

The torture stopped. Numbing sleep came.

Raba stood over Deborah and watched her cry in her sleep, curled like a fetus. Raba wanted to cry herself. Deborah was pale and her breathing was irregular. Never had she seen a human being so abased and abused. At last she put a hand on Deborah's shoulder. Deborah jerked awake. She opened her swollen eyes a slit. Raba gave her a drink and held her head. The water turned pink from the blood in Deborah's mouth and dribbled down her chin. She was trying to talk. Raba waited. Deborah's voice was thick. "Why have you joined them? You're no terrorist."

Raba stiffened. The last thing she expected was to be put on the defensive by this pathetic-looking creature. "Terrorism runs in families. You remember my brother, Ibrahim Masri, don't you?"

Deborah looked as if she was trying to place the name. She fell asleep. Raba felt ashamed that she had answered so roughly. She gave Deborah more water.

"I want to make a deal," Deborah said at length. "I'll tell you everything—betray those who sent me here—if you personally promise to get those girls out. They're only children. Innocent victims."

"I cannot act against my own people." Her words sounded vapid.

"Don't be asinine. This isn't your people and my people. It's your megalomaniacs versus mine."

It sounded like something Aunt Juni had said. Maybe women always saw war like this.

As if divining her thoughts, Deborah asked, "What if you have a baby girl? How will you look at her without remembering the faces of all those innocent high school girls you could have saved? They'll haunt you."

Deborah's swollen eyes were pleading with her. "Please. I'll make a deal with you. Each of us will betray her own self-righteous cause for a greater one."

Despite the heat, Raba felt cold. "Even if I agree with you, I have no way of getting those girls out."

Deborah took so much time to answer that Raba thought she had fallen asleep again. "You have to find a way. Everything depends on it."

Deborah reached for her hand. Raba saw the mutilated finger, and dry heaved.

"Yes. That, too," Deborah said. "This is the work of your leader. This is where he will take you—a world of coercion where your very soul is no longer your own. That's worse than the physical torture. Escape while you can. Raba, you're not like them. Take a paper. Write this down. I'm going to give you the first half of my confession to buy time. Tell them I've promised to give you the rest—names, addresses, everything. Think of some condition and then stall until you can cook up a plan. There must be another way out of this campus."

Raba searched her own heart. Deborah's words were an echo of her deepest feelings.

Inside Raba's briefcase was a pad and pencil set. She took it out and started to write.

"The office of the GSS is off Our Mother Rachel Street in the old Katamon neighborhood. The elevator doesn't work the way a normal elevator does . . ."

An hour later, Raba left Deborah, who'd been too exhausted to go on. She had a spy novel's worth of details on Israel's secret world. Raba wondered if Deborah would be put into prison if she survived. Evidently Deborah didn't care.

Each of us will betray her own self-righteous cause for a greater one, Deborah had said.

The children must be saved.

Raba retreated to the bathroom and locked the door. She wanted to be alone to think.

What she hadn't told Deborah was that she'd visited the girls. Several were already in shock. When she entered, one of them had been praying, standing with her eyes closed, swaying back and forth. One stared listlessly into space. Others wept, clutched each other, or talked nonstop, but their speech lacked coherency. Unfortunately, psychological damage would be harder to repair than physical.

Raba had insisted that they be taken to the bathroom and that food be brought. Food was in short supply, and she was told that the students had to be fed before the prisoners. Starvation would worsen their already precarious state of helplessness and confusion.

On one side of the balance hung the lives of these eight teenage girls. On the other side were her life and Ali's.

And the baby's.

Even if she wanted to save them, Raba felt helpless. She didn't know how to fix burners or knock out mechanics like Deborah. She made a mental list of her assets. She'd gained the terrorists' trust and had access to the girls. Abed seemed to have a crush on her and might indulge her whims. No one had checked her briefcase coming into the campus. In addition to the cellular telephone she had a pocket-sized can of pepper spray, bought long ago in Detroit. She wondered if it stayed potent indefinitely. Deborah would know that, too.

There had to be another exit. Barguth was an aristocrat like Ali. He would never allow deliveries through the front gate. New fence or not, there had to be a service entrance.

Let's say she found a way out. The campus was surrounded by the Israeli army.

If the girls made a rush for the exit, the army would provide cover for them. If the army knew that it was the girls getting out. Otherwise the girls might be killed by friendly fire.

Even if she dared to use her phone, there would be no way of getting the army. Information would be difficult. She'd have to work her way through operators who would be contemptuous because she didn't speak Hebrew.

Her home phone and the car phone were probably bugged.

Whom could she call?

Aunt Juni. She'd be in the kitchen now, stirring pots, passing on information. *I've worked for them all,* Aunt Juni had said. *The causes change and in the end it's your family that counts. . . . You'd be surprised how you can control people through their stomachs.*

Aunt Juni would have some way of getting through. Suddenly an outlandish plan came to mind. It was so simple, it just might work. What if it failed? She thought of Deborah and trembled. If she failed, they would torture her next.

She turned to the mirror to put on lipstick. She looked herself in the eye. I think I've made the right decision, she thought. She shuddered. Her skin was pale. She touched each cheek with lipstick, and with the heel of her hand rubbed in the artificial pinkness. With a steady hand she pulled her eyelids outward and traced them with black liquid eyeliner. Her eyes looked bigger and more mysterious. But would they fool Abed?

Doesn't he realize how silly his university Arabic sounds? Raphi woke from a stupor to hear Gil's voice uncharacteristically loud. Then he realized where he was, and the shock hit of Gil's being here in Bethlehem. Why was Gil here? What was he doing?

He looked down at himself in panic.

He hadn't been castrated.

He let out his breath.

Raphi had been beaten to unconsciousness. He remembered being tied and dragged to a supply room attached to Barguth's office. He'd been tied to the foot of a bed.

The last words he remembered were Abed's promise to castrate him.

What had stopped him?

Gil. Somehow his friend had come at the right moment and stayed the hand against him.

Gil was reading out loud a listing of Red Cross rules for visiting prisoners. He talked about Amnesty International and the Geneva Convention and pretended to be an advocate for the hostages.

Raphi assessed his injuries. His right hand was badly sprained, and, from the extreme pain, it felt as if several ribs were broken. He hoped his lungs weren't punctured. He took a deep breath and exhaled. They seemed to be okay. Abed had smashed a chair on Raphi's right leg, his so-called good leg, and it hurt like hell.

If Abed thought he'd be stalwart and hold out under continued torture, he'd be disappointed. The GSS golden rule in resisting torture was to be tight-lipped up to the point of serious permanent injury—then talk. Latter-day espionage believed it was more important for a person to gather strength than to protect government secrets. In the end, a clever interrogator could get anything, so why resist until you were cat food?

Raphi listened to Gil, trying to figure out what the GSS had come up with.

Gil used an authoritative tone: "The campus is surrounded by Israelis with commando units at every conceivable exit. There's no way you can escape without violence. I would be glad to personally negotiate a way out for you and to guarantee your safe passage to a sympathetic country of your choosing. Tunisia? Libya? Cuba?"

Raphi tried to figure out the strategy, but he was puzzled. If Moshe Cohen wanted to send someone in, Gil was not the logical choice. He hadn't done serious fieldwork for several years, and many Palestinians, including Raba Alhassan, had seen him in Jerusalem.

Then it hit him in the gut. Like him, Gil hadn't gained approval from Moshe Cohen or anyone else in the GSS. Nor was he connected to the helicopter rescue of Jacques and Uzi. The GSS hadn't sent anyone in to rescue him. Gil was acting on his own.

Raphi tried with all his might to break the bonds. His hands were tied behind him, which made his balance awkward.

His legs were shackled and his mouth gagged.

Gil was pretending to be a bloody Red Cross inspector, alternating between his university Arabic and British English, using words like "bits" instead of "parts," and complaining that "it wasn't well done of the terrorists" to deny him access, as if they gave a fuck. He went on as if delivering a filibuster in the House of Lords, explaining how he'd gotten in— "Even the Israelis are respectful of the Red Cross," he'd said. Raphi could imagine Gil crossing his legs, flicking lint off his lapel, examining his fingers. He was politely insisting on seeing the prisoners, and Abed sounded, unbelievably, as if he were wavering. It was, Raphi realized, a clever ploy—and the stalling technique, plus the doubt he'd created, had probably already saved his balls, if not his life.

He felt a glimmer of hope.

The office door opened. Raphi recognized Sami's voice. Sami knew Gil! In fact, he owed Gil a debt for protecting him from the border police. He could help get them both out!

On the other hand, Gil could expose Sami. Gil was the only one with whom he'd been in direct contact. Gil had personally heard Sami's confession and shaped his alibi. If Sami had decided to go back over to the other side, Gil could be in his way. If Abed suspected Sami, the redhead would have to prove his loyalty. He might already be suspect because he'd supposedly recognized Daud Bahar.

Killing Gil would be an easy way of showing his loyalty.

The more he thought of it, the more Raphi realized that was what Sami would do.

Again Raphi strained at his bonds. *Gil, Gil, Gil, watch out.* But it was too late.

"He's GSS," Sami screamed.

There was a noisy struggle, furniture scraping and curses in Arabic. Gil was a terrific fighter, but he was outnumbered and out-armed. It was over fast. Raphi heard the pounding, the scream, the gurgle of blood.

His best friend had been stabbed to death.

At that moment he wanted to die, too.

But not before he had his revenge.

Raba ran her fingers through her hair again and knocked on Barguth's office door.

Abed opened immediately, the rifle in his hand, his face fierce. Raba startled and pulled back.

His face changed instantly. "Sorry. I thought it was someone else."

"Do you mind if I come in?" Raba asked.

Abed looked uncomfortable. He slipped out of the room and closed the door behind him. "Let's sit out here. I've smoked a cigar and the odor might be offensive to someone in your condition."

She could smell the smoke through the door and imagined him helping himself to Barguth's expensive cigars. Abed took her arm and sat down with her in the outer office. With a hand gesture, he banished the student secretary from the room and Raba noticed the blood on the underside of Abed's sleeve. What was going on in there?

Raba spoke with an exaggerated breathlessness. "I thought you'd like to know, Deborah Stern has fully confessed. All she's holding back is the real names of the officers who recruited her. And she's willing to trade those for a sign that the hostages are being well treated. I've convinced her that we have no intentions of hurting them, that they'll be getting lunch soon."

Abed's eyes narrowed. "She has no right to demand anything."

"Patience," Raba laughed, showing off her dimples. "Remember, you catch more flies with honey. She gave me a lot of useful information. I took it in shorthand. I'll transcribe it this afternoon. We already found the listening device she confessed planting in the teachers' room. So what if she wants to make sure the children eat? In any case, I was about to propose that I do some cooking. Do you mind? Frankly, I'm feeling a little faint."

Abed's eyes flickered to her belly, and he looked sheepish. "I suppose you would be. I hadn't thought of it. I'm afraid we're out of sandwiches."

Raba forced another smile. "Leave that to me. They serve lamb every day in this school. There must be supplies in the freezer. I'll cook it plain for the students, but do you like *senyye maslouka?*"

What was it about meat pies that made men's eyes shine? *At least I got his attention,* she thought.

He smiled at her. "I didn't know professors could cook."

She whispered, with a twinkle in her eye, "Do me a favor and don't spread it around. The Alhassans might fire their chef. I once won a prize, and Ali's aunt has been giving me cooking lessons."

Raba knew that the next words would determine

the success or failure of her plan. "The supply room is locked."

She'd checked. The kitchen door led to a loading dock, where the supplies were delivered by truck.

Abed was thoughtful. "I'll have someone open it for you." He paused. "In fact, I'll send you a student to help you." He glanced at the clock. It was nearly three. The deadline was three hours away. "How long will the cooking take?" Abed sounded eager. Except for those pitiful sandwiches, no one had eaten a meal since the operation began. The whole campus was full of ravenous men and women.

"Not long," Raba smiled. "Just leave it to me."

The prospect of lunch with Raba cheered Abed. He should have made better preparations for food. Everyone knew that the Algerian terrorists who'd hijacked the plane to Marseilles had become thick witted from hunger. Raba was turning out to exceed his fantasies. He thought of her striking Deborah. Her fierceness had surprised and pleased him.

An assassin had been dispatched from Gaza. Her husband was certainly dead by now. According to Islamic law, she could remarry within one hundred days. Abed could tell she was attracted to him. Why else had she put on lipstick? Maybe I can get her to make love with me after lunch. He felt the beginning of an erection with its pleasant anticipation. He went back to Barguth's office. "Have the office cleaned," he ordered Sami. "I'm going to check the perimeter. Wash it, air it out, clean the bathroom." In the storeroom adjoining the office there was a bed where Barguth napped. "The storeroom also. Change the linens on the bed."

"What about the prisoner?"

Abed frowned. He'd planned to take care of this supposed Bahar himself. There was no time, now. Bahar had been beaten soundly enough so that he wouldn't be an immediate threat. "Make sure he's bound. Then put him in the chemistry lab. There's time for him later."

*   *   *

When the door opened, Deborah held back a horrified scream. Sami was dragging in Raphi—limp, dirty, and inert. *Oh my God. Let him not be dead.* Sami was tying Raphi, back toward her, to a metal radiator, so he couldn't be dead! Relief poured through her. She had to bite back a shout. Sami ripped off Raphi's gag in a way that had to be painful, then turned to her. "Here's someone to talk to," Sami mocked in Hebrew.

Deborah waited for the door to close and made her voice work. It came out in a whisper. "Raphi, Raphi, can you hear me? Are you all right?" It was the first time she'd spoken since Raba left and her voice had a different timbre, without modification and amplification, as if it came from a tape recorder. The problem, she suspected, was her head.

His voice was flat, inflectionless. "I've felt better. How about you."

The tension loosened inside her. He was alive and he was here! "Okay," she said, her voice hoarse.

Sami was conversing loudly with the guard in Arabic.

"What are they saying?" Deborah asked.

"The gist is that we have to get out of here."

"No shit."

He laughed. The brittle sound seemed so incongruous. Tears came to her eyes, and she felt vitalized.

Her thoughts shifted once again to her mother. After the war, she'd been despondent and close to suicide. While she was waiting for a public shower, a woman in line had taken pity on her and given her an early turn. That act of kindness had rekindled her mother's spirit. Now Raphi's laughter rekindled Deborah's.

Raphi spoke slowly, as if feeling his way. "I'm not going to patronize you and say everything will be okay. Unless we think of something clever, nothing is going to be okay. I'm not even going to ask you the details of how you're feeling, but that's not because I don't care. If we're not out of here soon, feelings aren't going to be relevant, because we'll be dead and the girls will be dead. Tell me how you're tied."

She described the ropes on her arms and legs left over from the torture session.

"I'm so sorry, Deborah. For this, and for getting you involved in the first place. Please forgive me."

Somehow that made her feel better, too. "I'm an adult. I could have said no. I'm doing okay. Just tell me if you have any ideas to get me untied."

Raphi sighed. "There is an old Houdini trick for getting out of ropes. Sami won't take me anywhere without permission, but I assume he takes you to the bathroom. Tell him you need to go. Before he ties you up again, flex and inflate your body as much as possible. That will give you slack to move afterward."

Anything was better than sitting here helpless. "I thought Houdini used handcuffs."

"He did most of the time," Raphi said.

"How did he get out of those?"

"He hid a key up his nose or in his ear."

That surprised Deborah. "Do you have anything hidden?"

"Sorry, only an old condom, and it's not even mine. I'm wearing borrowed pants." His voice sounded unbearably sad.

A condom. The kernel of an idea lodged in her fuzzy brain. Deborah shouted for Sami. He must have gone downstairs, because the guard in the hall called for him, too.

About ten minutes after she called him, Sami pushed the door open. He was smoking. "What do you want?" he asked gruffly.

"The toilet, please," Deborah said. He blushed, and then untied her. She could barely walk. Every joint ached, and the pain from her finger made her dizzy. As far as she could tell, the microphone was still in the electric lightbulb. Was anyone listening? Her throat was too dry to sing. "Are you going to kill me?" she asked him.

"Yes. But you will suffer again first."

"Why are you doing this, Sami? I can hear children in the next room. You must have little brothers and sisters. Let the children go. They'll speak in your behalf."

"Shut up," Sami said. "Next time, shit in your pants."

As he retied her in the room, she tried to swell her body. A pity she hadn't asked Raphi for more details about how to do this. She did the best she could, flexing her sore muscles, thinking that might add breadth.

After he'd slammed the door, Deborah checked the ropes. Sami hadn't bound them in ringlets around her arms this time, just once around her wrists, and looser. It wasn't much, but that's all she had. The ankle ties seemed the least secured. Raphi advised her to work on those first, moving them back and forth until the knot gave. Her ankles were soon worn raw, but it worked.

Raphi coached her. "Take off your shoes and try to work with your toes. I know it sounds crazy, but Houdini did it."

She was skeptical but found that she could tug at the knots by fisting her toes, then grab the end of the string between her first two toes. "How do you know so much about Houdini?"

Raphi, trying unsuccessfully to wriggle out of his own ropes, sounded out of breath. "As a kid I was fascinated by the idea that a Hungarian rabbi's son could become the world's most famous magician. But when I was thirteen I met my first martial arts teacher and he was better than a magician."

Deborah pulled another knot out. "Where was that?"

"In New York. Believe it or not, he was a rabbi named Zecharia who believed that protecting your body was a divine commandment and needed to be taken as seriously as morning prayer. He used to say that God had taken us out of Egypt 'with a mighty hand and an outstretched arm' to show us the way we had to take care of ourselves ever after."

She was silent for a moment. "Do you believe in God?"

"Sure. It's man I have trouble believing in."

"I'm surprised."

"I wasn't bullshitting you the night we went dancing. This wouldn't make sense to me if I didn't believe that there was a divine purpose in the survival of the Jewish people."

The night they'd stood together at the Wall seemed a million years ago, Deborah thought as she watched him struggle with his bonds. Her knots weren't yielding any further. "Is there anything you can use to cut the ropes? Look around," Raphi said.

A metal strip ran along the countertop to contain spilled liquids. She had a rim like this in her apartment, and it often became unattached. Maybe this one would, too. She slid her ropes under one edge of the metal strip and sawed back and forth. Sweat trickled into her eyes, but the effort paid off. Eventually the last rope fibers split.

As she knelt to untie him, he saw her face close up. "Poor Deborah. They really did a job on you." His first motion with his freed hands was to hug her. He pressed his lips to her bloodied hand. His right arm barely made it around her shoulder. She realized he was badly injured. "You're not in such great shape yourself."

He stretched his right leg painfully. "Could be worse."

She looked at his pants. "Whose are they?"

"Gil's. He doesn't need them anymore." Pain shrouded his eyes.

She hugged him. "Oh, Raphi, I'm so terribly sorry."

His eyes were wet. He sighed and squeezed her good hand. "We have to get out of here fast."

Deborah shook herself. A thought was nagging at the back of her brain, waiting to be articulated. She got up and touched the gas spigots. For safety against explosions, gas was always supplied by high-pressure tanks kept outside the building. It would run into the building with copper tubing. In the lab itself, a rubber hose connected the gas spigots to the Bunsen burners. Either the copper lead or the rubber might be so brittle that it would break when even slightly jarred so she'd have to work carefully. All depended upon whether the reducing valve on the high-pressure main tanks had been left open.

"I have an idea. No one ever turned the water off in this room. There's a chance the gas still works. We could possibly make a gas bomb."

"With what, exactly?"

"You wouldn't happen to have anything stretchy and impermeable, would you?"

Raphi caught on and his eyes lit up. He pulled the condom from his pocket. "Something like this?"

"Exactly what I had in mind," she said. Her torn lips tried to turn upward. *I can't believe I'm smiling.*

Cautiously she turned the valve that controlled the gas flow to the lab. The hose looked okay.

She tried to turn the handle but it had corroded and wouldn't move. "Shit," she said. "I need a monkey wrench." She looked around the room in frustration, trying again. Her hand ached, but the spigot wouldn't move. She stamped her foot in frustration.

Raphi placed his hands over the faucet, bracing his legs. He looked so intense. Then he moved, stifling a shout. There was a pop of air and the hiss of gas. He turned it off again.

"Fantastic!" Deborah whispered.

He bowed crookedly.

She was excited now. She might be battered and terrified, but for the first time there was cause for modest optimism. Maybe they'd get out of here after all.

The room already smelled of gas. Natural gas was odorless, she knew. Gas companies were compelled to add a bad smell for safety. She hoped it wouldn't alert their guard.

Raphi slid the light-brown rubber out of the wrapper. Deborah held it curiously to the light. She'd never actually seen a condom up close, having married before they had made their rebound on the contraception scene. Deborah examined it. There were bumps on the rubber, but the surface appeared whole.

In fact, for her purpose, the condom looked perfect.

Deborah grasped it in two hands. "How far will it expand?"

He grinned. She shook her head. "A lot of good you are."

Raphi turned on the gas tap while she held the condom around the edges. When it had ballooned out to three times its original size, she tried to tie it closed, but kept hitting her injured finger. The first time it slipped from her hands. Stop it, she scolded herself. You've done this a thousand times at birthday parties.

When she was ready, Raphi went back to the radiator, pretending to be tied. Deborah keened, "Sami, Sami, Sami."

The door slammed open. Sami walked in militantly. For the first time he wasn't smoking! "I told you not to call me," he shouted. "I'm not your personal servant."

She kept crying, "Sami, Sami, Sami, Sami."

Angrily, he lit a cigarette and approached her. Deborah let out her breath.

"What's the problem?" His voice was hostile.

"I have a terrible stomachache. Please help me."

"I told you I wouldn't take you again."

Nonetheless, he came closer. He must have noticed that her feet were untied, because he jerked back just as he got to her. She still managed to catch him with her feet, her back thrusting against the floor.

She threw the balloon at his lit cigarette.

The flame moved at 300 yards a second, just under the speed of sound.

There was a whoosh and a whip. A belch of flame enveloped Sami's face. His red hair and eyebrows ignited, filling the room with a putrid smell. He screamed and batted at his head.

Raphi grabbed the gas spigot and wrenched it fully open. Deborah and Raphi ran toward the door, slamming it closed when they were on the other side. Behind them was another sound like wind and then an explosion knocked the tiny window out of the top of the door.

"Hurry," Raphi said, though he was limping.

Deborah couldn't move fast. She hurt too much. He

was already opening the classroom where the girls were sequestered. There was a terrible peppery smell.

The guard was gone. It was eerily quiet. The room was empty.

25

After getting Abed's permission to cook, Raba walked back to the kitchen through the courtyard. She had to keep herself from running; now that she'd worked out her plan, she was eager to start before her courage ran out. The campus had fallen into a lull. Students were lying around the grassy areas under the trees. Every soda machine had been emptied, and the sandwiches were gone.

Abed, juggling his subordinates, had told the gate guard to help Raba. The kitchen door was padlocked, as was the huge refrigerator freezer. Anwar fumbled with the keys, while Raba became more anxious. She had barely two hours until the deadline.

Anwar was sweating when he finally unlocked the freezer. The cold frosted the air around them when he swung the doors open. Inside were shanks of lamb hung unappetizingly on hooks. Raba was short and lifting them off the hook took all her strength. "Could you, please?" she smiled at Anwar. He blushed and lifted one off for her. Then, trying to look as if she knew what she was doing, Raba took it from him and maneuvered it into a huge cooking pot. The food here was usually roasted on a spit, but she supposed that would require cutting it from the bone. On the wall was a block of enormous sharp knives. She didn't have a clue about how to transform this cold slab of meat into something that could turn on a vertical rotisserie. Betty Crocker, where are you now? she thought in frustration. She found a slicing knife with a ten-inch blade in the drawer and pretended to start trimming the fat.

Raba wiped her forehead with an apron, just as Aunt Juni had. She was already out of breath. She put the pot on the fire, and lit the gas with a long match. There was no water in the pot. How stupid can you get, Raba? she thought. Then, always the psychologist, she cautioned herself against negative thinking.

Using a plastic pitcher, Raba poured water over the lamb.

Even she, a noncook, knew that roasting a piece this large would take two days, not two hours.

Raba asked Anwar to bring in the empty glass dishes from the teachers' room. She prayed he wouldn't notice how premature that was. He left, glad to have something useful to do, and Raba was alone in the kitchen. She looked out to the loading ramp. To her joy, exactly parallel to the back door of the kitchen, there was an opening in the security fence, cleverly disguised so that it could only be seen from inside.

If she left right now she could escape!

The idea made her tremble all over. An inner voice shouted that she owed that to herself and her new baby. Then a second, stronger voice made her think of the children upstairs, helpless without her assistance.

Raba was pouring a whole container of coriander into the water when Anwar returned. The kitchen smelled wonderful. Soon the smell would permeate the campus, and, if Raba was right, the students would wake up, feel their hunger, and become restless. Arguments would break out as an expression of the tension plus hunger. She was counting on the unrest to serve as a distraction.

She prayed that no one would come and check on her progress.

Ad-libbing, she took out a knife and a rounded wooden hammer used to flatten cutlets. There was a second large pot on the counter. When Anwar returned with the pile of plates, Raba asked him to fill the pot with water and carry it to the stove.

"Fill it to the top," she said. "We need a lot of rice."

It was so heavy he put down his gun to carry it.

The water splashed over the top onto his expensive imported sneakers. He cursed and looked down to assess the damage.

That's when Raba hit him on the head with a metal frying pan, just as the characters always did in the cartoons she'd watched as a kid in Detroit.

The pot fell to the ground, spilling water everywhere.

He slumped to the floor, dazed, and then he closed his eyes. How long would he remain unconscious? Raba had no idea.

She took out her telephone and dialed. Chimes and an announcement in Hebrew answered her back! Her hands were shaking. She tried again. This time the phone rang. On the third ring Aunt Juni answered. Raba exhaled.

"Aunt Juni, this is Raba. How are you? I need some cooking advice. I'm making lamb. I need to take out eight portions immediately. How can I do it without ruining the whole roast?"

"Is it a young lamb, milk-fed, perhaps?" asked Aunt Juni. *Wonderful,* thought Raba. She understands. She must be following the kidnapping on TV. "You must cook it *sofrito* with just a cup of water and a few tablespoons of oil. When the meat is browned, turn it, and then cut off what you need. The rest will stew in its own juices. Don't worry, it won't fall apart.

"How are you feeling, little one?"

Raba's eyes filled with tears.

"I'm okay, Aunt Juni."

"Don't worry. Do you want me to come and help you?"

"That would be wonderful, Aunt Juni. I can't talk now. The lamb will burn. Peace be with you."

Both a GSS intelligence officer and a Manger College student picked up Raba's phone call. The Israeli soldier, wondering what lamb could stand for, sent the message for computerized decoding. The student, already giddy from the wonderful smell, smiled and licked his lips. He decided not to report the call. Abed had given strict orders not to disturb him this afternoon unless it was urgent. He was new at security, but any fool would understand that a recipe wouldn't constitute an emergency.

Aunt Juni took off her apron and phoned her oldest and best-paying customer: Moshe Cohen.

Anwar would awaken any second. Raba had to work fast. With shaking hands, she took a long aluminum ladle and pressed it to the bottom of the pot. It filled with dark, oily liquid, the first drippings of the lamb. Carefully, she filled a bowl. A few bread slices were caught beneath the blade of the slicer. Her narrow fingers slipped underneath and pulled them out. Raba arranged them in the towel with which she held the hot bowl and climbed the stairs.

The student who was guarding the girls leaped to attention when he heard her footsteps. "I brought you something to eat," she said.

He relaxed his stance, and Raba gave him her sweetest smile. Abed had permitted her to visit the girls. There was no reason for the guard to doubt her now. Raba watched him eagerly eye the food. He leaned his gun against the wall. "Could you unlock the room for me first?" she asked. "I'm supposed to check the Jewish girls from time to time."

He took out the key and snapped the lock open. Raba moved closer to him with the soup. The smell of the lamb floated up in the steam. "Careful. It's hot."

Despite her warning, he reached with both hands. The bowl burned his fingers. He looked for a surface to put it down, dancing against the pain. Raba pulled her pepper spray from her pocket. She aimed it at his face and hands. The guard collapsed in agony, howling and rubbing his face.

Raba started sneezing. She shook her head and squeezed her eyes. She flung the door open.

Inside, the eight girls looked startled and terrified. The room stank of urine and body odor.

"Come now, quickly," she shouted. Then she lowered her voice, "Quietly. Walk so you can't be heard."

At first they hesitated, suspicious of a trap. At last one girl shouted something in Hebrew and the rest broke out of their stupor and followed.

They raced down the stairs after Raba, trying to move quietly.

They went through the kitchen, past the cooking meat. Raba was still sneezing. The outside door to the loading ramp was stuck. "Help me," she shouted desperately. Anwar was gone. They had only seconds.

Two girls threw themselves against the door, mercilessly pounding their shoulders against it. Slowly it gave. Fresh air blew into the hot room.

Raba looked for the soldiers but didn't see any. Where were they?

"Call in Hebrew. Call for help. Call for help in Hebrew," Raba said in English.

Had Aunt Juni understood her? Had she gotten through?

"Ta'azroo lanu," one of the voices called. Then the others joined in, wailing, crying in Hebrew.

For a long moment there was no response. Raba heard shouts from the direction of Barguth's office.

There were no stairs down from the ramp. "Jump!" Raba shouted. "Jump."

The ramp was at least five feet off the ground. The first girl jumped and fell. The others followed, crying out softly. The last girl looked too frightened. Raba pushed her off the ramp and she screamed.

Then suddenly faces burst through the fence outside. Israeli soldiers, thank Allah. Raba never thought she'd be happy to see armed Israeli troops rushing toward her. The girls ran forward. One girl fainted, and a soldier put his hands under her armpits and dragged her away.

The rescue was happening so quickly Raba could hardly take it in. She counted six girls safe, and then finally the last two were on their way. One paused. *"Shukran!"* she shouted her thanks.

Raba took a deep breath to clear her head. Her heart was beating hard. She turned back to the kitchen. Now she had to get Deborah out.

That's when she saw Abed standing in the doorway, a rifle pointed at her.

Never had she seen a face so contorted in frenzy.

She backed up. She was at the edge of the ramp. If she pretended to fall, would he shoot her? Would the fall hurt her baby? Before she could move, Abed grabbed her arm with piercing fingers and dragged her back to the kitchen. He struck her cheek with his fist. She could taste blood. Amid the agony she saw colored lights.

"You would have had a future with me," Abed screamed at her. His scent was strong; he'd perfumed himself for their luncheon. "Now you will die like your husband. That's right. Ali Alhassan was killed this morning. His loyal wife will join him and his family line will end on this day."

Abed reached for her and slammed her down against the kitchen sink. She remembered the knives on the wall and tried to run for them. He guessed her intention and threw her to the floor again and kicked her savagely in the belly. She tried to protect her baby, but he kicked her fingers away.

She lay very still. She could both smell burning lamb and taste the blood in her mouth. *Let it be a lie*, she begged God. *Let Ali be alive.*

Upstairs, the fire was spreading quickly in the hall. Deborah was paralyzed. Raphi shouted, "Let's go!"

When they got downstairs, loud shouting in Arabic came from the direction of Barguth's office. "What are they saying?" Deborah asked.

Raphi paused, listening. "Most of the students are surrendering through the front gate. It appears that the children have escaped from the kitchen through a back exit.

"Quickly," he said. "Abed will never surrender, and there may be others loyal to him. The children's departure makes us his last card to play. He's coming for us, you can be sure."

In the kitchen, they found lamb splattering on the stove. Beside the stove, Raba lay in a puddle of blood.

Deborah ran to her and put fingers on her neck. The pulse was thready. "Alive," she said. "Thank God. Can you carry her?"

"I'll try. You go ahead."

As Raphi bent forward to pick up Raba, Deborah heard the hissing intake of his breath.

"You're badly hurt. Let me help," she said.

"Hoist up her legs," Raphi said.

When Deborah touched her, Raba's eyes opened briefly. They were stark with pain and she was ashen. "We have to get her out of here," Deborah said.

They began walking to the ramp. Raphi had already crouched to jump down when they heard the grating laughter from the direction of the kitchen. Abed stood facing them, his eyes blistering with fury. In his hands he held the eighteen-inch barrel of the Galil. He slammed the heavy kitchen door behind him, shutting off escape from that side. Deborah and Raphi stood motionless on the ramp, still holding Raba.

"Idbah alyahud," Abed shouted, raising the rifle in a powerful arm, calling again and again for the death of all Jews.

There was nowhere to run. Deborah remembered reading that although the Galil was rather heavy, it climbed rapidly in automatic fire. "Duck-down," she whispered, as Abed's grip tightened and he pulled it closer to his chest.

Raphi's thin mouth twisted in a mocking half smile that petrified her. They were still holding Raba. Deborah screamed and tried to stoop as Abed's long fingers closed on the trigger.

Nothing happened. His face was deformed with wrath, his eyes scalding with hate as he pulled the trigger again and cursed.

Raphi baited him. "Oh, dear Abed. Your passion for our Jewish weapons was so great that you neglected to check the Galil when I returned it. I was counting on that when I removed the firing pin."

Abed's fury seemed to bloat him, and Deborah thought he might charge at them, driving them over the ramp. Raphi must have felt the same thing. He shifted directions, taking all of Raba's weight in his arms, backing away from Abed, and laying her down in the kitchen.

In a paroxysm, Abed threw the gun at him. Raphi ducked it. The Galil clattered along the stone floor and slid under a table, dragging with it a forgotten onion.

The two professional fighters sized up the situation. It was a standoff.

"You've lost," Raphi said, in a reasonable voice. "The girls are free. Call it quits. Maybe you'll be traded in a prisoner exchange once the Palestinian Authority takes over."

Abed's face turned rigid at the suggestion. "A free dog is better than a shackled lion. Death is better than being mired in your jails."

"As you wish," Raphi said, his eyes turning cold and black as space. They focused on the slicing knife on the counter. Abed surged forward, lunging for it.

Deborah didn't think. Propelled by fear and her own rage, she hurled herself toward Abed, hitting him in the wrist as she'd been taught in Raphi's class. It caught him by surprise and the knife crashed onto the floor.

He recovered fast, but not before she'd grabbed a cooking hammer from the table. She stretched back with it, her aim to strike him in the nose. Abed reached around her and knocked it from her-hand. Her hair was caught in his fingers and it wound around his wrist until tears came to her eyes. He crimped her arm backward so that the pain ran through her shoulder. She cried out in agony and he laughed again. "Kike whore, you've given me more trouble than you're worth." His thumb and middle finger closed on her breast, pinching it hard.

She stamped hard on Abed's toe. It was enough to unbalance him. She dodged, but not before receiving a blow to the side of the head. A tray of glass plates fell with her, smashing into hundreds of sharp pieces. Deborah tumbled onto them.

Her hands were bleeding. *I'm still alive*, she thought,

her heart beating fast. Despite the pain, she felt a strange high, as if she'd taken amphetamines.

Abed had shifted his attention to Raphi. Smiling, as if pleased at his own cleverness, he stalked Raphi's right side. *He remembers just where Raphi's been hurt,* Deborah realized. "I should have castrated you when I had the chance," Abed said.

"Who's preventing you now?" Raphi asked. "Let Deborah leave. Then they'll be just the two of us. One Jew, one Moslem. Isn't that what this is all about?"

Oddly, Abed and Raphi were speaking English, as if locked into the neutral tongue of international athletic contests. But these weren't amateurs and this wasn't a demonstration joust. A few meters from her, a battle to the death was shaping up. It felt surreal.

To her alarm Deborah realized just how vulnerable Raphi looked. Abed pitched toward him. At the last possible moment, Raphi pivoted and changed directions, facing Abed with his left side. Then he stumbled.

Abed's smile grew wider with confidence.

He leaped forward, punching Raphi in his broken ribs. Deborah winced at the pain in Raphi's face, as he lost his balance and fell backward. Her hand edged toward the slim knife on the floor and she crouched, ready to spring when the chance came.

Raphi's eyes were squinting, as if he had to force himself to concentrate.

Abed rushed at Raphi's head. He was already up, his left hand forward again. When Abed tried to jab out again, Raphi stepped aside neatly. His eyes broadcast pain, as he side-kicked Abed with his left leg, hitting Abed in the chest and sending him sprawling.

Deborah tightened her grip on the knife, but Abed was too fast for her. Gathering himself quickly, he ran at Raphi. He pummeled Raphi's chest. He got in close this time so Raphi couldn't kick back. Abed seemed to draw strength as he sensed Raphi's fatigue. Abed was the larger man. A fighter could often dominate a fight with brute strength, Raphi had taught them. Abed was doing that, wearing away at Raphi's diminished reserves. He roared his success. My God, he's going to win, Deborah thought.

Abruptly, Raphi broke away and rallied. He smiled, as if he'd been playing with Abed. It was an act, she knew. Sweat gleamed across Raphi's forehead. How far could he go on pure will? She held the knife in striking position, ready to attack.

With a mighty fist, Abed struck out at Raphi. Raphi leaned back fast, the knuckles just grazing his face. While Abed was still swinging, Raphi grabbed his hand, pushing his head to the side, making him lose balance and stumble forward. Raphi forced air out of his lungs in a *kiai* of triumph. His left leg came out of nowhere. It struck Abed under the arm. There was a snap like twigs breaking. The Palestinian let out a grunt of pain.

Abed groaned and stayed down. Raphi closed in, limping. Somehow Deborah knew he couldn't make his legs kick even one more time. She heard voices and shouts from somewhere else on the campus. Where were the other soldiers? They were probably rounding up the students and would have to move room to room until they came to the kitchen. Abed heard them, too, scuttled backward, and slammed the outer door to the kitchen. He staggered, but then rose unsteadily to his feet.

Raphi switched to Arabic now, and the sounds were loud and guttural.

The smell of fire was stronger, as the blaze upstairs came closer.

Abed broke the stalemate. He dove forward to the block of deadly instruments on the wall: cleavers and knives long enough to slice a carcass in half. They had one side for crosscutting and the other for ripping.

Abed pulled out a gleaming blade from the butcher's block. Like the image of Moslem conquest, he held it high above Raphi's head. His eyes were glossy. He bellowed in a chant that sounded like the Koran. His ruby lips curved in triumph as he circled the blade around his head.

Deborah moved closer. Raphi saw the knife in her

hand and shook his head. He pounced forward and drew a longer knife, one that made her own look like a toy.

She let out her breath. At least they were evenly matched. Then her panic escalated as Raphi sank suddenly to his knees.

Abed too looked momentarily confused. He hesitated, the knife above Raphi's head. Raphi held the knife in his left hand, the tip of the blade at his elbow, as if he were waiting for Abed to strike the first blow.

His nostrils flaring, Abed struck down at him, the blade in his right hand. Raphi blocked the thrust with the side of his knife. There was a clang of steel against steel. Abed shouted in surprise and pain.

Raphi inhaled and forced Abed's knife to the left.

In a smooth movement, Raphi pushed up on his thigh muscles, his head held straight, his right shoulder pulled back. As gracefully as if the knife were part of his body, he cut horizontally with his left hand, slicing Abed across the chest.

Blood appeared instantaneously. A shriek of fury rose from Abed's throat, as he pressed one hand to the cut to staunch the bleeding. He went wild, like an injured bull, slashing with all his satanic strength.

Raphi stepped back, his knife dripping. He looked exhausted, as if he didn't have the strength to finish Abed off. He parried with the heavy knife, struggling to keep his left wrist unbent.

Abed was gaining the advantage again. In order for Raphi to block Abed's thrust, he dropped to his left knee. But this time Abed was prepared. His smile was cocksure. Raphi blocked each hit above his head, his forehead wrinkled, sweat plastering down his hair.

How long can he keep this up? Deborah wondered. She stopped herself from crying out, afraid she'd distract Raphi.

On the stove, the lamb sizzled.

With a quick thrust, Raphi managed to get in a slice at Abed's shoulder. Abed cried out, grasped his shoulder, giving Raphi a moment to gather dwindling strength.

Raphi's body acquired an unnatural stillness. Deborah gasped again, then noticed that his two feet were aligned in what looked like a ritual. Abed's on to you. There's no time for this martial arts hocus pocus, Deborah wanted to scream.

Raphi looked as if he'd moved into slow motion. He changed the position of his knife, taking it in both hands and holding it in front of him. Abed whooped as he moved in for the kill. Raphi remained immobile. Deborah had stopped breathing.

Abed's blade moved to decapitate him. Raphi lifted the knife vertically above his head, and then pulled it forward in a circle. In a savage, graceful motion he inserted the knife above Abed's navel, aimed upward toward the heart.

Abed had fallen into Raphi's trap. Both of Raphi's hands held the knife handle now. His face was impassioned as he moved his wrists right and left as if he were wringing out a towel. Deborah gagged Abed fell backward, a look of horror and fright distorting his face. He made low keening sounds. Raphi stood over him for a few seconds. Then, without saying a word, he went back to the sink and washed the blood from the long knife, as if compelled to carry through an ancient *kata*.

Deborah reached up and turned off the lamb. Her face was wet with tears, but she couldn't remember crying.

She ran toward Raphi. He held her in his shaking arms. She could feel the muscles pulsing and his heart beating fast. He gave a deep sigh, and then gently moved her away. "Lets's get out of here."

He limped outdoors, shouting instructions in Hebrew. In seconds hundreds of heavily armed soldiers rushed forward. Out in the campus, someone had thrown a smoke bomb. It burned her eyes. A soldier, his face singed, yelled to Raphi that there was nobody upstairs.

Sami was missing, Deborah realized with horror.

Yigor, the Russian guard from Hadassah Hospital, was among the soldiers. He smiled and as always the sun hit his gold tooth.

"What are you doing here?" she asked.

"My retraining, remember? Mining engineers—we're experts in explosives." He started to explain something about deactivating the complicated wiring in the Church of the Nativity even before the news conference.

She had no idea what he was talking about.

Sirens were blaring. Arab and Jewish firefighters pulled hoses together to put out the fire.

The smoke stung her throat. Her head was spinning. The activity around her speeded up so much it blurred, like a video in fast-forward. Soldiers were leading out small bands of the student rebels. She felt someone holding her arms, looked up and saw it was a blue-eyed soldier.

Joshua! In uniform!

She felt as if she'd awakened from a nightmare. Out of old habit she reached up for him and he closed his arms around her.

"Thank God you're all right," he said, a look of profound relief on his face.

She felt a confusion of joy, absolution, and anguish. She began to shiver uncontrollably and he tightened his arms around her. Her eyes closed so that the dizziness would pass.

When she opened them, she saw Raphi watching her from the kitchen ramp. He stood still, his eyes soft. Then he blinked, swallowed, and squared his shoulders. He moved back into the building and began barking orders at the soldiers.

An overwhelming sense of loss pierced her.

She collapsed. Joshua caught her. Medics came running with a stretcher.

The medics lifted her into the ambulance. Joshua got in, too.

"Thank God you're all right," he repeated, his voice thick.

Only then did Deborah's mind clear enough to remember that voice, Joshua's voice, threatening to take her children from her forever. The feeling of momentary asylum dissolved. Her voice wouldn't work, so she turned her face from him. That's when she saw Raba lying beside her.

26

Ali is alive! With her eyes still closed, Raba savored the relief she felt. Despite all the painkillers, she remembered his face leaning over hers as she was wheeled into the brightly lit operating room. Then a mask had been pressed over her nose and she'd slept. How long ago was that? She struggled to open her eyes. A strong smell of flowers reminded her of her garden. Her lids lifted and she saw an enormous bouquet on her night table: roses, gardenias, and birds-of-paradise from home. A helium balloon inscribed "To my love" rose above it, attached by a violet ribbon.

Ali was standing at the foot of the bed, his brows close together, listening to a woman wearing a doctor's jacket. He lifted the chart and whispered something to her. Then his gaze shifted and he saw Raba's open eyes. "Raba, you're awake. How do you feel?" He came closer, smiling, and squeezed her hand. The woman doctor also waited for her answer. "I'm not sure yet," Raba said. "I think I feel okay."

In a professional but unemotional voice, the doctor assured Raba she would recover from her injuries.

She hadn't mentioned the baby!

Raba's eyes asked the question. Her baby had been delivered dead.

Ali held her hand. Tears filled his eyes and Raba wept. Her baby was dead. It couldn't be true! When she caught her breath, the doctor was still standing there. The baby had been small for the fifth month, the doctor said to console her. An ultrasound revealed something was wrong with her kidneys.

"Her?" Raba asked.

"Yes. You had a little girl."

The tears flowed anew. Ali stroked her hair. The trauma to Raba's belly had ruptured the placenta, the doctor explained.

Raba pulled at the hospital blanket as she asked the doctor about her symptoms before the attack. "The baby's problem wouldn't have made you feel ill, or vice versa," the doctor said. "But you were under stress and that can cause muscle pain. The staining sounds as if the placenta was low and you had some seepage." The doctor advised Raba to come in as soon as she decided to get pregnant again. In the meantime, she should rest and watch out for signs of depression. If she wanted, the doctor could prescribe something preventive. She left Raba to her weeping.

Ali held her until she fell asleep. He was there when she woke up again, putting ice chips on her cracked lips. He, too, was concerned about depression. She could tell from the way he was censoring the news. Nothing of Abed, Manger College, the dean, or the Jewish children. A message had come this morning, he told her. From the PLO. Jericho would be the first West Bank city to gain autonomy. He was being offered a position as head of a new hospital in Jericho that would be built as soon as there was peace. He gave her all the credit: her heroism had accorded him new status among the PLO vanguard. He was suggesting to the PLO liaison committee that Raba should be placed in charge of psychological services.

She slept off and on all day. By evening Raba insisted Ali go home and get some rest since he had to operate the following day. "I understand that you can't come until evening tomorrow," Raba said. "Maybe you can ask Aunt Juni to stop by."

Right after breakfast the next day Juni arrived, wearing a bright purple dress and hat. She'd managed to get by the entrance guard who was supposed to limit hospital food packages to kosher food. Her huge pocketbook contained jars of pickled eggplant and prawns with rice.

She set the food down on the night table and kissed

Raba. Then she stood at the doorway, looked both ways down the hall, and closed the door.

Raba wondered at her need for caution.

Juni's news was less finely filtered than Ali's. It was Aunt Juni who told Raba about Ali shooting an assassin on the way home from work. Raba felt weakened by her husband's near miss. "He was very heroic. Just like the movies," Juni said, fanning herself with a Hong Kong fold-up fan.

In her inimitable way, Juni changed the subject to Raba's mother. Aisha had planned to visit today, too, but Juni doubted she'd be able to come. There had been riots in Gaza after the events in Bethlehem, and the Strip was sealed off. A fifteen-year-old Palestinian had been killed when his own bomb blew up in his face. We're our own worst enemies, Raba thought.

"Don't worry about her," Juni said, misinterpreting Raba's sadness. "As soon as you go home, your mother will come for a month. I'll work it out," Juni said. "She's still a young, handsome woman. It's about time she had a vacation."

Raba smiled. Juni would arrange it.

Juni sat on her bed and whispered. Dr. Barguth had been killed. Raba's eyes widened with shock and horror. "But who would want to kill him?"

"We're claiming it's the Israelis, but Abed killed him."

At Abed's name Raba grasped Juni's hand. "Then he's still on the loose?" she asked in panic.

"No," Juni said. "An Israeli operative gutted him. His home has been bulldozed. It was very pitiful to see his family on TV last night." She told Raba how one of the sisters, a blind girl, had been shown on the news, weeping over the bodies of pigeons killed by Israeli sharpshooters, who claimed, falsely of course, that she was sending messages to a terrorist network. "It's a shame," Juni said. "I don't see why the family has to pay for what he did. What did anyone know? When you get well, I'll take you with me to the Moslem Women's Auxiliary. We're raising money to help his family."

"What about Sami?" Raba asked.

Juni shrugged. "No sign of him."

Raba felt a stab of fear. "So it goes on."

Juni patted her hand, got up, and smoothed her dress. "You look tired. That's enough news for the day. Wassim will be waiting for me."

Ali had put him at her disposal for a few days.

He knows we owe you, Raba thought as Juni bent down to kiss her cheek.

When Juni left, a nurse came to give Raba her pills. Raba had taken a course in medications as part of her training in Michigan. She put the green and white capsule back on the tray. I don't need Prozac. I need my garden, Raba thought, looking up at her flowers. She longed to get home, to drink tea under the trees with Ali, to pretend that none of this had happened.

On the hospital table was her personal copy of the Koran. Ali must have brought it. When she had the strength, she'd study Islam. She was sure the message of the Prophet had more to do with loving kindness than the violence that had overcome the spirit of her people. Then she'd find a way to teach that, along with Freud and Piaget.

Deborah too was in a private room. She leaned over her bed and took her own chart to read: so far, officially she had shock and a mild concussion.

The nail would grow back on her finger, a dermatologist told her, adding cheerfully that in Russia nails were routinely pulled off to deal with fungus infections. The concussion would not have a lasting effect, she was assured. Assorted scrapes, bangs, and burns weren't serious. Nonetheless, she had been subjected to blood tests and pelvic, chest, and skull X rays.

She was bruised and sore, but felt remarkably well for someone who'd been beaten and tortured. She stretched her limbs. They all seemed whole. A miracle.

Her body would be all right. What about her soul?

She'd felt *hashgahah pratit,* that God had intervened and saved her and the teenagers. Joshua's rebbe had phoned, offering his blessing for a quick recovery.

He'd called her a heroine of Israel and compared her to the biblical Esther and Deborah.

Would reuniting her family be her way of paying God back for the help she'd received? She tried to convince herself that she could do it, but it felt hopeless. She was hurt and puzzled that Raphi hadn't come to visit her in the hospital. She couldn't believe that the closeness she'd felt to him had been imagined. Where was he? Were the events of Bethlehem so common to him that he had already forgotten them and gone on to the next assignment?

Deborah was searching for a possible explanation when Joshua appeared at the door. The children! He must have brought them. She craned her neck to the hallway, yearning to hold Ben and Sarah.

He came in and closed the door, making the room seem smaller. Her heart sank. He had come alone. She felt like crying. "Hello, Deborah," he began, pulling up a chair. He took a pile of magazines Rachel had sent from the chair, looked at the cover of one, shook his head, and put them on the floor before sitting down.

Why don't you ask me how I feel? she thought. He hadn't brought flowers, but he was holding a wrapped package in his hand. She sat up taller in bed. "Hello, Joshua. How are you?"

"Fine. Thank God," he answered. He put the package in his lap and put his black hat on the table. Beneath was a black skullcap. His hair curled around his neck.

He leaned on his elbows, pressing his thumb knuckles into his eyes. He began without looking at her. "There are some things I should have told you long ago."

Deborah felt breathless and scared. At last he looked up and met her eyes. He looked so sad. She was tempted to comfort him, but with an effort she refrained. "I have always considered myself guilty of Oren's death."

His face was drawn. He licked his lips and paused as if to evaluate her reaction.

Deborah was trying her best to look neutral. She leaned back on her pillow and kept her face impassive, trying to hide her relief. She'd guessed his guilt long ago.

"Old secrets," she shrugged. "I always knew."

Joshua looked surprised and sighed. "I turned to religion and eventually went to live in the yeshiva to find expiation for killing Oren. Oh, I know I didn't kill him physically. But my pride did."

Joshua drew a deep breath. "I resolved never to foist my will on anyone, and so I moved out of the house rather than insist you come with me. It was a mistake."

He sat up taller and cleared his throat. She remembered him doing that in court and tension coiled in her. "Deborah, I see now I was wrong. I should have insisted you come with me. None of this would have happened. God has given you a second chance at life. There is a message in what happened. You have to join me now. To make sure you do, I won't let you see the children until you come to live with me."

At first Deborah thought she was going to faint. She felt herself pale and inhaled. After everything that had happened he was still threatening her with the children! She thought of him in uniform. *You hypocrite!* Her voice shook.

"Did you see a burning bush on the way to the hospital? Do you know what you are? You're a false prophet! I happen to agree with you that there's divine significance to what happened. But what gives you the monopoly on interpreting it?"

He stood up and glared at her, pointing one finger accusingly at her, the cunning attorney making his final point. "I knew you'd be aggressive. You've always had a problem controlling your temper. That's why I'm not giving you a choice this time. It's for your own good, believe me. I don't blame you. I shouldn't have left. You were exposed to degenerate lifestyles and were almost killed. That's what the GSS is about. I know. I was in the army, remember? Don't you see where your association with these animals leads you?

What I'm offering is an orderly life, where good deeds are the norm."

Deborah lifted herself to sitting. "Don't you see the contradiction? You come here to the hospital. You don't even ask how I'm feeling. You take away my children and then insist I leave my home and my job to join you in your world. Where are the good deeds you keep talking about? I don't see you taking in strangers like Yocheved. I don't see you looking for the good in people like your rebbe. All you want to do is use religion as a weapon. I think you got the message wrong. What did the rebbe say about your ultimatum?" Deborah got a fit of coughing.

Joshua flushed. "I haven't discussed it with the rebbe. I'm sorry it came to this, but there's no other way. Either you live with me at the yeshiva, or Sarah and Ben aren't going to live with you."

"Don't be so sure," Deborah said. "If anyone has changed, it's me. And I've got powerful friends now."

The movement of his Adam's apple as he swallowed gave him away. She knew his body language and that she'd scored. Deborah looked at the man sitting across from her. She'd given him her love and trust, but he'd squandered it. After being so close to death, how could she settle for less than love? She'd be doing Ben and Sarah a disservice by bringing them up in a cold marriage.

Joshua was breathing hard. "Don't think your lover boy can help you. A woman who has committed adultery can never marry the man with whom she'd fornicated. It's the law."

"You always were good at the law, Joshua," Deborah said. "It's the love you miss. 'You shall love your God with all your heart. Love your neighbor as yourself.' Did you ever hear of those? They're the law, too."

He stood up and walked toward the door. He nearly walked out with his package and then turned and balanced it on the night table. He gave her one more condescending look, shook his head, and walked out the door without saying good-bye.

Deborah snatched the package and ripped off the paper. It was a book called *Gates of Repentance*.

Deborah wept.

She had no idea how much time had passed when she saw the technician standing at the door. Deborah needed another abdominal ultrasound.

She was wheeled in a chair down a gray corridor smelling of hospital disinfectant. Another patient was waiting ahead of her, lying on a cot on wheels with an IV pole near her bed. When Deborah got up close, the woman turned.

Raba! Deborah felt a surge of warm emotion. Here was the woman who'd saved her.

"I never got to thank you," Deborah said. "You saved all ten of us. We would have been dead without you."

"And you saved me," Raba said, just barely smiling. "From my point of view, I think we're even."

Deborah pulled aside the IV pole that was between them. "What will you be doing?"

"I'm not sure. I have the work at the clinic. If I feel strong enough, I may even go back to Manger College. But my health has to come first." Her voice thickened. "I lost my baby."

A lump filled Deborah's throat. "I'm sorry."

"Thank you," Raba said softly. "I'm sorry about a lot of things."

"I'd like to keep in touch. If there's peace, I'll come visit you in Jericho."

"Inshallah."

Deborah had learned enough Arabic to know that meant "God willing."

The next morning Deborah was dozing when she heard a gentle knock on her door. She jolted awake when she saw who was at her door: Rachel and Joshua's father with Ben and Sarah! She stretched out her arms and the two children went running forward. Deborah tried not to wince as they jumped on her. "Did I hurt you, *Ima?*" Sarah asked.

"No, of course not," Deborah said. "I'm so happy to see you that nothing could hurt today."

She looked over their heads to Dr. Stern. "Thank you," she said.

He shrugged. "The kids were staying with me, and I figured that at my age I could do whatever I wanted. Rachel and I are going to have coffee while you do some catching up." He gave a severe look to his grandchildren. "Remember what I taught you this morning about treating patients. Don't tire your mother out."

Deborah brushed away her tears of joy. She tapped the bed. "Right here," she said, motioning for them to sit down near her. "Ben, how's the basketball going? And Sarah, someone has a birthday coming up. We need to decide about a cake."

Raphi kept his word to Joshua by not coming to the hospital for the first three days.

Never had he regretted a vow more.

He drove by Deborah's house and wondered who was watering the pink hanging geraniums blooming wildly in her window boxes.

He tried working out, but his body hurt too damn much.

Drinking didn't help. He filled a garbage can with beer bottles.

The chain of meaningless relationships that had led up to his distasteful sexual entanglement with Anat disgusted him. He was nearly thirty-five, and what did he have to show for himself?

He was through with the GSS. Moshe Cohen's criticism of his acting on his own at Manger College still made him smolder. Raphi had written a scathing resignation, wishing his colleagues good luck in completing their helicopter plan to evacuate dead bodies. He reminded Cohen of his pledge to help Deborah receive a sympathetic hearing in the rabbinical courts. He'd make sure the judges understood what a duty she'd done for her country.

He'd nearly forgotten that in real life he was an

economics professor. Evidently the university was also concerned that he had neglected his obligations. The department secretary had called to remind him about the book deadline and that his students' papers were curling in the sunshine. There was time now. After seventeen years working for one intelligence agency or another, Raphi was finished spying.

His last act of intelligence was to read the report to the GSS filed by Deborah's nurse. When Joshua had visited, the nurse had heard shouting from the room. Deborah had wept. Joshua had walked angrily away. He hadn't returned.

Raphi prayed she wasn't one of those women who wanted time between relationships.

At last, he limped down the long gray corridor to her room.

Deborah woke up to find Raphi standing at the foot of her bed, his face covered by her medical chart. "I hope you feel as good as this looks. Do you?" said the voice she'd longed for every waking moment and even in her dreams.

She felt light-headed, as if the breath had been slammed out of her. At last she spoke, her voice high-pitched, the first banal words that came to her head. "I'm feeling okay, nearly ready to go dancing."

He came up to stand near her. Their eyes met. Hers filled with tears. She choked back a sob as she said, "Where the hell have you been?"

He smiled mysteriously but said nothing.

"No more secrets, Raphi," Deborah said, bristling.

He smiled more broadly. "You don't let a man get away with anything, do you? What if I promise to tell you on a different day?"

Deborah didn't want to be angry at him. She lay back, allowing herself to enjoy the pleasure of his presence. They'd been through so much together. They'd both nearly died. "Okay. I assume you've got a good reason."

He looked suddenly embarrassed. "Here, I've brought you something."

She gave him a mockingly stern look of disapproval. "I've been warned by the General Security Services not to touch, move, or cut tape, strings, or wrappings from any suspicious packages."

"This one won't explode. Trust me." The room was so silent they could hear the tick of her bedside clock.

She stuffed another pillow behind her head. "Oh, I do," she whispered, realizing how true it was.

In his hand, wrapped in cellophane, the sand seeping through it, was a bouquet of the desert flowers, roses of Jericho. Dried, barely green cactus curled into a tiny fist.

He had to have gone all the way to the desert to pick them for her.

Tears of appreciation spilled down her cheeks. Raphi kissed them away, reverently.

When Deborah finally looked down at the flowers she was holding, she saw that some of the tears had fallen on them. Rose of Jericho: a hand of mercy. A symbol of rebirth. A promise of the future. For her personally and for their country.

Like a miracle, the flower was opening.